Praise for *Trace of Magic*

Other Bell Bridge Book Titles by Diana Pharaoh Francis

The Diamond City Magic Novels
(urban fantasy)

Trace of Magic

The Crosspointe Chronicles
(fantasy)

The Cipher

The Black Ship

The Turning Tide (coming soon)

The Hollow Crown (coming soon)

Edge of Dreams

Diamond City Magic: Book 2

by

Diana Pharaoh Francis

Bell Bridge Books

Bell Bridge Books
PO BOX 300921
Memphis, TN 38130
Print ISBN: 978-1-61194-585-0

Bell Bridge Books is an Imprint of BelleBooks, Inc.

Copyright © 2015 by Diana Pharaoh Francis

Published in the United States of America.

We at BelleBooks enjoy hearing from readers.
Visit our websites
BelleBooks.com
BellBridgeBooks.com
ImaJinnBooks.com

10 9 8 7 6 5 4 3 2 1

Cover design: Debra Dixon
Interior design: Hank Smith
Photo/Art credits:
Woman (manipulated) © Haywiremedia | Dreamstime.com
Woman (manipulated) © Avgustino | Dreamstime.com
Background (manipulated) © Leeloomultipass | Dreamstime.com

:Lder:01:

Dedication

To Mom and Dad, who gave me everything.

Chapter 1

Diamond City had been hit with snowstorm after snowstorm. Every single one brought a foot or more of snow. The stuff was piled twenty or thirty feet deep in some places, and the city was dumping truckloads of the stuff into the river as fast as trucks could haul it. Most of the main streets had been plowed, but the side streets hadn't been touched. I'd been getting around on snowshoes for the most part, and the subway. I'd have gone out and bought a snowmobile, but apparently everybody else had had the same idea. My name was on a waiting list for the next shipment. It couldn't come soon enough. I was tired of being frozen.

"Here. This will help."

I grasped the coffee cup like it was the elixir of the gods, which it was. I sipped and groaned. Sweet, creamy warmth spread down into my frozen core.

"C'mon. I'll help you get your coat and boots off. You've got a new client waiting out front."

Patti shoved me down onto a wood bench in the mud-slash-storage room at the back of the Diamond City Diner and started digging at the boot's laces to loosen them.

"Stop," I told her, taking another swig of the coffee. I didn't even care if I scalded my tongue. As cold as I was, I would gladly have stood in the middle of a raging inferno just to warm up. "You'll break your nails."

"Screw my nails," Patti said, but she paused to check them all the same.

I grinned. Patti is my best friend and half owner of the diner. She stands about five foot three in her stiletto heels, which she wears without fail. Otherwise she's just scraping four foot eleven. She's also tough as razor wire. She's got several black belts in an assortment of martial arts, and she wouldn't back down from a starving grizzly bear. But her nails were her pride and joy.

I set my coffee on the bench and bent over with a tired groan. The laces were crusted with ice and frozen stiff. I wasn't going to get them off until they thawed out. Instead, I unzipped the sides of my snow pants and shimmied out of them. I unzipped my jacket and handed both over to

Patti. She hung them on the line stretched across the back room.

I bent my fingers around my cup again and leaned back against the wall. I was starving, but most of me was still numb from the cold.

"Is this blood?" Patti demanded. She spun around. Her only concession to the cold was a pair of indigo tights instead of fishnet stockings under her tight miniskirt. "Are you hurt?"

"Not really," I said. "It's nothing. It was barely even a knife."

"Barely a knife? It was enough of one to cut you, wasn't it? Let's see."

She dropped my coat and grabbed my arm to pull it straight. I was still too cold to feel any pain.

"What the hell happened? Who did this?"

"I was looking for that surgeon. The one who went missing a couple of months ago."

"Right. I remember the case. The wife was in here a few days ago. All designer glitz and dripping money. I think she had a chauffeur."

I nodded. "That's the case."

I'm a tracer. I can see the ribbons of light that everyone leaves behind and follow them. I can even see trace off dead people, which had been one of my biggest secrets, right up until a month ago when I'd been outed in front of the biggest Tyet kingpins in Diamond City—think mafia with magic. I'd come out of the proverbial closet with a big bang. I might as well have rented a billboard. The janitor in the local 7-Eleven probably knew what I could do by now. Since then, my private tracer business had gone through the roof. Now I could charge a grand for an hour's worth of work and still turn people away. As far as I knew, there wasn't another tracer in the world who could track dead trace. That's why the surgeon's beautiful and plastic wife had come to see me three days ago.

Today had been the first day I'd had time to go out to track him down. The wife seemed to be hoping he'd turn up dead. Most people thought he was dead. She probably wanted the insurance that came with a death certificate. I told her I was too busy for her case, but I'd read his trace and at least let her know if he was alive or dead. Not that my word would hold up in court. I wasn't a bonded and licensed death authenticator.

She'd handed me his running shoes. I'd been about to tell her the happy news that he was alive and send her on her way, when she mentioned the kids. That got me. My dad had disappeared when I was around sixteen. Just *poof!* Vanished. He hadn't left any trace behind, which was . . . impossible. I still don't know what happened to him. I figured the surgeon's kids deserved to know what happened to their dad. I took the case and then went under the knife, so to speak.

"He was down in the Bottoms, of all places." I braced myself for

Patti's reaction. She didn't disappoint.

"He was *where*? And you followed him? Alone? Crap on a cracker, Riley! Do you have a death wish or something? You're lucky you didn't end up worse off than this." She shook my arm for emphasis.

I winced as pain began to wake in my flesh. "It's not like I haven't been to the Bottoms before," I said by way of an excuse. I shouldn't have bothered.

"Let me understand this. Being stupid once deserves repeating it again and again until someone kills you for real? Is that it? For fuck's sake, Riley, you're wanted, now. You're like the tracer messiah. There's no one you can't find and everybody wants a piece of you, whether you like it or not."

She let go of me and tossed her hands in frustration. "Why do I even have to say this? You know it better than I do. Every Tyet crew has been nosing around here looking for you, not to mention the FBI, CIA, NSA, Homeland Security, and every other agency on the planet. Given what you can do, most everyone would rather see you dead than working for someone else. You seriously have to start looking out for yourself better. Did you at least shoot this asshole? Or did he just knife you and get away with it?"

I tipped my head back and looked at the plaster ceiling, exhaustion weighing me down. "It was the surgeon. He came at me with a scalpel." He'd been hiding in a shack down near Helo's, a ramshackle juice joint that served homemade liquor and surprisingly decent food.

Diamond City is built on the side of an ancient volcanic caldera. The higher you go, the more money you've gotta have to live. The people who lived in the Bottoms were dregs—those who'd fallen off the diamond dole, or who needed a place to hide from the Tyet or the law. My job took me down there fairly often. More often than Patti would ever know. What she didn't know didn't hurt me.

"What's he doing down there? Why did he attack you?"

"I expect the answer to both questions is Sparkle Dust," I said, and the words left a bitter taste in my mouth that the coffee couldn't clean out.

"Sparkle Dust?" Patti repeated. "But—Why? He's got money and a family. Why would he get on that stuff?"

I shrugged. "Who knows? Maybe he wanted to find out what talent felt like. Maybe he just wanted to feel good."

Sparkle Dust was an ugly new drug made from minerals found only in the Diamond City caldera. The stuff supposedly made the user feel invincible and orgasmically good, to hear dealers tell it. Plus, it gave those with magical talents extra, if temporary, abilities. Fat lot of good that did. The drug-induced abilities were totally unpredictable. For people without any magical talent, they got to experience it for a brief time. 'Course, without any knowledge or skills in using that magic, they often killed or maimed themselves.

As if all that wasn't bad enough, the drug had another side effect—this one fatal. It turned the users into what the street had come to call *wraiths*. I didn't know much more about how that worked, except users turned translucent from the outside in, fading away until they just vanished off the face of the earth. As Hollywood as that sounded, it seemed accurate. At least, you didn't trip over a lot of dead SD users lying around the streets.

"You know, that shit is expensive," Patti pointed out. "You wouldn't think he'd have to go to the Bottoms to find it. You wouldn't think anyone in the Bottoms would have any to sell."

That fact had been bothering me, not that it really mattered to my case. "He was holed up in a little flophouse." Sometimes those houses provided sexual company, but this one was just a warm place to sleep for a couple of bucks. Dirty, sleeping bodies had been squished inside like sardines. "I hadn't realized he was dusted at that point. I went inside to see if I could talk to him."

I ignored Patti's sound of disgust. It *had* been stupid, but it's not like I had options.

"When I put a hand on him, he jumped up and came at me with that scalpel." I'd scrambled out over the sleeping bodies, leaving him raving and stabbing at anyone who came near him. I hadn't even realized he'd got me until I was out the door. But one thing I'd seen for certain despite the gloom was the telltale opalescent shine of his teeth and the shadows of muscles and bone beneath his skin. He was going wraith.

I sucked down the rest of my coffee and set the cup down hard on the bench. I closed my eyes, trying to get rid of the memory. I didn't think his wife or his kids would be happy with my news, though not for the same reasons.

I sat up and twisted to try to get a look at the cut. I couldn't tell. Blood had clotted to my long-sleeved shirt, hiding the damage. I was beginning to feel a faint ache in it. I had a feeling it was going to hurt a lot worse. "Think I'll need a tinker?"

"Maybe I can superglue it," Patti said, rolling her eyes in pure disgust. "Don't be an idiot. Of course you'll need a tinker, if only to be sure you don't get infected with rabies or something."

I laughed. "I didn't get bit by a stray dog."

It wasn't until then that her first words to me registered. "I've got a new client?"

"Yep. She's been waiting awhile."

I groaned. "Not another cheating husband case."

"Probably not." Patti hesitated. "She's a cop."

I stiffened as a wild mix of emotions crashed over me. My stomach flip-flopped. "A cop?"

The last cop who'd hired me had been Clay Price. He also moonlighted as a Tyet enforcer. He hadn't given me a lot of choice on whether to work for him or not. When my not-quite-brother-in-law was kidnapped, Price had helped me get him back. On the way, I discovered Price's brother was one of the biggest Tyet kingpins in Diamond City. Rather than running for the hills, instead I'd fallen head-over-heels in love with Price. I'd never been much of a believer in love at first sight or chemistry—true chemistry—until Price. I fell fast and hard for him. I'll admit, he was sexy as hell, but there was more to it. He was smart and funny and annoying. He argued with me and tried to keep me out of trouble, then followed me into hell and had my back, regardless of the cost.

I admit that what had happened between us was near unexplainable for me. I'd never let anyone that close. I'd even blindly followed him into enemy territory, where I was promptly captured and nearly killed twice—four if you count the times I didn't bleed. We'd got out by the skin of our teeth. That's when I'd kicked the love of my life to the curb.

I had to. To get his brother to leave me alone, he'd promised to join his brother's organization. As bad as Touray wanted me, that made Price my enemy. I knew he would do whatever he could to protect me, but he had split loyalties and he loved his brother. Sooner or later push would come to shove, and I just didn't believe I'd be left standing. Before we could even think of being together, I needed to find a way to stand on my own two feet and protect myself and my family. Then maybe we could figure things out.

If this was real love and not just a crush.

If he still wanted me then.

If I was still breathing.

Patti was right to worry. Hell, I was so deep into the woods, I doubted I'd ever get out. Not without a helicopter, a bucket of hand grenades, and one or two miracles. Now that my secret was out—now that I'd gone head-to-head with the highest-ranking members of Diamond City's own magical mafia—I was on the top of every bad guy's to-do list, not to mention on the lists of a few of the good guys. Neither list made me happy. I supposed that meant I was still on the right side of a psychotic break.

I rubbed my hands over my face and winced as pain burned up my arm from the scalpel cut. I didn't want to think about Price or the trouble

I was in with the Tyet. Both made me want to curl up into an emotional ball. Since I was a grown-up, I wasn't going to do that. I told myself this firmly, and tried to believe it.

"I suppose I should talk to this cop," I said, focusing on the here and now, pushing Price's image out of my mind. I was more than a little bit curious what this potential cop-client wanted. "How long has she been waiting for me?"

"Through a dozen cups of coffee, two bathroom breaks, a grilled cheese sandwich, and a slice of pie," Patti said.

"That long, huh?" I smiled and started to stand up.

Patti put a hand on my shoulder and shoved me back down. "No, you don't. I'm going to bandage you up first."

I waited while she fetched supplies. My mind skittered back to the surgeon. What a waste. He'd been good, if his wife's appearance was anything to go by. You didn't make that kind of money by being a hack. In a world where he had to compete with tinkers and their magic, he must have been downright brilliant. Now he was nothing. What had made him start using Sparkle Dust? I'd probably never know. He was as good as dead. The addiction was awful. Most people couldn't shake it.

I thought of my almost-brother-in-law, Josh. I hadn't seen him since just after we'd rescued him. He'd been tortured and force-dosed with Sparkle Dust. My dreamer friend, Cass, had healed what the haunters had done to his mind. She had also done all she could to stop the effect of the SD, but I didn't know if it had been enough. For all I knew, he was dead in the gutter somewhere. Hell, he could be totally invisible and watching me right now.

I shuddered. Not a comfortable thought. He and I had not ended well.

Did I mention my sister isn't talking to me? She's pissed I let him walk away without dragging him to see her. Since then he's been nulling his trace so I can't find him. Of course, if he can afford the nulls to do that, maybe that's a sign he's not drugged out of his gourd. I can't be all unhappy he's off the grid. He was one of the people who tried to kill me. Sure, he was drugged up at the time, and they'd tampered with his head, but he'd never even apologized. He wasn't the same man my sister had fallen in love with. I was just as happy to see him stay away from her. Besides, he was as wanted by the Tyet as I was. Not to mention, he was tangled up with the FBI. My sister didn't need that kind of trouble.

Patti returned. She pushed up my sleeve to reveal the cut. It was about two inches long. I looked away as she cleaned it with warm water and a washcloth. I gritted my teeth and sucked in a breath.

"Hurts, doesn't it? Maybe you'll think twice about going to the Bottoms next time. At least take one of your goon squad. How did you lose them, anyhow?"

"I know the city better and I make good nulls."

It actually hadn't been that easy. I'd dodged through several buildings and into the subway, then switched lines and jumped off at a random spot. They'd followed me all the way to that point, but I had jumped the train quicker than they could, and by the time they could get back to where I'd ditched them, I was long gone. Nulling my trace meant that I hadn't left any trail for them to follow once they no longer had eyes on me.

"Any idea yet who's paying them to watch you?" Patti dabbed on some disinfectant ointment and then wrapped my arm with some gauze, followed by some hot-pink vet wrap. One of these days, I was going to buy myself some good heal-alls. Now that I had some money, I could afford a couple, and since I kept getting myself hurt on the job, it would be smart to keep one on me.

"My goons have got to be from Price or Touray. Neither of them wants me to fall into the wrong hands."

I was guessing it was Touray, not Price, though. I tried not to feel like I'd lost my pet kitten. After all, I'd told Price to stay away from me, and one of the things I love best about him is that he respects my boundaries. Or maybe he'd given up on me. It's not like I'd tried to call him or anything since I booted him out of my life. He might have figured out he wasn't all that into me, that it was all just a case of the two of us getting thrown together in an intense situation and hormones just took over.

Or maybe he figured I just wasn't worth it. After I'd ended us, I'd broken the tab he'd used to lojack me before I went home. I suppose that was a sign I didn't really love him as much as my heart seemed to think I did. I didn't trust him enough to let him know where I lived. He wasn't stupid. He'd have gotten that message loud and clear. So either he was respecting my wishes and letting me figure out my life, or he was over me. Why did both those possibilities hurt the same?

"I'm a contrary bitch," I told Patti as she pulled my sleeve back down. Hopefully the hole and the blood weren't terribly obvious. My arm was on fire. The rest of me was starting to throb and tingle as the numbness wore off, and I started to warm up. Deep inside, I could feel the fluttering of chills waiting to erupt.

"You won't catch me arguing with that," Patti said.

I laughed. "Tell me why we are friends again?"

"Because we both need someone to help bury the bodies, no questions asked. Plus, I'm not sure anyone else will put up with you. Oh, that reminds me, your stepmother called me."

"She called *you*?" I'd been dodging Mel's calls. After I'd recovered from rescuing Josh, I'd let my stepbrother Leo update the rest of the family. Or rather, I'd totally ducked out on the drama of telling my family how much trouble I'd gotten myself into and that I'd fallen in love with a Tyet man. That, and I wanted to keep them safe.

I loved Mel. She'd been just as much a mother to me as my own had been. I'd always felt ridiculously guilty that my father had left her and me and everybody else without a word. Worse, I couldn't track him. He was just gone. All his trace had vanished liked he'd never existed. It was totally impossible, and yet that's the way it was. Mel couldn't remarry, couldn't move on in any way—my dad wasn't dead. But this time it wasn't the guilt that made me avoid her. I'd become a danger to my entire family. I couldn't pretend they didn't exist, but I could pretend not to have any real connection. At least until I figured out how to protect them. And me. I needed to figure that out, too.

"Apparently she was tired of talking to your answering machine. She said she expects you for dinner a week from Saturday. Six o'clock sharp. She also said, and I quote, 'no excuses will be accepted.'"

"I guess I have Saturday night plans next week. My bathtub will be so sad. It'll be the fifth Saturday in a row I've broken our date."

"There's always this week."

"I already told Ben I'd help clean the kitchen this week after you guys close."

"I'd say you lead a very boring life, but getting shot, stabbed, and other various and sundry scrapes and scares argue to the contrary," Patti said. "You might want to get that wound tinkered before you help Ben. Most definitely before your dinner. Mel will notice real quick that you've got a bad wing."

"She probably already knows. I swear the woman has her own intelligence network better than the NSA or the FBI or anybody else."

"Good thing she doesn't work for the Tyet or you'd be in trouble. Maybe you should make her your secret weapon."

"Right. Get my stepmother involved in my mess. Good plan."

Patti shrugged. "That's what the mafia families all were—families. At least you can trust her. And your brothers."

"Seriously? My brothers are jewelers."

"Your brothers are expert metal tinkers. They are also jewelers. Your stepmother is a reader and a damned good one."

It was true. Mel had worked for a while as a cop consultant when she was younger, reading the emotions of suspects and witnesses. It wasn't legal to use dreamers, but you could use a reader, since they were picking up emotions, not trespassing into thoughts. After a few years, she'd gone on to work with mental patients and then to consult for the government. She'd spent a lot of time traveling to Washington and other places, helping with various negotiations and treaties.

She'd retired a few years ago at the ripe old age of fifty-two and now did some teaching at the university and spoke at conferences all over the globe. At dinner, she would read me like a book and make me talk about everything. I groaned. This was going to be a shark feeding frenzy, and I was going to provide the bait.

"Was that groan because you know I'm right about leaning on your family?" Patti finished packing up her medical supplies and shoved the box up on a shelf above my head.

"No. I just realized how painful next Saturday night is going to be."

"Better than being dead."

"Is that a choice? At the moment I'd consider it."

She put her hand out to help me up. I towered over her by a good nine inches. "You can't escape your family that easily." She looked me over.

I was wearing my gun in a nylon shoulder holster, both gifts, courtesy of Gregg Touray. He'd sent them over with a message about how he didn't want me to be defenseless. I'd destroyed my own gun with magic in the course of rescuing Josh. He'd also sent over a Kevlar vest, but I'd left it rolled up on my dresser.

Patti put her hands on her hips, her brows arching. "Did it not occur to you to approach that rat-bastard surgeon with your gun drawn?"

I flushed. It hadn't, really. Before a month ago, I'd forgotten to carry my gun half the time, much less draw it. I was going to have to get better about it. I used to carry a Chinese telescoping baton. I needed to get into a store and replace it. In my defense, until recently my cover had been that I was a not terribly competent tracer, and the cases which came my way hadn't been that dangerous. Except maybe for the occasional missing child cases I had worked anonymously and pro bono.

Patti shook her head at me. "Look up *careful* in the dictionary. You might want to learn about it. Now, come on. I'll introduce you to your next client, and then I'll have Ben cook you something."

I didn't bother to tell her what I wanted to eat. Patti didn't work that way. She decided what I needed, and I didn't complain or I might find myself eating liverwurst on burned toast for a week. I was not willing to go through that hell again.

I followed her up the hallway past the kitchen. I waved at Ben, Patti's partner and a cooker. It was a branch of maker magic. There are five major kinds of magic: tracer, maker, binder, dreamer, traveller. Then there are tons of minor magics that are offshoots of the others. So for instance, my stepmom is a reader, which is related to dreamer magic. My stepbrothers are metalsmiths, which is an offshoot of maker magic. As a cooker, there's nothing Ben can't do with food.

It was well after the lunch rush, but the diner was still busy. Ellie, a plump, bubbly waitress with curly hair that hung to her waist slung coffee and plates and chattered brightly with the customers. Before Patti could introduce me to my new client, the door jingled, and a man stepped in followed by another man and a tough-looking woman.

"Oh *hell* no," Patti muttered and stomped up the aisle to meet them. No mean feat in stiletto boots.

I hung back. These three were part of my bodyguard squad. They'd showed up on the diner's doorstep a day after I'd left the safety of the healer's house six weeks ago. They followed me everywhere, or tried. I didn't give them the slip often, but sometimes it was necessary. Like when I went to the Bottoms. It was also necessary when I went home. The first time they tried to shadow me there, I scraped them off and didn't come back to the diner for almost a week. By the time I showed up, they were going out of their gourds.

We pretty much had ourselves a Mexican standoff. That's when we had our come-to-Jesus meeting. I wasn't footing the bill for their protection, so they didn't figure they answered to me. On the other hand, they couldn't do their job if I sneaked off and got myself killed. They'd probably end up filleted or skewered pretty quick after, Tyet justice being what it was. So we made a deal. I'd come into the diner first thing every morning and report in, and they wouldn't try to follow me home. It was the only concession they were willing to make.

"What the hell good are you idiots if you let her go off and get stabbed?" Patti demanded of Dalton, the one in charge.

He had a long face with a large, blunt nose, straight eyebrows, full lips, and a close-cut mustache and beard. His skin was light copper. What always caught me up short were his eyes. Instead of the dark brown his coloring suggested, they were silvered steel. Definitely not natural. They were some sort of magical implant, but what they did was impossible to guess. He was a good three or four inches taller than me, and next to him, Patti looked like a child. If it came to a fight, I'd put my money on her.

As she continued to harangue him, he turned his silver stare on me, then strode up the aisle to stop right in front of me. I held my ground, unwilling to be intimidated. Everything about him was a threat. He had muscles on his muscles, and danger radiated from him like smoke off a bonfire. He wore animosity like a shield.

"We have to talk," he said, his lip curling in a slight sneer.

He always sneered. I wondered if he even did it when screwing a beautiful woman. Or man. I didn't know which way his bat swung.

He had a way of holding himself tight, like a lit piece of dynamite. There was no doubt he was pissed. I couldn't really blame him. By risking myself, I'd risked his life and everybody else in his crew, given that the typical Tyet poor job evaluation included death. I'd have been surprised and maybe a little bit disgusted if he *wasn't* enraged. Then again, as he liked to point out, he wasn't working for me, so I wasn't obligated to him in any way. Plus he's an asshole.

"I have a client."

His mouth twitched, and the muscles in his jaw knotted. Then his expression smoothed out. "I'll wait." He glanced down at the pink bandage showing through the bloody hole in my shirt. "How bad?"

"I'll live."

"I've got a heal-all."

I should have known. "Better save it for an emergency," I said. "I'll see a tinker later."

His eyes narrowed, but he nodded. "Your call."

I blinked. It was? I scowled. What was Dalton up to? He walked away without another word. He slid onto a seat at the end of the counter, with his back to the wall, where he could see everything. His companions took seats on either side. I felt his eyes follow me as Patti motioned me toward a booth.

"What's the point of having them around taking up space if you get mauled on their watch?" she grumbled.

"I lost them on purpose," I reminded her.

"So? If they were worth a damn you couldn't have done it."

"Maybe I'm just that good," I suggested.

"Maybe you're just that stupid."

"You really think I can trust them?" I asked, startled.

"I think you don't have a choice. For fuck's sake, Riley, you almost got yourself killed today. Again. What's it going to take before you realize you need a little help?"

I thrust my fingers into my copper hair, pulling it loose from its ponytail. "Dammit, Patti."

"You know I'm right."

"I—"

Patti glared at me, daring me to argue or maybe just because I was playing with my hair in the diner and she was worried it would go flying off into the food. Her blue eyes sparked with anger. Nope. This was about putting myself into too many dangerous situations. I wasn't going to win this argument. Not while I was still bleeding from the surgeon's attack, anyhow. I decided to save time and irritation and give in now rather than after a long argument.

I gave an exasperated sigh. "Okay. Fine. You're right, as usual. But that doesn't mean I can trust them." I hooked a thumb in the direction of Dalton and his two companions.

"So don't. Find your own people, but stop acting like you're Wonder Woman. You can *die*, Riley. Quit fooling around."

I glanced at Dalton. He held his coffee cup between his palms, his silver gaze locked on me. He had to have heard every word. I turned back to Patti, refusing to feel embarrassed or guilty.

"Okay. I will. Later. Where's this new client?"

"Right here."

A black woman with iron-gray hair rippling along her scalp in elegant cornrows stood up out of the booth behind Patti. She wore a navy-blue suit with an ivory turtleneck and heavy black boots. Underneath her jacket on her hip was a holstered gun. On her belt I could see the gold shine of a police badge.

I stretched out a hand. "I'm Riley Hollis."

"Good to meet you, Riley. I'm Lauren Morton." Her voice came out in a husky Southern drawl. That was about all I had time to register before she hit me with the big guns. "I'm here because rumor says you're about the best tracer around. I need your help. I've got five teenagers lost inside the mountain, and if you can't find them, they're going to die."

Chapter 2

The mention of missing kids woke me up like nothing else could. I motioned for the other woman to sit. "Tell me about it."

She hesitated, her gaze flicking at the door. "They don't have time."

"I've got to know more before I can help you," I said, sliding into the booth.

She gnawed her bottom lip and finally sat opposite to me. "You'll be paid, if that's what's concerning you," she said in a rolling Southern accent.

I examined her. Her skin was ashy, like she'd not slept for a while, and her eyes were sunken with bags around them. She linked her hands in front of her, weaving her fingers together. Her nails were oval and polished in a lilac color. She wore light makeup, and her lips matched her nails. I guessed her to be around forty-five or fifty years old.

I ignored the financial reference. I didn't trace kids for money. I traced them because I hadn't been able to trust anyone else to do their jobs and find them.

For a fleeting second, my mind fled back to the last time I'd helped recover a kidnapped little girl—named Nancy Jane Squires. It made me think of Price. He'd been the cop I'd taken my anonymous tips to. Now that I'd kicked him out of my life, I didn't know who to tell. Even if I were still talking to him, he'd left the force. Most cops were corrupt. I couldn't trust them to actually go after the kids.

I ignored the ache of emptiness that came with thinking of Price. I'd get over it. I pretended to believe the lie and focused back on the woman sitting opposite me.

"Tell me what happened. Who are these kids and how did they end up in the mines?"

Patti brought me another cup of coffee and topped off Lauren's. I noticed she gave the other woman decaf. Good idea. Lauren already looked wired to the gills.

She looked down at her hands, visibly collecting herself. She looked up, meeting my gaze. "I've been working on a case involving Sparkle Dust. The Tyet makers and distributers have been using kids as messengers and sometimes couriers. Couple of days ago, five of them vanished. I have reason to believe that this particular group of kids decided to start making their own drugs and went down into the mines to get some of the base mineral for making SD."

I leaned against the back of the booth and considered what she'd said. What had they been thinking? First—stealing anything from the Tyet was a ticket to the dead zone, and second, the mountain was a huge warren of passages and caves. Precious few of them were publicly mapped. Unless they knew exactly where they were going and had left themselves a trail of breadcrumbs, they'd probably gotten lost in the first ten minutes. I was betting on lost. The kind of breadcrumbs they needed involved high tech or good magic, and neither were cheap. Teenagers weren't going to just walk into Best Buy and find what they needed.

I frowned as questions clicked into my head. "They've been gone two days? How come the news doesn't have a hold of this?" Before the detective could answer, my suspicion doubled. "Why come to me? The cops have tracers." Not very good ones, admittedly, and after two days, they probably wouldn't be able to find the trace. But still, cops didn't go looking for outside help on cases like this unless they had more than a professional interest. From the looks of her, Detective Lauren Morton was deeply interested.

Lauren's mouth hardened. "The department isn't willing to allocate resources to an undermountain search. These kids are drug runners and don't merit the cost."

In other words, nobody important was going to care if they died. My hand tightened around my coffee cup. "Why do you care so much?"

She hesitated. "One of them is my nephew."

My brows went up. "Your nephew? How? You're a cop." The moment I said the words, I wanted to reel them back. Talk about a dumb question. Cops and cop families weren't immune to breaking the law. Hell, most of the Diamond City force was on the Tyet payroll. In a city run by the Tyet and an economy revolving around billions of dollars of diamonds and drugs, that was just the way things were done in Diamond City.

Lauren gave a weak smile. "We moved here last summer. My brother—Well, let's just say he couldn't be a good father and leave it at that. His ex, Trevor's mom, left years ago. Anyhow, I took a job here. Figured I'd get Trevor somewhere he could make a new start. He'd gotten a little bit wild back in Rock Hill. Hanging out with the wrong crowd. He'd been pinched for vandalizing and petty theft. I thought maybe being in the mountains and isolated, he'd get sorted out in school and straighten up. But then he made friends with this no-good excuse for a boy—Justin Barba. Next thing I know, he was involved in Tyet business."

She spun her spoon on the table. "It's my fault. The job takes up more time than I thought it would, you know?" She smiled again, and just as quickly it faded. "Trevor has no one else but me. I should have been with him more."

Even if I'd been leaning in that direction, which I wasn't, I couldn't judge her. She was taking care of a kid that didn't even belong to her. As far as I was concerned, that made her pretty close to a saint. I had some experience with being abandoned to the care of others.

"How old is he?"

"Seventeen. Just turned."

"He's not using, is he?" My stomach clenched as I remembered the surgeon and the way I could see the dark threads of his arteries beneath his skin.

"I don't think so. God, I hope not." She wiped away a couple of tears. "Sorry. I don't usually break down. I just thought maybe here he'd have a chance to be a normal kid. If only I'd—" She knotted her hands.

"If you'd what? Look, the boy's a teenager and he's trying to be a man. You took him from a bad situation and set him up in a better one. You've been a better parent than his own. What more could you have done?"

She grimaced and just shook her head. I understood. Guilt wasn't that easy to shrug off. I pushed in a different direction.

"The cops know he's your family? And they still won't go looking for him?" I really shouldn't have been surprised. I'd bounced off the corruption in Diamond City so many times that I practically had a PhD in bureaucratic greed. All the same, however corrupt law enforcement was, they tended to look after each other's families.

Lauren looked away. "I begged," she said. "But like I said, Trevor had a juvenile record before we came here. I'm a new face and they think I'm just a silly woman without sense enough to realize that he's off doing what he wants to do." She drew a breath and let it out, nodding. "That's true enough. He is off doing what he wants to do, but that doesn't mean he's not in trouble, and it sure doesn't mean I'm going to sit around waiting for his body to turn up."

I didn't bother telling her that it was a rare thing for anybody to be brought up out of the tunnels, unless it involved some sort of mining accident. Those people the Tyet dumped there tended to be lost forever.

I took a breath. It was up to me. If I didn't find him and his friends, they were likely going to die, if they weren't dead already. Two days is a long time in the mines.

Unless they'd nulled out their trace, I'd be able to find them fairly easily. That wasn't what bothered me. The location of the Sparkle Dust minerals was a closely guarded secret, one that those in the know were willing to kill for. On top of that, the method of converting them into the drug was a complete secret. If the kids knew, they were dead meat. With all that, looking for them became a serious risk. If we were caught, we'd be up shit creek without a paddle or a rubber ducky.

I caught myself. Was I really going to do this? I hated tight spaces. I rarely took elevators, and going into the subway sent my heart into overdrive. I usually came out soaked in sweat. Literally. The mine shafts would be a lot worse. Could I handle it? I jeered at myself. Better question was, could I live with chickening out and letting five kids die when I could have done something about it? The answer to that was a big *hell no*.

If I was going to do this, I was going to need help. The most convenient and quickest option was right here in the diner. I twisted around. Dalton was still brooding at me beneath lowered brows. I waved at him to come over. His brows rose, but he complied.

"How fast can you get gear together to go into the mountain? There'll be two of us—" I pointed to Lauren and myself. "Plus whoever you want to bring, and one more." I'd call my brother, Leo. A metal tinker would be useful in the mountain, especially Leo. Rocks talked to him, or so he said. I didn't know what that meant, but it couldn't hurt to have him along. He spent half his time underground.

Dalton scowled. "You can't go into the mountain. It's suicidal."

"Yet I'm going," I said. I gave him a long look. When he neither spoke nor moved away, I shook my head. So much for trying to trust him. "Fine. I'll find someone else who's willing."

I thumbed my phone on and hit my *Contacts* button. I knew where to get the gear, but finding backup was going to take time. More than I had. That meant it was just going to be me, Lauren, and Leo, though I was rethinking calling him. Without Dalton and his crew, we'd be sitting ducks. We wouldn't have a chance if we ran into any Tyet goons. I didn't want to lead my brother right to his death. I didn't have a right to risk him that way.

Dalton's calloused hand closed over mine, preventing me from dialing. "I'll take care of it," he said, grooves cutting deep into the sides of his nose and mouth. He definitely didn't look happy. "When do you need it?"

I looked at Lauren. "Have you got anything with you I can read?" I'd at least find out if they were still alive to be rescued before putting Dalton to work gathering supplies.

"I only have something from Trevor, my nephew."

She put her hand in her breast pocket and took out a toothbrush wrapped in a plastic evidence bag. Trust a cop to get something that had DNA evidence on it and keep it protected. DNA didn't matter at all to what I did. I only needed Trevor to have come in contact with an object and leave a bit of his trace behind.

I took the bag and opened myself to the trace. Two ribbons wrapped the toothbrush. One was a greenish yellow. It belonged to Lauren. The other was a mustard-orange color. That had to be Trevor. I blinked out of trace mode, feeling a wave of dizziness. I really needed food and some sleep. I was only going to get one of those before diving into the mine tunnels. My stomach clenched hard, and suddenly I wasn't remotely hungry. I shuddered and swallowed hard. Stupid phobia. I focused back on my new client.

"He's alive."

Lauren's shoulders slumped, and she clutched her hands together. "Praise the Lord."

I looked up at Dalton. "How soon can you get the gear ready?"

I hoped he knew what we'd need. He seemed more than competent. Mostly I wanted food, water, lights, and weapons. I'd provide the nulls.

"An hour, maybe two."

"As quick as you can. Soon as you're ready, we'll go."

"Where?"

I looked at Lauren. "Where was the last place you know these kids were?"

She nodded. "They were hanging out at a place near Vine and Reeder."

"I'll get to work," Dalton said. "Stay here and I'll be back to pick you up." He withdrew to speak to his two crew members.

I thumbed my phone to text my brother, Leo. I didn't want to explain beyond the bare bones.

Got a case. Missing teenagers. Going inside the mines. Could use some help. Can you come to the diner in the next hour?

I hit *Send* and set my phone aside.

My phone beeped with a new text. I checked it. It was from Leo. He was short and to the point:

On my way.

Just then Patti arrived with a bacon burger smothered under sautéed onions and bleu cheese, with a mound of crispy fries. I eyed it sourly.

"What's wrong?" she demanded, her brows winging down. "You don't like what I brought you?"

I shook my head. "That's not it. I'm just not sure I'm hungry anymore."

"Why's that?"

"We're going into the mountain." I glanced up at her with a pained look. She knew I didn't like small spaces. "I might be better off with just coffee."

Her expression softened slightly, but she shook her head, wisps of black hair dancing around her face. "You've been up for almost twenty-four hours, and I'm willing to bet you haven't eaten since you left here yesterday. You need the energy. So pull up your big girl panties and force it to stay down."

Having made that pronouncement, she smiled at Lauren. "Can I get you anything else?"

The other woman looked itchy. I understood. She wanted to find her nephew and the other kids, and this felt like wasting time. All the same, there wasn't anything we could do until Dalton returned and Leo arrived.

Lauren smiled weakly. "I guess I'm going to need a little fortification of my own. Can I see your menu?"

Patti cocked her head at the detective and then waved her hand. "Never mind. I'll bring you something. You'll love it." She twirled around, ducking behind the counter and vanishing into the kitchen.

Lauren watched her go, brows raised, her mouth hanging open. She looked at me. "I don't get to order?"

I laughed. "She doesn't usually do that to first timers, but once you've been in a few times, you start to realize that it doesn't matter what you order, she brings you what she thinks you ought to have. Sometimes it's even what you want. I warn you, though, if you refuse to eat it, you'll regret it when you come back. If she lets you come back."

I have to admit, I have always loved the bacon bleu burger, and with the sautéed onions, it was possibly the most perfect food on the planet. I started to eat, prodding Lauren to tell me about the other missing kids.

"There are three other boys and a girl," she said. "I can't tell you much about them. Once I realized that Trevor had come into extra money, I figured he was up to no good. He didn't have a real job.

"We had a come-to-Jesus meeting. He wouldn't tell me what he was up to, but for a few weeks, it seemed to work. The next thing I know, he's back being gone all the time and I found bundles of cash under his mattress. I've been working long hours. I thought maybe I could catch the people he was working for, so I started following him and his friends whenever I could. Most of the time I lost them. Sometimes they'd take a bus or the subway or their bikes. Few times I did manage to follow, they'd pick up a package in one part of town and drop it off somewhere else. Wasn't hard to figure out they were messengers. Just a couple days ago I realized they were hooked in with some of the people I'd been investigating for manufacturing and selling Sparkle Dust. I didn't even get a chance to warn Trevor before he disappeared."

She leveled a tortured look at me. "I'm a cop. I ought to be able to protect my own. I shouldn't have to come to a civilian for help."

"You can't keep people from doing what they want to do," I said. "Teenagers especially. Don't worry. We'll find him." The question of what shape he'd be in when we did, I left hanging. For now, he was alive.

Patti brought out a deep dish of something covered in melted cheese for Lauren, along with a glass of milk. She set it down and walked away.

"What do you suppose it is?" Lauren asked, looking wide-eyed at her meal.

"Tasty," I said. My hamburger was gone, but I was still chewing away at the fries.

She picked up her fork and dug in. White sauce bubbled up. With a look of trepidation, she took a bite, and then her eyes widened again and she swallowed. "Oh my! That is good."

After that, she ate rapidly. I fell silent. With any luck, the five kids had gotten terribly lost inside the mountain and were nowhere near a Tyet drug enterprise. Nobody knew exactly what sorts of minerals made the stuff, only that they were unique to the Diamond City caldera. That meant a monopoly on that particular drug trade, and it also made it incredibly expensive for buyers. That's why I couldn't figure out what the surgeon was doing looking for it in the Bottoms. He'd have been better off looking somewhere in Uptown among the über-wealthy.

Diamond City is built on the inside of an ancient volcanic caldera in the Rocky Mountains near Gunnison, Colorado. The caldera spans over a hundred miles in diameter, with the biggest diamond mines on the west side. The bulk of the city clings to several ledges along the eastern side. The highest and most expensive is Uptown, then a step down is Midtown, then Downtown, where most of the businesses are, with the dregs trying to survive in the Bottoms. There was no reason on the planet that anybody would be selling Sparkle Dust in the Bottoms. It simply made no sense.

"You said you've been looking into the Sparkle Dust trade?" I asked, twisting my coffee cup on the table. Maybe she had an idea of how the Bottoms might figure in. Sirens wailed faintly outside. Tough day to have to call an ambulance. I hoped whoever was sick got across the roads before they croaked.

Morton nodded and swallowed, eyeing me warily. "It's an ugly drug."

"You're preaching to the choir. Got any idea why someone would go down to the Bottoms to make a buy?"

She straightened thoughtfully. "What makes you ask that?"

"I was working a trace on a guy who turned out to be an SD wraith. I found him down there in a flophouse. I assume he was looking for more drugs, but that's not exactly where I'd expect him to find any. There's no money down there."

"Maybe he was down there for something else," Lauren suggested.

"Maybe," I said doubtfully. SD addicts had one-track minds: get more drugs and get them now.

"I can check it out," she said.

I could tell she was curious. That was probably a basic requirement on the detective test. That and nosiness and the enjoyment of confrontation and the willingness to get shot at. I've got the first two covered, but the second two—I'm more of a hide-in-the-shadows sort of girl. Not that I can't hold my own in a confrontation. I just don't get off on it.

"Don't worry about it," I said. "It doesn't make any difference to my trace. The guy was probably so fried he didn't know the Bottoms from Uptown."

"Sure. You're probably right." She wiped her mouth with her napkin and pushed her dish away. "I suppose we should talk about payment for your services before we go any further."

"You don't need to worry about it," I said. "This one's on me."

Her chin lifted haughtily. "I can't do that."

"Sure you can. It's easy. I don't charge you anything and you don't pay." I liked that she didn't want a handout, but finding kids was something I'd been doing anonymously for a long time. I hadn't had a chance in more than six weeks to even breathe, much less help save a child. I wasn't going to pass up this chance, and anyhow, Lauren seemed to be a decent cop. That was a rare thing in Diamond City.

"Is that supposed to be funny? I'm serious. I pay my own way and I don't take bribes."

"I get that. I'm still not going to accept any money from you. But you could do something for me."

She braced herself against the table, her hands fisting. She scowled at me. "What's that?"

"You can let me know if a kid's in trouble and if I can help. Anonymously. I don't want anybody else knowing."

"Why not?"

"I just don't." Because sometimes I couldn't get there soon enough. Sometimes the best I could do was help find the body. If I had to face the family after that, it would put a hole right through me.

Lauren was still scowling as she considered what I was asking. "It's illegal to reveal details about an ongoing case."

I shrugged and didn't say anything.

"And this is what you want in exchange for finding my nephew?"

"Nope. I'll find him anyway." I grinned because there wasn't anything she could do about it, and it clearly pissed her off. Okay, maybe I do sometimes like confrontation. I still would never have made a good cop. I don't follow rules well at all, and I really don't like getting shot.

"Why?"

"Because I can and because kids don't deserve to be pawns in Tyet games." I hated the way the Tyet used kids and families to leverage people to do what they wanted. They left a lot of dead bodies and broken families littering the city. I couldn't do a lot to stop them, but if I could keep the kids from dying, it helped me sleep at night. Sure, a Tyet faction wasn't involved in every case, but nine out of ten of the kids I'd looked for had been taken by or because of the Tyet.

"Even though my nephew is trying to commit a crime?"

"Sure. Don't get me wrong—there's no worse drug than Sparkle Dust. As far as I'm concerned, the dealers and the creators of it should all be dumped into a vat of boiling oil. Trevor is stupid, but then so are most teenagers. He shouldn't have to die for it. He deserves a chance to learn better. He just needs a good kick in the ass. I'm willing to bet you're going to make sure he gets one."

"Good Lord willing," Lauren murmured as she thought over my words. Finally, she sighed. "I'll think on what you've asked."

"Take your time. I'm going to go upstairs and collect a few things. I'll be back in a few minutes."

I ran up to Patti's apartment. She had a bedroom set aside just for me. I decided I had time for a quick shower. Actually, I didn't care if I had time, I was taking one. I needed to wake up and get my brain moving better. I wrapped the bandage on my arm in a plastic sack I found under the counter and hopped in. Despite the glory of the hot water, I was in and out in five minutes.

After dressing in jeans, a long-sleeved green shirt, a brown fleece vest, and heavy wool socks, I slid out the box of nulls that I kept under my bed. I'd been working on upping their power levels, but had been pretty hit or miss about getting that done. Recovering from my near-death experiences had taken a lot of my strength, and then I found myself unable to say no to all the paid work suddenly coming my way. The truth was I'd been in full-on avoidance mode. I was trying to pretend that everything was normal and all that death and murder stuff had been a fluke. But reality kept poking at my pretty little fantasy. I was on the wrong end of danger way too often.

I groaned, rifling through the bin. It looked like a thrift store "Free" box. It was full of Legos, marbles, polished rocks, glass figurines, and a variety of other knickknacks. Plastic, stone, glass, and metal were best for making nulls. They held magic best. The more magic they held, the bigger the object needed to be, though I was pretty good about cramming a whole lot of power into a small thing. I picked out some of the strongest nulls. Most of them were cat-eye marbles and a few ball bearings.

Tracing tends to be a defensive sort of talent. I can null out magic, but there really is no good way to attack an enemy beyond that. I can take an enemy's magical weapons away, but that does me precious little good if he's still left with all the normal ones like guns and knives and whatever else he might be carrying. At least, that's the way things have always been. I've got some theories on how to target someone and kill them. I just need to make time to figure it out.

I was going to have to work on it quick, though, because now that the word was out on me, sooner or later some Tyet asshole was going to come after me. Probably more than one. When I refused to do what they wanted, they'd go after my family to force me. I wasn't going to let that happen. Or at least, I didn't plan to, but the way I was taking jobs and ducking my deadly magic project, I was going to run out of time before I had a solution. I'm betting a psychiatrist would have plenty to say about avoidance or sticking my head in the sand or whatever.

"I'll get to it as soon as I find Trevor," I promised myself. I'd hole up at home for a week or so and do some experimenting.

"Talking to yourself?" Patti asked from the doorway behind me. "You know that's a sure sign of insanity, right?"

I twisted to look at her. She leaned against the doorjamb, hands hanging at her sides. Darkness shadowed her eyes, and her brow furrowed. She chewed her upper lip.

"What's wrong?"

Patti never loses her cool. When she worries, she snaps and snarls. It's only when things get really bad that she starts to look uncertain.

"I don't know if I should show you," she began.

"What?" My voice sharpened.

She drew a breath in and blew it out. "You know that since you got caught up in that Tyet business, I've been keeping an ear to the ground for news. I keep feelers out for information on Savannah Morrell and her Tyet buddies, Gregg Touray, the FBI, and of course, Price."

I breathed slowly to calm the sudden fear curdling the food I'd eaten. I clenched my fingers on the bedspread. "So?"

"So I get an alert when one of my search terms pops up somewhere interesting." She held still for a moment, then said. "There's been an explosion."

My heart clenched, and I could barely breathe. "Not Price," I said hoarsely, as if saying it could make it true.

She nodded. "A house that belongs to his brother. That's all the news is reporting."

I leaped to my feet and staggered a few steps and stopped. *Where was I going?* The next thought almost dropped me to the floor. *What if he's dead?*

No. I wouldn't go there. Price was tough and smart. He wasn't going to let himself get killed easily. But I wasn't worried about the easy; I was worried about the hard. Like getting blown up.

"Where?"

"Uptown."

"How bad?"

She held out her phone. The video didn't show much more than clouds of billowing smoke, emergency vehicles, and emergency personnel.

I dug in my pocket and typed out a text: *Are you all right?* I tapped *Send*.

I stared down at the screen, silently begging Price to reply. The bastard phone refused to do anything but lie there like a corpse.

"Maybe he doesn't have his phone on him," Patti suggested, taking pity on me.

"He should be out investigating crimes. If not for me, he wouldn't have become a partner in his brother's syndicate," I said hollowly. "He only did it to force his brother to stay away from me."

I'd wanted—I still wanted—to stand on my own two feet. Now that my secret was out, I needed to learn what I was capable of without relying on someone else to protect me. The irony that I was letting Dalton and his team do just that wasn't lost on me. I hoped that once I was able to protect myself and my family, I could find a way to fully trust Price. That I could protect myself against him if—when—he chose to turn on me in favor of his brother.

The words rang hollow in my mind. They'd made so much sense a month ago, but now the flaw in the logic stuck its tongue out at me with overflowing disgust.

It *had* come to a choice for Price, and he had chosen me. He'd blackmailed his brother into letting me go, and he'd sacrificed his police career to join the Tyet. To buy me time. What more proof of his loyalty and love did I want? Why the hell was I spending so much time feeling crappy about being apart and wondering if he was falling for someone else? Lately my dreams had been divided equally between erotic images of the two of us together that left my thighs aching and the rest of me more frustrated than an impotent priest on free fuck night at the local brothel, and erotic images of Price tonguing some other woman to screaming ecstasy, which left me wanting to skin him alive. I really have mental problems, I swear.

Interrupting my thoughts, Patti snorted at my charitable interpretation of Price's choice to join his brother. "Don't go rewriting history. He was always a part of his brother's organization. With or without you, Price could easily have been in that house just now. If he was, which there is no saying he was," she added, apparently by way of reassuring me. "And it's not like being a cop isn't a dangerous job, especially in Diamond City."

That was true enough, but I wasn't ready to be done tripping on guilt or wallowing in self-pity. "Still, he could be dead and it's all my fault."

"You are fucking kidding me. How could you possibly be responsible for some jackass setting off a giant weenie-roast in Uptown?"

Okay, she was right. The guilt was more about the time I'd wasted. The real issue was I wanted him. I missed him. I'd been smothering myself in work to avoid that particular truth. I'd probably sell my soul to have him back, which is why I couldn't trust myself before and why I second-guessed myself even now. "I should never have pushed him away."

"Are you nuts?" Patti snapped her fingers in front of my face like I needed waking up, then dropped her hands to her hips. "Really? You decide not to date a man who could get you killed or who might even kill you himself, and that's a mistake? For fuck's sake! Avoiding him is probably the smartest thing you've done in your life, besides being my friend. He's too dangerous to be with," she declared.

"Maybe. Okay, probably," I said when she just stared disbelievingly at me. "But it's been damned boring without him."

"You're saying you'd risk your life for entertainment?"

"No." I shook my head ruefully. "It's more than that. I don't seem to like my life much without him. There's no flavor."

"Who are you and what did you do with Riley?" Patti demanded. "You sound like a mental patient. Why don't you take up skydiving or bullfighting. Hell, try Russian roulette. You'd be safer."

"Probably." I shrugged helplessly. "I miss him, Patti. I've been missing him so hard. This bombing—what if he's dead?" The words nearly choked me. No. He was alive. He'd damned well better be or—I drew a harsh breath, refusing to even think of any other possibility. "I fell in love with him. He fell in love with me. Maybe it's doomed. Maybe we'll be fighting like cats and dogs by the end of our first date. But maybe not. All of a sudden I realize that I really want to find out whether we can be anything. This might be a once-in-a-lifetime thing. Why waste the time we have on what-ifs?"

Patti cocked her brow and crossed her arms. "The Riley I know doesn't usually throw caution to the wind. Are you sure this isn't your libido talking?"

"I already decided I didn't want to live in fear anymore. I'm tired of hiding in the shadows from all the big bad wolves of the Tyet. Then I went back to doing it all over again with Price." I looked down at my hands, then back up at her. I didn't talk about my dad much. "When my dad disappeared, I got cold, put up walls to keep people out. I didn't want to get attached to anybody and get hurt. Then I went and fell in love with Price, and half the reason I do love him is that my heart trusts him, even if my head isn't there yet. If I love Price, I have to believe he's not going to disappear on me. I've got to choose to trust him. He's not my dad, and keeping away from him is just another way to put up walls so I don't get hurt. I didn't really realize that before, but now—" I gave her a lopsided grin. "It seems I've gained a whole lot of clarity in the last few minutes."

Patti tipped her head, examining me. Finally, she nodded. "Okay. So long as you're sure he's worth it, I won't argue anymore."

"He is."

She closed me in a tight hug. I wrapped my arms around her.

"Thanks," I whispered. I knew I was doing the right thing for me, and I didn't need her approval. All the same, it was nice to know she had my back in this. My family was going to go nuclear.

Just then my phone chirped. I pulled away from Patti and read the text, my heart pounding in my chest.

Banged up, but safe.

I drew in a shaky breath and let it out slowly, sinking down onto the bed. I read the words again. Then I grinned. Time to jump into the deep end.

I typed out a text:

Dinner at my stepmother's a week from Saturday. Pick me up at the diner at 5:00.
I tapped *Send.*

A moment later he sent his reply.

About fucking time. And all it took was a bomb.

Chapter 3

I collected myself and returned downstairs to the diner. Hearing from Price made me both happy and itchy. I'd never had what anybody could call a boyfriend before, so I had no idea how to feel, except that I was suddenly nervous about seeing him again. I decided that was ridiculous, and in light of the missing kids, too stupid to even give brainspace to. I pushed it out of my head and hoped I'd get over it in the meantime.

Leo had arrived earlier than I expected. He sat at the counter talking to Ben and sipping coffee. When Leo saw me, he jumped up and wrapped me in a bear hug. I clutched him tight right back, ignoring the burn of pain in my arm when I lifted it up.

At last he pushed me back, hands on my shoulders, examining me closely. His hands and forearms were covered with burns, scabs, and scars stemming from his work with jewelry.

Leo was four years older than me, and about that many inches taller. He's my stepbrother, so we look nothing alike. He's über handsome, for one thing. His dark hair is thick, and he combs it back in sexy waves. His eyes are hazel with long dark lashes. He's got one of those chiseled up-to-something faces that make women pant. If he's got a flaw, it's that the bridge of his nose is flat and the whole thing is a little crooked. That, and he can't grow a beard to save his life. When he tries, he looks like he has mange.

I endured his scrutiny as long as I could. "What?"

"You said you were all right, but I haven't seen you since—" He tipped his head in a silent "you know what I'm talking about."

"Since I almost got killed?"

He winced and gave me a little shake. "Yeah, since then."

"You can see for yourself—I'm totally fine."

"Except for the stab wound she got today," Patti added as she stepped up beside me. "How's it going, Leo? Been too long."

He scowled at me. "Stab wound?" His fingers tightened on my shoulders.

"You're going to crack bone if you keep squeezing like that." I wriggled out of his grip. "It's not a big deal. A tinker will have me fixed up in no time."

He looked exaggeratedly around. "Where is this tinker you speak of? Because we sure as hell aren't going under the mountain until you're healed up."

I rolled my eyes at his kingly command. Like I was his peasant-girl servant to order around. "Yes, we are, because five kids are missing and they can't wait."

"Riley—"

"I have a heal-all," Dalton chimed in, having managed to come in the door without ringing the bell. Didn't he know that the whole point of a bell was to warn people he was coming?

I glared at him. "Mind your own business."

"Who are you?" Leo demanded at the same time, turning so that I was behind him.

They faced off like two bulls about to charge each other. If they did smash heads, it wouldn't knock a lick of sense into either one of them. I resisted the urge to kick Leo in the ankle. Instead, I pushed him aside. Rather, I tried to push him aside. He's slender, made of not much more than skin, sinew, bone, and muscle, but I had no more effect on him than a fly on a dinosaur. He might as well have been a boulder. I stepped around him.

Dalton was staring back at Leo with that shuttered look he liked to wear. He was like a book written in unintelligible code. Not for the first time, I itched to slap him, just to see if his expression would change. Being the smart cookie that I am, I didn't follow through, as I prefer being alive.

That's when I noticed that the edges of his silver irises glowed faintly blue. What the hell? Obviously he had tinker-mods, but I had no idea what exactly his eyes could pick up. Another reason not to trust him. For all I know he had Superman's X-ray vision and was looking right through my clothes. I have to admit that while the possibility squicked me out, it also made me want to go shave my legs and other more personal bits. I hadn't had time when I showered upstairs.

Oh hell. I *should* be in a loony bin.

I pushed aside all thoughts of my pubic hair and focused on taking control of the situation.

"Leo, this is Dalton. He's my bodyguard. Or possibly a stalker, I haven't entirely decided yet. No, I didn't hire him. No, I don't know who did. No, I can't get rid of him. So far he's a pain in the ass, but otherwise neither he nor his team has tried to kill me. Dalton, this is my brother, Leo."

"This man has been following you?" Leo asked in an icy voice.

"Him and his team," I said. Then anticipating his next question, I added, "ever since I found Josh."

Josh was a sore subject with Leo, and now he had his underwear in a wad over Dalton. Not that I could blame him, but he was wasting time.

"Before you two decide to go fight a duel or make out in the back of the diner, can I remind you that there are five kids who need our help? If we don't find them soon, they might not survive. Dalton, do you have the gear?"

I wasn't getting away with the change of subject so quickly.

"We're not going into the mountain with him," Leo declared. "We're already looking at running into Tyet soldiers. I'm not going to let us get trapped between them and whoever this guy is." He jerked a thumb at Dalton.

"She's not going without my team," Dalton said, his jaw hardening. His shoulders squared. If he'd had fur, it would be bristling all down his back. My brother and my bodyguard/stalker—a matched pair of macho idiots. If Price were here, I wouldn't be able to breathe for all the testosterone in the air.

"*She* is going to do whatever *she* damned well pleases," I said. "If necessary, *she* will scrape both of you off and go in alone. It wouldn't be the first time." I gave Dalton a pointed look, then continued. "*She* is getting pissed off and *she* is going to kick both your asses if you don't stop acting like dogs fighting over who gets to pee on a fire hydrant. Is *she* clear?"

Leo glanced at me. The corner of his mouth pulled up, and his eyes danced. "Yes, ma'am. The fire hydrant is very clear," he said.

Dalton's lips may have shaped into a fleeting smirk, but I doubted it.

"You're an ass," I told my brother. "So are you," I told Dalton. "Now, did you get all the gear?"

He nodded, but his eyes narrowed. "You will use the heal-all before we go."

Before I could say anything, Leo jumped in. "Absolutely."

I started to open my mouth. My brother cut me off.

"It won't take much time."

I blew out an aggravated breath. "I wasn't going to disagree."

I flopped into the seat across from Lauren and scooted across to leave room for Leo. "Detective Lauren Morton, this is my brother, Leo Calvert. Or stepbrother, if you want to be more accurate. Leo, meet Lauren. Her nephew is one of the missing teens."

He flashed his rogue smile and said hello before sliding in beside me. Dalton stood at the end of the table. I about fainted when he offered Lauren a greeting and a slow smile. A real smile, like a real boy. Man. Whatever. And here I thought he was made out of ice and salt.

"May I sit?" he asked in a tone I'd never heard before. Apparently when he wasn't annoyed with me, he had a sexy growl. Or maybe his Riley voice was also his drill-sergeant voice.

Lauren got a flustered look and moved over. I didn't blame her. When he smiled, he was dazzlingly handsome. Seriously. He could have been a cover model.

He melted gracefully down onto the seat beside her and began fishing in a pocket. He wore one of those military-style flak jackets with a billion pockets and a Kevlar lining. It was black, which, from what I'd seen of him so far, matched the rest of his wardrobe. He seemed to have taken clothing advice from Johnny Cash.

He pulled out an amethyst crystal about the size of my thumb. A silver cap covered one end and a heavy silver chain threaded through the bale on top. He set the necklace down on the table in front of me. I picked it up, turning the crystal in my fingers. I could feel a heavy power in it. This would easily heal my arm and a whole lot more.

I glanced up at Dalton. "Isn't this a little overkill?"

He shrugged. "It's the littlest one I've got."

I lifted one brow. "Again, overkill?"

"Your reputation precedes you," he said, his expression reverting to his habitual sneer. He voice had also returned to drill-sergeant mode.

I frowned. "What are you talking about?"

He started listing stuff, ticking each off on his finger: "getting shot, nearly freezing to death, getting hit with tear gas, getting yourself diced to ribbons, getting beaten within inches of your life, and now . . ." He pointed at my arm. "You really have to ask?"

His list just about confirmed that Touray or Price had sent him. I don't know how else he could have learned about all my mishaps.

He pointed at the crystal. "You ought to use that. We're burning daylight."

Leo stared at me. "Beaten?" he squawked.

Yeah, because that's the worst on the list. On the other hand, I'd deliberately left out that detail in recounting my recent adventures to him, since I hadn't wanted to tell my family that Josh—my sister's former fiancée—had been the one to beat the crap out of me. He'd been drugged out of his mind, and since he'd totally vanished out of Taylor's life since his rescue, I figured it was kinder to let her think he was just broken, not homicidal.

"I'll tell you about it later," I lied.

"Yes, you will," Leo said, his mouth pulling thin and his eyes glittering fury at me.

Inwardly, I sighed. "It wasn't that big of a deal."

"Then you should have no problem telling me about it."

Dalton snorted softly. I glared at him.

"Is something funny?"

"Most definitely," he said, and his expression was positively gloating.

I supposed he figured this was karma for me giving him and his team the brush-off this morning. Last night? Sometime between sunset and sunrise, anyhow. "Remember that snort next time you can't find me," I said with a sweet smile.

His grin faded. "We made a deal—" he began.

I cut him off. "Our deal says that you won't follow me home, and I'll show up for work at the diner so you can stalk me to your heart's desire. I never promised to make it easy."

"What the hell is going on?" Leo demanded.

"Nothing." Dalton and I said it in unison.

I lifted a brow at him, and this time his lips ghosted into a smile before he turned into Mr. Roboto again.

"Are you going to use that or just look at it?"

I thought about making a smart-ass remark, but decided against wasting time. Dalton really rubbed me the wrong way. I settled the necklace around my neck, tucking it under my shirt. Skin contact wasn't necessary, but I didn't know if the crystal would light up like a disco ball. Some tinkers liked a little showiness. Maybe they thought it was a way to get free advertising. Or maybe they thought the sick and wounded needed a little light-show pick-me-up. Plus the customer usually appreciated a sign that the heal-all was working. Like flesh and bone knitting up wasn't evidence enough. At any rate, I didn't need everybody in the diner rubbernecking to see what was going on.

I touched the amethyst lump between my breasts and activated it. It flared with scorching heat. Instantly I started sweating, making my shower fairly pointless.

The heat spread around me in a sheath before sinking inside. It broke into wormy fragments that oozed and slithered through me, nosing around for something to fix. Maybe I should have put the pendant right over the wound so it would focus on my actual problem. Then again, it wasn't called a heal-*all* for nothing. This sort of magic was meant to be thorough. If I had a canker sore or an ingrown toenail, it would fix those, too.

Eventually I could feel it focus on the scalpel wound. I gripped my coffee cup tightly as it burrowed into the wound, summoning reinforcements from the rest of the oozy little bits. It was like having a few hundred maggots wriggling around in my flesh. I was starting to feel really glad that the last time I'd suffered a heal-all healing, I'd been unconscious.

Everybody was watching me. I looked at them, sweat running down the sides of my face, not to mention everywhere else. "Should I do a dance or something?" I asked.

"Watching you squirm is entertainment enough," Leo said, but he still frowned.

Dalton, on the other hand, was grinning. I gave him a withering look. He only smiled wider.

"What are the eye mods for?" I asked, deciding that I didn't need to be the only uncomfortable one at the table.

His smiled vanished. "None of your business."

"I don't know. Apparently you want to be my bodyguard. Seems to me I ought to know your skills and capabilities, don't you think? How do I know if you're any good?"

"Just who the hell are you?" Leo demanded, glaring at Dalton through narrowed eyes. "Who are you working for? What do you want of my sister?"

I could have chanted the answers along with Dalton, I'd heard them so often.

"I work for someone who wishes to remain anonymous, but wants to see Miss Hollis stay safe. My job is to protect her."

Leo looked at me. "And you're okay with this?"

"No. But I can't seem to do anything about it at the moment."

He looked back at Dalton. "What have you done to protect her?"

Now *that* I hadn't actually bothered asking.

"We've blocked three attempts to kidnap her just this week, and two attempts to kill her. We have also captured several people carrying various charms designed to incapacitate her or lure her away."

My mouth fell open, and my stomach wriggled queasily. Dalton gave me a "so there" sort of look. Because apparently we were still twelve. I, however, did not stick my tongue out at him, though I really wanted to. On the other hand, I felt like I'd been gut-punched. I'd known I'd be a target once word about my skills got out, that and I'd developed some new enemies among the Tyet elite, including Savannah Morrell and Alexander Briandi, both of whom would like to skin me alive for ruining their plans to take over the city. But I'd convinced myself that *I* was the one who was keeping me safe; that I was being so ultrasmart and careful that they couldn't get at me. I was an idiot. And now Leo knew it, too.

Leo does this thing when he's mad where he sucks it all in and turns into something like volcanic ice. I could feel his rage vibrating off him in frigid waves.

"So how did she get knifed?" he asked in a calm, conversational voice. Anybody who knew anything about him would know he was about to come unglued.

"She ducked us and went to the Bottoms by herself," Dalton said, and he looked like he'd eaten a porcupine. He probably didn't like confessing that I'd given him the slip.

"Ah," Leo said, nodding his head. "So what you're saying is you're not particularly competent at your job."

Unexpectedly, I found myself wanting to defend Dalton. After all, I'm pretty damned good at my job, and mine included being sneaky. It was possible he wasn't incompetent, but I was just that good. I didn't say anything. The healing sensation was making my stomach churn dangerously. Keeping my mouth shut meant that Lauren stood a better chance of not wearing my last meal.

Dalton's cheeks flushed brick red, and his mouth compressed into a white line. "It doesn't help that your sister refuses to cooperate in her protection."

I couldn't let that one go. "Excuse me, but I don't know who the hell you are or who hired you. As far as I know, you're just trying to lull me into a situation where I calmly walk into your spider web, Mr. Black Widow. No fucking thanks."

I sucked down some coffee to force my rising breakfast back down. Right about then, the heat of the heal-all intensified, and I started considering stripping naked to cool off. Suddenly it shut off, and the heat began to dissipate. I lifted my arm and rotated my shoulder a little. All that remained was a slight ache and tightness where the cut had been.

"Looks like I'm good to go," I said. I started to slip the heal-all back over my head to give it back. It wasn't used up yet.

"Keep it," Dalton said. "Knowing you, you'll need it."

"Like you know the first thing about me," I snapped back.

His nostrils flared, and his lip curled. "More than you know, Princess."

Princess? *Princess?* What the hell was that supposed to mean?

Leo snorted. "Princess, my ass. Or no! I'd say you are Princess Pain In the Ass." He grinned. "You need a crown, your highness."

"You need a kick in the balls," I returned, then looked at Dalton. "Call me 'princess' again and I'll make you regret it."

He didn't look cowed in the least. That's okay. He'd learn different when the time came. If I had to, I'd pay a tinker to make sure he couldn't get a hard-on for a month. Maybe I'd have them turn his balls blue, too, just for fun.

Lauren had sat through all of this without saying a word. Now she cleared her throat, reminding all of us that we had work to do.

I sobered. Business. Lives were at stake.

I took one last sip of my coffee and nudged Leo to get up. "Let's go."

"Where?" Dalton asked.

"Let's start at Vine and Reeder where Lauren last saw him. I'll pick up Trevor's trace there," I said. "We'll follow it in."

He scowled. "We could easily be walking into trouble."

"Doesn't change the fact that these kids need help and we're all they've got. But by all means, if you want to sit this one out, do." I sounded nonchalant, but I have to admit, even not fully trusting him, in the tunnels I'd rather have him at my back than not.

Dalton said nothing, but stood and headed toward the door. Lauren followed, collecting her coat, hat, and gloves. Leo did the same. I ducked into the back to slide on my spare snow pants and grabbed my coat. I drew on gloves, a hat, and a scarf before returning to the others.

Outside, Dalton had a pair of charcoal-gray Hummers waiting. I was surprised. The dealership must've been out of black models on car-shopping day. Both were outfitted with studded off-road tires. He motioned for me to get into the first one with Leo and Lauren, while his four-member team climbed into the other.

I slid into the front seat. I didn't buckle. I figured I'd rather be able to jump out if necessary. Dalton started the engine and touched his fingers to the dashboard. Instantly magic enclosed the vehicle.

"What was that?"

He looked at me. "What was what?"

I almost backpedaled. If he didn't know I could sense magic, then maybe it should stay that way. Then again, he wasn't stupid, and he'd figure it out soon anyhow. "The magic you just activated."

He looked away, scowling. "Shielding. It'll keep us safe from magic attacks and it also nulls us out."

"Nice," Leo said.

"Expensive," I said.

"The trucks are reinforced against bullets and explosives," he added. "You are safe inside."

"Uh-huh," I said. I could shred the magic shields if I wanted. At least I was pretty sure I could. After escaping a powerful null cage a month ago when I was exhausted, breathing tear gas, and bleeding, I felt pretty good about being able to take down the Hummer shields after having just benefited from a heal-all. If I could do it, chances are others could too, even if they had to work together to do it.

I opened myself to the trace of the shield. A shimmering sheath of pale blue encompassed the truck. It reminded me of light reflecting off a swimming pool. I couldn't touch it without rolling down the window or putting my hand into the trace dimension. I wasn't going to try either in front of an audience. Instead I let my eyes unfocus, trying to get a sense of the spell's nature. It was binder magic, for sure. Not a surprise. Most shields were. Binder spells could deflect attacks, and occasionally absorb them. Not a lot of people could make magic-absorbing spells. I was the only one I knew who could, though I'd seen evidence of other magic workers who could do it. The few absorbing spells I'd seen were at Tyet fortresses.

Just looking at this spell, I couldn't tell what it could do. I blinked and closed off from the trace. I settled into my seat and turned to look out the window. Snow lay thick over everything. Dirty mountains of it filled alleyways and formed ranges on sidewalks. On roofs, it lay in tall slabs, glittering like diamonds in the sunshine. Luckily, most people reinforced their roofs with magic, otherwise the buildings might have collapsed under the weight.

We drove through the center of Downtown. The high-rises loomed over us. The streets were pretty drivable down here. Money's got to get made, after all. We crossed the river, where a long line of dump trucks dropped snow into the fast-running water. You'd think that someone would figure out a magical solution to clearing snow, but there wasn't a good one. Melting it would only cause floods, and you couldn't make it move itself.

Dalton turned off onto a side street. The Hummer's engine roared as it bounced over ruts and trenches in the snow. I had a feeling we were going to have to start slogging on foot soon. Sure enough, he pulled over into an empty parking lot and shut the truck off and disabled the shields. He hopped out, and we all followed, as the other Hummer pulled in beside us.

I retreated to the back, where Dalton unloaded snowshoes and backpacks. He handed them out. I buckled the aluminum frames over my boots. Magic tingled in my fingers as I did. My guess was that the snow-shoes would repel snow a bit, keeping them from getting weighed down, and also lend a little lift to my strides. I put on my backpack and fastened it around my waist. I didn't bother to ask what was inside. I was pretty sure we had the basics—lights, food, water, rope, first aid, nulls, possibly weapons, and some sort of emergency beacon. The latter wouldn't do much good in the mines if we got ourselves lost unless the searchers got close, but it was better than nothing.

Dalton passed out walking poles next. I extended mine and tightened the nut to keep the length where I wanted it. Leo had just finished getting ready and turned to help Lauren get her gear sorted out.

"Walking isn't that tough in these," he assured her. "Lift your foot and turn your toes out. Use your poles for balance. I'll warn you, though, you're going to feel it in your butt and hamstrings later."

"I'll be fine," Lauren said, putting her hands through the pole straps. "Let's get going."

"The carabiners hanging on the front of your packs are shield nulls. Activate them now," Dalton ordered.

We all grasped them in our hands and ordered the nulls to activate. A voice command or strong mental command was all it took. Then Dalton gave quick orders to his team, and the two women swung into place just ahead and two men flanked us. Dalton fell in to the left of me, and Lauren and Leo came behind. All five bodyguards carried automatic weapons dangling from shoulder slings.

The sun had turned orange in the western sky by the time we got to Vine and Reeder. We kept to a slower pace, as Lauren quickly wore out. Snowshoeing is hard work. Good for your ass, but hard work. I glanced back at her periodically to ask if she wanted to rest, but she remained dogged.

"I'll be fine," she said each time. "Don't need to waste any more time."

When we got to the convenience store on the corner where the missing kids liked to hang out, I didn't bother going in. The snow gave the place an air of quaint cottagey beauty, but I knew that underneath the paint was peeling and the cement walls were eroding way, and the place was infested with rats and vermin. I'd been inside once years ago, and I refused to ever return. If I went in, I'd probably come out with a case of lice.

I searched for Trevor's trace outside. I found it within a few minutes. As I expected, it headed east toward the escarpment. Then I quickly picked up trace from his companions. One was a plum-black, another gray with streaks of red, the next was faded brown, and the last was a rosy apricot. It was a relief to see that all the kids were alive.

I considered reaching into the trace dimension to touch their trace. That would tell me more about their states of mind and give a better sense of when exactly they'd passed by, but I wasn't about to do it in front of witnesses. Not too many people knew I could do that, and I wasn't ready to broadcast the secret.

The good news for us was that their trail didn't meander around before it entered the tunnels.

The entrance they'd used was to an old mine shaft. It was a little over a mile from the store up Reeder Street, which dead-ended into the easement that ran along the length of the escarpment. Train tracks, sidewalks, and roads ribboned out in both directions. A few shacks and piles of snow-mantled slag filled in between.

They'd had to dig out the entrance to the old mine shaft. It was little more than a hobbit hole along the base of the escarpment. A square, rusted steel door covered the entrance. I didn't sense any magic from it. By law, all mine entrances had to be magically and physically sealed. The teens had broken the chains that ran through steel loops fastened into the rock. My guess was that the magic lock had long since dissolved. That sort of thing happened a lot. A powerful magical vortex fed by multiple ley lines swirled deep under the mountains. It tended to eat away at other magics if they weren't reinforced regularly. Most of the in-city mining claims had been abandoned because of increasing regulations, which meant the mine entrances were no longer tended. The city claimed not to have enough resources. Getting inside the mountain these days took almost no work at all.

Getting out, now that was a whole other story. Odds were in favor of you dying, either by running into Tyet operations, by starvation or thirst, or by Mother Nature giving you a stone spanking.

As Dalton pulled open the door with an ominous creak, I felt my insides tie into macramé knots. I swallowed. He bent and removed his snowshoes, setting them aside behind a pile of rocks and snow. He returned to the entrance and leaned down to look inside and then in a bonelessly graceful move for such a big man, he disappeared into the darkness. A moment later his hand appeared, his fingers curling to indicate it was safe to follow.

One of the women from the team removed her snow shoes and squatted down to crab-walk inside. Now there were two people guarding our entry. I should have been next, but I hung back. Lauren went instead. Leo frowned at me.

"Are you sure you want to do this?"

"No," I said, mechanically unbuckling my own snowshoes and setting them with the others.

"Better to stay out if you're going to become a liability inside."

"Can *you* find the kids?" I retorted, my heart battering at the inside of my ribcage. I was starting to feel light-headed.

"About as well as you if you decide to faint," he said.

"I'm not going to faint."

"Mind telling that to the rest of you? You're about as white as a ghost and you're shaking like an aspen leaf."

"I'm white? Me? A redhead? In the dead of winter? Well, hell. I suppose I'd better get to a tanning bed as fast as humanly possible."

"Riley," he said in that big-brother warning tone of his.

I rolled my eyes. "I'll be fine."

He crossed his arms over his chest. "Then get going already."

With a silent sigh, I forced myself to the entrance. As I crawled inside, I couldn't help feeling like I was walking out in front of a firing squad. I told myself not to be an idiot. After all, not only was my stepmother expecting me for dinner a week from Saturday, but I had a date with Price. There'd be hell to pay if I let either of them down. Neither was going to accept dying as an excuse.

Chapter 4

Rocks chewed into my knees as I crawled through the opening, every movement I made stiff with reluctance.

Dalton had clipped toe lamps to his boots. He gave me a hand up. The rock roof overhead allowed me to straighten, but he was forced to stoop.

"You've got toe lamps in the left side pocket of your pack," he said, then reached down to help Leo through.

That was handy information. It would have been even handier if I'd had a chance to find them outside where there was still light enough to see by. I dug for them, using the distraction as a chance to get myself under control. I breathed in, counting silently in my head: 1 . . . 2 . . . 3 . . . 4 . . . 5 . . . And out: 1 . . . 2 . . . 3 . . . 4 . . . 5 . . .

I kept that up as the rest of our party joined us inside. There wasn't much room. A pile of rocks and rusted equipment heaped up on one side, cutting what had been a reasonably spacious area into a hallway. I guessed that this had once been an easy in-and-out shaft for workers, and when the mine went defunct, it had turned into a dumping ground.

I was squeezed between Dalton and Leo. The former blocked the passage out so that no one could go past him. Likely that's where the foreman had checked miners' pockets in the good old days to keep them from stealing. The outer rims of Dalton's silver eyes gleamed dark orange, almost red. I wondered again what he could see. Then again, maybe his eyes were just human disco balls. Better yet, maybe they were mood eyes. If so, he was feeling fiery. I snorted to myself. Right. As far as I could tell, he only had the one mood—pissed off. I could sympathize.

I was still shaking with the cold of pure fear. The longer I stood around doing nothing, the worse it got.

"Let's get going," I said. I sounded belligerent. Dammit. I swallowed. "One of the kids could be injured," I added. Maybe everyone would think I was just worried instead of terrified.

"Not yet," Dalton said. He unhitched a length of rope from his backpack and unwound it. Every four feet was a pair of double knots, two inches apart. A carabiner hung in between. "Latch yourself on to the rope," he ordered. "Use a belt-loop or one of the metal rings on the side of your pack."

Clearly we weren't moving until we were all attached, so I hooked the rope to my backpack. I wanted to be able to drop it and run if needed, and clipping to my pants was counterproductive to that plan. I was beginning to feel a lot like one of the seven dwarves. Maybe next we could all start singing. Hi-*ho, Hi-ho, it's off to death we go, with magic traps and mine collapses* . . . The rhyme needed a little work.

I was in line behind Dalton and one of the female members of his team. I should learn their names. Her chestnut hair was pulled into two tiny pigtails just behind her ears. Bangs curtained her forehead above a rounded face. She looked over her shoulder past me, then turned to murmur something to Dalton.

I took advantage of the murky gloom and everybody's distraction over clipping on to the line to grab hold of Trevor's trace. I bent down, pretending to adjust my toe lamps. I slipped my hand into the trace dimension. Instantly my skin and bones turned icy. The cold slipped into my blood and crept up my arm and into my chest. I grabbed Trevor's trace. Something against my hand, then thin fingers grasped my wrist. I yanked back. As I did, someone called my name.

"Yeah?" I asked, rubbing the numbness circling my wrist where I'd been grabbed.

"Yeah, what?" Leo said, tugging on the rope and letting go when he was satisfied it wasn't going to give way.

"Someone said my name."

He gave me that patient worried look, like I was going out of my head. "Are you sure you can handle being down here?"

I made an exasperated sound and shook my hand. "I'm fine." Except someone had called my name. I looked around. No one else had heard it. Had it come from the trace dimension? The idea sent spiders crawling down my spine. Who—what—had touched me? And called my name? How did it know me? What the hell was going on?

I looped Trevor's trace ribbon around my wrist and shook my hand to get the circulation going and warm myself back up. I'd never had the cold of the trace dimension strike me so swiftly or with such a vengeance before. I flexed my fingers and curled them into my palm, my nails cutting into my skin.

I'd often wondered if something inhabited the trace dimension. Spirits, maybe. It was the only explanation I could think of for the feeling of beings rubbing against me when I reached through. I'd always thought the encounters were accidental, like fish nudging against swimmers in a small pond. But now—someone, some *thing*—had tried to grab me. Something more solid than a spirit. If it had got hold of me, would it have tried to pull me fully into the trace dimension? Would it have frozen me solid? Or did it have another plan that I couldn't begin to imagine? It knew my name. Did it want something from me?

I shuddered. I wasn't going to cross over that line again any time soon unless absolutely necessary. I take great pride in not being that girl in the horror movies who knows a serial killer is axing people out in the woods and so decides that a nature walk is a brilliant idea. I'm the lock-myself-in-the-basement-with-a-shotgun-and-some-napalm sort of woman. So given that the metaphorical ax-murderer was in the trace dimension, I planned to stay the hell out of the woods.

I know, famous last words, and I've been known to blindly run into a burning building to help someone out. this time would be different, I told myself firmly.

I didn't have time to worry about what might be waiting for me in the trace dimension. I had more pressing problems. Focusing on the reason we were in the mines, I turned my attention Trevor's trace. Its mustard-orangey hue was still vibrant, though I could feel fear racing through it, along with a healthy dose of curiosity. I wonder if anybody ever told him that curiosity killed fewer cats than it did humans and that it never paid to get nosy with the Tyet.

I gave a quiet sigh. He was a teenage boy, and stupid by virtue of his hormones. Teenage girls were no better. At that age, after my dad disappeared, there wasn't a single line I didn't cross, and no rules I didn't break. I was lucky I didn't get myself killed. I came close more than once, and goodness knows I wouldn't have cared much if I did.

Lauren didn't appear to be having much better luck straightening out Trevor than Mel had with me. You can lead a horse to water, and while you can beat it senseless, you can't actually make it drink, short of putting a hose down its throat and pumping its stomach full. That probably defeats the purpose.

I was hoping Trevor didn't learn his lesson by getting his throat slit.

Happily, I realized that thanks to getting grabbed, for a few minutes, I'd forgotten I was standing inside a mountain, the roof and walls of the shaft held stable by fading magic and old timbers. Not so happily, I suddenly remembered, and instantly my body dampened with cold sweat. I snorted at myself. At this point, though I *knew* the Tyet was the most dangerous threat around, they seemed like mere gnats to the circling vultures of my fears.

"Are we ready?" I asked, trying to keep my voice steady. Movement always helped. I knew I wouldn't get lost. Or rather, I might get lost, but so long as I could find trace in the maze of shafts knotting through the mountain, I'd find a way out eventually. Of course, that was presupposing the mountain didn't collapse on me, or I didn't fall down a deep shaft.

A chorus of readies down the line behind me indicated that, in fact, we could start looking for the teens.

"Where to?" Dalton asked me.

Inconvenient though it was to be the third in line and have to lead from behind, I knew he wasn't going to let me get around him or the woman in front of me. Maggie. That was her name. I'd heard it before, but now it clinked down into my brain like a pebble down a drainpipe.

"Straight ahead," I said.

We started off. It was like being in a chain gang. We shuffled along, the rope pulling taut between us, then slackening, then tightening again. I couldn't see anything ahead. Dalton's toe lamps only illuminated a few feet in front of him, and he and Maggie blocked most of that view.

The ceiling was low, and here and there Dalton called out a warning to duck. We went on for a hundred feet or more.

"Left. About ten feet up," I called.

Turning the corner took a while. Behind me, the rope jerked as Lauren, Leo, and the other three members of Dalton's team snaked around. If the snake was an epileptic in the middle of a seizure.

We had only just straightened out when I called out a right, another left, then down a long, rough-cut stairway that jigged and jagged according to whatever drunken whim had overcome the people cutting it into the earth. The walls on both sides scraped my shoulders, and I had to hunch over to keep from scalping myself on the roof. Chunks of stone littered the steps, and once I slid on one, barely catching myself before I dominoed over Maggie and Dalton.

A wider space at the bottom led away into four branch tunnels. Metal tracks ran through, with a circle roundabout where we stood.

"They split up," I said. "Three of them went to the far right, two others went to the second left."

"Which way did Trevor go?" Lauren asked. She sounded faintly winded and the last word trembled off her tongue.

"With the three," I said. "We should split up."

"And how do you expect to follow both trails? We only have one tracer," Dalton said.

I could hear him sneering.

"Leo can ask the metal," I said, before looking at my brother. "Can't you?"

The light from the toe lamps hollowed at his face, making him look harsh and dangerous. "I don't think it's a good idea," he said.

"What if the others are hurt? Maybe dying?" I dug my heels in. "We have the means to go after both. We should."

"No," Dalton said.

I ground my teeth together. I couldn't make Dalton do anything he didn't want to do. Unless, of course, I decided to run off on my own into the mines. That was a spectacularly bad idea, so much so that even I understood it. I looked over my shoulder.

"Leo?"

He sighed heavily and shook his head. "I agree with Dalton. Better we stick together. We'll come back and get the other two after we find the three."

I flexed my fingers. I could grab the trace of the two, and then I'd know if they were in danger. But I'd have to put my hand back into the spirit dimension, and that was enough to make me think twice. Plus I didn't want Dalton or his crew to know I could do it. Basically, there was no way I was going to argue myself into a win. I decided to give in gracefully.

"Fine," I said. "I hope to hell they don't die." Or maybe not so gracefully.

Dalton strode out down the far right branch. Maggie followed quick on his heels. The two yanked me after them before I had a chance to think about moving. I stumbled forward, stepping on Maggie's heels. She swore and twisted sideways.

"Walk on your own damned feet, would you?"

"But yours are so much more comfortable," I said. "Hey, that reminds me. Where were you when I went down to the Bottoms earlier today?"

She scowled at me. "Fuck off."

"Trying to, but damn if you and your buddies can't take a hint."

"Maggie," Dalton said before she could retort, his voice cracking like a whip.

She flinched and spun away from me.

After that, I lost all track of time. It was clear the teens had quickly become lost. They coiled and turned, twisting back on their own path. I was able to follow the most recent trail, which saved time, but it didn't seem to bring us any closer to our quarry. I couldn't tell how far we'd gone. We climbed up and burrowed down, marching down oddly straight shafts for what seemed like miles. We saw no one else. Occasionally, distorted noises filtered through to us. Every time we heard something, we stopped and waited to see if someone was coming. Leo's talent came in handy for that. If enough metal veined in the walls or floors, he could reach out along it like an antenna. The more metal, the better his information.

Eventually we found functioning mining claims. Most were booby-trapped, miners being paranoid about people jumping claims. Dalton seemed to have a sixth sense, or maybe he saw things nobody else could. I could only pick up on active magic, and could only tell vague things about a spell, like whether it was binder magic or maker magic or what-have-you.

A lot of the traps didn't require magic. They were good old-fashioned blow-you-up sorts of things. Trip wires spanned the passages every-where—from ankle high to head high. Each time we had to unclip from the guide rope, and each one of us had to go over or under with two of Dalton's team members holding lights on the wires so that we didn't accidentally blunder into them anyway.

After a dozen of those, I was getting ready to scream with frustration. We were going too damned slow.

"Don't get ideas," Leo said as I waited for the last member of Dalton's crew to pass over the most recent trip wire.

"Ideas?" I repeated innocently.

"Of heading off on your own."

"Wouldn't think of it," I lied.

"You'd be dead by now," he said. "All these traps—you wouldn't have seen any of them."

I shrugged. It was true, but that didn't mean I had to admit it. I frowned. That begged the question—how were the teens still alive? How had they managed to avoid triggering the traps? I asked Leo.

Now it was his turn to scowl and shrug. "It's been bothering me, too."

"What's bothering you?" Dalton asked. Apparently he had bat ears.

I bit back my unhelpful and sarcastic knee-jerk reply—the man brought out the worst in me, I swear—and focused on being a team player. "How come the kids didn't trip these traps?"

"A good question," he said. "I have been wondering the same."

"Maybe they had some sort of map," Lauren suggested.

It was the simplest explanation, which made it also the most likely explanation. If true, it meant that the kids might not be in danger. At least, not from starving or getting lost. Though why the two had split from the three was a question that gnawed at me. If they had a map, they could have stuck together; they *should* have stuck together. Still, they'd been alive when we'd crossed their trail. Maybe there had been two maps.

But why? Why give the teens the means to come down into the mines at all?

Foreboding washed through me. Something here was way off-kilter. Danger prickled over my skin. I wanted nothing more than to run, and not just because of my claustrophobia. I might have bolted if Lauren hadn't sniffed and wiped at the corners of her eyes. That left me with no choice.

I cast a worried look at Leo, and he nodded. He'd sink himself deeper into the metal to give us what warning might be had. I wasn't entirely sure what that would entail. Neither of my brothers were ever particularly clear on what the metal had to tell them or how. But I'd never once won a game of hide-and-seek with them. They always knew exactly where to look for me. They always just smiled and went cryptic, saying the earth talked to them.

We continued our slow march. Our path began to lead downward. I couldn't tell what direction otherwise. I was sure we were well below Downtown, but I didn't think we'd reached the level of the Bottoms. Other than that, we might have been heading east deeper under the mountains for all I knew. The idea made me shudder.

One of these days, I was really going to have to figure out how to get over my claustrophobia. Without going to a dreamer.

Just the possibility sent chills rushing through me, and my mind slammed it down with an instant *never!* Dreamers go into minds and can do everything from erase memories to implant new personalities, as well as heal psychological issues like phobias. I'd never trusted them—even though I'd become friends with one in the course of finding my kidnapped almost-brother-in-law. Much as I liked Cass, I had no plans to let her back in.

I caught myself. That wasn't entirely true. At some point, I was going to have to let a dreamer into my head. Cass had discovered someone had tampered with my mind. Other than Cass saying it had been a long time since the damage had been done, I had no idea what they'd done or when. Just thinking about it sent my blood pressure thundering through my head and twisted my stomach inside out.

What had been done to me? What had I lost? Who had done it and why? When? So many questions, and no answers except what might still lie in my brain. I didn't know if Cass could repair it. I definitely wasn't ready for her to try. I wasn't sure when I would be. I couldn't put it off forever. It had something to do with my mother's murder and father's disappearance. I was absolutely sure. Nothing else made sense.

Now was *not* the time, I told myself firmly, as we came to yet another trip wire. I needed to stay focused.

We all unclipped again and stepped through. Before we could reattach ourselves, shots rang down the tunnel to us. I couldn't tell from which direction.

Instantly, Maggie and Dalton took up defensive positions. "Lights off," Dalton whispered. Leo pushed me up against the wall. He bent and switched off both our toe lamps, then shielded me with his body. I tried to push him off, but he'd braced his hands on either side of me.

"Stop it," he muttered against my ear. "Can't you see I'm working?"

I did as told, but made a face in the darkness. Ever since my dad had married Mel, my stepbrothers had treated me like I was glass. They were obnoxiously protective, to the point I'd considered moving to Timbuktu just so I didn't get the ninth degree every time I went to the grocery store. After my dad disappeared and I'd gone wild, I'd driven them nuts with all the crazy chances I took. But at least now they let me have my life. That had something to do with how paranoid-careful I was about keeping my head down and my nose clean. Hence me not wanting to hang out and chat after the whole finding-Josh episode. I'd kept a lot of details to myself, and once Leo knew Josh had used me for a punching bag, I was pretty sure I was headed for a Spanish Inquisition–style interrogation about the whole episode. Despite the situation, I couldn't help the smile that quirked the corners of my mouth. Wait until Leo found out Price was coming to dinner. That would pop his cork with a vengeance.

"We've got about a half mile before I sense people. There's an empty cavern a ways up on the left. It gets us close and we can figure out a plan from there." He spoke quietly, barely more than a whisper.

With his bat ears, Dalton had no trouble hearing.

"Where did the gunshots come from?"

"Hard to say. There's a lot of metal up ahead. It would take me a while to find a single gun, and I don't know that I'd find the right one."

"Fall in behind me," Dalton said, not wasting words. "I'll check for traps. Everybody clip on," he ordered.

I reached out to grip the rope, but didn't attach myself. Leo went ahead of Maggie. Lauren came behind me.

We'd gone a little ways when the sounds of thumping and grinding started rolling down through the tunnel. It was soft at first, like a snoring dragon, then grew louder. A glow penetrated the stygian darkness ahead.

Just as predicted, Leo led us into a cavern room on the left side. Light erupted as we entered. I'll admit I jumped and grabbed for my gun. But the lights were automatic.

Boxes and various equipment filled the metal shelves lining the walls. A little alcove contained a kitchenette with a small counter, a stove and oven, a microwave, a sink, a fridge, and a small table. Next to it was a door. I looked inside. Within was a large bathroom, complete with urinals, stalls, and gang showers, the kind I remembered from high school. Blue lockers lined the far wall.

It was a pretty typical mining setup. A lot of employees worked long shifts, spending their nights down close to their jobs. They'd work seven days on and seven off. Somewhere close by would be dormitory rooms or, more likely, several larger rooms with stacked bunk beds, as well as an actual cafeteria. This kitchenette was set up for times when the cafeteria wasn't available to employees, or when they might not want to use it.

"What do we do now?" Lauren asked. She looked at me. "Trevor, he's—?"

Her fears for his safety were palpable. Sweat slicked her forehead, and her chest rose quickly.

"He's alive," I said. His trace looped around my wrist told me he was probably sleeping. His emotions had gone soft edged and quiet.

"You're still going to find him?" she asked. Pleaded, really, as if she were holding me to a promise no matter what. Maybe she thought I changed my mind after hearing gunshots.

I nodded. "We will."

I wasn't going to come this far without something to show for it. And Lauren's desperation touched me. Unlike the surgeon's wife, she clearly loved her nephew. I hoped when we got him back, he'd find a way to straighten out.

"Why aren't the tunnel lights coming on automatically?" Maggie asked. She was looking out the way we'd come. Two of her cohort were guarding the entrance. She looked at Dalton. "These lights came on. Clearly this part of the mine is in use. That means there should have been sensors to turn up the lights when we came through, or they should already have been on."

I disliked the woman, but I couldn't argue with her logic. That sense of something being off banged in my skull. It was beginning to feel like a trap. But how? And why?

I looked at Lauren. She was looking at me sadly, her faced lined with guilt. "He threatened to kill him," she said. "All of them, if I didn't bring you down here. He said you'd come for the kids. You have a soft spot for them."

My mouth opened. Words stuttered on my tongue and dissolved into silence. I'd trusted her; trusted her very real worry and loss. In that moment, I hated her. I felt betrayed. Reason tried to remind me that her nephew was being held hostage, that I'd have done worse to get back my own flesh and blood. But the truth was that I wouldn't have. I'd kill myself to get them back, but I wouldn't sacrifice innocent people.

I'd thought she wasn't corrupt. Turns out she was just as bad as all the rest of Diamond City's cops.

"We have to get out of here," Dalton said, reaching out to grab my arm.

Like I needed dragging. I was more than ready to go.

"No. You can't. They *will* kill Trevor." Lauren's voice hardened. She'd backed up so that her back was to the shelves. Her gun pointed straight at me. It looked like a cannon. Funny how big a gun suddenly gets when it's pointed at your chest. In her other hand, she held small black block. She activated it, and I felt magic pulsing off.

"I only need her," she said. "The rest of you can go."

Nobody moved, which left dealing with the situation sensibly up to me. I forced myself to draw breath, never tearing my eyes away from the gaping barrel of the gun.

"Go," I said. "Get out now. I expect to be rescued."

"I'm not leaving you, Riley," Leo started, but I chopped a hand in the air to cut him off.

"Yes, you are. Because everybody else is lost without you. Keep your senses peeled. I'll make sure you can find me."

"Fucking hell," Dalton swore. "This—" He broke off. "Fuck."

"Damned right," I said. "You're running out of time. Get out."

I guess I was convincing. One by one they slipped away until only Dalton and Leo were left.

Leo grabbed my hand in his hard grip. "Don't get dead."

"I don't plan to," I said, fear coiling through me. I breathed slowly, trying to focus. I felt like crying when he disappeared out into the tunnel. I should have given him some last words to tell my family and Patti. And Price.

Then only Dalton was left. He hesitated off to my left. I could tell he was thinking about attacking Lauren.

"I'd rather you didn't risk it," I said. "She's very motivated."

"So am I," he snarled. Fury crisped the edges of his words.

"All the same, she's pointing the gun at *me*." I hesitated. "Gregg Touray and Clay Price will help. Get them."

Whether he worked for them or not, he had to know the names, and know the power behind them. Those two would bring an army. Touray would do it just to keep me from falling into enemy hands. I *would* be rescued.

Whoever wanted me wasn't going to kill me. The danger was that they'd haul me off and make me disappear. I was already halfway doing their job by nulling my trace, but my captors would make sure that continued. They could hide me next door to Price, and he'd never know. Leo's talent would only find me if he was in the near vicinity.

That said, I wasn't helpless, by any stretch of the imagination. I'd broken out of captivity before, I could do it again. I made myself look away from the barrel of the gun, up into Lauren's face. I wanted to punch her. Her mouth tightened, reading my expression.

"Get lost, Dalton," I said. "Try to do better about finding me this time, will you?"

"As you wish, Princess."

With that, the bastard slipped out, leaving me alone with Lauren.

"What now?"

"He'll send someone for us."

"Who?"

She shrugged. "I don't know. He has Trevor and his friends. He called me, told me that I could have them all back if I brought you down here. He said you'd trace them. All I had to do was ask. He never said who he was and the call couldn't be traced."

"And if you didn't do what he asked?"

"He'd kill all of them. Send them back to me in little pieces." Her mouth twisted and set. "I couldn't say no."

"Sure you could."

She shook her head hard. "No."

"You can, however, sacrifice me. Have you thought about what they might want? What they plan to do to me?"

She swallowed convulsively. "I have."

"And you're okay with that?" I knew I wasn't talking her out of anything. I also wasn't trying to make a run for it. I was pretty sure she wasn't going to give me the chance. She was a cop, after all, and she knew how to stay focused on her mission. She also knew how to use a gun.

"It's better than the alternative," she said after a moment, her voice rough. "I'm all Trevor has. I *am* sorry."

"Maybe it's better. Maybe not." I smiled. "You trust these people to keep their word? That's a little naïve, don't you think? Chances are better than good that they'll kill you and Trevor and his friends."

"I don't have any choice."

"Are you trying to convince me or yourself?"

"What would you have done in my place? Let him die?"

"I'd have rescued him, without trading an innocent life," I said.

"I haven't the means."

"You didn't try," I retorted.

I fell silent at that point. I was angry, but less at her now than myself. I'd trusted her blindly and walked into the trap like a lemming. I'd never thought it could be a setup. She'd been genuinely worried. After all, her nephew had been kidnapped for real. There was no reason to suspect her.

Except that I knew for a fact that people were out to get me. Dalton and his crew were a daily reminder, but I'd been acting like one of those hear-no-evil, see-no-evil monkeys, covering my ears and eyes and blundering around like a fool. Or more accurately, I'd stuck my head in the sand like an ostrich, with my ass waving in the air for anybody to come shoot at. Surviving what I had, had made me cocky.

Basically, I'd chosen to screw myself because I was too busy acting like nothing had changed and I could go on with my life, business as usual. I'd pretty much asked to be suckered into a trap. Should I be surprised that someone accepted the invitation?

The minutes ticked past. I didn't hear any sounds of fighting, so hopefully everybody else had made it somewhere reasonably safe.

I never heard the footsteps of my new captors. One minute they weren't there, the next they were. I'd almost have said they travelled in, but travelling was rare enough I doubted it. Touray was a traveller, and only one of a handful I knew about. The others were likewise high up in their Tyet organizations. Probably because that particular talent gave them a massive edge up on their competition. They could be two places almost at the same time. They could go into locked rooms and take things, or put them in. Only good null walls or binding circles could stop them.

But these two weren't travellers. They were something altogether different. Magic radiated off them like beacons in a lighthouse. I'd never seen anything like it. I almost had to squint. That wasn't all. The magic moved around them, rippling and swirling. It shone with rainbow colors. A sound that wasn't quite sound filled the room. I covered my ears, but it made little difference. The sound drilled down through the marrow of my bones and turned them to taffy. I sank to the floor, my body too heavy and too graceless to move. My head thudded against the stone floor. I heard the clunk of Lauren's gun as it fell, then the sound of her body slumping to the ground.

I dropped out of my trace vision, letting go my hold on Trevor's trace. I blinked my eyes slowly. It took most of the strength I had left to manage it.

In the chill blue fluorescent lights, the two men who'd come for us looked ordinary. The taller one had broad shoulders and a barrel chest. He wore his brown hair in a ponytail. The other one was shorter and just as broad in the shoulders, but his stomach overlapped his belt, and his legs bowed slightly. His blond hair curled around his ears. He'd not shaved for at least several days.

They looked at me and then at Lauren.

"She had people with her," the blond said, nudging her with his boot. "Where'd they go?"

Lauren attempted to say something, but the sound came out garbled.

"Dammit," the ponytailed one said. He went to a box on the wall and flipped down the metal cover. Inside was a phone. He lifted the receiver and stabbed in a three-digit number. In just a few seconds, someone answered.

"We've got the cop and the tracer. The rest are on the run." He waited for the other person to reply. "Right. On our way."

He hung up and closed the box. Magical communication didn't work reliably in the mines, any more than radios. A lot of magic permeated the mountain. Maybe Diamond City's strong node of ley lines gave too much interference, or maybe the lines knotted up there around the diamonds and other gems hidden in the mountain—it was an ongoing debate in scientific circles. Either way, it made magical communication tough underground. Physical lines were necessary.

"Grab the wagon," ponytail told his companion. "Random says the boss wants them ASAP."

Blondie went out the opening and returned with a four-wheeled cart. He pulled me up in a fireman's carry and dumped me inside, shoving me over to leave room for Lauren. He dropped her next to me. She landed on her side, her face pressing up against my left breast like she was looking to nurse. I tried to push her upright, but my body still wasn't answering. Except for breathing and blinking, I was essentially paralyzed.

I decided not to think about how scary that was. Panic wasn't going to help me. These people wanted to use my magic talents. They needed me whole. This paralysis was, therefore, not permanent. I kept repeating that in my head as ponytail got in front and blondie got behind to push us.

We went through brightly lit areas. I could hear machinery and people. No one paid attention to us. Maybe we weren't all that unusual. Maybe these men did this on a regular basis.

At one point, the cart stopped inside a closed-in space. Our two guards disappeared. Shortly after, the air filled with a sweet, putrid miasma. It sank down over us in a heavy blanket. The smell coated the insides of my nose and mouth until I could taste nothing else. I swallowed the bile that rose in my throat and, with it, that thickness in the air. It congealed into thick honey in my stomach, then expanded, pressing outward even as it seeped inward through my skin. It was repulsive. I shrank away from it, while at the same time I trembled with hungry eagerness. My body pulsed and throbbed with electric pleasure. Soon I teetered on the edge of an orgasm. Lauren moaned and twitched as if she'd gone over delight's edge. If it weren't for the fact that Sparkle Dust cost a ton of money and it wasn't airborne, I'd have thought we were getting dosed.

Magic shot through me in hot streaks. Barbed-wire twisted into me, down into deepest places where my talent grows. Instant agony. Inwardly, I rolled and twisted, heat roiling and crashing into me. Pain sharpened in my head until tears rolled down my cheeks. All that, and still my body fluttered and hummed with growing euphoria.

I tried to think. What was happening? My brain kept spinning back to Sparkle Dust. But that wasn't possible or likely. And yet—there seemed no other answer. I wanted to scream and force it back out of my lungs. The stuff hung thick in the air. Every breath pulled the poison into my lungs and bloodstream. I fought to move. Inside, I kicked and raged. Outside, my body remained still. I felt like a marionette with the strings cut. Or one of those people who wake up in the middle of the surgery to feel all the pain but remain paralyzed, screaming into endless silence.

I couldn't let this happen. I couldn't stop it.

Could I?

I had a weapon. I didn't know if it could do anything. I had two null tattoos. One was in the shape of a purple calla lily circling my belly button. The other was done in white in my scalp. I kept both charged at all times. The ink didn't tend to hold magic for that long—a month maybe—but as dangerous as it was to wear a null on my flesh, I liked the fact that if I ended up naked and alone, I'd have a last line of defense.

Since the null on my scalp was the nuclear option, I chose the calla lily. Because it was already a part of me, I didn't need to touch it to activate it. I just needed to focus on it. That turned out to be harder than I liked. The euphoria of the drug sanded away the edges of my mind. I felt myself wanting to yield to it. Instead, I sent a pulse of power into my belly tattoo.

Magic exploded. Pain surged, overwhelming the Sparkle Dust bliss. My body convulsed. My arms and legs flailed, my torso arching and twisting in agonizing spasms. My head banged against the cart, and I tasted blood. Mewling gasps squeezed through my throat.

The barbed-wire tendrils ripped away. Pain smashed into me, crushing me under its weight. I passed out.

Chapter 5

I was strapped to a chair when I woke up. My head dangled forward, and drool dripped from my mouth onto my chest. The coppery taste of blood saturated my taste buds. I blinked, remaining still, trying to pull myself together before anybody noticed I was awake.

The chair I was strapped to was a whole lot like a dentist's chair. My ankles and wrists were buckled in tight with new leather straps. The stench of Sparkle Dust was gone, though I could still smell the odor of sweet rot drifting off my hair and clothing, along with the sour stink of my own sweat and fear. Wherever I was now, smelled of machine oil and the cool damp of the underground. And pizza. I wrinkled my nose. I'm almost always hungry, but at the moment, the idea of food was about as enticing as the idea of taking an acid bath.

I could hear muted sounds that made no sense to me. Rumblings and clangings and beneath those, an insistent whine. I felt it more than heard it. My ears ached with the pressure.

I took stock of myself. I felt like I'd been tossed into an industrial dryer with a couple of cannonballs and left to tenderize. My body throbbed all over. Something felt like it was drilling through my left shoulder, and my right wrist and hand were swollen to three times their normal size. My middle finger stuck out straight and when I tried to move it, pain shot up my arm. Something was definitely broken there.

My belly null remained active, though its strength was nearly gone. I'd designed it to nullify only magic in my body or on my skin. The idea was that it wouldn't sap itself on unimportant exterior magic.

On the positive side, the null had clearly worked hard against the SD. I froze a moment as realization sank into me. I might be on my way to becoming a Sparkle Dust addict, not to mention a wraith. Before I could panic, I took a breath. I might be able to get over the addiction. Cass had helped my almost-brother-in-law Josh do just that, when he'd been given Sparkle Dust. His captors had been trying to pry information out of him and figured the SD would help lube the process. Since I hadn't seen him since Cass had treated him, I didn't know how well it had worked. I liked to think he was free and clear, especially since I was staring down the same gun.

As far as I knew, there was no cure for what changes the drug made in a body. I looked at my hands but didn't see any differences. Maybe there wouldn't be any. Maybe they'd show up in a week. I didn't know enough about Sparkle Dust to say. Hopefully my null had worked in time.

Worry chewed at my stomach. When would I start craving it? Would they give me more? Turn me into an addict? Would I be able to walk away from them if they did? I had no doubt that the whole point was to break me, to make me beg to help them with whatever they wanted. They'd reward me with the drug. Whoever they hell *they* were.

I gritted my teeth together. It wasn't going to happen. I was never going to beg. A snotty little voice gophered up inside my head and laughed. Like I had a choice. I stomped it back into its hole. I refused to consider the possibility that I didn't have a choice.

I figured maybe a minute or two had gone by since I woke up. There didn't seem a whole lot of point in playing possum any longer. I wanted to know where I was, and I wanted to know if I could move. I lifted my head with a groan, totally not faked. My neck ached with whiplash. My convulsions from the null's magic had been violent, and every inch of my muscles protested movement. It was more than a little bit nice to be able to move of my own volition, despite the pain.

My chair sat on a polished wood floor facing a large glass-topped desk that sat on a thick woven rug. A man sat behind it, his feet set together on the floor, his back straight. He wore a charcoal-gray suit with a blinding white shirt and a cobalt tie. His light blond hair hung down to his shoulders. His hands were laced in his lap, his head tilted to the side as he watched me.

I stared back, saying nothing. His expression didn't change. He didn't acknowledge me in any way, shape, or form. My gaze roved over him. His skin was pale, his eyes light blue. His eyelashes and eyebrows were so light they were almost nonexistent. His hair was thick, and he definitely used hair spray.

After I'd gotten an eyeful of him, and he still said nothing, I checked out the rest of the room. The walls had been drywalled, and colorful paintings hung on them. They had no frames. The ceiling was stone. Veins of gold and quartz ran through it, the vaulted surface polished to a high shine. The light came from several freestanding brass and blue-enameled lamps.

Aside from my chair and the desk, the only other furniture consisted of two cushiony chairs against the wall. I didn't know where Lauren was. I'm not sure that I cared.

I resumed looking at my captor. He was going to have to speak first, though I didn't know how long before he'd get bored of looking at me.

Another minute or two passed with the two of us staring deeply into each other's eyes before he finally looked away. He fished a silver box from his inside breast pocket. He flicked it open and drew out a cigarette. It was terribly James Bondian of him, and I almost had to laugh. Except I was shackled to a chair, my null was sucking the life out of me, and I might be turning into a wraith. So pretty much there was nothing funny about my situation. The corners of my mouth still turned up, despite myself.

He set the case down and tucked the cigarette between his lips. He picked a lighter up off the desk and thumbed the flame to life. The tip of the cigarette glowed orange as he drew deeply on it. He closed the lid of the lighter and set it down beside the crystal ashtray. At the same time, he blew the smoke out. It was a rich, spicy smell. Unusual.

"Welcome, Miss Hollis. I have been looking forward to meeting you." He sat back, crossing his legs and watching me. His voice was higher than I expected, with just a hint of gravel in it. Like he'd strained it. Maybe he'd been singing his boy band songs in the shower. Maybe it was his smoking habit.

"So go ahead and meet me," I said. "What are you waiting for?"

His brows rose, his forehead wrinkling. He chuckled. It was a dry sound that reminded me of a rattlesnake. "Charming," he said. "I believe I will quite enjoy our acquaintance."

That made one of us. *Charming?* Who the hell says that? Where was this guy from? Since he still hadn't actually made an effort to meet me, I decided to hurry him along. "Who are you?"

He answered slowly, drawing on his cigarette again. He closed his eyes to savor the smoke, then opened them again. He set the cigarette on the ashtray and slowly breathed out his dragon breath. "My name is Caldwell. George Percival James Borden Caldwell the fourth. I go by Percy."

"That's a mouthful. Your parents couldn't squeeze any more names onto the line when they were filling out your birth certificate?"

He smiled, his teeth straight and white. I bet they were fakes.

"How do you feel?" he asked.

"Like I've been drugged and then run over by a tractor," I said, not bothering to hide my irritation. When I'm scared, it helps to be a smart-ass. Makes me feel more in control, even if I'm totally screwed. I was hoping that my rescue team was on their way, but I had serious doubts that Leo or Dalton had summoned help. Both were too stubborn and both would have been afraid I'd vanish while they were gone. I glanced up at the ceiling. With all that gold, Leo might be able to tell where I was. I could hope.

I glanced down at my chair to see if there was any metal I could touch to help him find me. None. The Amish must have made it.

"Yes, I was surprised at your reaction to the Sparkle Dust fumes. I've never seen that before."

Percy went back to smoking and watching me. I felt like an experiment he was trying to figure out.

"I guess I'm special that way," I said.

"Let's hope next time goes better for you," he said.

"Next time?" My heart dropped into my stomach.

"Of course. No need for concern. By then you'll want it. Even with your rather violent reaction, I expect the addiction has already taken hold. Within a day or two you'll be sweating and aching for it."

I did my damndest to keep the horror from my face. "And then what? You'll happily provide?"

"Absolutely. So long, of course, as you do as I ask. Sparkle Dust is quite expensive, you know. You get your first taste free, but after that, it costs. Of course, the fumes are less potent, but I understand they are quite enjoyable, as I'm sure you discovered. They also make a slower impact on the user's body. The process of turning wraith is much more gradual. Given your talents, I thought it best to prolong your life as long as possible."

"Why give me the drug at all?" I hated the tremble I heard in my voice. If he'd been more threatening, I might have been able to stir up more anger to control my fear. His matter-of-fact revelations were so much more terrifying just because he seemed unconcerned.

"Quite simple, Miss Hollis. When I have something you would die to get, you not only stop fighting me, but you cooperate enthusiastically. I will get far more from you addicted than I would if you were not. Using the fumes instead of letting you inject or snort it, you should survive for six months to a year. That should be ample time for my plans."

"What plans? Who the hell *are* you?"

Percy tapped his fingers on his chin, smoke curling around his face from the cigarette. Finally he set it back into the ashtray before sitting back and crossing his legs.

"Scuttlebutt claims that you are a valuable asset and that a number of various people would like to have possession of you. Anyone who procured you could offer your skills up for a fee. Sort of like a prize stud." He frowned and shook his head. "You do realize that you've been charging ludicrously low prices for what you can do. As for security—you must be mad, the way you go about. Surely you knew that *someone* would come for you?"

I didn't answer. I *had* known I was at risk, but I'd been swimming in denial. That will be the cause of death on my death certificate. In red letters and all caps.

He waved his hand. "At any rate, I have no need of stud fees. I have something else planned for you entirely. Something that requires your complete and utmost cooperation and enthusiasm."

His expression took my breath away. It wasn't just cold, it was evil. True evil. I shuddered. When I didn't answer him, Percy rose and turned away. He adjusted a perfectly straight picture of what appeared to be somebody's version of an acid trip, and wandered around to the side and behind me. I tensed, ears reaching for every sound. What was he up to?

"I've been told you can see dead trace. Is that accurate?" he asked finally.

I didn't answer that either. Instead I went with a question of my own. "What did you do with Lauren?"

"Do you care?"

Oh great. A game of ping-pong questions. "Would I have asked if I didn't?"

"I believe she explained that she lured you down here. I should think you wouldn't care what happened to her or perhaps you want to know that she has suffered for her crimes."

"I just want to know what you did with her." I honestly didn't know why I cared. The woman had led me into a trap. She deserved whatever crap this guy dumped on her. On the other hand, maybe she was eating peeled grapes while muscular men massaged her. A grand reward for capturing me. "You exposed her to the SD fumes, too. Why?"

"My, you certainly are curious." He came back around to stand in front of me. He folded his arms over his chest. "Very well. Detective Morton served her purpose well. However, I am not one to waste manpower. She could prove useful again. I have now made her willing to provide her services to me without having to go to the trouble of blackmail."

"You're a fucking bastard."

He tilted his head at me, then before I even saw him move, he slapped me. My head twisted to the side with the force of it. My eye felt like it was going to pop out, and blood seeped where I cut my cheek on the edges of my teeth. I turned to look at him again, wincing from the pain radiating across my face.

"I don't care for insults," he said, no sign of anger in his voice. "I suggest you curb yourself. It will be more pleasant for both of us if you do. Now, back to my question: can you see dead trace?"

I considered whether or not I wanted to answer. I was at the bastard's mercy, and he was willing to beat the answer out of me, or worse. It wasn't like he couldn't get the answer from somebody else. He already had. All the same—

"I would much prefer to keep our relationship civilized," Percy said, pulling out another cigarette and lighting it. He drew a deep breath and let the smoke out slowly, watching me through the curling blue tendrils. "However, my personal preferences must be set aside from time to time. It's the price of succeeding at business."

He took another deep drag and eyed the glowing tip of the cigarette a moment, then leaned forward and gently touched it to the top of my hand. I tried to jerk away, but the shackles held me firm. I bit my lips as my nerves registered the heat and then pain. I refused to make a sound.

He lifted the cigarette away. I stared at the wound, too shocked that he'd so casually burned me to even think. A band of dark pink surrounded a white circle on the back of my hand. I could smell burned skin. My stomach lurched, and I turned my head barely in time to throw up onto the floor.

My captor eyed the mess with furrowed brows. "Very poor manners, Miss Hollis. I should think you'd know better."

"What the fuck do you think you're doing?" I gasped.

"Isn't it obvious?" He examined the tip of the cigarette and relit it, drawing deeply to get the cherry going again.

Once again, he leaned forward and set it on my skin. I jerked back, kicking and twisting, but I wasn't going anywhere.

"Jesus fuck!" I yelled, pretending tears weren't burning the back of my eyes. "Stop it already!"

He waited until he was done and then drew away. This time the circle around the white burn was darker red. The pain drilled down through my hand and skewered steel knives up my arm.

"I want to be sure you learn the lesson I'm teaching you," Percy said, relighting the cigarette. "I expect my employees to behave politely and with respect." He touched the burning end to me again. "That means behaving yourself politely and obeying my orders promptly and without question."

I clamped my teeth together, refusing to scream or cry. He lit another cigarette and another, until he'd covered both hands with burns. Milky white blisters bloomed in the center of a few, the rest were white and red. Both hands throbbed. Pain lay over me in a fiery blanket.

By the time he was done, tears ran freely down my face. I hadn't made a sound. It was a pitiful victory.

"Now," he said. "I ask you again. Can you see dead trace?"

Everything inside me told me not to answer. Don't let him win.

"Yes," I muttered. I didn't doubt that he'd continue his burning until I answered. I didn't know how long that would be, but I knew I would eventually. People were coming to find me. If they didn't, I would escape on my own. Either way, I had to be alive and able-bodied. I could still feel the amethyst heal-all hanging around my neck. It should have enough juice to handle these burns. Not answering out of pride was just a good way to get hurt.

"Very good, Miss Hollis. Now tell me, what other skills do you have? Do speak up."

I closed my eyes. I couldn't stand looking at him. "The usual. I make nulls, I track people."

"Come, now. Don't waste my time."

My eyes flicked open as he lit another cigarette. My stomach heaved, and I swallowed. He smiled faintly at my reaction.

I needed to give him something. "If I'm close enough to an active spell, I can sense it and what kind of magic made it."

Percy nodded. "Interesting. That could come in handy. What else?"

"I've been able to take apart a null wall, but it almost killed me."

"Very good. What else?"

I shook my head. I couldn't tear my gaze from the cherry glow of the cigarette. "Nothing most tracers can't do. I just tend to be better at it."

"Ah. Are you sure?"

I wasn't going to tell him about being able to touch trace or reach into the spirit dimension, or the fact that I had made a blood null—even though it was almost as deadly for me as for anybody else. I shrugged, tensing against what he might do. "That's all I've got." I barely pushed the words through the fear choking my throat.

"Hmmm."

He stood and walked around behind me again. His fingers brushed the nape of my neck. I shivered. I waited for the heat of the cigarette to replace his touch. Nothing happened. Maybe he was waiting for me to break down and babble out more confessions. How many burns would it take before I vomited up everything I knew?

Finally he returned to his desk chair. He stubbed out his cigarette in the ashtray with the butts of the others he'd used on me. He rested his elbows on the table, steepling his fingers like he was going to pray.

"Very well, Miss Hollis. I will believe you, for now. We will revisit the subject after your next Sparkle Dust treatment." He smiled without teeth.

He waited for me to say something. No, not just something, I realized. He wanted me to say thank you. Like I should be grateful he'd chosen not to torture me some more. Worst thing was that I was grateful.

"Thanks," I said, hardly moving my lips.

He heard it and nodded. "You're quite welcome, I am sure. Now, I will escort you to your room so that you can rest and eat. Later we will continue your initiation and training."

"Initiation and training?" I repeated, turning cold. "What does that mean?"

"It means that I wish to trust you, Miss Hollis. In order to do that, you must learn my rules, and you must demonstrate your eagerness to obey them. Don't worry. You are a smart woman. I'm sure you'll do well. And as they say, pain cements the lesson in your mind far better than reward, though there will be rewards for you as well. Not the least of which will be more Sparkle Dust."

"No!" I said before I could stop myself.

His brows arched. "No? Perhaps you should review the last half hour and reconsider. Not that you have a choice. By tomorrow, your opinions won't make any difference. You'll be begging for SD. You *will* do as I ask, whenever I ask. Things will go much more pleasantly for you if you accept that."

That would happen when pigs flew and screwed butterflies.

Because I was smart enough not to antagonize him into hurting me again, I kept that to myself.

I wondered if I should deactivate my belly null. I didn't want Percy to know I had any protections. He'd probably cut it out. On the other hand, I didn't want to get sideswiped with a magic attack.

After a long moment, I chose to deactivate it. I might need what was left of it later. Right now, I expected I was safe enough. Percy liked the personal touch in torture.

I don't know how Percy summoned his minions, but the door opened with a rush of sound and air. I heard the trundle of wheels. Two women unbuckled me and unceremoniously hooked their hands under my arms and knees, lifting me up and none-too-gently laying me into the cart. My head banged the edge. My broken finger hit the side. Jagged pain flared through my hand and into my chest. Despite myself, I whimpered.

"Careful," Percy admonished sharply. "She's far more valuable to me than you are."

"Yes, sir," one of the woman said, fear curling around the words. "I apologize."

"I prefer good work to apologies," Percy said. "Remember that."

If his people were afraid of him, maybe I had a chance to worm help out of them. Maybe they'd want to get away, get out from under his thumb. The hope filled me for a bare second and then died. It didn't work that way. Not fast enough for me, anyhow.

I was now almost positive that somehow my null had prevented the SD from taking hold. I had felt the magical barbs pulling out of me. It wouldn't be strong enough to do it again. I had maybe a day or two at most before he exposed me again. He'd do it faster when I didn't show the right signs of addiction. I didn't even know what those were, beyond groveling for the drug.

I still had my scalp null. It was the nuclear option and stood as much chance of killing me as saving me. It would send out debilitating pain to everyone around me, and was a powerful null besides. All well and good, but once it used up its own magic, it would suck the life out of me in order to power itself, unless I deactivated it. If I didn't, I'd die. So if I passed out or got hit on the head, it would kill me before I woke up.

Unlike the last time Percy's minions had come for me, I didn't go paralyzed. They didn't have the brilliant auras surrounding them, nor did I hear the sound-not-sound drilling down through me.

They wheeled me out, following Percy. We passed through several caverns. One looked more like a hospital. It was full of bright lights, stainless steel tables and tubs, and smelled of antiseptic and the same sweet rot of the Sparkle Dust fumes. I almost gagged and fought against activating my belly null again, but stopped myself. I didn't feel its corrosive magic digging into me.

Percy slowed. "How is progress today, Dr. Inawa?" he asked someone I couldn't see. A woman answered, her voice low and scratchy.

"We should be wrapped up by the end of the week. We've only a little stock left to finish ripening before harvest, and of course, to finish testing the effectiveness of the SD we've used for fumigation."

I could hear the frost in Percy's voice. "I was unaware further testing was required."

The doctor was uncowed by his anger. "I thought it useful to continue the research to learn how long before the SD becomes ineffective altogether once it's become a fume source. Once we establish the lifespan, we can stop short and package it. A less powerful dosage could be sold more cheaply, and build our consumer base. If not, we could use it on the stock to shorten harvest times. Either way, it would be a more efficient use of resources."

Percy considered. After a moment he nodded. "Your rationale is convincing, Dr. Inawa. Write me up the details when you are done. Be sure to finish before migration."

"Yes, sir. Thank you, sir."

With that, Percy resumed walking. I lay there, trying to piece together what I'd heard. *We could use it on the stock to shorten harvest times.* If that meant what it sounded like—

I swallowed, icy cold trickling through my veins.

Percy was giving his so-called stock SD. A drug so expensive it sold for five thousand dollars an ounce. Who was this stock? And what was Percy harvesting from them?

Every possible answer I could come up with was too horrible to contemplate. Percy had some sort of Hitleresque Mengele project going on down here, along with manufacturing Sparkle Dust.

What the hell had I gotten myself into?

Chapter 6

My prison was a stone cell about twelve by twelve feet. It had a twin bed, a table with two chairs, a toilet and a sink, and nothing else. All the furniture was bolted to the floor. The door was made of heavy metal mesh. The two women lifted me out of the cart and set me on the bed, more gently than previously.

They left when Percy dismissed them. I sat up, eyeing him warily.

"Someone will bring you something to eat and drink," he said. He glanced at my hands. "I'll let you reflect on your pain for a while. You may benefit from contemplation."

"What were you talking to that doctor about?"

"Nothing to concern you."

With that, he left, swinging the door shut and bolting it. I followed. My entire body ached. The convulsions had wrenched muscles I didn't know I had. My head ached, and I didn't want to think about my broken hand or the burns. I felt like I was wearing flaming gloves.

I limped across the stone floor to the door. I pressed against it. The damned thing was as solid as the rest of the place. I glanced up at the roof. I couldn't see any veins of metal running through it. It was low. I could reach up and touch it if I wanted. For a second I froze, feeling the mountain collapsing on top of me. I panted, my mind going blank.

I slipped down to sit on the floor, hyperventilating. My head spun, and tingles circled my mouth and then spread down my arms to my fingertips. I tried to slow down, to count breaths in and out, but the next thing I knew, I pitched sideways onto the floor.

When I woke up, I felt worse than before. My headache had ratcheted up from a ten to a hundred, and when I'd tipped over, I'd landed on my broken hand. Now it was screaming at me. I sat up, leaning against the door as I gathered myself. I wondered if the mesh was telling Leo where I was. How long before he and Dalton came and got me?

I reached under my collar and pulled the heal-all out, clutching the pendant in my fist. I was going to have to thank Dalton later for making me keep it. Reluctantly, I tucked it away. I couldn't heal myself. Not yet. Not until I had an escape plan. Percy would only repeat the lesson. I frowned. What else did I still have?

I fumbled at my pockets. Nothing. Sometime after I passed out, his people must have cleaned me out. Thank goodness they hadn't cared about my jewelry. Or maybe they were just sloppy.

I snorted. That could get them killed, working for Percy. He wouldn't easily forgive that sort of mistake.

I needed to get up. That was harder than it sounded. I rolled up onto my knees, bracing myself with my unbroken hand. Leaning my shoulder against the door, I slowly levered myself up. My legs shook, and I forced them to steady.

When I was upright, I staggered back to the bed and collapsed on it. I closed my eyes so that I didn't have to see how low the ceiling was. I counted breaths until my breathing was steady and my head stopped spinning. I must have dozed off.

The sound of the bolt on the door shooting back woke me. A girl came in carrying an orange plastic tray. She *might* have been legal to drink. A broad-shouldered man in khaki army pants and a black shirt blocked the doorway so that I couldn't make a run for it.

The girl glanced at me and gave me a shy, apologetic smile before withdrawing. A couple seconds later, she returned with a pint-sized carton of milk and a gallon jug of water. She set those down, along with a disposable plastic cup.

"Tray pickup is in an hour," she said. Her gaze locked onto my burns. She went green. "Oh my God! Are you—"

She broke off, flicking a nervous glance at the door guard. He scowled. She tossed her blond ponytail and persevered.

"Are you okay?" she asked, then shook her head, recognizing how stupid the question was. "I could get you some bandages or ice or something. Maybe some aspirin or ibuprofen."

Her escort made a noise. I shook my head.

"Thanks. I don't think that's in your best interests. Your boss wants me to suffer."

She recoiled, and her eyes got shiny like she wanted to cry. It was like watching Bambi find out his mother was dead. How the hell did someone so innocent get involved in Percy's operation?

"Run them under cold water at least," she urged, not giving up. "You could make bandages from the pillowcase."

I held up my broken hand. "Not going to be tearing anything anytime soon. But thanks. I appreciate your concern."

"Let's go, Madison," her khaki goon said. "You're wasting time."

She leveled a furious look at him but complied, shoving through the doorway past him, elbowing him in the ribs as she went. He eyed her back and shook his head before shutting the door.

Madison was feisty. I wondered if I could get her to help me. I caught myself up short. And if I did? Would Percy kill her? I didn't even have to think to know the answer to that. If she helped me—if anybody helped me—I'd have to find a way to get them out and protect them, or else I wouldn't be any better than Lauren—selling out someone else to save my own ass. I wouldn't do it.

I wondered what had become of her. Was Percy even now conducting his little interview with her? Was she getting her hands burned? I shuddered. I wouldn't wish that on anyone. Well, except maybe for Percy.

I figured Madison's advice on the cold water for my arms was smart, so I headed for the sink. Before I got there, I was sidetracked by the food on the tray. I stopped to investigate. The tray was heavily loaded with a butter-and-bacon-heaped baked potato, a steak, a pile of roasted vegetables, and a cup of soup. A chocolate bar finished off the meal. It was accompanied by a plastic fork, spoon, and knife.

Dared I eat? Would they have sprinkled Sparkle Dust on the food? I bent to sniff it. It smelled good—without any of that sweet rot that seemed to characterize the drug. I picked up the candy bar and tore it open. I stuffed chocolate in my mouth, then went to the sink and ran my hands under the cold water.

After that, I returned to the table and sat. The chair was too far from the table, and it was bolted down. I gritted my teeth and started eating. I broke the tines of the fork within a minute. I mashed the potato as well as I could with the knife and ate it with a spoon. I ate the vegetables with my fingers, then just ripped at the steak with my teeth.

I drank the milk despite the fact that it was fat free. Disgusting. Why even bother milking the cow? Still, I needed the calories and protein. I guzzled about half the gallon of water. By then my arms were hurting again. I returned to the sink.

I was still running water when the door unbolted and swung toward me. Madison came in with tall, broad, and burly standing in the doorway again.

"Sorry about the silverware," she said, stacking my dinner debris on the tray. "Plastic is all prisoners are allowed."

"Prisoners?" I repeated. "How many are there?"

She shrugged. "Only a dozen or so right now."

I blinked. That many? And from the sounds of it, fewer than normal. "Who else? And why?"

"You don't need to know that," growled her companion.

Madison rolled her eyes. "Don't be such a jerk, Luke."

"I'm following orders. You should pay attention. You don't want to end up—" He looked at my arms. I turned off the water. Thankfully, it was ice cold. It felt like it had come from deep underground. Tasted like it, too. I'd tried a sip. Nothing like drinking down tea made from quarters, nickels, and dimes. Yum.

"You don't want to get yourself in torture trouble," I finished for him. "How'd someone like you get roped into working for Percy anyway?"

Madison's already-pale face blanched. She averted her face. "It's a long story."

I looked at Luke, whose expression had gone savage. Oops. I'd stepped on a land mine. "None of my business, anyway," I said. All of a sudden, the food combined with my exhaustion to make my knees weak. I hadn't thought I'd sleep, but now I could barely stay awake.

"That's right," Luke said. "Let's go, Madison."

Her jaw jutted, then she picked up the tray. Luke stepped aside as she went by. He gave me a dour look as he jerked the door shut with an echoing clang that had shrapnel dancing through my skull. My head hurt too much to think about what was going on between Luke and Madison. Instead, I decided to use the toilet and go to sleep.

It isn't that easy to go to the bathroom when the door is nothing more than a heavy-duty screen. Not to mention pulling my pants down with a broken finger was no fun. No one walked by, but my bladder got really shy for a while. Finally the tide grew too strong, and I was able to go. Afterward, I washed up and searched for a light switch. It was just inside the door. I flipped it down. Instantly, darkness filled the cell. I stumbled over to the bed, knocking my knee into it. Swearing, I crawled onto the mattress and sprawled flat.

It was as hard as a board. I like soft. Something I can squish down on. I felt like a nun, lying on this bed. Like Percy had decided an extra bit of torture or sleep deprivation was a good idea. Maybe that's exactly what he thought.

My pillow was a hard rectangular piece of foam inside a gritty pillowcase. I was too tired to really care. Still, I forced myself to plan. My cell was entirely magic-less. I couldn't null the locks or the walls. The bolt was on the outside of the door—impossible for me to pick, even if I had the tools, and even if my hands were working properly. No windows. On the other hand, it was full of metal—the table, the bed, the chairs, the sink, the door—enough that Leo should be able to find me. I sighed. So either I had to hope that Leo and Dalton would rescue me before I got turned into an SD addict, or I had to convince someone to help me break out.

Madison might, but Luke didn't seem inclined to let her out of his sight.

There wasn't anything else I could do for myself at the moment but to sleep and recuperate as best I could. As I drifted off to sleep, I wondered where Dalton and Leo were. Did Price know where I was? He was going to be pissed if I missed our date. On the other hand, he might be so furious that he'd track me down. 'Course if he did, he was as likely to kill me as not, so maybe I shouldn't get excited about that.

It couldn't have been more than a few hours later when I jerked awake. I listened. I wasn't alone.

"Are you awake? It's me, Madison." Her voice came from the other side of the door.

I breathed out slowly and sat up. "What are you doing here?"

"I just wanted to see if you were all right. I brought some aspirin."

"You shouldn't have done that. Your boss isn't a nice guy." All the same, I edged my way over to the door. I didn't turn the light on. I didn't want anyone to notice it and come investigate.

"I'll slide them under," she said.

I bent, feeling for the pills. I found three oblong tablets and picked them up.

"This is nice of you, but I need to get out of here," I said. "Can you help me?"

"I—I can't," she whispered.

"Just pull back the lock. I'll get out on my own. You know what's going to happen to me."

"It already has. He's got you—don't you see? You don't feel it yet, but tomorrow you'll start. You'll need the Sparkle Dust. You'll do anything to get it, even crawl back to *him*. You'll tell him everything."

With that, she fled. I bit my tongue to keep from swearing. Instead, I took the pills with a swallow of water from the jug on the table, then clambered back into bed. This time I didn't fall asleep so quickly.

My hands throbbed. I couldn't find a position to ease the pain humming through them. My brain scrabbled to come up with an escape plan. The primary hurdle was getting out of my cell. Nothing in the cell was usable for tools, except for maybe the toilet innards. I got up and turned on the light and went to have a look in the toilet tank. It was your typical setup, with more plastic than metal parts. Not terribly useful. Next I examined the door lock. It was on the outside. The mesh door fit solidly into a lip of stone, with the bolt shot snuggly into steel housing anchored to the rock. The only gap was at the floor where Madison had pushed through the pills. It was only a finger-width high. The mesh covering the door was fine—too small for anything bigger than a soda straw. The hinges were on the outside.

After an hour of consideration and searching for ways to get at the lock to pick it, I gave up. I wasn't escaping that way.

I shut off the light and returned to my bed. My mind zigged and zagged. The best chance of escaping would come the next time they took me out of my cell. I had a feeling that would be for my next SD fumigation. After the treatment, I would be useless for a while if my body flipped out again. So I definitely needed to escape before that happened.

That brought up the next problem: when they came for me, would they paralyze me this time? I had no idea if my belly null had counteracted the paralysis last time, but it stood to reason. I could activate the null after they put me in the cart. I had no idea how long it would last. I needed to wait as long as possible to activate it, both to save its strength and to keep myself from accidentally giving myself away. If they happened to jam my broken finger loading me into the cart, I'm pretty sure I'd react no matter how much I tried not to. Then I'd be screwed.

Again.

Once I was in the cart and activated my null, then the major problem was going to be getting back out away from my two guards. They wouldn't be expecting me to be able to move, but they'd get over that by the time I hefted myself up onto my feet. With my ribs hurting and my hands in crap shape, I wasn't going to be moving quickly. Not unless I used the heal-all first. As in, before I activated my null, otherwise the null would kill it. That meant using the heal-all before anybody showed up to take me. But if Percy came along first and realized I'd healed myself, he'd have at me again. He wouldn't take my defiance lightly. This time his torture would be worse. Plus, he wanted me to suffer my burns and was going to make damned sure I did just that.

I had to pray that didn't happen. I'd heal myself after breakfast so no one would notice what I'd done, but before Percy's paralytic goons came for me. Then I'd activate the null once I was in the cart. After that, I had to find a good spot that would give me a chance to escape into the tunnels *and* get lost before anybody could catch me. If there was a spot like that. Finally, I had to find my way back to the surface without tripping a booby trap and blowing myself to bits.

I squeezed my eyes shut. Fuck me. My plan was full of prayer, what-ifs, and *I hopes*—all of those hanging by a thread of good luck. My luck was rarely good.

Maybe this time would be different.

Fat chance.

Chapter 7

Despite my wounds, at some point I fell asleep. The sound of the lock snicking back woke me. I jerked up straight and groaned as pain flared all along my body. The burns were the worst, but the convulsions had pulled muscles, and bruises throbbed everywhere else. I held my hands up in front of me like a surgeon waiting for gloves, hoping the blood would run down out of them and they'd stop hurting.

I had a better chance that leprechauns would rescue me.

The door swung open, and Madison brought my breakfast tray in. She set it down and looked at me, her gaze gravitating to my arms. She gasped and put her hand over her mouth. I didn't really want to see the damage, but I couldn't help myself now that she was looking.

Most of the burns had turned into pink-and-yellow blisters, each the size of a nickel. I'd have thought they'd be smaller. The edges along my skin were white, red, and gray. A couple of blisters had popped at some point, crusting my skin with pus and other seepage. The wounds were purply-red with puckered centers. I looked like I had smallpox.

I decided that I was definitely not going to throw up, and instead slid off the side of the bed. "Good morning," I said to Madison, firming my knees up before crossing over to the table. I really needed to pee. I really wasn't going to do it in front of guests.

I lifted the cover off the tray. Underneath was a vegetable and cheese omelet, hash browns, sausages and bacon, and a cup of canned fruit. There was also a can of V8. No coffee. Somebody was a sadist.

I picked up the plastic fork and knife, and started eating. I made a face as I swallowed the first bite. Epic bland. "Is there any salt or pepper? Maybe hot sauce?"

"This isn't a restaurant," Luke said from the doorway. He was either wearing the same clothes as the night before, or he had a drawer of black shirts and khaki pants and not a lot of taste. Probably wore tighty-whities, too. Two sizes too small if his expression was anything to go by.

"Right. It's a prison. How could I have forgotten I wasn't at the Ritz?"

"C'mon, Madison," was Luke's only reply.

"I'm really sorry I can't help you," she said to me.

"Me too," I said, then decided that she deserved a little more civility. After all, she'd brought me pills for the pain. "I understand. I don't want Percy going after you. You're right not to take chances. I appreciate that you want to."

If I thought that would ease her mind, it did anything but. Her chin crumpled and tears welled in her eyes. She clutched her hands together.

"I really want to," she started, but then Luke grabbed her elbow and pulled her outside, giving me an icy stare as he did.

The bolt shot into place, and the two trundled away with the serving cart. I could hear Luke's oppressive silence and Madison's sniffles. Maybe I was crazy, but I felt more sorry for her at that moment than for myself.

Taking advantage of the momentary alone time, I relieved myself on the toilet. After I'd washed up and let the ice water run over my arms for a few minutes, I returned to my breakfast. It had gone from decently hot to barely more than cool. I made a face but finished anyway. After all, this was prison, not a restaurant.

Afterward, I paced. I had no idea what time it was. I wished I could do more to try to contact Leo. I knew he could sense things through the metal of the room, but it wasn't like I could talk and he'd hear me. It was more that he would know where I was, maybe even how I was doing. I wished I knew Morse code. He'd probably hear that. Note to self—if I got out of here alive, learn Morse code.

I also didn't know when I'd be dragged back to the fume room or to see Percy. I'd decided he probably wasn't going to come visit me. If nothing else, there was no comfortable place to sit.

In what I assumed was an hour, the bolt shot back on the door again, and it swung open. This time Luke was alone. That was probably better for Madison.

"I don't suppose you'd be willing to tell me what's next on the agenda for me," I asked.

He looked at me, he eyes narrowed. "Don't involve Madison in your mess," he said. "She's a good kid and she doesn't need an extra helping of shit to make her hell worse."

I blinked, not expecting that. Curiosity got the better of me. I refuse to say *stupidity*, because, after all, it's not like I could do anything to help her. "What's her story?"

"None of your damned business," Luke snapped. "Just stay the fuck away from her."

"It's not like I'm bringing *her* food," I pointed out. "I'm in the jail cell, remember?"

He growled in frustration. "You know what I mean. She feels for you.

You could talk her into helping you. Don't. I swear I'll make your life hell if you do."

Wow. He must have it bad for her. "Don't get your panties in a wad, Fonzi," I said. "I'm off to the gas chamber soon, remember? After that, I probably won't even remember my own name."

He frowned at me. "You don't act like you've been smoked."

I shrugged, wondering what I could do to fake it better. "What do you want, more convulsions? Maybe I could dance around with a lampshade on my head?"

A faint smile made him look almost human. It vanished. "Just leave Madison out of whatever game you've got planned."

"I'm not a child, Luke."

He spun around. The young woman in question stood just within the doorway, hands on her hips, her mouth pressed flat in fury.

"You act like one sometimes," he said, thrusting the tray at her.

She didn't take it. "Says Grampa Luke, right? Ten years older than dirt? Been everywhere? Seen everything? Give me a break. I'm twenty-four years old, and maybe I haven't done a lot with my life yet, but that doesn't make me a baby. So quit treating me like one."

I blinked at her. Twenty-four? I'd figured she was scraping up against twenty-one, tops. Even though I was only a few years older than she was, I felt about a hundred and two. She didn't seem like she got out much.

"You need to get out of here and stop thinking what you're thinking," he told her.

"Now you're a mind reader?" she asked, not giving an inch, despite the menace in his stance.

I was starting to like her more and more. She had backbone.

Before Luke could say anything else, more company joined us.

"My, my. I didn't think to find you with so much company," Percy said in that slick, oily voice of his. The smell of cigarette smoke invaded my cell with him. Turns out he *had* decided to visit me this morning. Thank goodness I hadn't used the heal-all yet.

Percy studied Luke from head to toe. The other man flushed and straightened like someone had shoved a hot poker up his ass. Percy smiled faintly, and his attention shifted to Madison.

"Did you forget how to do your job, my dear?" He motioned at the tray that Luke still held.

"Of course not," she said in an ultrapleasant voice. Probably the same one Norman Bates used. "Let me have it, please." She held her hands out to take the tray and went out to the cart. She rolled it away without waiting for watchdog Luke.

"Did you sleep well?" Percy asked me, walking around to inspect the room.

I half expected him to pull out a white glove and look for dust.

"I had a little trouble getting comfortable," I said. "The bed might as well be granite. And by the way? The breakfast is a little on the bland side. You probably ought to mention that to the chef."

He chuckled. "You *are* a delight, my dear. I am going to enjoy having you in my stable."

Stable. Like a cow or a donkey. "Lucky me," I said.

"How do you feel today?"

He studied me, and I wished I knew how to fake like I was getting addicted to Sparkle Dust.

"Sore," I said, holding up my blistered arms and broken finger. "In fact, I hurt like hell. Pain seems to be crowding every other feeling out."

"Nothing else?" His brows arched.

"Like if I am getting period cramps or something?"

"Don't be crude," he admonished, examining his fingernails. He reached inside his coat jacket and pulled out his cigarette case.

I watched him open it and take out a cigarette and tuck it between his lips. He put the case away and drew out a gold lighter. He flipped the lid and lit his cancer stick. I didn't even breathe.

He drew in a breath and blew out cloud of smoke. "I shouldn't like to give you a lesson again. What else do you feel?"

I really wanted to tell him to fuck off, but I wasn't interested in another lesson. Defying him would only get me hurt. I opted for the truth. "Tired. Irritated. Filthy. I could use a shower."

He eyed me for a long moment. "Interesting," he said at last, taking another drag on his cigarette.

I didn't like the sound of that. I started pacing again. I needed him to think I was on my way to addiction. If he figured out I had nulls that worked against the SD, he'd cut them out of me.

Up until now, I'd been managing to distract myself from my claustrophobia by pretending the cell was just another room in a house somewhere, and keeping my mind occupied with figuring out an escape plan. But all of a sudden, I realized that my claustrophobia might be just what I needed to convince Percy I was succumbing to the SD. It didn't hurt that Percy's presence was smothering. The cell felt twenty times smaller with him in it. I had to resist the urge to press myself up against the wall in case he decided to burn me again.

I let myself think of the mountain, and the walls closed in around me. I broke into a cold sweat, and my head reeled. My breakfast started swirling in my stomach. I felt like I'd swallowed a half-dozen snakes. I felt the color drain from my face as I turned cold.

"So what happens next?" I asked, not fighting the shake in my voice.

"That depends on you."

"How so?" I started to shiver, even as sweat beaded on my forehead and trickled between my breasts.

"You seem agitated, my dear. Why don't you sit?" He dropped his cigarette to the floor and stepped on it.

"Why don't you answer my question?" I retorted, walking around to the other side of the table. I wanted to keep something solid between us.

He linked his hands behind his back. "Perhaps we should talk later when you feel better."

"I'm not going to feel better until I'm out of here," I panted. I couldn't seem to catch my breath. Pretty soon I was going to start hyperventilating and pass out entirely. Percy would like me falling down at his feet. I decided to sit on the bed.

"That will happen as soon as I feel you can be trusted. As soon as you realize that you belong to me now."

He turned away and went to the door. Luke followed him.

Percy stopped and turned back to look at me. I was huddled over, my feet dangling off the floor. My shivers had started to make my teeth chatter. He started to say something else, then changed his mind and left. Luke clanged the door shut behind them, shooting the bolt back into place.

I tried to pull back on my claustrophobia, focusing on breathing and closing my eyes and imagining I was outside.

Slowly, I pulled myself together until my shaking was just a tremble and my breathing was just a little fast.

I still had no idea when to expect the fumigation squad to come for me. My short acquaintance with Percy said that he'd want me to go through a day of desperation first. I assumed he'd translated my fear symptoms into drug symptoms. I never thought I'd be glad to have claustrophobia. Then again, if I'd not shown symptoms, maybe he'd want to expose me again that much more quickly and I'd be able to make a move. As it was, I wasn't sure what I should do.

So I sat.

Then I paced again.

Then I sat.

Lunch came eventually. My stomach was growling, and my arms were on fire. I kept running them under the faucet, but the relief lasted only a few minutes each time.

Luke brought me my tray. He opened the door and practically slammed it onto the table, making everything on it jump. He left and returned with another gallon jug of water. He left without a word.

Even though I was starving, the thought of food made me nauseous. I lifted the lid off the tray. I'd been given a lettuce salad, steamed green beans, a BLT, and French fries. A can of Coke and a bowl of tapioca finished the meal. Not bad for prison food, but then I supposed I was getting the same things that Percy's employees were getting. I snatched up the soda and gulped it down. Cotton stuffed my head. I needed caffeine. After that, I picked at the rest of the meal. I drank the water and hurried to relieve myself before Luke returned.

It seemed a lot longer than an hour before he came back. By that time, I'd managed to choke down about half the meal, and I'd climbed back on the bed and dozed off. I blinked at him when he walked back in, but didn't bother to get up.

"You don't look so bad," he observed.

"Kudos to me. I feel like crap."

"You should look worse."

"I've got great genes."

He snorted. "Sparkle dust doesn't give a shit about genes."

"What am I supposed to look like?"

He shrugged. "Red eyes, sweats, shakes, kind of shiny in the eyes."

"I've had the sweats and the shakes all day."

He frowned. "Still . . ."

I closed my eyes and sighed. "Don't you have somebody else to bother?"

"So that's it. You're giving up already? Not even going to beg me to help you get out?"

"Why? So you can laugh in my face? I'll save my sadomasochistic urges for when Percy wants to slap me around or burn me some more, thank you very much. You can go get your jollies somewhere else."

"What if I'm prepared to help you?"

Something in his voice sent a jolt of electricity through me. I opened my eyes and sat up slowly, studying him. He glared, his jaw jutting, his entire body braced like he was expecting a tornado to rip him off his feet.

"You're serious. Why would you?"

He grimaced, his teeth clamped together. "Madison will if I don't. She doesn't need that kind of trouble."

"But you can handle it."

"I will."

The lines around his mouth dug deep. He was afraid of Percy, and I didn't blame him at all.

"What do you have in mind?"

"You don't need to know. Just be ready when I come for you."

With that, he walked out, shooting the bolt home behind him. I stared blindly at the door. I actually believed him.

Chapter 8

I dithered about using the heal-all for the next half hour. Luke had sounded like he was coming back soon, but I still worried that Percy's people would drag me off to get fumigated before Luke came back, and they'd report that I'd been healed.

In the end, I decided to risk it. If Luke came for me first, I wanted to be in decent shape to run. The heal-all filled me with its wormy magic. The heat was worse than back at the diner. I practically sizzled. It was all I could do not to peel off my clothes and stick my head under the faucet. I panted as the worms invaded my body. I thought they'd concentrate on my arms and broken finger, but they dug deep inside, down where the Sparkle Dust magic had ripped out of me.

I hadn't realized how raw my insides had been until the heal-all withdrew its awful touch. I lay on the bed, my body tingling and pulsing with leftover pops of healing energy. I stared at the ceiling as I took a mental inventory of myself. My arms no longer ached, and my finger curled and bent like brand-new. My bruises were gone and so was the ache in my face from Percy's slap. Most of all, I felt an easing inside, like I'd been bleeding to death and hadn't even known it. I sighed and sat up.

I was going to have to thank Dalton for the heal-all. I blew out a disgusted breath as I stood and stretched, reveling in the fact that I didn't hurt. Amazing how good just not hurting could feel. I really didn't want to thank the smug bastard. Still, I owed him that much. If I saw him again. Where the hell was he? And Leo? Please God, I hoped they were safe. Even Dalton.

The faucet lured me over. I rinsed my face and hands, wetting my towel and rubbing it along the back of my neck and under my shirt. My hair was a rat's nest. How long had it been since I showered?

I'd been in the cell nearly twenty-four hours, if the mealtimes were to be believed. My little team and I had taken three or four hours just to get to the tunnel entrance, and then spent another five or six finding our way into the trap. So it had been maybe thirty-six, give or take, since we'd left the diner, plus a little more depending on how long I'd been in the fume room and with Percy getting myself cooked, one little burn at a time. Even if I were a fan of polka dots, I'd be giving them up forever after that experience.

Several hours went by without any sign of Luke. Every person passing in the hallway made me jump. The cart rattled outside my doorway, and I pushed myself back against the opposite wall as if that would protect me. I could see the brilliant light surrounding the men pushing it. My body started to go numb, and the high whining sounding from before drilled into my skull and vibrated down to the marrow of my bones. I was getting tired of being in pain.

I bit my lower lip to keep from moaning my misery out loud, silently urging the fuckers to go faster. Apparently they got paid by the hour, because they weren't in any hurry. By the time they moved out of range, I felt boneless. I sagged to the floor. At least I wasn't paralyzed. There was something to be said for that, anyhow. The range of their magic was maybe ten to fifteen feet.

It took me a good five minutes before I could trust my legs to hold me up. I wobbled over to the bed and sat on the edge and proceeded to do weightless arm and leg lifts until I began to feel normal again.

I began to wonder if Luke had changed his mind. If my stomach was anything to go by, dinnertime was close. I'd just gotten up to pace again when the lock on the door shot back. Luke brought in my dinner tray and set it down.

"Come on," he said.

"Now?" I asked stupidly, because obviously he meant right now.

"Do you want to stay longer?" he snarled. He was clearly in a foul mood, like a porcupine had crawled up his ass and decided to have a litter.

I started to follow him, but paused to take a deep swig from the water jug before joining Luke at the door.

"What now?" I asked.

He scraped his bottom teeth over his upper lip, hard enough that I thought he was going to draw blood. He shook his head hard as if dismissing something, probably his own sanity, and blew out a long breath.

"Stay with me. Don't get separated."

He turned away. I opened myself to the trace. His was a vibrant blue and white, like a bolt of lightning. He was my lifeline out of here. I didn't dare lose him. I took a quick breath and reached into the trace dimension and snatched hold of his trace. Instantly something grabbed me, almost like it had been waiting for me. It pulled on me. I clutched Luke's trace and yanked back. The grip loosened but didn't let go. Icy cold fingered its way up my arm.

"You must . . . come to me," a voice said in a whisper. "Riley. Before . . ." I jerked back again as aching cold fingered across my shoulder and into my chest. This time the hand let go. I stumbled back and bent over, putting my hands on my knees.

"What's the matter with you?" Luke said, spinning to look at me. He grabbed my arm and pulled me up straight.

"Nothing," I rasped. "Just dizzy." I looped his trace around my wrist. Now there was no danger that I'd lose him.

I didn't think about the voice. It was clear Luke hadn't heard it, any more than my other companions had heard it the first time it had talked to me. It had been in my head. Who was it? *What* was it? A ghost? Something else? Goose bumps prickled all over my body. I shivered and thrust away the mystery. For now, it didn't matter. I had to escape from Percy. Then I could worry about it.

I waited for Luke to hustle me out into the passage. Part of me had this idea that he was going to stuff me inside the food cart and roll me to safety that way. Instead, we stood there just inside my doorway. He faced away to the wall and put his hands on the rock and just stood there. His muscles bunched, and then I felt a pulse of magic move through him and out into the stone. It started to burn.

Low flames spread over the wall and out of the doorway into the hall. They rippled in a rainbow blanket. An acrid smell drifted through the room, and black smoke billowed.

"Don't breathe too much of the smoke," Luke said, his voice thick with concentration. "It's poisonous. You'll probably want to see a tinker when you get out."

"What about you?" I asked.

"I'm not your problem," he snapped.

"You are if you pass out before I get out of here," I retorted. He didn't need to know that for a nanosecond I'd actually been concerned about him.

"You can always trace your way out."

"Right into a booby trap."

He dropped one of his hands and put it into his pocket. He pulled out a smoothly polished piece of white quartz. "Once it's activated, it glows red when you get close to a trap, white when you head toward the surface. Don't follow the blue or you'll end up back here."

"Thanks." I plucked the stone from his hand and pocketed it. The flames had traveled far along the passage ahead. I could hear cries of warning. Black smoke bubbled along the ceiling, dimming the lights and filling the air with chemical stench. Luke's calloused hand closed around mine. He pulled me into the hallway. He kept one hand on the wall, fingers dragging lightly along. Magic continued to pulse through him and feed the fire. It ran down ahead of us and behind.

"Won't Percy suspect you?" I asked.

"He doesn't know I'm talented," Luke replied, pulling me along. He ignored the terrified yells from the cell doors as we passed by.

"What about them?" I asked, pulling back against his grip. "We can't leave them to burn up or suffocate."

"They won't," he said, yanking on me so that I stumbled forward. "As soon as we get to the end of the corridor, I'll melt the doors."

"Then what? They'll stumble around in the smoke to get caught again?"

He growled. "They aren't my problem. *You* are."

I dug in my heels, hauling back against him. He only tightened his grip and kept going. I staggered after, unable to resist without popping my shoulder out of its socket. "Those people need help."

"They're getting help. They are getting freed. The rest they have to do for themselves."

"What about the booby traps? They have no idea how to get out." I put my other hand against his back, trying to get leverage to pull away. It was like wrestling with the Hulk. He didn't even notice.

"It's a chance they didn't have five minutes ago. Percy's bugging out of here at the end of the week. He wasn't going to leave anybody alive. They were all dead in the cells, they just didn't know it yet. Now they might live. Not that it's your problem. You need to get out of here. And you're going to have to rescue your friends. They got stuck in a trap."

That sucked all the fight right out of me. I quickened my pace to catch up to him, my chest knotting up. "What kind of trap? Are they okay?" No wonder they hadn't shown up to rescue me.

"They're alive."

"Are they okay?" I repeated, and then started coughing as I sucked in smoke.

"Stop talking," Luke said. "Cover your face with your shirt. Breathe through your nose."

I did the best I could one-handed, and concentrated on keeping up with him. We heard more yells and screams, and then someone glanced off me, knocking me sideways into Luke. He shifted his grip to my wrist and plowed onward.

Since he wanted to play bulldozer, I dropped back as far as I could and let him take the brunt of whoever came barreling down the corridor. As doors melted away, more and more people tumbled out of the cells, all of them shouting and looking for a way out.

My head pounded and spun from the acrid vapors. I wasn't ready when Luke veered off to the left and then to the right. He no longer touched the walls, and the fire and smoke stayed behind.

"Neat trick," I said, leaning on my knees and sucking in clean air. "Next time I want to make lava, I'll know who to call."

"Don't bother. I won't be answering. Come on. You're wasting time."

He set off again, and I fell in behind. The lights popped on ahead of us as we walked. My lungs refused to let me go faster. Luke turned again and then again.

"Where are the booby traps?" I wondered out loud.

"There aren't any through here."

"Why not?"

"You'll see."

That sounded ominous. Clearly he wanted me to stop asking questions. So I didn't. "Where's Madison? How did you keep her from food deliveries?"

He glared at me and didn't answer.

"What about Percy? Why don't you tell him you're talented? Seems like you'd get paid more and wouldn't have to be a glorified food delivery boy if he knew."

"If he knew, I'd be a wraith by now."

"What? Why?"

I was surprised when he answered.

"He thinks having talents around SD production throws off the process. Plus, he doesn't trust us. He'd give me SD to keep me loyal, and then when I turned too far wraith, he'd turn me over to Doctor Inawa."

"For what?"

He stopped dead, then glanced at me. "Do you really want to know?"

Something in the way he asked sent ripples of fear chasing through my entire body. I didn't want to know. And yet I didn't want to walk away without knowing who had taken me. I needed the full truth.

I nodded. "Yes."

He snorted. "Why?"

That caught me up. In the blink of an eye, Madison's scared face flickered through my head, then Lauren's, then Percy burning me, and his and Dr. Inawa's cryptic conversation, and then the fumigation. It wasn't just that he was stone-cold evil, it was that nobody else seemed to know he existed. I'd never heard of him before he'd captured me. Right now, I was the only one who might be able to bring him down. And oh, Lord, but I wanted to. I hated him more than I'd hated anybody ever before.

"Because I'm the only one."

Even though that didn't make a lot of sense when I said it out loud, Luke seemed to understand what I meant. His brows rose.

"You could get caught again," he pointed out.

I hesitated. It wasn't just about me. Leo and Dalton and the others were trapped somewhere, and they were depending on me.

Luke gave a thin smile that made me feel about an inch tall.

"Figured as much." Luke started to turn away.

He might as well have dared me. I have more sense than to do the schoolkid reaction and accept the dare. That's not what made me grab his arm. No, what made me stop him and delay my escape despite the risk to myself, my stepbrother, and Dalton and his crew, was Percy and the fact that I wouldn't be able to live with myself if I didn't try to stop him, and that meant finding out all I could about his operation.

It wasn't just the fact that he was making SD, though that was part of it. The drug was horrible, and I had a chance to maybe shut down some of the production. Mostly, it was about Madison. Percy was holding her captive somehow. That much I could read. She was just a kid, really, even though she was just a few years younger than me. She wasn't the only one. He'd used the five teens to lure me down. Were they even still alive? It's one thing for adults to get sucked into evil, but another thing to be innocent and young and have someone like Percy take advantage. After my dad left, during those years when I was running wild, I'd lived that. I'd seen it up close. I wasn't going to stand by and watch Percy do it to others. I couldn't.

Luke eyed me narrowly, then nodded. "Then come on. I'll show you the horror show . . . What's left of it, anyway."

I didn't get a chance to ask what he meant. He turned and ducked down another tunnel. This one smelled stale and old—it clearly wasn't used often. There were no lights. He pulled a headlamp out of his pocket and fit it onto his head, clicking it on. I could feel his agitation through the ribbon of trace wrapped around my wrist. Whatever we were going to see was bad enough to send him soaring on all the fear, loathing, and hatred charts.

Why was he taking me to see this? If we were caught, Percy wouldn't be kind. Hell, Percy wasn't going to be kind anyhow.

"Why are you doing this?"

"I have my reasons."

"Which are?" I pushed. "Why are you willing to risk getting caught helping me?"

He didn't answer right away. We both had to watch our feet. Rocks and old boards littered the ground, which was gridded with ore cart crossties and rails. Ragged stubs of rotting wood thrust out from the walls every so often. I kept expecting to see rats nosing along and bats hanging overhead. The tunnel shrank the farther we walked down it. I began to sweat. I balled my hands into fists and made myself count breaths—five in, five out. I had to duck when my head scraped stone, and I nearly screamed. My heart thundered in my chest.

I didn't realize I'd stopped until Luke turned around and shined the light in my face. I squinted and looked away.

"What's wrong?"

I didn't speak. If I opened my mouth, the sounds that would have come out would only humiliate me. So I stood there, my entire body shaking. In the back of my head, I was praying I didn't pee myself.

"Hey!" Luke snapped his fingers in front of me, and then he put his hands on my shoulders and gave me a little shake. "Snap out of it."

Oh, good. I was afraid I'd never be cured, and he'd done it. A quick *snap out of it* and I was over my claustrophobia. If I could have, I would have rolled my eyes. I opened my mouth. Something like "ack" came out.

"Fucking hell. You've got claustrophobia."

Thank you, Doctor Phil. I didn't know. I'd have said it out loud if my lips weren't made of frozen rubber.

"Jesus." He shook me again and then made a frustrated sound before he slapped me.

I suppose it was a gentle slap. Admittedly, it didn't hurt quite as bad as when Percy had hit me. It also woke up a little fire in my stomach. My hands rose mechanically, and I shoved against his chest. Or maybe my hands just fluttered like butterflies there. I liked to think there was shoving. In my head I was pounding him to a pulp.

"Riley—Get over it."

I'm not sure whether the *get over it* is what got me going, or the fact that he actually knew my name. It shouldn't have surprised me. After all, I'd been deliberately lured down into Percy's trap. All the same, it was the first time he'd used it, and it shocked me. Between the two, it was enough to get my blood flowing to my head again.

"Don't ever hit me again," I mumbled. He still got the gist.

"Don't stand around like a wooden puppet and maybe I won't. Are you ready to get this over with? Or do you want to turn tail and run? Quit before you even get in the game?"

The light of the headlamp cast his face in demonic shadow, and there was no missing the derisive twist of his lips as he stared down at me.

"I'm not bailing," I said. "Tell me why you're showing me this. I get that you want to save Madison before she gets into trouble, but why add to your risk?"

He laughed, short and humorless. "Once I freed you from your cell, I lost all my choices," he said. "You're right. I hate Percy. Showing you his secrets is a Hail Mary to cut the bastard's legs out from under him and put him the ground and keep him from hurting anybody else."

And by anybody else, he meant Madison. "If you hate him so much, why do you work for him?"

He gave me a look like I'd said something so stupid it didn't deserve an answer. Abruptly he spun around, calling back over his shoulder. "Do me a favor and try not to turn into a statue again."

"Do *me* a favor and try not to turn into an asshole again. Oh wait, you never stopped," I muttered. I didn't know how he'd come to work for Percy, but he stayed for Madison. I was sure of it. He'd made himself her protector, and so long as she was here, he wasn't going anywhere. That made him less obnoxious, so maybe he wasn't a total asshole after all.

In response to my comment, he actually made a sound that might have been a laugh. It was hard to tell. He could have been choking, or maybe he swallowed a spider.

I kept that thought in mind as we went deeper into the tunnel, imagining spiders crawling out his nose and dangling out his ears. Luckily, the passage had shrunk as far as it was going to, and all I had to do was tolerate it. Easy peasy. Almost as easy as sitting through Percy burning me.

We turned off into a little side passage that went about ten feet and ended in a little nook about the size of a bathroom. There wasn't anything in it except for a boulder that protruded a couple of feet out from one wall.

"*This* is what you wanted to show me?" I asked, turning to see what I'd missed.

"Keep your voice down. And no. We have to go through there. If you can."

The last was a flat-out taunt, and my hackles rose. I'm sure he meant to piss me off enough to keep me from freezing up. It worked. I followed his pointing finger around the jut of stone and into a darkened corner where a small opening hunched low. It was all of about two feet tall and maybe eighteen inches wide. I was going to have to crawl through.

I didn't let myself think about it. I gripped my irritation at Luke in both hands and dropped down on my hands and knees. *It's just a doorway*, I told myself. *You'll be through in no time to something bigger.* I took a couple of deep breaths and crawled forward before I let myself consider how insane I was. I couldn't see anything ahead of me. I should have asked for the damned light, but at this point I wasn't going to give Luke the satisfaction of seeing me scared again.

Chills curled around me, and I shuddered. It took everything I had to go forward. I stuck one hand out in front of me to keep from banging my head. Or worse, sticking it into a bunch of cobwebs. Once I was all the way in, I eased to my feet and stepped out of Luke's way.

When he came through, the light revealed a similar sized room as the outer chamber. Luke pointed at a rope ladder hanging down one wall. Looking up, I could see that it led to a narrow niche about ten feet up. It looked to be about a foot and a half wide. Oh yay. I was about to be the meat inside a rock sandwich.

"Can you get up there?"

"Yep." I didn't move.

"Are you going to?"

"Yep." I still didn't move.

"Today?"

"You're a fucking bully, do you know that?"

"I thought I was saving your ass. That won't be true if you don't get it in gear." He sounded more worried than angry.

Remembering that Percy would be looking for me and possibly finding me was enough to get me started. I clambered up, trying not to think of the mountain sinking down to crush me. The rope ladder required concentration—they aren't easy to use—and that got me to the top. I lizard-crawled onto the stone platform. The opening was more like two feet wide, maybe a little more. Light gleamed about ten feet ahead. I inched forward while Luke crawled up beside me. He'd turned off the headlamp.

The light came through a small chiseled window, maybe three feet long and not quite a foot tall. I should have been catatonic from fear, but I was too distracted.

"What the hell is this?" I whispered.

"The horror show," Luke whispered back.

I could feel his agitation through his trace ribbon wrapping my wrist. No, agitation was too tame. Rage and horror and fear and frustration all tumbled together in a torrent.

Forty or more feet below us was a cavern. Cages made of the same mesh as my own prison door lined the walls and made aisles across. They were each large enough for one bed with maybe two feet to walk around. There had to be a couple thousand, if not more. Most were empty. A half-dozen people wearing various colored scrubs pushed metal carts around, collecting trays. Four others in lab coats carried clipboards and wandered from cage to cage, pushing more carts and doling out something to each of the prisoners. There were all clustered at the far end. I guestimated there were maybe fifty to a hundred people in the cages.

"What is this?" I breathed, my mouth going dry.

"Wait," Luke said.

Bursts of magic erupted down the line of cages where the lab coats had just passed. It was like dominoes falling. As each flared, nulls answered, shutting each down as fast as they occurred. That's when I realized that the cages were the nulls. Then the other pieces fell into place.

"They're giving everybody in those cages Sparkle Dust," I said, much louder than I intended.

Luke slapped his hand over my mouth. "Sh!"

I pushed his hand away and glared at him. "I'm right, aren't I?" This time I whispered.

"Seems so."

"Why?" But I was remembering what Doctor Inawa and Percy had talked about. *We've only a little stock left to finish ripening before harvest.* These prisoners were the stock they were ripening. But what the hell did that mean?

"Come on," Luke said and wriggled backward.

I was more than ready to get out of there. I scraped my knuckles getting back down the ladder. Luke had turned his light back on to let me see. Before I could ask any questions, he crawled back out. Again I followed. He barely waited for me to stand before he started off again.

This time I was the one to grab his wrist. He didn't stop.

"What's going on in there?"

"You're not stupid, figure it out," he snarled.

I could feel the emotions boiling up in him. One of the biggest was sheer terror. He wasn't the kind to be afraid. But he was afraid of Percy and his farm project. He pulled away from me and stalked away. I followed automatically as I considered what I'd seen. There's no doubt they were deliberately feeding prisoners SD. The null cages were designed to protect against the sudden random magical talent side effect that came with taking the drug. Even non-talents would have a temporary talent. It didn't last long, though I had no actual facts to back that up. Most of what I knew was rumor and word of mouth. So the cages kept the magical talents bound. But why give an expensive drug like that to so many? Why keep them caged?

We've only a little stock left to finish ripening before harvest. Stock. Dr. Inawa had said something about using the fume source SD on the stock to shorten harvest times. What were they harvesting from the prisoners?

The answer came to me. But it was wrong. It *had* to be. It wasn't possible or even likely. Besides, no one would do anything like that. No one could be that evil.

Percy's face rose in my mind.

I stopped, hardly aware that I had. Luke turned around, his face harsh in the light.

"What are they doing?" I demanded. I needed him to tell me I was wrong, that I was crazy.

He gave me a long look. What he saw must have satisfied him somehow, because for once he gave me a straight answer.

"Sparkle Dust is people."

Chapter 9

"What?" Even though I'd already figured it out, I wasn't about to accept it without a fight. The idea that Percy could be farming people to make a drug was too awful to let it be true.

"Sparkle Dust is people," he said again. "Just like Soylent Green, except for real." Luke turned around and started walking again.

I hurried after him. "But that's insane and impossible. How?"

Luke sighed. "I don't know how they figured it out. One story says that someone found a stash of miners who'd been trapped near an underground spring. Over time, as the spring overflowed and retreated, the minerals in the water leached into them and turned their bodies into pure Sparkle Dust. More was found near the spring—it can be distilled from the water. That takes time, like getting salt from the sea, only there's a lot less SD in the water. So eventually Dr. Inawa and Percy worked out a plan to experiment on manufacturing the drug by using people. Those with talents give a stronger Dust, but anybody can be turned. Percy would use you until you couldn't trace for him, then stick you in a cage until you were ready for harvesting."

"Why the hell do you work for such a sick bastard?" I demanded. I wanted to be yelling at Percy. I wanted to be pounding his face in with a brick. Luke was the only enemy in front of me.

"I've got my reasons," he said, and I could feel the cold reserve drop around him as he recoiled from me. I felt his hurt and rage and doubt tumbling through his trace in a torrent. I forced myself to be calm. Madison was his Achilles' heel. She was the reason. I didn't have to hear him say it to know it for a fact. So I focused on her.

"Why does Madison work for him?"

"She doesn't." He snapped the words off like an alligator snapping legs on a wildebeest.

"That's weird, because serving food certainly looked like her working for him."

Luke sped up without replying. I broke into a jog, just to keep up. I stepped on a piece of loose rock, and my ankle twisted. I yelped and hopped, but he didn't even slow down. I caught up, grabbing hold of his arm and leaning hard on him. He started to shake me off, but I gripped harder.

"If you want to go fast, then you'll have to put up with being a crutch," I gasped.

"You'll breathe better if you shut up, then," he said.

"I'll breathe better when Percy's hanging up by his balls and can't hurt anybody anymore."

Luke snorted. "Who's going to stop him? You?" Despite his doubt, I could feel his hope.

"Maybe. Clearly it won't be you."

"Just be grateful I'm helping you escape," he said. Under my fingers his muscles went rock hard. I didn't need his trace to know he was furious. His trace told me that anger was mixed with healthy doses of fear and fatalism. Like he knew something bad was coming and couldn't do anything about it.

"I am. I owe you," I said.

"You're damned right you do. I plan to collect. With interest. Now, this is where you're on your own."

We came around a corner, and in front of us was a barn-sized cavern. Just inside the door was a rotating crossing circle with rails on it. It could be turned to let ore carts from the various passages emptying into the cavern pass onto one of the four tracks leading up and out of the cavern. Chains and pulleys dangled from above, and old carts lined the wall, some tipped on their sides, others upside down or missing a wheel. They weren't what caught my attention.

In the middle of the floor sprawled five bodies. I dropped into trace sight, and gasped with relief. All were alive. Leo lay to the left, Dalton to the right, with the rest of the team flopped over onto each other between. They tangled in the same magic that had wrapped my paralyzing captors. Sheets of it hung haphazardly across the passage, guaranteeing that anyone wandering through would blunder into one, if not more.

"What are those things? What kind of magic is that?" I demanded, pointing at the sheets. "What's it doing to them?"

The sound of the magic grated on my nerves. This time it wasn't just a high sound, it was a full-on symphony that scraped my bones and made my skin crawl. I shivered like a horse trying to twitch off a swarm of flies. It didn't work.

"You can see them?" Luke asked, startled.

Yay. I surprised him. Points for me. I decided to act like I couldn't always see magic other people couldn't. "Can't you?"

He shook his head. "Paralyzes them mostly," he said, answering my last question. "Puts them to sleep. Might cause some pain. Depends."

"On what?"

"How're they made. You're lucky. Usually Percy collects up the victims and puts them in the cages as soon as they trip the trap. He's bugging out of here at the end of the week, so he didn't bother with them. He'll send someone to collect up the magic and kill them."

"How do we get them out of there?"

He snorted, giving me a sidelong look. "*We* don't. You do. You're supposed to be the Wizard of Oz when it comes to trace magic. Null them out."

He crossed his arms and looked at me. I resisted the urge to shake him, mostly because I didn't need him dumping me on my ass when I tried. At least I wasn't half-dead anymore. That would help. I bent down and searched along the ground with my fingers. I found a bolt about as big around as my middle finger and just as long. That should do it.

Before starting, I released Luke's trace. I didn't need distractions.

Creating a null mostly requires a tracer to pour magic into an object, all the while molding it into what you want it to do. Making a null that absorbed wasn't that tricky, for me, anyhow. At least not for something small-scale like a defined space. The hard part was making it strong enough. Normally I'd take time to build the power—add to it daily until it reached the strength I wanted. If I was really desperate, I could suck the magic out of one null and feed it into another and build it up that way.

I dropped to the floor, crossing my legs and holding one end of the bolt in each hand. I focused, drawing magic up out of myself and feeding it into the metal. I wove it with my intent, winding power around the barrel of the bolt like thread around a spool.

I reached out beyond me, looking for bits of natural power that I might be able to use. The reason Diamond City was so magical had something to do with ley lines and the depth of the prehistoric volcano that had caused the caldera in the first place. Magic was in the dirt and the water and the air. Unfortunately, this area seemed to be a desert of magic. That meant I was depending only on myself, and I didn't know if I had the strength to null out those swathes of magic, whatever the hell they were.

Unless—

What if I used one of them? I could dismantle magic. I'd done it before. And when I had, I'd been able to use the power to fuel nulls. It was dangerous without knowing what exactly the magic in the tapestries of magic could do, but even so, I'd demolished serious magic before and survived.

I stopped winding power around the bolt and stood.

"Done?" Luke asked, clearly surprised.

I gave a little shake of my head and walked toward the closest sheet of magic. His arm thrust out in front of me.

"If you go out there, you'll end up like your friends."

"I don't think so," I said.

He dropped his arm. "Your funeral."

"Let's hope not."

A strand of the sound got louder when I got near the shining sheet of magic. It swirled and twisted uneasily, almost like it was alive. I squinted at it. It almost seemed like there was a pattern in it. Or maybe like it was a bunch of pieces sewn together. But pieces of *what?*

I lifted my hand and hesitated. If I was wrong, I'd be trapped, just like Luke said. My hand tightened on the bolt. I could try it out and see how well it worked. I could feel the magic in the sheet, and I knew the null wasn't strong enough. It needed a lot more power, which only the sheet could provide. I had to risk this.

I reached out and touched my fingers to the magic. Instantly, the sheet dropped over me, shrouding me from head to foot. My skin prickled, and energy crackled over it. It was like standing in a jar of Pop Rocks. The sounds I'd been hearing whined louder. It began to sound like a chorus of voices straight out of an insane asylum. I had a sense of being stung by bees from the bottoms of my feet to the top of my head. That, and invisible fingers started pinching at me.

I turned into Gumby. I teetered on the balls of my feet and started to fall. My fingers were still lifted. I channeled energy into them, sending out tentacles to suck the power out of the shroud.

At first, the magic resisted, then the fabric knotted into sticky clumps. It felt like clumps of tapioca. I fed the power into the bolt null clutched in my other hand.

Thirty seconds passed, and then the whining turned to screams. What was left of the sheet coruscated and rippled outward, tearing apart into patchwork tatters. Threads of binding power tangled with the seeking tentacles of my power. It was as if the binding power had been sewing the other bits together. The rags of leftover magic drifted in the air like dande-lion fluff caught on a summer wind.

As the shroud tore apart, I regained strength, catching myself mid-stagger. The stinging and pinching subsided. I hardly noticed. I reached out and captured one of the tatters in my hand. It fluttered and twisted as if trying to get away. Then it flattened, pressing soft against my skin. It sent a chill through me—not ordinary cold, but the kind I associ-ated with the trace dimension. The kind that frosted the untouchable places deep inside me. I shook my hand to get it off, but it didn't slide away. "What the fuck?"

"What's wrong?" Luke rasped.

I glanced at him. Grooves cut deep lines around his mouth. He had his arms crossed over his chest, every muscle bunched tight. If I didn't know better, I'd have thought he was nervous.

I didn't know how to explain what had happened, even if I wanted to, which I didn't. "Nothing." I rubbed the back of my hand against my pants, but the cling-wrap magic stayed stuck.

"Can you hurry up? I want to get back before someone misses me."

"You should come with me."

His mouth twisted. "Why don't you worry about yourself? Can you get your people out of the trap?"

Right. He wouldn't leave Madison behind. My fingers tightened on the null I'd made. Was it enough? I wasn't sure. The shroud hadn't acted like any magic I'd experienced before. On the other hand, something about it felt familiar. I just couldn't place it. I rubbed the back of my hand against my thigh again. Where the patch of magic clung to me, my skin had gone numb and a chill ached deep inside me.

"Well?" Luke demanded.

I glared at him, then went to kneel beside Leo. My brother and two members of Dalton's team were wrapped in the same blanket. It shimmered and pulsed with rainbow color. I activated the bolt null and thrust my hand inside.

Cold closed around my wrist, and once again, I felt the sensation of pinching and stinging where the shroud touched me. I'd created the null to suck in power like a battery, rather than just stamp it out. I hadn't realized I'd done it that way. It was harder to do than just make a normal null, but far more efficient in the end. Once again, the shroud tore apart into tattered bits that drifted through the air and along the floor. I frowned at them. Why did they seem so familiar?

I didn't get a chance to think about it. Leo groaned and blinked.

"Hey," I said, relief making tears well in my eyes. I blinked them away, swallowing the sudden ache in my throat. "Are you okay?"

He stiffened and sat up with a jerk. "Riley? Where did you come from?"

He pulled me into a hug and then caught sight of Luke behind me. "Who's that?" Leo jumped to his feet, staggering and then steadying himself. He tried to step in front of me to shield me, but I held him back.

"This is Luke. He's helping me escape," I said. "Luke, meet my brother, Leo."

"I don't give a fuck who he is. Get on with it," Luke said.

Right. He was on borrowed time, and so were we.

"Can you see if there are any batteries in the packs?" I asked Leo. His toe lamps were dead, as were everybody else's. Luke had the only light, and he was taking it with him. I didn't wait for him to answer. I turned to Luke.

"You can go if you want." I winced. That sounded obnoxious. I didn't mean it to be. "What I mean is, thank you. I owe you big-time. You should go back before someone misses you."

Luke glowered at me beneath his headlamp. For all his eagerness to leave, he seemed firmly rooted to the rock. "What about the others?" He jerked his chin at Dalton and the rest of my unconscious bodyguard squad.

"It won't be a problem."

"Then do it."

"Where did you meet your new friend? Nazis-are-us?" Leo asked, handing me a headlamp he'd fished out of his pack.

"He was my prison guard."

"Was he?" Leo eyed Luke with narrowed eyes.

My brother didn't have the bulk that Luke had, but I'd give him odds in a fight. He might be a jeweler, but he was all muscle and tough as hell. I figured their talents were pretty even, though I knew better than most the tricks my brother could do with metal. He'd tortured me with them as a kid. I'd learned to null out his power in sheer self-defense.

"Relax. He's a good guy." I smiled when Luke's mouth fell open. I bet he didn't get compliments that often, and getting one from me was probably grounds for a heart attack. "He helped me escape and brought me here to help you. I owe him."

Leo nodded, still watching Luke, his face flinty. "Yes, we do. Thanks." He looked at me. "Why don't you get to work on the others?"

I repeated the nulling process on the rest of our team. Dalton had been tangled by himself in two different blankets, while the others had been wrapped together in one. By the time I was done, the bolt null was pulsing with power, and a confetti of magic tatters floated through the cavern. As they brushed against me, several fastened on my skin, sticking to me like patches of silken ice.

I could have activated the bolt null again to see if that would get rid of them, but they didn't seem to be doing any damage, and I wanted to examine them later. The magic was totally unfamiliar. I could feel bits of various talents in all of it like different body parts all Frankensteined together. Only that wasn't possible. Talents didn't meld that way. Two people with different talents could weave them together into something like a song, but this felt different, like a patchwork. I growled inwardly at myself. I couldn't find the words to even make sense of it to myself. It was why I wanted to examine the bits later.

I extended my hand to help the last two bodyguards to their feet—Mac and Sharon, if I remembered right. Both looked dazed, and they leaned heavily against each other as they stretched their arms and legs. Mac had a bruise on his forehead. Sharon's chin had a scrape, and dried blood clung to the corner of her mouth. Dalton looked none the worse for wear, but he was absolutely seething.

He glowered at me. "Are you all right?"

"Thanks to that heal-all you gave me," I said, which was probably the only thank-you he was likely to get on the subject.

He didn't crack a smile. His gaze shifted to Luke, and he slipped his gun from its holster. At least he didn't lift it. Yet. "Who's this?"

I repeated the introduction I'd given Leo, who'd none-too-subtly shifted to put his hand on an ore cart that remained on the rails. Luke also stood on the rails. With his metal magic, my brother could bind Luke or kill him in less than a heartbeat.

"You've got the rock; you should be safe enough from traps," Luke said to me, ignoring the others. "One more thing: Percy won't give up. He'll be coming after you. If he finds out the fumigation didn't take, he's going to want to know why. Hell, *I* want to know why. And don't think he's the only one. Just because you've seen one claw of the monster doesn't mean you've got a clue what the rest of it looks like."

He stopped, his tongue pressing out against the inside of his lower lip, like he was trying to make up his mind. All of a sudden, he gave a little nod. "Wait here."

He swung around and disappeared up one of the side passages. My companions had found their packs and their lights, as well as protein bars and bottles of water.

"What's he up to?" Dalton said, then looked at me. His silver eyes were rimmed blue again and shined as if lit from within. It looked a little too Terminator for me. "Do you trust him?"

"Why would he help me escape and then screw me over now?"

I couldn't tell if that reassured him or not. Luke reappeared about thirty seconds later. He was cradling a body against his chest.

I didn't have to see her face to know it was Madison. Her long blond hair gave her away. That, and I didn't know who else Luke would be carrying around as carefully as he was holding Madison.

"What the fuck?" Dalton said.

"Take her out of here," Luke said to me. "That's what I want for helping you." Frustration, desperation, and a more complex cocktail of emotions flooded his trace. He was a volcano—all rock and ice on top, and below a molten mess.

"What did you do to her?" I asked. Madison hung in his arms like a rag doll.

"Her bracelet's a sleep charm. She'll wake up when you take it off her."

Something wasn't right. "Why aren't you coming out with her?" I didn't say it, but I knew he got the message—why aren't you escaping, too, when the whole reason you breathe is leaving?

Luke's teeth bared in a snarl. "I've got reasons." He looked at my companions. "Who's going to carry her?"

Dalton folded his arms. The members of his squad just stood like statues, like kids in science class who hadn't done their homework and were hoping the teacher didn't call on them. Finally Leo glanced at me and stepped forward, taking Madison. Luke looked like he'd rather cut off his arm than let her go. Instead, he stepped back.

"Tell her not to worry. I'll take care of everything," he said to me, and then disappeared back the way we'd come.

What the hell did that mean? I started after him, but Dalton grabbed my arm. "We've got to go."

I shook away his hand. As much as I wanted to argue, he was right. I looked at Leo. "Thanks."

He gave me a lopsided grin, then frowned. "I won't be able to carry her far."

"Not a problem." I grabbed the bracelet circling her wrist. The silver and blue glass beads were strung on a stretchy cord. I pulled it off Madison's wrist and tucked it in my pocket. Instantly, she stiffened and blinked awake. She frowned up at Leo.

"Who are you? Let go of me!" She pushed against him and kicked. Hard.

"Easy now," Leo said, setting her on her feet, and raising his hands up in surrender. "I'm friendly."

Madison backed away, then caught sight of me. Her brow creased in confusion. "Riley? What's going on? Where are we?"

"The quick and dirty version is that Luke helped me escape, then charmed you to sleep and told us to take you out of the tunnels."

Even in the gloom I could see the color drain from her face. Her eyes widened. "No! I can't. I have to get back. How do I get back?" She twisted around, looking at the various tunnels.

"You can't," I said firmly. I didn't care what Percy was holding over her head, I wasn't leading her back, even if I could find the way. Luke said he had her covered, and I was going to trust him. Mostly because I didn't figure I had a choice. Neither did Madison. "We're heading to the surface. Luke said to tell you not to worry. He'd take care of things for you."

Madison startled me by swearing a blue streak. Abruptly she stopped, her lips clamped white. She closed her eyes and drew a breath and slowly let it out. She opened her eyes again. She looked at me.

"Percy has my family. If I escape, he'll hurt them." Her voice broke on the word "hurt."

"Shit," Leo said.

He took the word right out of my mouth. "Luke seemed to think he could take care of them." It was the most reassuring thing I could come up with. Pathetic.

"How?"

I thought of Luke's talent for burning stone. Madison probably didn't know about it. "He's got more going for him than you know. Besides, he doesn't have to hold the fort long. We're going to get reinforcements and go back in. We're going to put Percy out of business."

At least, that was my plan. I didn't know if Price and Touray were going to agree.

Chapter 10

I introduced Madison to everyone. I even remembered everybody's names: Dalton, because I'd never forget the most irritating man on the planet—though Luke gave him some serious competition—Maggie, Bret, Sharon, and Mac. Lastly, I introduced Leo.

Madison eyed Dalton warily, no doubt disturbed by his eyes, though I suppose it could have been the cold brutality of his expression. On the other hand, After Luke, Dalton wasn't a whole lot worse. She nodded to the others. Her gaze lingered on Leo. I wasn't surprised. My stepbrother was serious eye candy. The startling thing was that he seemed to be blushing. Or maybe it was the way the shadows fell on his face. Finally, she looked back at me.

"I have go back," she said.

"Not now," I said. "Not without help."

She considered that, turning it in her mind like a jeweler examining a diamond. Once again she surprised me. She looked so young and seemed so sheltered. Then again, she'd been dealing with Percy for who knows how long. As young and innocent as she looked on the outside, she had a core of iron.

"How long is it going to take to get help?" she asked.

"I'm not sure. The faster we get moving, the faster we find out."

"This help of yours is strong enough to handle my uncle?"

"Uncle?" I repeated.

She hunched her shoulders. "Not by blood. He's my mom's sister's first husband."

"This is all very interesting, but we should get moving before we get caught," Dalton said. Grooves cut deeply into his face. The flashlight shine of his eyes had begun to dim, but he still radiated anger and menace.

"Everybody ready?" He didn't wait for an answer. "I'll take point with Sharon and look for booby traps. The rest of you stay twenty feet behind. Mac, you lead them, Bret and Maggie, bring up the rear. No straggling." He glared meaningfully at me, Leo, and Madison, then started across the cavern to the tunnel opening that they'd probably entered from.

"Stop!" I yelled, just before he stalked into one of the still-intact magic blankets. He ought to have been more careful than that, given his paranoid nature. He was off his game. But then, he'd been unconscious and bound in magic for who knows how long. Plus, he'd let me get kidnapped, and I'd escaped, and rescued him. That had to be humbling. At least it ought to be. I grinned at that thought. I'd be reminding him of it, regularly and often.

At my shout, Dalton froze in place. He twisted his head to look at me. "What's wrong?"

"Back up three steps."

To his credit, he obeyed without question, setting each foot carefully.

"There are magic blankets hanging from the roof," I said. "You guys got wrapped up in four of them, so this area down here is safe enough. There are five others. I'll have to guide you out."

The placement of the blankets seemed haphazard, but looking now, I realized they'd been hung with an eye toward getting people all the way inside the cavern before the trap sprung, increasing the odds that no one would escape. Impressive, in a pathologically insane villain-of-the-week sort of way.

I guided everyone out, one at a time, leaving Dalton until last. As I led him out, I glanced back. I hoped Luke would be all right. I hoped he really could protect Madison's family until we could bring the cavalry.

I snorted to myself. Some cavalry: Gregg Touray, Tyet kingpin, whom I feared more than just about anyone else on the planet. Still, as monsters went, as far as I knew, he wasn't as bad as Percy.

Of course, that all depending on convincing him to help me. I was fairly certain the SD production would be enough to get him motivated. He claimed to want to shut it down. I hoped that when Touray found out that Sparkle Dust was actually made from people, he'd be as horrified as I was. On the other hand, trusting him with this information was a definite risk. There was no doubt SD was hugely profitable, and no doubt that Touray's business had come under siege by other Tyet factions. Maybe he'd want to take over operations for the income potential. At the very least, he'd want something in exchange for his help, and I already knew what his price tag was. He'd better not expect me to come wrapped in a red bow.

I sighed. I'd worry about handling Touray after I survived the battle with Percy. *If* I survived the one with Percy.

As for Price—whatever we had together just got *more* complicated.

I smiled. He would come help me, if only to hopefully save some lives and make sure Percy didn't come after me again. I bit my lips, suddenly longing to feel his arms around me, his chest warm and solid under my cheek. As much as I worried about the Tyet end of things in our relationship, there was no arguing that being with him made me feel safe and loved and just *happy*. Even when we were getting chased and shot at. I sighed. Clearly, I needed to be in a mental hospital.

Once I got Dalton to the cavern entrance, I pulled the white quartz stone out of my pocket and held it up. "Luke gave me this. It will show where the traps are and how to get back to the surface."

Dalton thrust his hand out to take it. I pulled away, unwilling to hand it over. Not only would the stone get us out, it would get us back in. I didn't trust him to return it when we escaped.

"I'll lead," I said.

He scowled at me, but for once, didn't argue. Instead, he motioned Sharon to hang back with the others. Leo made no effort to fall back, standing firm beside me. Madison hovered close behind.

"It's suicidal to stick too close together," Dalton said slowly, explaining himself as if to a group of particularly stupid children. "If we trip a booby trap, if you're hanging back, then at least you might survive and get out."

"It's a good point," Leo said. "But I'll take my chances."

"Me, too," Madison said, edging closer to Leo.

Once again she impressed me. She'd decided to play the cards she had instead of whining about Luke betraying her or freaking out about her family—which I'm pretty sure I would have done. No wonder the over-sized gorilla had a thing for her. I was half in love with her myself. Of course, when she got him in her sights again, she was going to rip him a new one at the very least. I was hoping for a ringside seat.

Getting out wasn't as straightforward as it might seem, even with our quartz disco rock. More than one passage led to the surface. It lit white over and over. Since I didn't want to blunder into any Tyet operations, or worse, give the impression we were trying to move in on someone's diamond claim, we had to go carefully. The passages were peppered with ordinary traps we had to find without the help of the stone. Between Leo's metal skills and Dalton's—whatever was up with his eyes—we got past those with relative ease. I was doing my best not to have a panic attack, especially when the tunnel turned into a pipe and I had to crawl through on my stomach.

I closed my eyes and wriggled through, pulling myself with my elbows and shoving with my toes. My head clouded, and all I knew was I needed to get out. I couldn't breathe. I hunched upward and crashed into stone. My head reeled, and blood trickled warmly down my forehead and onto my nose. I wiped it away with a fist and forced myself to keep going, tears of pain dripping onto the ground.

It was a twenty-foot crawl, give or take. On the other side, I flung my-self to my feet and bent, leaning on my knees as I panted, trying to get my breathing under control.

"Fuck, Riley, what did you do?" Leo said as he caught sight of the blood. He dug in his pack and came out with a tube of disinfectant wipes. I almost laughed. Who packed one of those? Apparently, my brother. He wiped my face with one, and then pressed another against the wound to stop the bleeding.

I put my hand over his. "I've got it. Thanks." I sounded like I'd chain-smoked a carton of cigarettes, then drank a fifth of bourbon.

"What's wrong?" Madison asked as she came through behind me.

"Banged head."

"Claustrophobia."

Leo and Dalton spoke at the same time. I glared at the latter. He didn't need to sound so condescending about my fear. I bet he had a skeleton in his closet somewhere. Probably more in his pantry, laundry room, spare bathroom, and garage. Likely real actual skeletons, but somewhere in there was probably an embarrassing quirk of some kind, even if it was only toe fungus or an troubling inability to hit the toilet when he peed. A girl could hope.

"Are you okay?" Madison put a hand on my shoulder. "God, this whole thing has been hell for you, hasn't it? You must've been going crazy in that cell."

I straightened and gave her a crooked smile. "Yeah, well. I'm out now, right?"

She shook her head. "I'm so sorry."

"Not your fault."

"He's my uncle."

"He's a giant jackass and it's not like you gave him lessons in how to be Josef Mengele."

She frowned and looked away without answering. I wanted to kick myself. Sure, remind her how awful Percy was when her family was at his mercy.

"We'll get your family out," I said softly, gripping her hand.

She didn't reply, but her fingers tightened on mine for a moment be-fore she let go.

The other members of the team came through the pipe, and we set off again. My whole body was shaking. I don't know if it was the fear or exhaustion, the effect of dealing with the magical blankets, or flat-out hunger. Probably all of the above.

I started off again without a word. Dalton swore and trotted to catch up with me. He grabbed my shoulder and shoved past me. I let him. If he wanted to get blown up first, no skin off my nose. Right now, the quartz rock was glowing white. No signs of imminent danger.

Before too long, we came to a spot where water ran out of a crack up at the top of a wall. It washed to the floor and turned into a little creek. My heart lifted. We were getting closer to the outside. Maybe hope was getting the best of me, but I was certain this was surface water leaking down into the cave system. That meant the surface had to be close. I squeezed my eyes shut. *Please, please, please, let us get out soon!*

We marched onward. I got antsy enough to step on Dalton's heels a couple of times. Finally, he swung around and pushed me back.

"Back off," he growled.

I met his silvery gaze. Words spilled out before I had a chance to consider them. "What do your eyes do?"

He gave me an "are you for real?" look, then shook his head. "They see. Eyes do that, don't you know."

With that, he swung back around and stalked off. Okay, it might have been a rude question, but what did he expect? Inquiring minds wanted to know, and he wasn't exactly Mr. Manners. I sighed. I really needed sleep and food. And air. I could use a whole lot more air.

The stream followed us down a steep passage that reminded me a little bit of a log ride without the logs. Grooves and holes in the floor revealed that it had once had an ore cart line running down it, which had no doubt been in use before it became a creek bed. I kept stepping into the water where it had pooled behind little rock debris dams. It was cold. Pretty soon my feet were numb, matching the little ice patches made by the clinging bits of magic. I was a patchwork quilt of cold.

We reached the bottom of the passage. Four other tunnels led away, all of them offering the white light of the surface. Trace led through all of them, though trace said that two of them had a lot more traffic. That was both potentially promising and equally dangerous, depending on their destinations. I glanced at Leo.

"Can you tell anything?"

He ran his fingers along the wall, searching for a vein of metal. He paused and closed his eyes. I felt the pulse of his magic as he sent his awareness out through the rock. After a minute, he opened his eyes. "The second from the right. Shouldn't be far."

It was all I could do not to sprint. I gripped my hands together and forced myself to keep to the slower pace. I swear Dalton had slowed down just to torture me.

I caught the first hints of pine and fresh air. I tried to squelch my moan, but didn't succeed even a little. Leo put his arm around my waist and squeezed, then took my hand. I clutched it hard enough to break bones. He didn't pull away.

Light that wasn't from our headlamps filtered through the darkness. I swallowed, my heart pounding.

"Easy now," Leo said as the passage narrowed.

I splashed through water. The slope of the floor had eased and the creek had widened, spreading to the wall on this side. Leo swore and took the forgotten quartz from my other hand. It had turned ruby red. That meant a trap nearby. I said so.

"Dalton, hold up."

I didn't pay much attention to what they did at that point. My body had gone taut as a guitar string, and I vibrated with the need to get out. I forced myself to stay still, even as I leaned forward against the wall, inhaling the scents of the outside. Finally, Leo grabbed my hand again.

"It's safe. Come on."

He led me across the little creek to the other side of the passage, where a narrow bit of path was still above water, then let go of me and pushed me forward. Madison waited to take my hand. Leo and Dalton made sure the others made it past, and then we went another twenty steps and turned a corner to freedom.

The exit was no bigger than the entrance we'd used to get in, and the stream ran straight through the middle of it. An ice dam had formed just outside, backing the water up inside the cave until it created a pool that was more than waist-deep. Water ran over the top of the dam and tumbled down the mountainside. It sounded like there was a steep drop waiting for us. I didn't care. I was ready to plow through the water and take my chances.

"What now?" Madison asked. "I'm not a fan of a February swim."

"Maybe we can get a signal." Leo took out his phone, as did Dalton. Neither had any success.

"I'll try near the entrance," Leo said, and splashed through to the circle of gray sky. He held his phone out through the hole and squinted. He shaded the screen. "Got one. We can get a text out. Now the question is who do we call?"

I was hysterical enough to want to answer with *Ghostbusters*. Somehow, I didn't think Dan Aykroyd and Bill Murray were going to be a lot of help.

"I can activate a tab. We're close enough to the outside that my people can follow it. They'll rescue us shortly," Dalton said, and dug in a pocket and put his plan into action.

I had a different idea, and my idea might get us out of here faster.

"Gimme your phone," I said, holding my hand out to Leo, who'd joined us back on dry land. He was dripping, and he'd clenched his jaw to keep it from chattering.

"Who are you calling?"

"Trouble," I said. "Helpful trouble." I punched in Price's phone number and then typed out the text:

Need help. Stuck inside the mountain with no way out. Have your brother travel *to us.*

I eyed the screen and wondered if there was any way this was a sane move. We could wait for Dalton's help to show up. It was coming from the same source in the end. I started to hit the delete key and hesitated. Touray could get Leo out right away instead of waiting for someone to follow Dalton's tab. Leo was shivering. Even inside the cave, which was warmer than outside, it couldn't have been more than thirty degrees. My breath plumed in the air. How long before he got hypothermia? If getting wet from the crotch down could do it . . . I didn't know, but I sure as hell wasn't about to gamble with my brother.

I handed Leo the phone. "Go send this," I said.

He read it and flicked an eyebrow up at me, but didn't ask any questions. He waded back to the cave entrance.

"I've got it covered," Dalton said, not moving out of the way. He'd gone to the opening to send a message of his own.

"All the same," Leo drawled, thrusting his phone up over the other man's shoulder until he had bars. He thumbed the *Send* key. A few seconds later, he lowered his arm and returned to me, followed by Dalton, who managed to stomp through the water.

"Who did you send that message to?" he demanded, skewering me on his silver gaze. He still had his phone in his hand.

"Like you don't know," I said.

"Who?" His voice was a gunshot.

I sighed. He really wanted me to spell it out? "Your boss. One of them. Who else?"

He swore, then whirled away. "Come on. Let's go. Double time. Full retreat."

My other four bodyguards straightened at his whip-crack voice, spinning around and heading back the way we'd come.

What the fuck? "What are you doing?" I demanded, shock and sudden doubt crashing through me. I was putting two and two together fast and not liking results one bit.

Dalton looked over his shoulder as he followed his people up the passage. "You'll see me again, Princess," he said with a sharp grin, and vanished.

My mouth fell open, and I exchanged looks with Madison and Leo. "What just happened?"

"I don't think they wanted to be here when your buddies showed up," Madison said.

"But—" I stopped before I said something extremely stupid, like, for instance: *but Dalton works for Touray!* Because it was pretty obvious that that was not even close to the truth. Which meant I'd given that asshole and his team access to me, my friends, and my brother. I'd risked all of our lives. My stomach quaked as I imagined what they could have done, who could have been hurt. "Who are they? Who sent them?" Panic—way, way too late—made my voice rise.

"That is the twenty-four-dollar question," Leo said, ice crusting his voice. "Didn't you check them out?"

"I just—" What? I'd tried to follow their trace, but they'd nulled it out. I'd followed them, trying to find out where they lived, but they only went where I went. I had no idea where they slept or ate. I'd been recovering from my earlier injuries, then I'd been too swamped with new jobs, with worrying about who was out to get me, and the constant misery and heartache of missing Price. When a hacker friend hadn't found anything, I'd let it go; I'd decided I knew who Dalton was working for and that I could live with it.

I'd been criminally stupid.

"Just what?" Leo demanded, shoving his fingers through his hair and looking like he wanted to strangle me. "Holy hell, Riley! How could you be so careless?"

Unable to meet his gaze, I covered my face with my hands and swung away. Tears burned in my eyes from emotional overload and exhaustion, plus hefty helpings of humiliation and self-recrimination. Dalton came and went from the diner when he wanted. He could have hurt Patti or Ben at any time. What if I'd relaxed my guard more than I had? Would I have led him to my family? He could have slaughtered them, or worse, taken them as hostages against my cooperation. Had that been his game? Or something else?

I didn't have time to contemplate much more. The air rippled and bent. Magic exploded outward in thundering waves. It rammed me up against the wall. I twisted so that my left shoulder and hip took the brunt of the impact. That, and the side of my head. It's not like I was using it much, anyhow.

My vision went blurry, and my head spun. I slid down to my butt and yelped as I landed on a sharp rock. Brilliant. On top of everything else, I'd managed to bruise my ass. At least the water I was sitting in would numb the pain at some point.

I touched my hand to my cheek. I'd cut it. The wound on top of my head had begun to bleed again, as well. I tilted my head back against the wall and closed my eyes, bracing hands in the water on either side of myself, trying to keep to the right side of consciousness.

"What the hell is going on? Where's Riley?"

Damn, but I'd missed that voice. Even full of brutal menace, it sent jolts of electricity sizzling over my skin. I lifted my hand and made a dying kitten sort of sound. It was enough. I heard splashing, and hot hands ran over my hair and gently cupped my face, then moved down to grip my shoulders. Price gave me a hard little shake.

"God dammit, Riley. I can't trust you as far as I can throw you. What the hell was I thinking letting you out of my sight? Fuck your rules. You got that? I'm not leaving you alone again. Not if you're going to go around trying to get yourself dead." Price punctuated his little diatribe with more shakes, fury ratcheting up in his voice until he sounded like his head might pop.

"Can you stop shaking me?" I asked. Whined, really. "My head hurts."

He swore and swept me up out of the water, clamping me tight to his chest. My head flopped onto his shoulder, and I whimpered as sharp metal pinwheels whirled through my brain. He growled in response. Seriously. Growled.

I rubbed my face against him. He smelled amazing. Like soap and heat and something delectably *him*. If I'd been standing up, my knees would probably have melted. God, but I'd missed him.

"Get us out of here," he demanded.

"I'm not sure she can handle the trip," came Gregg Touray's low baritone. "She's in rough shape. Again. I'm beginning to think your girlfriend is suicidal."

"You're not taking her anywhere," Leo said, and he grabbed me around my bicep like an anchor. "Not without us."

His hand jerked away. No, all of him jerked away. I heard a grunt, and he crashed down into the water. "Don't make me kill you," Touray told him.

Fear gave me energy. I stiffened and struggled against Price's iron hold, elbowing him in the neck and kicking my feet.

"Leave him alone! He's my brother! Let go of me, you big rhinoceros," I told Price. He was nothing more than a blurry shadow. His only response was to tighten his grip. I gave up trying to escape and turned my attention to Touray, who was a blocky shadow, his arm extended. I didn't need to see well to know that he had a gun trained on Leo.

"Stop! He's my brother!" I practically screamed it as I started struggling again.

"Gregg. Enough. Put it away." Price's chest rumbled against me.

Touray's hand dropped to his side, but he didn't holster his gun. I melted in on myself. Whatever strength I had had washed away with the adrenaline. I was too done even to shut my eyes or blink. I must have looked like roadkill.

"Riley?" Price's voice roughened as he gently rocked me in his arms.

I didn't move, didn't answer. I couldn't. I no longer had bones or muscles. I was rubber.

"*Now*, Gregg," he snapped. He shifted his feet in the direction of Leo and Madison. "He'll be back for the two of you. Then I want to know just what the hell happened."

I didn't know if Leo was going to try to stop them again or not. Didn't matter. He had no time. Magic spun around us in a white cocoon. It *wrenched* us. We crossed into a between place—not the trace dimension, but somewhere else. It was full of morphing shapes and colors that made me go cross-eyed and feel seasick. The next thing I knew, I separate from my body. I swallowed—could I really swallow if I wasn't in my body? My throat felt dry.

This is normal, I told myself. *Touray told you how travelling works. Your mind and body split and get reconnected when you arrive.* It's normal. I didn't remember him telling me it was like a hallucinogenic drug trip.

My mind hooked on something, and I felt myself wrenched in a new direction. I rocketed through the dreamspace, as Touray had called it, pulled on an invisible cord.

I didn't think *this* was normal. I scrabbled to remember what else Touray had told me about travelling. He'd said that the body and spirit separated on the journey and sometimes had trouble melding back together on the other side. I had had no idea what he meant. As my mind raced farther and farther away from my body, I had a sinking feeling I was about to find out.

Chapter 11

I tried to stop myself, to return to my body, but I was like a fish hooked on a line. No matter how I wriggled or fought, I couldn't free myself.

Abruptly, I stopped. Something that looked like a soap bubble swallowed me. Inside it was still. Outside of it, shapes continued to morph and change, twisting and bubbling and splashing and rippling. There was no place to look that wasn't moving. My absent stomach lurched. It really wasn't fair that I had no body and still felt nauseous.

The bubble drifted and spun slowly, but seemed immune to the speeding currents beyond its walls. I lifted what passed for a hand—a crooked branch of pale blue energy—and touched the walls of the bubble. It sizzled, and little red flakes spun out around my hand. They settled and absorbed into me. As if I'd opened a mental dam, images rushed at me. They battered my mind, making no sense, even though they felt familiar. I thought I recognized something, and it melded with something else and something else again, and my head whirled with overload. It was like an acid trip gone way out of hand. I started to panic.

I pressed blue twig hands to what might have been my head and called on my null power. As depleted as I was, I expected nothing. Instead, it roared up inside me like a forest fire.

Calling up power with no place to put it wasn't entirely wise. It swelled inside me, looking for an outlet. I had no good place to send it. I pressed my twig hands against the bubble and let it go. White light burst into stars, and the influx of images stopped. I pulled my magic back and held still as shock waves rocketed back through me. It felt like I'd thrown a massive rock into a small tank and the water was crashing back into me, except it was magic.

After a while, or maybe only a few seconds—I had no sense of time—the waves subsided, and I was sitting in stillness.

I tried to figure out a plan. Could I tear the bubble walls apart with my magic? If I did, could I find my way back to my body? Though I figured Touray was looking for me, I didn't know if he would find me inside the bubble, or be able to save me if he did. I wasn't going to wait to find out.

I pushed my twig fingers against the bubble's wall again. The skin of my prison felt warm. I pressed harder. It stretched like a balloon, but sprang back as I pulled away. I did it again, this time trying to absorb its magical energy. Nothing happened.

More time passed as I tried to get my head to focus. The seventies lava lamp lights outside kept distracting me. They were hypnotic as well as sickening.

I would have closed my eyes, but I didn't seem to be able to. So in spirit form, I could get nauseous *and* get a full-on down-to-the-bones body ache, but I couldn't blink. Where was the sense in that?

I did appreciate the silence. Either my ears weren't working, or dreamspace was dead silent. After a while, though, the lack of sound started wearing on me. I got twitchy. I kept jerking around to see if something was sneaking up on me. I looked up and down and all around. Pretty soon paranoia set in, and I began a counterclockwise rotation, twisting to scan every quadrant of the hypnotic churn outside the bubble.

That went on for a while until I got bored with the constant fear. I couldn't maintain that level of vigilance. I let myself slow to a halt, pulling myself into a ball. I wished I knew how to meditate. Then I could while away the next centuries or however long I was trapped.

I was settling in for a massive pity party when I noticed a droplet forming in the top of the bubble. When it was about the size of a softball, it broke free and dropped lazily down. When it got to eye-level, it stopped and hovered, spinning slowly. White mist swirled inside, turning it opaque and reminding me of those crystals balls you see gypsies use in *Scooby-Doo* cartoons.

Color seeped into the mist and slowly resolved into shapes. I gasped. The first was of my mom, my dad, and me when I was maybe three. I was in the middle, with each of my parents holding my hands. We stood in front of some pine trees on what looked like a hiking trail. I didn't remember. My throat swelled, and tears burned my eyes. My mom smiled at me from the image, looking radiant with life and health. My dad was looking at her, over my toddler head, his expression full of love. I reached out to touch them, and the image faded.

"No," I said brokenly, and was startled when the sound bounced around the bubble walls, making them vibrate.

A new image rose to replace the first. This time it moved, like I was watching a movie. A horror movie. My stomach knotted. I hadn't been there that day. I'd been out with my dad. I remember how someone said after that we'd have been killed, too, if we'd been home.

She was in the kitchen at the sink. In the middle of the window hung a purple glass heart. The same one that I thought had been burned up in a fire, but later turned up in our investigation to find Josh. Mom's fiery hair hung loose around her shoulders. She wore a purple sweater and jeans. From the back, she almost looked like me.

I made a little squeaking sound as she shut off the water in the sink. She turned around and said something. She frowned, looking more angry than scared. Was this real? Had it happened this way? Then someone moved. A big man wearing a black knitted cap stepped into view. I could only see his back. I didn't recognize anything about him.

My mom grabbed a plate off the drying rack and threw it at him. He knocked it aside and lunged for her. He had a knife.

I pressed my twig fingers against my mouth. *No, no, no!* I wanted to scream, to tell her to run, to fight, but my throat squeezed the sound into a tiny squeak.

My mom fought. She kicked and hammered at the man with a dirty pot. She smashed his head, and he dropped his knife. Then she kicked him and ran for the doorway. He caught her, driving his knife into her stomach. I saw his face. It was . . . Gregg Touray.

For a moment hate filled me, pressing out everything else. I wanted to kill him. I *would* kill him. I shook with the emotions crashing through me. I couldn't breathe.

Touray's arm rose again and again as he stabbed my mom. Thirteen wounds altogether. I'd found that out later when reading the police report. I watched every one, horror twisting my stomach and knotting my lungs.

The image faded to white. I sat gasping, trying to understand what I'd just seen. But before I could put any of the puzzle pieces together, a new image appeared.

Dalton. At the diner. I was there, too. My forehead was bloody and bruised, and I was wearing the same clothes I had been in the mines, the clothes I was still wearing, somewhere. Patti threw her arms around me and then around Dalton. She was smiling and crying. Then I saw Dalton hold out his hand to me. I took it, and he pulled me out the door. The picture honed in on our linked hands, then faded. The bubble swirled white, and then melted away into smoke. It rose and melded back with the walls of my prison.

I couldn't say how long I sat just replaying my mom's murder in my head. Each time I felt sicker and sicker. I could almost hear the sounds of the knife pulling out of her flesh.

I was so wrapped in misery and rage that it took a while for reason to return. I focused on the last scene. It bothered me. Or maybe I just wanted to stop reliving my mother's murder. For one thing, though it had looked incredibly real, I couldn't imagine Dalton and me ever holding hands. Or

Patti hugging him. That the scenario was a message to me, was obvious. It told me I could trust Dalton, that I should go to him for safety. Of course, that implied I could trust whoever was sending me the message, and I wasn't so eager to jump off that cliff.

Another thought struck me—as real as that scene had looked, it obviously wasn't. So how much of the murder scene was made up to manipulate me? A lot, if they expected me to believe Touray had been the killer. That was more than twenty years ago. He'd have just been hitting puberty, maybe.

I made myself consider the images of my mother's murder. The scenario had got the kitchen right, down to the paint on the walls and the glass heart in the window. It all looked perfectly plausible, and of course, my mom *had* been stabbed. Of course, somebody could have picked all that information out of crime-scene photos, and I didn't trust my four-year-old-kid memory enough to believe I'd spot any minor differences. Besides, I'd already been burned by stupidly trusting Dalton without asking enough questions. I wasn't about to swallow this performance without verification. But even if I did believe it, I couldn't get around the question of just who was doing the sending. If this scene, minus Touray, was accurate, then the sender of the image could very well be the murderer. Who else could get the details right? There didn't seem to be even one logical runner-up for the Oz behind the curtain.

And that raised another big question. What did they want from me? Clearly, they wanted something, because they wanted me to go to the diner, and then from there, go off with Dalton. Maybe they thought the promise of knowing who murdered my mom would be enough to lure me. They were wrong. That sort of gift had to have strings attached. Or maybe I was supposed to believe that whoever murdered my mom was out to get me and this Good Samaritan wanted to save my life. Maybe I was supposed to knee-jerk freak out about Touray being the killer and immediately run away from him.

It irritated me that anyone could think I'd fall for that. Like I was an idiot. Like I was Little Red Riding Hood, unable to see past some pajamas and spectacles to notice that her grandmother was really a wolf. *My, but don't your teeth look big, Granny,* I thought sourly. I wasn't falling for it. I wasn't going to let the wolf get me that easy. This smelled like a trap.

At that point I lost it just a little bit and let go a primal scream of absolute and total frustration. A sound erupted from me, ricocheting through the bubble. I could see it—a harpoon of ice and fire. Everywhere its tip touched, cracks appeared in the bubble. I held still, hope wrapping me in barbed wire.

The power of the scream faded, and soon the harpoon vanished, but not before a spiderweb of cracks ran through the entire sphere. I collected myself, not even thinking before punching my twig fingers into the side of the bubble.

It shattered. Fragments flew off in all directions. I was left drifting in the dizzying shift of colors and shapes. *Now what?* I kicked my legs and swam with my arms. Nothing.

I was just starting to consider panicking when something enveloped me in a hot, sticky net. It dug spiny hooks into me, then dragged me in sharp yanks through the dreamspace. My panic went to DEFCON twelve, and I twisted against it. The more I fought, the more tangled inside it I got, until I could no longer move.

At some point, I checked out. I don't know if it was the pain, or something else altogether. All I know is the black curtain dropped, and I was gone

"RILEY? RILEY! C'MON, baby, wake up for me. You can do it. Just open your eyes."

Price's hands stroked over my hair. He cupped my face between broad, rough palms. He sounded belligerent. I'd have thought he was totally pissed at me, except that the fear lacing his frantic words suggested he might be more than a little worried about me. Until I'd texted him however many days ago, I'd been half afraid he'd forgotten me. Another thing I'd gotten wrong.

I made myself open my eyes. My shoulders and neck ached, and my head throbbed. Of course, I'd banged myself up a bit in the tunnels, so it was only to be expected.

I stared straight into Price's brilliant sapphire eyes. Long black lashes framed them, and his silky black hair fell over his forehead. His skin was porcelain white stretched over chiseled cheekbones. His nose was a stone wedge above a square chin. He hadn't shaved in a while. At least a couple days. Dark circles bruised his eyes.

"Riley?" he whispered when I said nothing. One hand smoothed over my hair again. It might have been shaking just a little bit. "Tell me you're here."

Duh. But I suppose half of me had been here awhile when the other half was lost in psychedelic drug land. I guess he deserved some slack.

I gave a faint nod. "I'm here."

"Thank God."

He kissed me. His lips brushed mine, opening an unexpected flood of emotion. His touch was delicate, like I might shatter. I wanted more. He drew away.

I made a wistful noise in my throat. "You can do better than that."

At my words, his fingers curved into hooks around the back of my head, but he held himself back, much to my eternal disappointment.

He let go of me and straightened out of his crouch. He turned to look at someone. "Tell her you're okay, and then get out. She needs to rest."

Turns out he was talking to Leo, who dropped down in front of me, taking one of my hands in his and squeezing. "You scared the hell out of me, Riley. What happened?"

"I'd like to know that, too," Touray growled from somewhere down by my feet.

I lifted my head to look at him. It weighed a thousand pounds. He looked bad. His face was gaunt, and his skin was gray. His short hair stuck up in spiky clumps. His black eyes were sunk deep into their sockets. They skewered me, demanding answers. "I know you didn't kill my mom." I dropped my head back onto the pillow.

"Your mother?"

"What the fuck does that mean?"

"Why would you think he killed your mom?"

The three men responded together. I don't even know why I said it. I knew it wasn't true—except for the first few seconds before I'd had a chance to think it through—and for whatever reason, I felt guilty about that. Especially given that he rescued me and looked like he'd gone through hell doing it.

I sighed. "Long story."

Silence. Clearly that answer wasn't going to cut it. I sighed again. "Something grabbed me in the dreamspace and dragged me off." My voice scraped thin through my vocal chords. Before I could say more, Touray pounced on that.

"Something grabbed you?" He repeated, and now he loomed above Leo. "How? What? Explain," he demanded. Magic swelled around him, driving the air out of the room.

I gasped, feeling an invisible weight pressing down on me.

"Enough!" Price grabbed Touray by his collar and spun him away. He planted a hand in his brother's back and shoved him hard. "Get. Out. Now." The ferocity in his voice promised anything short of complete cooperation would be met with violence.

"You, too," Price said, hooking his hand under Leo's arm and dragging him to his feet. "You can talk to her later, when she's rested."

Leo, entirely unaware of the danger, or else having a death wish, jerked out of Price's grip and shoved the other man back. "That's my sister, buddy. I'm not going anywhere."

Price practically purred. "But you are. Feet first if necessary."

Leo snorted. "I'd like to see you try."

Time for me to intervene. I attempted to clear my throat loudly, and that quickly turned into ragged coughing. That's when I realized I was parched. My bones felt like kindling, and my tongue was leather. Price leaped to my side, sitting down on the edge of my bed and pulling me up against him. He tipped my head onto his shoulder and stroked my back.

"Shhhh," he crooned, "I've got you, baby. Easy now. Just breathe."

I melted against him. I didn't really have a choice. Once the coughing settled, I didn't have the strength to do anything else.

This was ridiculous. I mean, sure, I conked my head a couple of times and I hadn't eaten for a while, but I shouldn't be pancaked like this. "What's wrong with me?" I murmured into Price's shirt. Black, per his usual. Wouldn't want any maverick color sneaking into his closet. He and Dalton apparently shopped in the same stores. "Why am I so weak?"

"It's spirit-sag. Happens when a body and soul are separated too long," Price said, running his hand over my hair.

How long was too long?

Leo anticipated my question. "You were lost for twenty-seven hours."

Twenty-seven? It hadn't felt like that long. I wrinkled my nose. "That doesn't seem so bad."

Price's arms tightened convulsively. "Much longer, and your body would have quit on you. You'd almost stopped breathing."

Oh. That was bad. Yes, I'm really good with the obvious. "Sorry," I muttered, because I didn't know what else to say.

His chest jerked at he laughed. A harsh bark. "Wasn't your fault."

"You won't say that when I tell you everything," I muttered. He has bat ears.

"What?" He pushed my head up so that he could look at me. His black brows slashed together, and his eyes blazed. "What did you do?"

"I got a little bit kidnapped." I hunched into myself, waiting for him to explode.

He only gave a restrained scowl. "Yes, Leo mentioned that."

Speaking of Leo, he stood at the foot of the bed, staring at me, arms folded, face forbidding. He saw me looking back at him and flicked a glance at Price, lifting his brows meaningfully.

Oh. Right. That. If Price having kissed me didn't clue him in, me snuggling up to the man no doubt demonstrated my woeful lack of self-preservation. I gave a weak smile. "I take it the two of you have met?"

The two men exchanged a smoky look.

"We did," Leo said, his upper lip curling. "Once his brother took the gun out of my face."

Oops. I'd forgotten. I grimaced. "Sorry."

"We'll talk about it later." His grin promised that I would be getting an earful. He looked again at Price. "It seems you left one or two things out when you told me about your adventures to recover Josh."

"That's because my love life is none of your business."

"Love life?"

"Price is—" What? My boyfriend? That sounded like I was about fourteen. Lover? I wasn't ready to announce that. "He's my date for dinner at Mel's." That should pretty much get the point across. I'd never, ever, taken a date to Mel's.

Leo blinked, and then his expression fractured into merriment. He laughed long enough to be irritating. Finally, he wiped the corners of his eyes. "This is going to be the best dinner ever. I can hardly wait."

I scowled. "I don't see what's so funny."

"Of course not," Leo said. "The sacrificial lamb never does."

Before I could answer, someone knocked on the door. Without waiting for an answer, Touray strode in carrying a mug. Soup. It smelled heavenly. He handed it to me. I fumbled it, and Price took it from me.

"You'll need calories to recover, and sleep. Your body's been healed, but a tinker can't do anything about the backlash from a body/soul separation. Because you were split for so long, it will take a few days to recuperate. You'll be dizzy and tired and your muscles will be rubber," Touray said as Price held the cup to my lips.

Chicken noodle soup. Luckily, it was only lukewarm, because I put my hands over Price's and gulped it down in three swallows. It was possibly the best thing I'd ever tasted in my life. Warmth ran down my throat to my belly and leached out into the rest of me. I licked my lips. "More?" I asked plaintively.

Touray made an exasperated sound and snatched the cup back. He marched out without a word.

Price chuckled, his chest rumbling. "He'll regret serving you when he finds out how much you can eat."

I smiled, grateful for a joke to lighten the mood. "He will, won't he?"

Touray seemed to have learned a lesson, though, because this time he returned with the mug and an insulated pitcher full to the brim. Under his arm was a roll of whole-grain crackers flavored with herbs. He set them down on marble-topped nightstand beside my bed. He poured some soup and held out the mug, then watched me drink.

His eyes were hooded, and I could almost hear his brain whirling with questions and no little fury. I'd endangered myself, and he wasn't at all happy about it. To him I was an irreplaceable commodity. Then someone had stolen me in dreamspace, and when I get back, out of the blue I tell him I don't think he murdered my mom. He probably wanted to wring me like a sponge to get answers.

Price, on the other hand, was going to flip out when he found out that Percy had burned me with cigarettes and fumigated me. Stir in the fact that he was harvesting innocent people for Sparkle Dust—I could imagine Price storming into the mountain to take Percy down all by himself and damn everything else. Touray wasn't exactly a cool head, but he seemed to be far more calculating than emotional. Hopefully, he could help rein his brother in from a suicide mission.

While everybody watched me, I drank three more mugs of soup and ate half a sleeve of the crackers. When I was done, I could feel energy sparking back into my body, and my head wasn't so foggy.

Price took the mug and set it down on the nightstand, then settled me back down on the pillows.

"I'll leave you alone to rest, then," Touray said and headed for the door. Leo hesitated. I waved at him, and he nodded, then followed.

I squirmed into a more comfortable position against the pillows. That's when I noticed I was wearing one of Price's shirts and some lacy underwear I didn't recognize. I scowled. "Please tell me you did not dress me in underwear that your girlfriend left behind on her last sleepover."

Just the thought of Price wanting someone else made my heart cramp. I fisted my hands on the feather comforter he pulled over me.

"What girlfriend?"

"You tell me."

He glared at me. "For your information, that underwear came out of a package. I sent someone to get it. I figured you'd want something clean if . . . when you woke up."

On the last, his voice ground to a halt in gravel. I stared at him.

"I'm sorry," I said, averting my eyes and hunching down into myself.

"You're damned right you are," he said. He stood near the foot of the bed, arms crossed, feet braced.

He didn't say anything else, just stared down at me, his upper lip curled, the lines of his body taut. His jaw knotted. After a long minute of that, I started to twitch.

"Well? Are you just going to stand there?"

"You're right. I've been awake since we hauled your corpse in here. I need some sleep." He turned on his heel and headed for the door.

I struggled to sit up. Lethargy weighted me down like stones in a pond, but his walking out on me hit me like a cattle prod to the ass. "Alone?"

"I sure as hell won't be curling up with the imaginary girlfriend you've got me playing house with."

He was punch-the-wall pissed. I tried not to smile and totally failed. I probably looked like the cat that ate the canary.

"You think that's funny?"

He stalked back to the bed, looming over me, and while I'm sure he meant to be intimidating, I was delighted by his outburst. But pushing pins into him wouldn't get me what I wanted.

"I apologize. I was jealous," I confessed, my cheeks flushing. It was still so very hard to admit my feelings to him.

The bed sank as he knelt beside me and caught my face between his hands. He tipped my head so that he could look into my eyes. His had darkened, glittering like moonlit waves. In their depths, I could see the tangled currents of his hard-held emotions.

"If I had, for even a single inconceivable second, thought that I wasn't in love with you anymore, nearly losing you again—" He broke off, clenching his jaw until I could hear his teeth grinding together. A shadow rippled across his face. His grip tightened, and he pulled me closer until his forehead pressed against mine. "If you'd died, it would have been the end of me," he whispered raggedly.

His words stabbed me through the heart. Tears burned in my eyes, and my throat knotted.

His chest bellowed as he sucked in a harsh breath. "I'm done waiting, Riley. I'm done letting you walk around like you're safe out there. You need a keeper. Fuck that, you need to be kept. You're *mine*. I'll help you do whatever you need to do, but I won't be cut out of your life again. Do you understand?"

I licked my lips, my heart pounding. What a Neanderthal. Yet I loved every word, the desperate catch in his voice, the way his hands shook even as he handed down his imperial orders. His whole body was braced, like a fighter waiting for the first punch. It was the fighter image that jarred something loose within me. In my life, the two most important people, my mother and my father, had left me. And it meant something to me that Price would be willing to fight like hell to stay in my life. I believed him, and that made another brick in my protective walls go tumbling down.

I toyed with the edge of the comforter. "I can't tell. Does that mean you're still going to go pout by yourself? Or that you're planning to stay here with me?" I looked up at him from beneath my lashes. Yeah, I was flirting. Not all that well, and Price only glowered harder at me, his mouth tightening into a thin, white line. He said nothing.

"I *did* ask you out on a date," I pointed out. The circumstances of that text came rushing back to me. "You know, you've got balls calling me out on getting into trouble. *You* haven't exactly been Mr. Safety. You nearly got blown up. At your brother's house, which was supposed to be so impregnable. Hell, should I be worried there's TNT in the toilet? C-4 in my shoes?" I managed to sit up straight by bracing my hands on either side of myself and shoving forward. "Don't go getting all high and mighty and calling my kettle black, Mr. Pot. You've been no safer than I have."

"You *texted* me for a date," he said, as if that was the only thing that mattered. "You can call for a pizza delivery, but you can't be bothered to actually call me."

I flopped back onto the pillows again. My eyelids were getting heavy. "Sorry. Next time I'll have my secretary call yours. We'll do lunch." I couldn't summon the sarcasm the last line needed, but hopefully he got the point. I burrowed farther down under the covers and heaved a sigh. A real bed. Soft and oh, so comfortable.

The covers drew back, and a rush of air chilled my back and legs. I murmured a protest. The mattress sank, and Price snuggled up behind me, wrapping a hard arm around my ribs and draping his thigh over mine. He pulled the covers back up around us.

"We are not done with this conversation," he said.

I laced my fingers through his as he wriggled his right arm under me and pulled me tight against his chest.

"Yeah, we are," I said.

"Not a chance, Riley. We're having it out."

I smiled as I felt myself sinking into sleep. I yawned hard, my jaw cracking. It took all the effort I could muster to have the last word. "I know," I said, loosening my fingers from his and patting his hand. "But when you find out the rest of the story, you'll be far too pissed to come back to this." Whatever *this* was. I wasn't entirely clear.

He might have said something else, but I didn't hear. I'd already fallen asleep.

Chapter 12

What woke me was a combination of the need to pee and my skin's prickling awareness of Price curled around me. I'd been too tired to get turned on before, but all of a sudden, heat pooled in my stomach, and my breasts ached with the need to have Price touching them. To have him lick and suck and—

I groaned. Talk about bad timing. What was my body thinking, anyway? I'd been tortured, imprisoned, and then separated from my body. You'd think sex would be the last thing I wanted.

Deciding a cold shower was in order, I edged toward the side of the bed. Sex wasn't on the agenda. Even if Price wasn't still pissed, there was always the issue of Percy and Madison's family. Indulging my libido would be selfish. Not to mention I didn't know when Leo or Touray would bust in to wake us up. That thought doused my desire better than any shower. I did not need either of our brothers critiquing our performance.

I'd almost made good my escape to the shower, when Price woke up.

"Where are you going?" he asked, pulling me onto my back and lifting himself over me.

His hips still rested on the bed, but he caged me between his arms, his chest brushing against mine. My nipples hardened into peaks. I clenched my thighs together as an ache burst to throbbing life between them. Price's eyes were sleepy, his hair tousled. I've never seen a more beautiful man. I reached up and smoothed the long locks out of his face. They fell back down. He twisted his head and pressed a kiss into the palm of my hand. His tongue flicked my skin, and my whole body reacted. Tingling swarms ran over me in waves. I pulled my hand away and balled it into a fist.

"You shouldn't," I gasped.

"Shouldn't what?" he asked with a pirate smile. He bent to nibble down along the side of my neck.

I made a whimpering sound and arched my back, twisting my head to give him access. He chuckled and nipped me, then lifted his head.

"Something bothering you?" He nibbled down the other side of my neck, then across my throat and down. The scrape of his beard stubble sent chills down to my toes. I curled them tight as I put my hands on his shoulders and gripped his shirt in my fists.

"I thought you were mad at me," I said breathlessly. How could I feel this good with just a few kisses? And after a near-death experience? Another one, that is. Was I insane?

Apparently so, because instead of pushing him away, I tried to pull him closer. He didn't budge, but neither did he stop kissing me. His tongue slipped down into the cleft between my breasts, and I shuddered. He laughed again. Fucker. He liked torturing me. I liked it, too. So, so, so *very* much.

He licked between my breasts again. "I *am* mad," he said huskily. "You have no idea. But given the choice between having my guts tied in knots and my head shooting off like a rocket versus this"—he paused to nibble up my neck—"I decided to enjoy myself a little."

"Logical," I said. Gasped really. With some squirming and maybe some panting. Definitely panting.

As much as I wanted to take this further, nature wouldn't wait. My bladder was about to explode. I grimaced. "Can you hold that thought? I really have to go use the bathroom."

He bent and gave a quick, hot suck on my right breast, then flopped away onto his back. I lay there, my head spinning with the rush of sensation from that one small caress.

He lifted back up on his elbow, looking down at me. "Well?"

"I'm not sure I can move."

"I'd rather you didn't wet the bed." He nudged my hip with his knee. "Get your ass up."

I rolled over and sat up, swinging my feet to the floor. I looked back at him. "Touray says I need sleep, but I've got a feeling unless I go home, I'm not getting any. Not with you around." I leered at him. The way he made me feel, I didn't want rest. In fact, I was pretty sure that a little attention from Doctor Price was all I needed to feel better than new. A wash of heat swept over me as my imagination took that thought in all its possible directions at one time. I fled to the bathroom before I went up in smoke.

Once inside, I eyed the shower longingly, then decided Price wasn't going to wait for me to get clean. On the other hand, I could see if he wanted a shower . . . I shivered. We could have both the bed *and* the shower.

I used the toilet and washed my hands and face, then examined myself in the mirror. Aside from the orangey-red rat's nest my hair had become, I didn't look that bad. All my wounds had been healed while I was zonked out. At least I didn't look scary, though my teeth were a little furry and my breath was probably rank.

My stomach growled. I glanced down at it and noticed the exhausted amethyst heal-all pendant still hanging around my neck. I jerked it over my head and dropped it into the trash. Empty of its magic, it was now only a pretty necklace. As grateful as I was for its healing, it was a reminder that I'd let potential enemies get too close to me, and far too close to the people I cared about.

I didn't want to leave Price waiting any longer, so I rinsed my mouth out with a cup on the sink and returned to the bedroom. Only he wasn't on the bed. He'd changed his shirt and pants and was buckling his belt. He'd put on a black cashmere polo shirt and black jeans, both of which clung to his body like a second skin. My fingers itched to trace the ridges and planes of his muscles. I sighed quietly and leaned against the bathroom doorjamb, watching him. If I'd known my going to the bathroom would screw the mood, I'd have risked wetting the bed.

He moved like a hunting cat, lithe and powerful. He pulled open the bottom drawer of the highboy cherry dresser beside the closet and lifted out a shoulder holster. He strapped it on and picked his gun up off the end of the bed. He must have had it under the pillows. He checked to make sure a bullet was chambered and the magazine was full. Because apparently the tooth fairy steals bullets when she find guns instead of teeth under the pillows.

After he was done getting dressed, he turned to look at me. My heart iced. His face was a blank mask, but his eyes seethed.

"I guess you decided to go with having your head shooting off like a rocket," I noted when his imitation of a museum statue started to get on my nerves. "You may as well lay it out for me. I don't read minds and while I know full well why you're *going* to be pissed at me, don't know what your damage is right now."

His brows rose. "You don't know," he repeated slowly.

"That's right."

He made a sound of disgust and shook his head. "You fucking-well should know, after that comment you made."

I scrambled to remember what I said when I got up. Something about him not letting me rest. I so didn't see what the problem was. "Enlighten me."

He flung himself down into one of the two blue wingback chairs in the little seating area on the other side of the bed by a bay window. He slouched down so that he could tip his head back and watch me from between slitted lids, his long eyelashes hiding the furious glitter of his eyes.

"You say you love me, but you don't trust me, which is fucked up because I'm the one you call for help when you get yourself into deep shit.

So you're willing to let me save your life, but not let me inside it. I'm not interested in being a toy you pick up when you want to play and drop in the box when I'm not convenient."

I opened my mouth to ask if he'd rather I hadn't called him, but before I could, he held up his hand to stop me.

"I'd have ripped you a new one if you'd called anybody else, but that's not my point."

I rubbed my forehead, trying to think. What had sparked this? What had I said? Then I realized. I'd told him I wouldn't get any rest unless I went home. I'd thought I'd been making a joke, but I'd only been reminding him that he didn't know where I lived. That I wouldn't tell him. That I didn't trust him enough to tell him. I wanted a place I could hide from him.

I closed my eyes and rubbed my hands over my face. Six weeks ago I'd decided I had to protect myself from him. That sooner or later he'd decide I wasn't the priority that his brother was. Now—I was surprised to find I didn't believe it anymore. Maybe because when I needed him, he dropped everything and came without question. Maybe because he'd proved he was willing to fight for me. I needed to fix this. Whatever it took.

I looked at him. He waited, his expression detached, almost like he didn't care one way or another. The taut lines of his neck and the hard stillness of his body—like he was set for a blow—said otherwise.

"Got a pen and paper?" I asked. If trusting was about choice, I was choosing Price. Maybe it would take my instincts time to get on board, but they would, even if I had to have my dreamer friend Cass go into my head and move things along. I froze. Had I really thought that? But I had, and that, more than anything else, convinced me that I wanted to do this.

"What?" Price said, taken aback.

"Paper. Pen. Do you have them?"

"What for?"

"Generally one takes the pen and writes on the paper."

"Now?"

"Can't think of a better time." I smiled. He was so going to get revenge on me for this, but just saying I trusted him wasn't going to be convincing. This would prove it beyond any doubt.

He made a growling sound and dug in the top of the far nightstand. He pulled out a four-inch square of paper and a pen. He thrust them at me. "Are you going to write me a letter? Dear John, maybe?"

What a high opinion he had of me. Deserved. I had to admit that. "You'll see." I went to the dresser and set the pad down. He stayed where he was. I glanced over my shoulder at him. "You can't see from there."

He stared at me a long moment, then curiosity got the better of him. He walked over to me. "What?"

I tapped the pen on the paper. "You know where the old Karnickey Burrows are? Up by the north wall?"

He nodded. "I've been past. Nobody goes in there. It's not safe."

"Safe enough. I live there." I started sketching a map of just exactly how to get into my place.

"What?" Price said, sounding hoarse.

"I'm showing you I trust you."

He put a hand over mine. "Not if you aren't ready."

I snorted and shook him off. "If you let me get away with running off, I might never be ready."

He took my hand, rubbing my palm with his thumb. "I'm serious, Riley. I want—I *need*—you to trust me. But I need it to be real, not just something you feel you have to do because I get a little bit pissed. I don't want you to fake it."

I couldn't help my lopsided grin. "I've *never* faked anything with you, I'll have you know."

He didn't smile. "No point starting now."

I scraped my teeth over my lower lip. "When my mom was murdered, my dad and I sort of went into hiding for awhile. We didn't know who'd done it or why. Cops said it was random—stranger-on-stranger killing. Dad never believed it. He married Mel and had Taylor before Mom had been dead a year."

That had hurt. He'd forgotten Mom so fast. It made me wonder if they'd really loved each other, especially with how much he seemed to love Mel. I wanted to believe he'd remarried because he wanted a mom for me, and a family. It took me a long time to realize that my distrust of the world had its seeds not just in Mom's murder, but in Dad's marriage so soon after. I doubted everybody, including the man I was supposed to love most in the world.

I'd never lost that doubt. In time it grew into general distrust. I loved my stepmom, my sister, and my stepbrothers with all my heart, but I didn't share myself with them. I kept myself apart. I kept secrets. When Dad disappeared, I'd practically become paranoid. The only person besides family that I kept close to was Patti, and that's because she refused to let me vanish. But I didn't tell her where I lived, either.

Price was waiting for me to finish. I drew a breath and let it out slowly. "I stopped trusting people then. Everybody. I'm not entirely sure I even know how to, anymore. But I *want* to trust you. I think I do. I just need to break a really old habit. So let me."

I turned back to my map.

Frank Karnickey had come to Diamond City at the beginning of the rush back in the early 1800s. He had no education and no money, but he was going to build an empire. He was a minor talent—supposedly he could calm animals like nobody's business. In today's world, he'd have been some sort of zoo whisperer. He'd staked a diamond claim, and then he'd built himself a compound to protect it. History said he'd had a rough charisma and he didn't mind killing anybody who got in his way, but he'd do just about anything for the people who proved their loyalty.

The Karnickey Burrows, as the place came to be known, was a ramshackle pile of buildings inside a box canyon that wriggled back into the mountain in a snakelike chute. Trees on the heights cut off most of the light. With heavy snows every winter, the community inside had been linked by covered passages and underground tunnels. It had been a safe and comfortable place for Karnickey's employees, if dark and gloomy. That is, it had been safe right up until a rival for Karnickey's mistress had unleashed a tinkered virus into the canyon in the dead of winter. It killed most everyone in the Burrows within a week. After that, Karnickey Burrows was abandoned. The place was said to be cursed. Eventually, it was all but forgotten. The buildings collapsed, and the place turned into a ghost town.

A couple hundred years later, I moved in. With the help of my brothers, we'd built me a two-story house of rock and wood and a whole lot of scrap metal they'd used to hold it all together. Six different escape routes—above and underground—meant I'd never be trapped. A variety of turn-away spells made sure anyone who thought of investigating the Burrows changed their minds. If an intruder carried good enough nulls to get past those, he'd run into a gauntlet of briar magic that would lead him away and leave him disoriented and hurting, and telling the rest of the world the place was still cursed.

I liked my place—it's spare, but warm and comfortable. Thanks to magic and several cisterns, I had plenty of hot water. I got stolen electricity from lines run by my brothers, no problem for metal tinkers. I didn't have cable or Wi-Fi, but then those could be tracked. I turned my cell off before I got anywhere near home and didn't turn it on again until I was far away. What mail I got went to the diner, and I was always über careful about not taking the same routes home, nulling out my trace, and watching my back. And I never, ever, told anyone where I lived.

Until now.

I finished the drawing and shoved it at Price. "There you go," I said.

I waited until he'd looked the page over, then when he looked up at me, I snatched up the page and marched into the bathroom. I ran it under the water in the sink until the ink bled away, then I shredded the wet bits between my fingers and dropped them into the toilet bowl and flushed.

"Overkill much?" Price asked from where he leaned in the doorway.

I couldn't tell what he was thinking. I put the seat down and washed my hands, drying them on a fluffy sea-green towel.

"Habit," I said, turning to face him. "Are we okay?"

Silence spun out, too much silence. He didn't seem all that happy. Was it too little, too late? What else could I do? Suddenly, I needed to retreat and think.

"I haven't showered in days. I itch and I can't imagine how bad I must smell. So if you don't mind shutting the door behind you, I'm going to get clean." At least it didn't have to be a cold shower. I was no longer ready to rip my clothes off and jump his bones.

I probably shouldn't have been disappointed when he turned and closed the door. The only reason my eyes started watering was because I stunk so bad.

With a sigh, I opened the linen cupboard and grabbed a couple of towels and a washcloth. On one shelf was a collection of soaps, shampoos, conditioners, and lotions. By the time I reached for a bottle of honey-jasmine shampoo, I'd gone from wanting to retreat to a kind of wild desperation. I had to find a way to fix this with Price. How epically ironic. I hadn't trusted him, and now he couldn't trust I'd had a change of heart.

I swung open the door, then stumbled back a step when I found him standing right outside, his hands braced on the doorjamb.

He looked at me, his eyes turbulent pools. "I've missed you so damned much," he grated. "Don't run. Don't go finding a new place to live. I won't trespass; I won't tell anyone. Promise me."

At this last, the starch went out of my legs, and I sagged against the wall to hold myself up. I put my fingers over his lips to stop whatever he might say next. Every word was a knife in my heart. He wasn't the sort of man to beg, not from anyone, not for anything. Yet I'd made him do that. Me and my paranoia and my all-about-me attitude. It had been a miracle he'd even fallen in love with me. It was a bigger miracle that he was *still* in love with me.

I needed to fix this before I broke both our hearts. Exactly how to do that was the big question. So I said the first insane thing that popped into my head. "Want to move in with me?"

His head jerked back. "That's not funny, Riley."

"It wasn't supposed to be funny. It's a bona fide offer. If you think you can stand to live with me, that is. I'm fairly house-trained, though I only have a queen-sized bed and you'll be moving way down on the style and luxury ladder. I don't cook and cleaning is mostly doing laundry and occasionally—"

His lips swallowed the rest of my chatter. He engulfed me, lifting me and pushing me against the wall. His hands slid down my sides to my hips to hold me. I wrapped my legs around him. We fit together like a lock and key. Bubbles spiraled through my chest. I tightened my legs, putting my arms around his neck and pulling myself tighter against him. He smelled so good.

His tongue was velvet on mine, dancing and tasting. He devoured me, twisting his head to delve deeper. I made encouraging sounds as I flexed my legs and undulated my hips up and down. Curls of aching delight rolled through my belly as I rubbed my soft heat against his hard shaft. He groaned and thrust against me, then stilled, pinning me so that I couldn't move. He tore his lips from mine and held me there. Both of us were panting raggedly. I was barely coherent. My body was an inferno. My hair practically crackled with the flames. His breath puffed across my neck in short, hot bursts.

"I swear, you're going to kill me," he whispered, when he finally found his voice.

"Does that mean you're saying no to moving in with me?" Despite the heat of his kiss, I still doubted.

"Fuck no. That's a yes. *Yes.*" He kissed me again, hard and deep, then lifted his head and pressed his forehead against mine. "Much as I want to celebrate properly"—he rocked his cock against me, and I gasped— "neither of our brothers is going to wait much longer. Go shower. There are clothes for you in the closet."

"You could join me," I suggested, sliding my fingers under his shirt. His skin was hot silk.

He groaned and kissed me once more and eased away. "Don't tempt me. You still need to recover."

"I feel fine." I reluctantly let my feet drop to the floor.

He rested his hands on my hips and brushed his lips against mine, flicking his tongue out like he couldn't resist one more taste. "I love you."

"Do your best to remember that later."

He scowled. "What's that supposed to mean?"

I widened my eyes and blinked and did my best to look innocent. "Just what it sounded like. You might get distracted and forget that you love me. Try not to."

"Why would I forget?" he asked, his voice turning dangerous as he enunciated each word with careful precision.

"Because I hear that happens when a person goes homicidal."

"I think I'm going to strangle you," he said, looking up at the ceiling like a divine light of patience would suddenly pour down over him. No such luck.

"Likely," I said. "If you don't drown me or shoot me first."

"I swear to God you're trying to drive me around the bend, over the edge, and out of my ever-loving mind. You're damned good at it, too."

"Thank you. I think," I said, putting my hands flat on his chest. "Seriously, though. I got into some trouble in the tunnels. I also learned something ugly. Really ugly. Just remember I'm out safe, and don't dwell on that part, okay? Because I'm going to need you to be, well, you. Focused, sharp, relentless, and stone-cold."

He glared at me. "Why don't you stop beating around the bush and tell me just what the hell happened?"

I shook my head. "I don't want to have to tell it twice, and your brother needs to hear it, too. Same with Madison and Leo. They don't know the whole yet, either." I remembered the fumigation. I wanted to be checked out to be sure there was no permanent damage from the SD. There was only one dreamer I trusted to go into my head and check. "Can you get Cass here?"

Price's brows rose. "Why?"

"I might need her."

"God dammit, Riley. Are you going to explain or am I going to have to guess?"

Would it have been asking too much of the universe at that point to have Touray come barging in and interrupt Price's interrogation? Or maybe a squad of ninjas could have overrun the place. I glanced hopefully at the door, but it remained closed and unassailed. We were wasting more time arguing than not, so I gave in.

"Fine. You win. Here is the nutshell version: Fact 1: Sparkle Dust can be made from the bodies of wraiths. Fact 2: I was exposed to SD. I think I nulled it out of my body, but I'm not sure. I'd like Cass to check me out. Fact 3: Whoever kidnapped me in dreamspace tried to make me think your brother killed my mother, which is really ridiculous, and why anybody would think I'd fall for that I don't know—"

"Stop." Price's face had gone pasty gray. He lifted his hand and ran his fingertips over my cheek. They trembled. "You were exposed to SD?"

I nodded. "They call it fumigating. They put you in a chamber and pipe in an aerosol version of the drug. It turns you into an addict, but the process of becoming a wraith is slower. Makes you a loyal lapdog willing to do most anything in the hope you'll get a fix."

"But you—*nulled* it out?" He scrutinized me, examining my eyes, skin, tongue, and teeth, searching for the telltale signs of becoming a wraith. Not that I would be turning yet. I didn't think. "That's not possible."

"That's what I thought. I invoked the null when the fumes were just starting to infiltrate. There's a magical component to SD. It makes sense that it could be nulled. Took a lot of power, though, and it hurt." I shuddered at the memory. "I don't know if I could have nulled it after it had a chance to take root in me. I don't know if I'd have wanted to."

Price crushed me to him, burying his head in my neck. Just as quickly, he let go and spun away. His back and shoulders knotted as he pressed the heels of his hands against his forehead. Without another word, he strode away and out the door, shutting it hard behind him.

I stared after him, my stomach sinking down into my feet. Fear etched away the warmth of his touch until I shivered with the cold. Price didn't even know about Percy burning me, yet. Maybe I should duct-tape him down before I revealed that little bit of news. Otherwise, he might go off to wreak vengeance on his own.

Unless . . . I glanced again at the door. Unless he was already on his way.

Chapter 13

The shower did a lot to revive me, though it did nothing for my anxiety about Price. I washed quickly and got out, hoping to track him down.

I found jeans and long-sleeved shirts in the closet, all new, all in my size. There was pretty much an entire wardrobe for me in there, including bras, underwear, and socks. As I was dressing in the closet—which was also big enough to contain a sitting area with a love seat and a couple of chairs—I caught the divine scent of coffee. Where there was coffee, maybe there was Price. I hurriedly put on socks and followed the airy trail of nirvana.

I went out the other side of the massive closet and through a pair of frosted glass double doors. On the other side was a spacious room containing all the comforts a guest might want, including a gas fireplace, an enormous television, fluffy couches and chairs, and most important of all, coffee.

Nobody else was there. I decided to grab a cup of joe before going in search of Price. It was more medication than vice. I went to the sideboard and filled a cup, stirring in a healthy dose of sugar and cream. I inhaled the rich fragrance and sipped. Ambrosia.

"I think we should talk, don't you?"

I jumped and gave a little shriek before spinning around. Coffee sloshed onto the thick blue and ivory rug. Gregg Touray stood just inside the doorway, looking malevolent. I could see the resemblance between him and Price. They both had black hair, pale skin, and a potent intensity that made it difficult to breathe around them. But where Price was like a mountain lion, Touray was more a bear. Slabs of heavy muscle bulged beneath his gray sweater. Lines fanned from around his hooded black eyes. Demons moved beneath the obsidian, inexorable and menacing. I forced myself not to squirm beneath his scrutiny.

"Couldn't you warn a girl?" I demanded, looking for something to wipe up the mess. "Where did you come from, anyhow?"

"I was waiting for you," he said, nudging his chin toward a chair in the corner I hadn't noticed.

I set my mostly empty cup on the tray and grabbed a handful of napkins.

"Leave it," he ordered. "Someone will take care of it later. We don't have a lot of time. Your brother is eager to see you. He won't wait much longer."

"I'm surprised he isn't knocking down the door," I said, ignoring his orders and cleaning up what I could. Afterward, I prepared another cup of coffee. My stomach was doing flip-flops. I leaned back against the sideboard and eyed Touray over the rim of my cup.

He'd taken a seat in one of the cushiony chairs in the middle of the room. He watched me. His look sliced me like a scalpel, peeling me back to reveal my insides.

Even though I was determined not to, I broke the silence first. "Something in particular that you wanted?"

"Yes."

I waited for him to clarify, edify, or otherwise explain, but he just kept looking at me with that smothering gaze. I sipped my coffee and forced myself to breathe.

"Sit down," he said, pointing at the chair across from him, and then said, "please," as an afterthought.

I topped off my coffee and obeyed. The truth was that he scared me almost as much as Percy did. They were peas in a pod: businessmen who didn't mind killing and maiming to get what they wanted. Touray claimed that he was trying to stamp out the bloody territory wars that had been increasing among the Tyet over the last few years. For Price's sake, I was trying to believe it, but mostly all I saw was a thug in a cashmere sweater.

He tipped his head. "You don't like me much, do you?"

I cradled my coffee in my hands and hoped he couldn't tell that I was shaking. "Can't say I know you that well. What I do know I find . . . unpleasant." Terrifying. Malevolent. "You did, after all, lock me in a cage and then tried to force me to work for you."

He smiled. The expression sent a chill down my spine.

"Fair enough." He said nothing after that, just watching me drink.

My heart revved into high gear, and my lungs contracted so that I could hardly breathe. "My, what big teeth you have," I muttered.

"What did you say?"

I gave him a level look, deciding I might be afraid, but I didn't have to be chicken. "I said, get on with it already. Flay me, fry me, fricassee me, but quit playing the menace-me-to-death game."

"Fricassee you?" His brows rose, and he grinned. It changed his face. If he learned to do that all the time, he could hide his true nature. He'd be tearing out his enemies' throats before they ever knew they were supposed to fear him.

"What?" he asked, reading more on my face than I wanted to show. "Why are you looking at me like that?"

You'd think I'd have learned self-preservation by now. I'd had years of successful practice, and Percy had definitely taught me a lesson on spouting stupid like Old Faithful spouts water. A lesson I clearly needed to work on because my mouth started moving before I could stop it. "When I first met you, when you had me locked in that cage and didn't realize yet what I could do as a tracer, you decided to kill me. Do you remember?"

He cocked his head. "I don't believe I ever said any such thing."

Not denial. "You didn't say it, but it was all over your face. Price was telling you how he'd hired me and how I'd got shot. Somewhere in there you figured out he had feelings for me, and you weren't going to let some girl come between the two of you. Do you deny it?"

"All right. Suppose, for the sake of conversation, that I did make a decision to kill you. Obviously I didn't. Water under the bridge, no harm no foul, and all that. What does it matter now?"

He might as well have been discussing his golf game or what he wanted for breakfast, for all the emotional investment he had in the subject. *Ha!* The subject. Killing me.

"It matters because you're as cold-blooded as they come. Just because you haven't killed me yet doesn't mean you won't get around to it today or tomorrow or next year. So don't bullshit me with the friendly act. I don't believe it anyway. I'd prefer you say what you came to say and then we can go to our separate corners and get on with the fight."

"You're very direct."

I shrugged. "My mother was murdered before she could teach me tact. My dad didn't seem to think it was a survival skill."

Touray's eyes narrowed. "Yes, you said you knew that I didn't murder her. I didn't realize I was a candidate. Explain."

"When I was in the dreamspace, I had a vision of her murder. You starred as the killer."

His brows rose almost to his hairline. "A vision? And me the murderer? Explain."

Even the thought of replaying the killing of my mother made my stomach churn. "I'd rather wait until I can tell everyone at once. Maybe we should do that now. Where's Price?"

"I haven't seen him since I left him with you."

Crap. I started to get up. "I'd better find him."

"Clay's in love with you," Touray said baldly.

That took the air right out of me. I sank back down and drew in a slow breath, trying to ease my impending stroke. I cataloged my symptoms: adrenaline rush, spinning head, dry mouth, pounding heart, trolls dancing on my bladder, and a desperation to dig a hole and climb inside. People paid a lot of money to feel this way. They jumped out of planes and climbed mountains without ropes and swam with sharks. I was getting the thrill of walking on the edge of life and death for free.

"So he tells me," I said, eying Touray warily.

"My brother has always been self-contained. He relies only on himself," he went on as if I hadn't spoken. "His romantic entanglements have always been strictly physical. When I first met you, I assumed it was business as usual. You had little enough in common. You both found yourselves in a dire situation. It is unsurprising you fell into bed. A physical outlet relieves stress, and no doubt it was enjoyable for you both. At any rate, when you cut ties six weeks ago, I expected he'd forget you and move on. I was"—he waved a hand at an invisible fly—"incorrect."

He paused like he was expecting a response. I had nothing. I just nodded. That was safe enough.

"He's hurting. I don't like to see him hurting." He scowled.

I could get behind that. I licked my lips. "Me neither." I could have said something about him being the wedge driving me and Price apart, but that elephant was already stomping around the room.

He looked down at his hands, opening and closing them in his lap. "I believe you share my brother's feelings, but obviously have your doubts about me. I want to clear any obstacles you may have imagined."

He leaned forward. I leaned back. I couldn't help it. The man may not have intended to be threatening, but he was still doing a good job of it.

"Let me make myself very clear so there's no possibility of misunderstanding: while you are with my brother, you are family. I assure you that you have nothing to fear from me. No harm will come to you from me, and I will protect you as I would Clay." His lips curved in a scythe smile. "Whether you like it or not."

Oh. Fuck. I suppressed my whimper. You'd think having him on my side would make him less scary. Nope. Not even a little. "I don't need protecting."

He lifted a brow. "No?"

"No." I wished my response didn't sound so much like a question.

He tipped his head. "Odd. From the story that Leo and Madison have been telling about your adventures underground, I would have argued otherwise." Again that taunting smile. He'd moved on from his guilt over me and Price and was enjoying messing with me.

Stress destroys any filter on my mouth I might ordinarily lay claim to. "I'm sure you have dicey moments in your line of work," I said. "Do you have a nanny running around after you keeping you from running out into the street?"

"So you admit you were in danger?"

"Duh. Of course I was. In fact, you have no idea," I said airily. "Leo and Madison don't even know. Suicide was starting to look like a good option."

He blinked, his arrogance unsettled by my ready admission. A predatory tension ran through his body, like he was readying himself to strike. "So you agree you need protection."

"Nope. Though I could use a small army. Got one of those I could borrow for a bit?"

His brows drew together. I'd thrown him off balance again. I took no small measure of pride in that. I had a feeling it wasn't easy to surprise him.

"I don't understand."

"You said Leo and Madison filled you in. I'm assuming they told you about her uncle."

He nodded. "Percy Caldwell."

"Actually, it's George Percival James Borden Caldwell the fourth. I might be missing a name or two. I was a little out of it when I met him, and he was burning me with cigarettes. That hurts, by the way."

In the space of a breath, he went from calm to nova. The rage roiling inside him stole the oxygen out of the air. His eyes went feral and deadly. It was like staring down an F5 tornado. My stomach curled in fear. Every instinct I had told me to flee, to get out of his way. If he reacted this way, what was Price going to do? And Leo?

"He what?" he said, leaning forward, his voice grating like tearing metal.

I pressed back against my seat, wishing I'd kept my mouth shut, at least until I had friends in the room.

"He wanted to teach me a lesson. So he burned my arms. I used a heal-all. I'm fine. All better. No worries."

"I will cut him open and strangle him with his own intestines," Touray said in a toneless voice.

I had a bad feeling he wasn't exaggerating. "Feel free," I said, collecting myself. "He needs to be dead." I raised a brow at him. "If you don't change your mind."

"Why would I? I told you; you're family. No one touches you and lives."

Just what I needed: a new big brother with a homicidal streak. "Did

Madison tell you what he's up to?" I asked.

His scowl deepened as I shifted the subject. "He makes Sparkle Dust. Not exactly news to me."

"Do you know *how* he makes it?" I hoped not. Because whatever respect I could ever have for him hinged on that answer.

He shook his head. "No one knows the secret." He leaned forward again, eyes lasering through me. "I take it you *do* know?"

"I know enough to want to drop a nuclear bomb into the tunnels to put a stop to it." My jaw jutted. "I'd like to think you weren't interested in taking over his business."

Touray recoiled. His cheeks flushed red, and if I thought he was pissed before, I was wrong. He thrust out of the chair and leaned over me, bracing his hands on the arms of my chair so that I couldn't escape. He dropped his head so that we were nose to nose. His eyes glittered like black diamonds. It was all I could do not to slide down into the chair.

"Never, ever, suggest to me or anyone else that I support or condone the SD trade," he said, though I'm not sure how he was able to get the words out through his clenched teeth. "I will forgive you your ignorance once, but never again. Understand?"

"Because we're family now and you'll protect me unless I piss you off?" Oh, good, Riley. Way to poke the raging bear with a sharp stick. Maybe I should just have my mouth sewn shut. It would probably add years to my life.

He jerked away, his chest heaving as he stood above me. His hands clenched and unclenched, and I was pretty sure he was wishing they were around my throat. I stared up at him, refusing to back down now that I'd walked across the coals this far. You were supposed to be able to trust family not to kill you when you pissed them off. It was time for him to put his money where his mouth was.

For a second I wanted to giggle. I mean, talk about jumping on the trust wagon with both feet. First I ask Price to move in with me, and then I piss off his merciless and cold-blooded brother and expect him not to hurt me hard. At least I should get points for style.

Finally, he looked up at the ceiling and drew a breath, letting it out slowly. Then he shocked the hell out of me.

"I was wrong. You are perfect for Clay."

"Say what, now?"

"I understand now why Price could fall so hard for you," he said. "You are his match. Just as hardheaded, and brave, as well."

He took my cold coffee and set it aside, pouring me a fresh cup and adding cream and sugar in near perfect amounts. He'd been paying attention. He handed it to me, then poured himself a cup, no cream, no sugar. Nothing to sweeten his personality. He sat back down, leaning back and crossing his legs like he hadn't just threatened my life. He ran his fingers through his short hair, making it stand up.

"I apologize for losing my temper. I abhor the Sparkle Dust trade more than I can say. I'd like nothing more than to shut it down, permanently." He paused. "If you know how it's made, then you know how to stop it. I need to know that. Will you tell me?"

Trust was a two-way street. Three-way, now that it wasn't just Price and me. I nodded. "I will."

He eyed me, the fingers of his left hand tracing a pattern on the arm of the chair. He must have read the doubt in my voice. "You really do have a low opinion of me, don't you?"

I laughed at his surprise. "Shouldn't I? Look at your track record with me."

"Maybe I can change your mind."

That sobered me. He was going to be a fixture in my life now. *Family.* The word finally sank in. Christmas and Easter and the Fourth of July. "Fuck me," I muttered, rubbing my forehead.

He chuckled, and I glared at him. "You think that's funny? Guess what, buddy. If I'm stuck with you, you're stuck with me. Your friends will be mortified."

"My friends, such as they are, will be delighted. If not, they can go to hell with my blessing. Clay has been miserable since the two of you split. I want my brother happy; you make him happy. End of story."

That's when I remembered the way Price had walked out on me. I sat up straight, sloshing hot coffee onto my legs. I didn't notice. "What the hell have I been doing? We have to find him!"

I leaped up. I hadn't gone two steps before he grabbed my arm and jerked me around to face him. His face had gone thunderous. "What's going on?"

"I told him about Percy. I think Price might be going after him on his own." If he was caught, if he was fumed—"Let me go!" I jammed my hand against Touray's chest to help lever me away. It was like wrestling with the Hulk.

He grabbed my other arm and gave me a hard shake. It rattled my teeth. "Calm down. Tell me what happened."

"There's no time! Price can't go after him alone." Panic had set in. I was shouting. I kicked at his shins and twisted away. "Let me go!"

A blur thrust between us. I heard the sound of a fist hitting flesh. Suddenly I was free of Touray's grip. I staggered back and fell over a table.

Sharp pain bit into my thigh and shoulder as I went ass over teakettle. More thuds and grunts and a crash as bodies crashed into a table. Wood splintered and glass shattered. I scrambled to my feet.

Price and Touray were locked together. Price's face was twisted with animal fury. Touray was holding on to him in a bear hug, trying to keep Price from punching him.

Price must have seen Touray grabbing me and had put two and two together and come up with his brother attacking me. Which, technically, was sort of true. Touray had been worried about Price, though, so I could forgive him. Not that he'd hurt me. Maybe a couple bruises on my arms and a little bit of whiplash. I could live with those. But I couldn't let Price go after his brother. He wouldn't forgive himself later.

I jumped out of the way as the two of them barreled past. "Hey!"

They didn't notice me. I wasn't about to jump between them. I may not be the smartest bulb in the box, but I did have some sense of self-preservation. I grabbed a pillow and smacked at them to no effect. Price was still wearing his gun in his shoulder holster. What if he decided to use it? That spurred me to think creatively. I resorted to a movie scream. I braced myself, sucked air deep into my lungs, and screamed with all the force I had.

That got Price's attention.

He shoved his brother away and whirled to find me. He put one hand on my shoulder and pushed my hair away from my face with the other. He looked me over from head to toe. "Are you okay?"

"Are you insane?" I put my hands on his hips and curled my fingers through his belt loops. "You just mauled your brother."

He cupped his hand around my neck, his thumb rubbing gently along my cheekbone. "Did he hurt you?"

I shrugged, not wanting to lie. "I was panicking. I didn't know if you'd decided to run off after Percy on your own. Touray was trying to get me to tell him what was going on. I wasn't exactly coherent."

He closed his eyes and tipped his head back, then pulled me against him, his arms wrapping hard around me. His body coiled so tight he was shaking with the tension. "No one hurts you." I could feel him twisting to look at Touray, keeping himself between us. "No one."

I leaned back so I could see him better. "Which is what your brother's been explaining to me."

"By restraining you. No. We can go to my place. It's safe."

Touray snorted. "Like hell it is."

"Shut up," Price snapped over his shoulder. "I told you to stay away from her. You weren't supposed to talk to her without me in the room."

Not that I wanted to sit around shooting the breeze with Touray by myself, but still—"Shouldn't I be the one to decide who I spend time with?"

"Exactly," Price said. "I know he scares you. I know you don't want anything to do with him."

Again, I'm not the smartest bulb in the box, but I translated that just fine. Price didn't want me to be so scared of his brother that I dumped him. Again.

I tightened my grip on his waist. "He thought you'd be here with me. He wanted to tell me I was safe from him." I couldn't believe I was actually defending Gregg Touray, Tyet crime boss. Two months ago, I'd have crawled through a vat of snakes rather than sit on the same park bench. "We've decided we're family."

I wish I had a picture of Price's face in that moment. He looked like I'd just told him I was a Martian.

"I won't hurt her, Clay. I promise. I promised her, too. As for what you saw—can you blame me? I knew once you found out that that bastard burned Riley with cigarettes, you'd be on the warpath. I didn't think she'd told you, or—"

Price was no longer listening. He turned back to me, his voice so cold and quiet I could hardly hear him. "He did what to you?"

His blue gaze wouldn't let me look away. I was pinned in place. "Burned me. On my arms, with cigarettes. He was making a point. I'd been rude."

Price's lips opened, and no words came out. He pressed them together and nodded as if making a decision. "There were no signs. I'd have seen them when—" He broke off and swallowed. "When you were lost in the dreamspace."

"I had a heal-all."

The corner of his mouth quirked and flattened. "I'm surprised. You don't usually make of a habit of carrying one of those."

"It wasn't my idea," I admitted.

"Whose was it?"

"Leo's and—Leo's." I wasn't going to tell him about Dalton, not yet. He wasn't over the news of the fumigation and Percy burning me. Finding out I'd been letting a squad of potential assassins follow me around me for weeks would send him over the edge.

"Leo's and Leo's?" He wasn't fooled.

I licked my lips, and his gaze fastened on the movement. Heat flared in his eyes, and a burst of inappropriate feminine delight at his reaction suffused me. I'd never lit such a fire in any man before, and to do it in this tough, unyielding man—it was breathtaking and thrilling. I wanted to drag him off some place private to have my way with him, despite his brother looking on, despite me having just escaped from Percy, despite the war we were about to ignite together.

Price's pupils dilated, and he sucked in a sharp breath, all too aware of my response to him. All the same, he wasn't going to be distracted. "Leo's and Leo's?" he prompted again, his voice rough.

He was right. He and I had to wait, which meant I needed distance. I shook my head, uncurling my fingers from their hold on his waist and stepping back. Instantly, I felt cold. "I'd rather explain when you get everybody together. Telling the story in bits and pieces is making a hash of it. Besides, I could eat."

"I'll get everyone. Be downstairs in fifteen minutes," Touray said briskly.

"I sent for Cass. She's on her way." Price slid his arm around me and latched me to his side. He faced his brother. "Don't ever touch her again."

Touray flinched from the hostility and threat dripping from Price's words. "I won't."

He stepped around the broken furniture and slipped out the door, closing it firmly behind him.

"Where were you burned?"

"My arms."

He lifted each one, turning them and examining them carefully. When he found nothing but healthy skin, he took both my hands and pressed a kiss into each palm, then looked at me, his eyes haunted. "I hate that I almost lost you. I wouldn't even have known it. You have to stop risking yourself."

I shrugged. "I'll work on it."

The corner of his mouth lifted. He knew as well as I did that my life wasn't getting any safer. "About the Sparkle Dust you ingested. You're not . . . craving?"

I shook my head. "No. I was told that I would have been begging for it a while ago, so I think I'm okay."

He closed his eyes and let go of a quiet breath. Almost like a prayer. "Okay."

"So," I said, stepping back and looking down at myself. "I'd better change. I'm covered in coffee." I didn't wait for him to respond, but simply unbuttoned my jeans and shoved them and my underwear down to the floor. I kicked them away. "Oops. Looks like my shirt got some on it, too. Can't have that." I yanked it off. "Damn. How did my bra get soaked?" I unhooked the totally dry garment and dropped it on the floor.

I stood in front of Price, bare-assed naked. I cast a challenging look at him. My ego took a bruising as he impassively stared back, totally unmoved by my striptease or my nudity. Maybe he needed a bigger hint.

"Thirteen minutes and counting before we have to be downstairs."

He gave me the once-over from head to foot and back up, his gaze lingering low and then higher. Finally, he returned to my eyes and gave a faint shake of his head, his mouth curving in an irritating smile. "You've been through too much. Exposed to SD, burned, and nearly lost in the dreamspace. Sex is the last thing you need."

I wasn't so easily discouraged. "Wrong," I said, closing the space between us, my fingers working the button free on his jeans before he his hands closed on mine. I wriggled my fingers under his waistband. "It's the thing I need most. Are you saying you're not interested?"

He gave me an arrogant look down his nose. "You're in no condition for sex."

I lifted my brows and stepped back. I spread my arms and looked down at myself. I'm no stick. I've got hips and boobs. Price's gaze dropped, and I jiggled a bit as I slowly turned around in a circle. "Really? I know I'm not that familiar with my own body, but I sure feel like I want to make love to you."

I slid my hands slowly over the sides of my breasts and down my belly. I was rewarded by a groan from Price. Taking that as encouragement, I moved forward again and unzipped his pants. This time he didn't stop me. His hands hung at his sides; his head tipped back. He wasn't on board yet.

I slid my hands under the waistband, reveling in the silky warmth of his skin and the way his body shivered like a plucked guitar string in response to my touch. I went up on my tiptoes and flicked my tongue along the taut cables of his neck. He caught his breath.

"I need you," I murmured as I nibbled his neck. "Skin on skin. I need to feel you inside me. I need to hear you lose control for me. I need to feel alive and whole. I need—" I needed him to be sure of me. I needed to show him how much I loved him.

"You need?" he prompted, his voice unsteady.

"You. Now. Please." I nudged his pants down so that they hung on his hips and looked up at him. I didn't even try to hide the tears that burned my eyes. "Don't say no."

He held himself still for a breathless few seconds, and then he pulled off his gun holster and let it fall to the floor. His arms wound tight around me. He lifted me off my feet, grappling me to him, his mouth slanting over mine. The kiss was raw and desperate with need. I clamped my legs around his hips and held on to him like he was a rock in a hurricane.

He carried me through the massive closet and back to the bed. Instead of laying me down, he turned and sat down. With my legs behind his back, I was helpless to fulfill the raging hunger inside me. Somewhere between the sitting room and the bedroom, he'd kicked off his pants, but his underwear still kept me from him. I rocked my hips against his hard length and made a complaining sound.

His chest shook as he laughed. He stroked his hands over my back and hips, his touch sending sparks dancing through my blood. His lips moved down the column of my throat. He licked the tops of my breasts. I arched to give him better access. Doing so pressed me harder against his cock. He groaned. I did it again. He got revenge by bringing his hands up to push my breasts together, lifting them so that he could lick and suck my nipples. Electric delight made me cry out. I gripped his shoulders, pulling him closer.

"*Please*, Price."

That was all he needed to hear. He pushed my legs down and lay back, leaving me straddling him. His sapphire eyes glittered. He rubbed his thumbs over my taut, wet nipples. "Take what you want, Riley."

I reached down between us, pulling his cock from his boxer briefs. I cupped his balls. He hissed and bucked in my hand. I smiled and gripped his rigid flesh firmly as I lowered myself down onto him. We didn't have time to play, and I didn't want it. I just wanted to be full of him. I moaned as he slid inside me. Pleasure spiraled through me, adding to the delicious ache winding me tighter and tighter.

When I didn't move, savoring the feeling of his rigid length, he thrust his hips gently. "Riley," he grated. "You feel so damned good. Don't make me wait."

I didn't need more encouragement. I lifted myself until I almost lost him, then I lowered myself just as slowly. I did it again, then again. Price's eyes thinned to slits as he watched me ride him, his hands running over me, cupping my breasts, tugging my nipples, drawing down on my hips.

It wasn't long before the pleasure inside me turned to a searing agony of need. I moved faster, clutching Price's shoulders. He leaned up and took my breast into his mouth. At the same moment, he slid his thumb across my clitoris.

I exploded. I shuddered and shook as euphoria crashed through me, clenching and contracting. As my pleasure crested, Price rolled me over, hooking his elbows under my knees and thrusting into me. He caught my pleasure and stoked it higher. Another orgasm roared through my body. I was helpless before it. Price groaned my name as he came, his body shaking and shuddering over me.

I was boneless. My body quaked with the aftershocks of extraordinary bliss. I let my eyes drift closed. Even if Price's grip on my legs hadn't held me pinned, I couldn't have moved. He drew his arms out from under my knees and held himself above me on one elbow as he brushed the hair from my face with his free hand.

"Riley?"

"Mmm?" I couldn't form coherent words yet. I felt whole in a way I hadn't since I'd kicked him out of my life.

"Are you okay? I didn't hurt you?"

"You killed me," I said. "In a good way." I rubbed my cheek against his arm, breathing in his scent. "I could stay here forever."

"But you won't."

Hearing a hint of bitterness in his voice, I opened my eyes. "No. Would you want me to?"

"I want you to be safe." He traced a finger over my lips. "You could have died. Or worse."

"I know. You could have, too. Remember the explosion? Neither of us lead safe lives. That's why I'm not wasting any more time. I want to be with you."

He pressed a kiss to my lips, pulling away before I could respond. "Then you have to promise me one thing."

I eyed him warily. "What's that?"

"Two weeks."

I frowned. "What do you mean?"

"Two weeks. Just the two of us together. No tracing, no family, no friends, no Tyet business. Just us. So we can figure out what 'us' is and how to be us."

I smiled. I could definitely do that. "When?"

"As soon as we take this asshole, Percy, down. Is it a deal?"

I hesitated, then shook my head. "I'm afraid we can't."

He scowled. "Why?"

"We have a date for dinner at my stepmom's on Saturday. She'll hunt me down with dogs if I miss it. Besides, if you're moving in with me, you have to meet her and my other brother, Jamie, first, or they'll come after me with pitchforks and torches. Taylor will be there, too."

His thunderous expression smoothed. "All right. Dinner with your family Saturday night. Sunday we start our two weeks. Even if we have to go find a deserted island to hole up on. Deal?"

"Deal. But if we're staying at my house, you should know I only have some ramen, a jar of peanut butter, some chocolate-chip cookie-dough ice cream, and a couple boxes of mac and cheese. We'll need to stock up on some groceries. I don't want you to starve." I smiled slyly. "Or run out of energy."

"I'm a good cook, but even I can't make anything out of that revolting collection." Price nuzzled my neck, sending delightful chills down to my toes.

"It's why I spend so much time at the diner. Patti and Ben make sure I eat well."

"Uh-huh. Grease and more grease, with a side of toxic fat and a pile of salt."

"Never say that where Patti or Ben can hear you or your life won't be worth living."

Price bit my neck lightly. I shivered and groaned, then rolled away. "We are not going to make your brother's deadline downstairs if you keep that up." I sat up. "So you plan to make me healthy, is that it?"

"I plan to make sure *you* don't run out of energy," Price said, running his hand up my leg to just above my knee.

"Never," I said, and then scooted off the bed. The last thing I wanted was to get hauled out of bed by Touray.

"Riley."

Something in Price's voice stopped me cold. I turned. His face had turned to stone. Only his eyes revealed the turbulence of his emotions. My heart clenched. "What now?"

"I'm going to kill this Percy, you know that, right?"

"I know that someone will."

He sat up. "Not just someone. Me. Not for justice. Not to save a life or in self-defense, but for what he did to you."

"Revenge," I said, my mouth dry. I knew what he was saying. Asking really. I'd feared his Tyet side, the enforcer who killed on the orders of his brother. I'd come to understand that Price didn't kill without good reason. He wanted the law and justice on his side. But this time would be different. Price was no longer a cop; even if Percy surrendered without a fight, Price would kill him. He wanted to know if I could live with that. If I could accept murder and still love him.

Could I? But it wasn't murder. It was extermination of an evil man. Eradicating him would make the world a safer place. It was no different than exterminating Hitler or Ted Bundy. No matter why Price did it, it was the right thing to do, the necessary thing.

"I understand," I said at last.

"Do you? I have to do this. It's about more than revenge. It's about keeping you safe in my world. I can't let anyone get away with touching you. They have to know they'll pay and pay dearly. I've got to make a lesson of him."

I sighed. This was a part of his life I didn't like thinking about, but he was right; I needed to face it. I didn't like it, but I lived in a Tyet world, and this kind of violence was how business was done. If I couldn't live with it, then Price and I were over before we started. For a moment I couldn't breathe. No. I wasn't living without Price anymore. I wasn't sure I even could.

"I can't promise not to have issues in the future," I said. Price started to say something, but I held up my hand. "Even if I have issues, I won't walk out on you. I promise." I said it like a wedding vow. Maybe it was. All I knew was that it was the truest thing I'd ever said.

"But as far as Percy goes, he needs to be killed. What he's doing—" I shook my head, nausea churning in my stomach as I remembered the cavern of drug-feeding pens. "Putting him in jail just makes him a recipe book for someone else to take and use. He needs to be put down and everything about his Sparkle Dust manufacturing has to be destroyed. Whatever your reasons for wanting him dead, the fact is that Percy's too dangerous to let live."

Price stood up. The stone mask had dropped away and his expression was a mixture of hesitation and doubt. "Be sure, Riley."

"I am sure." I leaned against him, feeling his skin feverish against mine, feeling his heart thundering in his chest. I licked the spot where his pulse fluttered madly in his neck. "I'm all in. Body and soul."

He caught my head between his palms, searching my face for hints of uncertainty. I had none. At last he nodded, the tension releasing from his body. "About fucking time."

He'd said the same thing in his text when I'd asked him to dinner. Ordered him, really. Only now, I could feel the relief pouring off him as he held me close and kissed the top of my head with something that felt like reverence.

That's when it dawned on me that he was mine as much as I was his. Body and soul. That's also when I realized exactly why he was going to kill Percy. Because if anybody touched Price, I'd slaughter them. Literally. He was mine to have, mine to hold, mine to protect. I was never going to let him down.

Chapter 14

It was more like forty-five minutes before we came downstairs. As we approached the dining room, I could hear impatient voices inside. Price's hand enveloped mine. He pulled me around to face him. I lifted my brows.

"They are waiting for us," I said, but made no attempt to pull away.

"Just remember I have your back. I won't let my brother bully you."

"*I* won't let him bully me," I said.

Price scowled. "He gets tunnel vision. He doesn't let himself get derailed."

"No worries," I said airily. "My specialty is derailing. I knocked you off your feet, didn't I?" I swung around, unable to resist the lovely scent of breakfast any longer.

"That's for sure. I'm still floundering," Price muttered behind me.

We stepped into the wood-paneled room with its long, polished granite table and heavy carved chairs. That was all I could take in before Leo snatched me into his arms.

"I was getting ready to come hunt you down. How do you feel?" He hugged me hard.

I hugged him back. "I'm good," I said. "I could eat, though."

He laughed, his chest jerking. "That sounds like you." He loosened his arms enough to scrutinize my face. "You're really well?"

"I'm fine," I said firmly. "How are you? And Madison?"

The girl in question stood a few feet away. Her eyes were bruised looking, and she looked like she'd lost a good ten pounds or more. She clung to the back of a chair, biting her lower lip as she watched my reunion with Leo. Touray sat at the far end of the table, his lips bowing down with impatience.

"We're well enough for a couple of prisoners," Leo said, sending an angry glance down the table at Touray.

"Prisoners?" My voice sharpened. I looked at Touray and then Price in silent demand.

"It seemed unwise to allow it to be known that you had escaped from the mountain," Touray said. "I thought it best to keep things quiet until you were awake and we knew what we were dealing with."

I nodded understanding. "He's right," I said to Leo. "If Percy thinks we're stuck in the tunnels somewhere, he's less likely to be on guard. I'm sure he's got people watching to see if we've made contact with anybody. Me and Madison, if nobody else, since he didn't really know about you and Dalton. Since no one's heard from us, he probably thinks we're lost or dead in the mines."

"Dalton?" Price echoed.

"Who's Dalton?" Touray demanded at the same time.

Damn.

I'd hoped to get some breakfast in me before the interrogation started. I eyed the sideboard longingly before answering. "Dalton was—is, I guess—the leader of a protection squad that I figured had come from one of you two. They've been guarding me since right after—Since the stuff with Josh went down."

"You thought he worked for one of us?" Price asked, his voice an icy knife. Hard to believe that he'd just been screwing me into oblivion. Just at the moment, he sounded like he wanted bang my head against the granite tabletop. "Surely you checked him out. Hell, why didn't you call and ask?"

"I didn't call because I was trying to figure out my life without your interference. I had someone check him out, a hacker friend of mine, but there wasn't much to find. Since I figured he was one of yours, that seemed normal. If you'd sent him, you'd erase his history and anything to do with you. I traced him as far as I could, but he had good nulls and he used them. That was another thing that made him look like yours. Add to that the fact that he was constantly on my ass about safety, and never once lifted a finger against me, the logic seemed sound."

"Christ," Price said. His jaw knotted, and he turned like he was looking for something to hit. "Why couldn't you just pick up the damned phone?"

I'd been asking myself that question, too, but I wasn't going to give him the satisfaction of knowing that. "Again, he didn't hurt me." I remembered the dreamspace vision. Somebody was working extra hard to get me to trust him.

"How the hell do you know? Maybe he hasn't triggered whatever plan he set in motion. Maybe he's just biding his time. Fuck, Riley! You know better!"

"He's right," Leo said. "Why the hell didn't you get in touch with me? I could have looked into it. Mom could have. She's still got contacts with the feds."

My stepmom was a reader. A strong one. She'd been recruited into various government agencies. She'd retired early, after my dad vanished, but she still got called in on hard cases. She could have done some digging. But I hadn't wanted to call her. Mostly because I didn't want her to use her empath magic on me. I'd been too torn up over Price, and I hadn't wanted to explain.

"She's the reader, correct?" Touray asked.

I rolled my eyes. "Should I assume you know everything about me? What deodorant I wear? The results of my last Pap smear?"

He smiled slowly, his eyes hooded. "I think it's a safe enough assumption."

I glared at Price. "I suppose you know all that, too?" No wonder he'd got all my clothing sizes right.

"I didn't know about Dalton," he said, still furious. "I kept my word. I backed off. I trusted you to take care of yourself, and then you let someone you don't even know worm his way in? Are you insane? Or just incredibly stupid?"

"I don't know. Let me think about that one," I snapped. "Right now, I'm feeling a lot like both, not to mention pretty damned irritated."

He stormed over to me, standing so close that I had to lean my head back to meet his gaze. "Irritated? That's nothing. I'm fucking pissed as hell. You have no right to take chances with yourself." He poked a finger into my chest to emphasize his point. "What happened to all your paranoia? Shit, you wouldn't let me be in the same room with you, but you let a total stranger under your roof twenty-four/seven."

"No," I said. "I didn't. I let him and his squad follow me around during work hours. I repeat, I thought you'd sent him. Besides, I—"

I'd been overwhelmed with the flood of work, with the sudden public outing of me being a tracer, and my loneliness from missing him. I'd been a hot mess. I wasn't going to admit it, but it was true that I hadn't been thinking all that clearly. I *should* have called. I *should* have double-checked with my stepmom. I should have gone to ground until I knew I was safe.

"You what?" Price prompted, looking angrier than I'd ever seen him. That was saying something.

I'd been so damned tired of hiding that I'd fooled myself into thinking I was looking after myself well enough. "I could have done better," I admitted. "Are you satisfied? I fucked up. I done wrong. Are you done stroking out for now? Can we get on with the rest of the story?"

He opened his mouth, then shut it. He shook his head and spun on his heel and strode stiff-legged across the room as far from me as he could get. He sprawled in a chair, his arms crossed over his chest, waiting.

Was he pouting? I marched over to him, my anger and embarrassment simmering hot. I put my hands on my hips. "It's the strangest thing, but suddenly I've got a feeling like a sore throat coming on. So if you don't come sit at the table with the other grown-ups, there's a good chance you're not going to hear much."

He glared at me. "If I do, I might kill you."

"I'll kick your balls up into your throat if you try. Besides, I told you that you'd be hearing things that would make you go homicidal. Didn't I ask you to keep remembering that you love me? Did you already forget?"

He snorted, and his lips flashed a momentary smile. It vanished as fast as it arrived. "I'm not sure I can take it. How bad is it going to get?"

"You've heard all the bad parts. Now it's me just fleshing out the rest."

I decided to leave it at that. I went over to the sideboard and served myself. There were thick-cut potatoes fried with peppers, onions, and marinated cabbage; four different kinds of eggs; steak, bacon, and sausage; steamed vegetables; biscuits; fruit; yogurt; pastries; and a half-dozen sauces and gravies. I loaded up two plates and put them on the table, then filled a tall glass with what turned out to be fresh-squeezed orange juice. Carafes of coffee were already on the table. I took a cup and filled it, adding cream and sugar. Price sat across from me. Madison slid in beside me, and Leo sat beside Price.

When I sat down, I realized we were missing someone. "Where's Cass?"

"She's on her way," Touray said, serving himself. "They had a flat."

Once everyone had loaded up their plates and settled around the table, I started to talk. I began with Dalton's arrival, then skipped forward to Lauren hiring me to find her nephew. Touray, Leo, and Price peppered me with questions. I answered each one, finishing both my plates of food and returning to the sideboard for pastries and fruit. I hadn't had room for them the first go-around.

I sat back down. When I got to the part about the fumigation, Leo lost it.

"What? You were exposed to Sparkle Dust?"

He sat slack in his chair. He looked like he'd been punched in the gut. Like Madison had looked when we made her leave her family behind. Like I'd felt when I thought Price might have been blown up. Helplessness and horror.

Quickly, I explained about by belly null, which ordinarily would have earned me a lot of grief from my audience. Investing a tattoo with magic risks that an enemy might cut it out of you. In this case, however, the fact that it saved me from SD had them conveniently overlooking that fact. I had a feeling I'd be hearing about it later, though.

Leo pressed the heels of his hands against his eyes, his fingers digging into his scalp.

"I don't think I'm addicted. I'm sure I would have been craving it by now," I reassured him. "Cass is coming. She's a dreamer. She'll be able to tell for sure."

Madison nodded, speaking up for the first time. "I've seen a lot of victims. Usually it takes less than twenty-four hours before they are shaking and begging for a fix."

For once my brother seemed out of words. He lowered his hands and nodded, his expression turning blank. "Okay."

I hesitated, but he didn't look at me. He'd gone liquid-nitrogen cold, and whatever he felt was locked inside that fortress of frost.

Nobody asked what would happen if I was wrong and Cass found evidence of SD addiction in me. Since I hadn't shown symptoms, I was pretty sure I was fine, but there was a lot of room for fear between *pretty sure* and *definitely sure*. I could tell they all thought it. No point in bringing it up now.

I then told about Percy and the way he'd burned me.

"I will kill him," Leo whispered. "Painfully and slowly."

"Get in line," Price said. "He's mine."

"She's *my* sister."

"She's my *life*," Price snapped back. "Get used to having me around, Junior, because I'm not letting her out of my sight."

I rubbed my hands over my face. I'm sure this was flattering, somehow. If you got past the fact that neither of the two men had a very high opinion of my ability to take care of myself. I couldn't blame them. Not after I'd confessed about Dalton, and then getting lured down to the tunnels by Lauren. It was clear they both thought I was touched in the head. Half-witted. Simpleminded. Idiotic. All of which I could agree with. I was determined to do better. Arguing about it at this point wasn't going to get me anywhere. I'd fight that battle later, when I actually had something to win.

Unfortunately, my two-second mental time-out had given Leo enough time to teach Price a lesson. Touray growled, and his heavy chair went flying against the wall. Madison squealed.

"What the fuck?" Price roared.

"Do not call me 'Junior,' and I am more than a match for the likes of you, Tyet man," Leo crooned in a voice I was all too familiar with. He didn't lose his temper often, but when he did—

I dropped my hands resignedly, already knowing what I'd find. I was right. Price was contained in a filigree suit of metal from neck to ankles. Leo had pulled it from everywhere in the room—metal buttons, screws, nails, hinges, silverware, electric cords, and anything else metal. It was beautiful to look at—my brother was an artist, and even something like this had to have flair.

Price struggled against his prison to no avail. I knew exactly how he felt. Leo had captured me like this a dozen times over the years. Even though his head and feet were free, Price would be feeling claustrophobic and helpless. After a moment of struggle, he held himself still, glaring furiously at Leo, who stared smugly back.

Touray reached fruitlessly into his rear waistband for a gun that no doubt had vanished into Price's bonds. His expression had gone deadly. "Free my brother or I will cut your throat."

Leo sneered. "Can you?" Ribbons of metal flowed up Touray's legs and around his hips, fixing him in place. More snapped around his wrists. A spike formed and lifted, nudging against the hollow of Touray's throat. "Don't ever threaten me."

Before Touray could do just that, I slapped my hands down on the table and hoped it didn't collapse without its metal parts. "Enough! You all called me 'stupid' and 'ridiculous' and 'idiotic,' so apparently you recognize it. Have a look at yourselves. Leo—I love you, but you can't go around attacking your new family whenever they piss you off, which I suspect will be often. Yes. I really did just say new family. I love Price, he loves me, we're moving in together. That means Touray comes with the territory, like it or not."

"As for the two of you," I said, whirling on Price and Touray. "Same thing applies. He's my brother, and if I'm your family now, so's he, and so's the rest of the bunch. Get used to it. Embrace the crazy. Now, this pissing match is canceled. If you all can't behave, I'd just as soon go back to bed until you come to your senses, though I'm sure Madison would like to see her family rescued sooner rather than later."

Seconds later, the metal pulled away and reshaped itself into a freeform wall decoration. It was ridiculously lovely. If Touray had had to pay for it, it would have cost him several hundred thousand dollars. That Leo could make it in a fraction of a minute was a testament to how over-paid he was, and how skilled. He gave me a little shrug of apology. All I would get. Touray eyed the wall and then Leo. I could almost hear his thoughts. Another tool for his toolbox. Over my dead body. He gave Leo a little nod of appreciation. Price lifted his chin in a little salute. *Men.*

I quickly told the rest of my story, from Madison's kindness to Luke's help to rescuing Leo and Dalton and the rest of the squad. I mentioned what Luke said about Percy clearing out within a week. We didn't have a lot of time left to catch him before he abandoned his lair.

Touray frowned as I mentioned the weird paralyzing blankets that Percy's people had worn, and the others that had been hung to trap intruders.

"You've never heard of anything like that before?" I asked, glancing around the table.

The men shook their heads. Madison stared down into her lap. She'd hunched in on herself, almost like she wanted to disappear.

"Madison? Do you want to tell us about your family? Percy's holding them?"

She flinched when I said her name, her lips pinching tight. Tears rolled down her cheeks, but she didn't wipe them away. Leo reached out to put a hand on her shoulder. She shook him off.

"It's my dad and my little sister," she said, so quietly I could barely hear her. "Percy has them. I'm supposed to be a hostage against their good behavior. If I run, if I escape, then he'll hurt them."

She looked at me, her eyes haunted. "Robin is barely eighteen."

Percy wouldn't hesitate to torture the teen. Maybe he'd burn her, maybe he'd find something else.

"Why does he have them? He hasn't fumed them?" He used the SD as a tool for guaranteeing loyalty. I was surprised he hadn't fumed Madison.

She shook her head. "He doesn't want them going wraith and dying. Me either, since threatening me makes them do what he says."

"What's that?" Price asked. "What does he want from them?"

Madison looked down into her lap again, then raised her head, firming her chin. Clearly this was a secret she didn't often reveal. I knew exactly what she was feeling. I gave her an encouraging nod.

"My dad has a fairly unique ability. He can tell what someone else's magic talent is, just by touching them. My sister can do the same."

Touray rubbed a hand over his lips and jaw, his eyes narrowing thoughtful. "Handy, but hardly a reason to hold a family prisoner."

Madison nodded. "Have you heard of ragpickers? Or quilters?"

Price answered. "Quilters are what they sound like. They can piece together broken things. Most of them are pretty minor talents and work with a single textile, like leather or cloth or ceramics. I've never heard of ragpickers."

"No reason you should. It's not all that useful a talent. They usually end up working with the dead."

"Why? What do they do?" Leo asked.

"They can see spirits. When people die violently, a lot of times their spirits are torn apart. Rags. The pickers can collect them. Strong ones can even snatch a spirit right as the body dies and keep it from passing across."

Leo frowned. "Why? And what does that have to do with Percy?"

But I'd already made the jump. "That's what felt so familiar!"

Everybody looked at me. Shit. I hadn't meant to say that out loud. Only Price knew I could reach into the trace dimension, and I hadn't said anything about the fact that sometimes I could feel things bumping me, or that lately someone had been trying to grab me and called my name. I'd realized that the blankets were bits of spirits quilted together. They felt a little like trace, but more like the sensation I got when the dead bumped into me.

"What felt familiar?" Leo asked.

The other three looked expectantly at me.

Did I tell them? Everything in me said, No! More than that. I could feel myself retreating inward and madly putting up walls behind me. I couldn't seem to stop it. I wasn't in control.

I needed to be alone.

"I have to use the bathroom," I said, standing up fast. "Where is it? Never mind, I'll find it."

I headed for the door. I'd gone about three steps when I found Price at my back.

"Riley, what's going on?"

"I need to pee."

"You didn't a minute ago."

He put his hand on my shoulder, but I didn't turn around. I felt . . . wooden.

"I'm a girl. This sort of thing happens."

"What are you hiding?"

"Just—give me a minute. Please." At that point I'd have said anything necessary to get him to back off and let me go. I was fighting off a paranoia attack, the kind that makes me want to change my name and find a new place to live. I thought these were over. I hadn't felt one of these in a few years. After my dad left, I had them all the time, but once I'd settled into a routine—albeit a seriously paranoid one—they'd quit happening all that often. I couldn't even remember the last time I'd had one. I stepped out of his hold, and this time he didn't try to stop me.

I didn't understand it. Why now? I trusted Price and Leo. Madison couldn't hurt me, and Touray—I'd decided I was going to trust him, too. But reason didn't make a difference to my panic. Chills ran over me, and my heart pounded as my lungs tightened into fists.

Adrenaline spiked. My skin was electric. Every instinct I had told me to run. But that was wrong. I had no reason to go anywhere! My brain fuzzed gray with static. I made myself stand still and leaned my forehead against the cool wall of the hallway, trying to think through the manic maelstrom in my head.

I was having a fight or flight reaction, which meant I was trying to protect myself. But I didn't need protecting. Not here. I was safe. This wasn't *me*.

If it wasn't me, then who was it?

An invader.

A wave of gray rose up to smother that thought. I fought it back, feeling a sticky residue clinging to the insides of my skull.

"Riley?" Leo stood beside me. That look of helpless horror was back. He put a hand between my shoulders and rubbed. "What's going on?"

I gave him a cracked smile and looked over his shoulder at Price. He no longer looked concerned. He looked sinister and dangerous.

No. That wasn't real. *Not real.* Something deep in me resisted the possibility that Price was a threat to me.

"I—" Before I knew what I wanted to say, another gluey gray wave crashed over my mind. It was like someone didn't want me talking, didn't want me *here*. Maybe the same person who'd kidnapped me in dreamspace. Had he wormed into my mind then?

"Cass. Get Cass," I gasped, then I lost all control and sprinted down the hall like an Olympic runner.

Chapter 15

I ran headlong into a bathroom, slamming the door behind me. For a long minute I leaned against the door, my body frozen in place. Finally, I unlocked myself enough to move again. Without thinking, I locked the door, then went to the sink. I ran the water and splashed my face. I stared at myself in the mirror. I looked wounded, somehow. Vulnerable. Needy. Weak. Deep inside I was shaking, trying not to crack apart.

This isn't real.

Someone changed me.

Someone invaded my head and *changed* me.

The magnitude of that hit me, and my stomach jerked. I threw up in the toilet, heaving hard. I started to sob and crashed to my knees in front of the toilet. I curled up into a ball on the floor, lacing my hands over my head. It hurt. Pain wrapped my head in a spiky helmet. Smoke filled my head. My ears rang. I couldn't hear beyond the clanging. I moaned.

What was happening to me?

I tried to remember if someone had touched my mind. Flames erupted. My body shuddered, and adrenaline roared through me. My brain went blank except for a need to *run. Escape. Hide. Fight.*

I wasn't aware when I leaped to my feet. I kicked and screamed, clawing to get out the door. I ran into flesh walls. I bit and kicked and punched, and when I was subdued, I bashed my head and bucked and writhed. An image rose in my head. My dad. He was looking down at me, like I was lying in bed. He stroked my head.

"It will be all right, Riley. This is for your own good. It will help you to protect yourself. Sometimes we don't always know who the enemy is. Better for you if everyone is. Now say the words again, slowly."

Run.

Escape.

Hide.

Fight.

Forget.

FLAT. PAPER THIN. Paralyzed.

Riley? I'm with you. I don't know if you can understand me right now, but you went rabid and flipped out. Like frothing at the mouth, head-spinning-around, bit-ing-your-tongue-off cuckoo. Then you went into convulsions. They put a sleep charm on you until I could get here. They sent for Maya, too. She's trying to keep you from stroking out or blowing your heart. She can't find anything wrong with your body to cause it, and they hit you with serious nulls, so it's not likely a spell. That means it's got to be in your head somewhere. I know you hate having me muck around in your skull, but I think you're going to die, otherwise.

Recognition. At last. Cass.

We took the sleep charm off and Maya's making sure you don't move. You have to be conscious for this. Damn, but I wish you could tell me what set you off. That would help.

Snow. Fog.

All right then. If and when you can, talk to me, okay?

Tug. Prod. Yank. Invasion.

Sink. Retreat.

Run.

Escape.

Hide.

Fight.

Forget.

Jesus. No wonder. . . . You've got serious landmines. This goes back a long way. Years. I've never seen anything like this. This is isn't going to be a walk in the park. Hold on tight.

Ripping. Agony.

Sink.

Retreat.

Sink.

Snow. Soft, cold, sweet.

Gray nothing.

Disintegration.

Release.

RILEY? COME ON, girlfriend. Talk to me. I'm reaching my limits. You ran far, but it's time to come back before all the testosterone chokes me.

Gray.

No.

FOR FUCK'S SAKE, Riley! Get your ass up and going, already. Time to get your shit together and quit lying around.

Pinch.

Feel that? I'll keep it up until you can't stand it anymore. If I have to, I'll start singing Justin Bieber songs. You should know I can't carry a tune.

Pinch.

Pinch.

Pinch, pinch, pinch.

What's it going to be? Damn. I don't know any Justin Bieber songs. Okay, I'll just do "A Hundred Thousand Bottles of Beer on the Wall." How about that? Get your shit together already, and come out of whatever hole you've dug for yourself. Dammit, Riley! What's it going to take to get you to pull your head out of your ass and climb back up into reality?

Pinch, pinch, pinch. Prod. Pinch.

Move it, girl!

Itch.

Itch.

ITCH!

Yeah, that's it. That's getting to you. Wake up or it won't ever stop.

Itch . . . itch . . . itch . . . itch . . . itch.

Stop it.

Riley? About fucking time! Come on, now. You're still too inside. Keep coming to the surface. You're going to have to stop doing this sort of thing to Price. He's out of his gourd. Batshit crazy.

Memory. *My dad.*

What about your dad?

Did this. To me. Not supposed to tell.

Tell what?

I—

Try, Riley. I'll help you. What aren't you supposed to say?

I can touch trace . . .

I know. I've been in your head when you do.

When I do, trace dimension. Spirit dimension.

Pain. Recoil.

Sorry! Missed that one.

Release.

There. I got it. Better now, I think. Keep going. Tell me.

I can touch spirits . . . in the trace dimension.

I tensed, waiting for punishing pain. Nothing happened. Inside, I felt raw, and my head still throbbed. But my mind was clear.

Touch spirits? Cass repeated.

Why is that such a big deal? I wondered.

Can you communicate with them?

I've never tried. One grabbed me a few days ago. Maybe called my name.

Whoever put those triggers and blocks in your mind wanted to be sure you never said anything about it, even if it killed you. Not just that. I found memory wipes. Totally gone. Your father did this to you?

I—Yes. I'm certain. But—I never knew he had talent. Betrayal burned like acid. He'd messed with my head—programmed me. My own dad. For my own good, he said. That's what people said to make themselves feel better when they stabbed you in the back.

Why would he do that? Didn't your father like you?

I thought so. If I ever find him, if he's still alive, I'll be sure to ask.

What kind of father did that to his kid? Deep inside, something cracked. Everything I'd been sure about my whole life was now in question. I'd been lied to. I'd been tampered with. For your own good. He'd told me that. Like hell. I wasn't sure what was real at all.

I'm real. Price is real. Your brother Leo is obnoxiously real and terrified for you. We'll help you sort it all out. I promise. But now you have a little farther to go. I know you're tired. I'm going to pull you up to the surface and let you wake up. We'll go slow in case there are any other landmines. Remember that Maya is holding you paralyzed. I'll tell her to let you go, but it could take a few minutes. Don't panic.

I won't. Maybe. No promises. But her words comforted me. I still had family, and I had friends, and I had Price. All of that was real. Those things helped me fight my father's mutilations. I couldn't think of another word for it. He'd mutilated me.

Ribbons of warmth fluttered around me. I fought the urge to resist as they clung and turned into muscular tentacles. I felt myself rising, expanding, stretching. I contracted, instinctively fighting.

Easy. You'll be fine. I rooted out a lot of the trouble, but your subconscious is going to cling to the habits for a while. You'll have to fight them. I'm guessing you already were and that's what triggered your meltdown.

How? It was all I could squeeze out as I tried to make myself relax.

You had a series of behavior constructs, along with mental barriers set up. The behavior stuff focused on keeping to yourself, keeping hidden, not trusting people, and that sort of thing. The deeper it went, though, the tighter the mechanisms. So you could break some of your rules with only minor mental repercussions—fear, guilt, anxiety, nightmares. But when you started breaking more serious rules—or even thinking about breaking them—that set off a series of—let's call them discouragements. *When you broke through some of those, you hit crisis level and your blocks shut you down. Thing is, I'm not sure you'd have recovered. Riley, I know this is hard to hear, but those stops were designed to kill you if you pushed them too hard. They almost succeeded.*

My father did that to me. I was trying to not feel the horror and pain of that realization, but it wasn't working. It engulfed me in a tide of black tar. Sadness and exhaustion netted me, and I felt myself melting apart, dripping out of Cass's embrace.

Shit.

Twist and scrape. Prickle and stab.

Hold on. This may sting.

Electric skewers plunged through me. A sheet of fire swallowed me. Nerves sang with pain, breaking and curling into ash.

Abruptly, the pain evaporated.

Sorry. Every time I think I've got it all taken care of, something new pops up. That last one was elegant. The dreamer who worked on you was an artist. Admiration resonated through her mental voice.

That artist was *my father. Glad to be so entertaining.*

All right, almost back up to where you'll just be asleep. You know, your dad might have figured you'd be better off dead than revealing what you can do.

Not for him to decide, I said grimly. *He mutilated me. My own father.*

People sometimes love in stupid ways.

Was Cass trying to make what he did better somehow? *It's not love.*

He might have thought it was.

He was wrong.

I'm sorry.

Yeah, me too. I'd always idolized my father, but after my mom died, he'd become the center of my world. Losing him had been—easier than it should have been, now that I was thinking about it. I'd cried, I'd mourned, but looking back, I'd moved on quickly. Too quickly? Had he arranged that, too? And if he had . . . did that mean he'd planned to leave me? Suspicion scraped claws over me.

Cass?

What?

Would it be possible for my dad to have taken my ability to see his trace away, like it never existed?

Say no. Please say no.

Sure. If I were doing it, I'd substitute a different trace memory so that even if you saw it, you wouldn't know it. The other thing he might have done is selectively blinding you to seeing his trace. I've done that kind of thing before when working with mental patients. Helps with PTSD especially.

It didn't really matter how, only that it was possible. Now I had the answer to one of the most painful questions of my life, and the assurance that I hadn't failed to find my father. He'd made sure I couldn't look.

Only now I'd substituted one painful question with another: Why had he done this to me? How was not finding him for my own good?

One thing was certain, if Cass could lift my blinders, I'd do whatever it took to find the answer, to find my father.

As if reading my mind, and likely she was, Cass spoke again. *You need to heal a little first. In a week or two, I can see what I can do. It could take a little while to undo everything, though getting back memories will be impossible. They haven't been buried, they've been wiped.*

I couldn't tell if I was more angry or hurt that my father had robbed me of those memories. Both emotions twisted through me like brambles on steroids. I pushed the emotions away, slamming them inside a little box, along with the billion other questions that kept popping into my head. I couldn't handle them now. They were too big. It was all too big, and I still had Percy to deal with. At least I knew where to find him.

Thanks, Cass. I'm ready to return to the land of the living.

Good. I'm backing out.

The pain of her withdrawal seemed like nothing more than a bee sting compared to all that I'd been through. The next thing I knew, I felt myself wake.

Because Cass had warned me that I might not be able to move, I didn't panic when my eyelids wouldn't go up and the words I wanted to say piled unspoken behind my teeth.

"Give it a moment," Maya murmured in her rich, husky voice. A Spanish accent melted the edges of her words. "I worked on your body while Cass worked on your mind. You should feel very good."

It was true. I felt energized. She'd repaired whatever damage I'd done to myself when I'd flipped out in the bathroom. I was, however, back to feeling hungry and hollow, though the hollowness surrounded the void in my soul where I'd hoarded all my memories and love for my father. That had all rotted into nothing.

Tears leaked from the corners of my eyes.

"What's wrong? Why is she crying?"

Leo.

Price was notably silent. Where was he?

"She's had a lot to deal with," Cass said tiredly.

"What do you mean?" Leo again. "What the hell happened to her?"

"That's her story to tell."

Finally, I pried my lids apart. It was only a fuzzy crack. Maya leaned over me, her long dark hair loose around her rounded face. Her eyes were eerie white. She smiled at me, a merry grin. "There you are, *querida*. It is good to see you again."

"You too," I rasped. My throat and tongue were stiff and unwieldy.

"Thanks for your help."

"Anytime. Now others wish to see you." She stood and moved away.

Next to fill my vision was Leo. Worry lined his face. He gripped my hand, and brushed at the tears rolling down the sides of my face. "How do you feel? Are you in pain?"

"No pain." Not physical, anyhow. I glanced past him. Cass sat at the foot of my bed. They must have moved me here. As usual, she looked almost anorexic, her blond hair wispy and short, her face all sharp angles. Where was Price? I looked back at Leo, tightening my fingers on his. "I'm okay."

"What happened?"

I squeezed my eyes shut. I couldn't make the tears stop. They kept leaking out. How did I explain that my father—his stepdad—had tampered with my head, stolen my memories, and nearly killed me.

"Where's Price?" I couldn't stop the words.

"Here."

I turned my head. He leaned against the wall on the other side of me, arms folded, face haggard and gray. Why was he so far away?

"I can touch spirits," I said. "I can reach inside the trace dimension and touch them. My father put blocks in my head so I couldn't say it. He wiped out some of my memories. I don't know what I've lost, or what other landmines he left inside me." The words tumbled out, no internal restrictions stopping them. My tears flowed harder.

Price didn't respond. He only stared, unmoving.

"Wait—your dad would never hurt you," Leo said. "He adored you. He'd do anything for you."

I couldn't argue. I didn't want to even try. Between Price's indifference and finding out about my dad, I hurt too much. I rolled onto my side and pushed my face into the pillow as tears kept spilling from my eyes. I squeezed them shut.

"Why don't we give her a little bit," Maya said. "Come on, now. All of you."

Leo squeezed my hand again and stood. I heard the rustle of clothing and the thud of footsteps, then the sound of the door closing firmly. Quiet surrounded me, and I began crying in earnest. My father's betrayal was a gaping wound, and Price's indifference cut deep.

I thought I was alone, and then the mattress sank behind me and Price's arms came around me. He pulled me into his lap as he sat back against the headboard.

"Shh, baby. It's going to be all right," he murmured against my forehead.

I swiped at my runny nose. "Easy for you to say. Your dad didn't scramble your brain. Why are you mad at me?"

"I'm not mad."

I snorted. "Could have fooled me. You looked like you wanted to cut my throat."

"No. My throat, maybe, but not yours."

I raised my head, trying not to let him see how much his words hurt. "Oh? When did you become suicidal?"

"I don't know. Sometime between you dying yesterday and you dying today."

My body turned to lead. I didn't know what to say to that. I couldn't blame him for feeling that way. Love was supposed to be joyful, not torturous. At least he was honest.

"Okay," I said at last, when nothing else came to mind.

"Okay, what?"

"It's too much, too hard, to be with me. I get it. You can't trust anything about who I am."

He was silent. Then, "I didn't say that."

"You'd like to cut your own throat. I think that pretty much covers it." Every word bruised my heart, but I wasn't going to make this tougher on him than it had to be. "It's okay, though. I understand. There's got to be someone out there you can love who doesn't make you suicidal. Even if there's not, being with me isn't healthy for you. You aren't happy. I can't even promise to look out after myself. My head's so fucked up that I don't know what I might do. You're better off not being with me."

His body hardened, his arms tightening. "That's not what I said."

"Either way, it's true." I should have been trying to push away, but instead I tried to breathe him in, to carve the memory of his touch and his scent into my brain so that I'd have that forever.

"Are you going to stop crying?"

"I don't know. I've got a lot to cry about, just at the moment." Like a shattered heart. I was losing my dad and the love of my life all at once. Maybe I should consider a little throat cutting of my own.

"I'm not going anywhere. I couldn't, even if I wanted to, which I don't. I'd rather be in hell with you than in heaven with anybody else. And before you go making jokes about us being in hell, I don't know what else you'd call it when I'm having to watch you sliding away from me and I can't do shit to stop it. I've never been so helpless. I am not good at being helpless, Riley. Now please stop crying. You're killing me. And making a mess out of my shirt."

I laughed and straightened up a little. "Got any Kleenex?"

"In the other nightstand, I think."

I crawled off his lap and pulled open the top drawer. It was empty. In the second drawer was a box of tissue, a fingernail kit, an alarm clock, a pad of paper, a couple of pens, a package of earplugs, an unused eye mask, and a little sewing kit. I grabbed a handful of tissues and blew my nose and wiped my eyes. When I'd gotten myself better under control, I faced Price, sitting cross-legged. He turned to lie on his side, propping his head on his elbow, his sapphire gaze locked on me.

"My dad messed with my head. It almost killed me," I said, and the tears started to roll again. I rubbed them fiercely. "When I was taken in dreamspace, I was shown my mother's murder." I fell silent, leaving Price to arrive at the same conclusion I'd arrived at.

"You think your father kidnapped you in the dreamspace."

I looked down at my hands. "Him, or my mom's murderer." I lifted my gaze again. "I don't want to think they are the same person."

Price sat up and wrapped my knotted hands in his. "He loved your mom, right? He wouldn't have killed her."

I shook my head. "I don't know. I don't know if anything I remember before he disappeared is even real."

"Fuck," Price said.

"Exactly." I ran my fingers through my hair. "I have to find him. But first, we have to take care of Percy." I frowned. "Truth is, I'd like to focus on something else."

"All right then. Gregg's working on a plan. Madison's helping him with the layout of Percy's underground compound."

I lifted my brows at him. "Good. Then we'll be able to get going soon."

"You could stay out of it. Let us handle it." Price continued to fake calm relaxation, brushing away imaginary lint on his jeans.

I gave him a long look, unsure how to answer. "Are you asking me to?"

"I want to."

"But?"

"You'll say no, because that's who you are. I love you, so I'd better learn to deal with it. Besides, there's no way I'd hang back in your place. The fact is that our attack team will get into Percy's lair with fewer problems if you follow the trace and lead us, not to mention no one else can see these spirit blanket traps. I'm sure Percy's rigged more of them since you and Madison disappeared. I would have. Besides, given that your father may have made a play for you in the spirit dimension, leaving you above ground puts you at risk. You're probably safer with me going after Percy than not."

I wasn't sure if he was explaining to me or talking himself into his logic. Either way—"I won't take unnecessary chances," I promised.

"You'd damned well better not."

I thought he might kiss me, but instead he rolled off the bed and picked his shoulder holster up off the floor. He'd dropped it there when he crawled into bed with me.

"Let's get going."

I got up and came around the foot of the bed. "At least I make your life interesting."

"If by interesting you mean insane, frustrating, and completely fucked up."

"At least the sex is good," I pointed out.

"The sex, in fact, is glorious."

The corner of my mouth rose. "And here I thought I needed more practice."

He gripped my hand, pulling me out the door. "Come to think of it, you do. I'm happy to help you with that, no matter how long it takes for you to learn to do it right."

"It could take a while."

"For you, sweetheart, I've got all the time in the world."

"You say that now, but wait until you're living with me and I put my cold feet on you in the middle of the night." I wanted to prolong the light-hearted ease between us before we blundered into the lion's den.

"I'll get you socks."

"I hog the hot water."

"Tankless water heater. Or I'll shower with you. I'll definitely shower with you."

"I tend to stay up all hours."

"I'll adjust."

He pulled me into his arms at the foot of the stairs. His expression sobered, his eyes drilling into me. "I won't ever walk away, and I won't ever give up on you. Count on it."

Unlike my dad. I knew that's what he was thinking about. But more than that, he was telling me that if something changed, if he *did* walk away or give up, then it wasn't real. For that to happen, he would have to have been tampered with the way my dad tampered with me, and I shouldn't trust it.

"I'll keep Cass on speed dial."

"Do. And never forget I love you."

I wish I could promise him that. Unfortunately, I knew better.

Chapter 16

Everyone had gathered back in the dining room, except for Maya and Cass, who were resting. Large papers littered one end of the table where Madison and Touray had been working up a map of Percy's lair. I was able to add some slight detail, with the overlook of the drug-farm cavern and some of the tunnels where Luke had taken me. I wasn't certain of any of them, and made sure that Touray knew it. Leo offered more insights from his time with Dalton and his readings from the metal.

"Before we get down to your plans for Percy," I said, serving myself from a new buffet set out on the sideboard. After getting so sick and going through a healing, I was starving again. "Let's finish with what's going on with your sister and dad, Madison."

"We left off that story with you," Leo said, lowering one of the pages he held to look at me. "You said something felt familiar, and then you ran off like your butt was on fire. Please don't do that again. For the record, it was unnerving and upsetting." He gave me a hard look, then an impish grin.

I forced myself to grin back. "For the record, that wasn't my fault. My dad set it up in my head so that I couldn't tell you—tell anyone—that I can reach into the trace dimension and touch trace, touch spirits."

Everybody looked at me. All except Price, who stood behind me and rubbed the tension from my shoulders.

"So what felt familiar?" Touray asked, quicker to start putting the pieces together.

"When I dismantled the spirit blankets, some of the pieces clung to me. I knew they felt familiar, but I didn't realize why. Then I forgot about them." Though really, how I'd managed to do that, I wasn't sure. They still patchworked my hands, arms, neck, and face, feeling like chilled cellophane.

Price's hands clamped on my shoulders. "Are they still on you?" he asked quietly.

Trust him to go right to the potentially dangerous part. I nodded.

Touray frowned. "I don't understand. I would have seen them when I took you into the dreamspace."

"Maybe you weren't looking. They attached to my skin." I pointed to the spots. Eight of them, though three were no bigger than pennies, and the rest ranged up to the size of my palm.

"Attached?" Leo asked, dropping the papers he was looking at and focusing all his attention on me. "They are still on you? Did you think maybe you might have wanted to mention that? Maybe back in the tunnels?"

I was pretty sure this was what it felt like to be stalked by hungry vultures. "What were you going to do about them? What are you going to do about them now?"

"You need a ragpicker," Madison inserted. "That's what they do."

"Is she in danger from them?" Leo demanded.

"I don't know."

"Hold on," I said, trying to get back on topic. "So far, they haven't hurt me. I'm not saying I don't want to get rid of them, but we have more pressing issues, like taking Percy down and rescuing Madison's father and sister." I paused. "What about your mom?"

A shadow flickered over Madison's face. "I never see her. She left us when I was a kid. She lives in Tahoe, I think, or maybe Reno. I haven't heard from her in a while."

"Okay, it's just your sister and father. Percy's using them to make those blankets, isn't he?"

Madison looked surprised that I'd figured it out and then nodded. "When the ragpickers collect the spirit tatters, my dad and Robin can sort them according to talent. Then the quilters piece together a blanket or cloak that lends that talent to the wearer. So when you were taken, that paralysis you felt came from the talent cloaks the guards wore. The blankets are usually a blend of different abilities designed for whatever the buyer needs. The power of the blankets is too much to be worn."

The silence that followed her explanation choked the room. Price's hands on my shoulders went boneless. Even Touray, always in control of himself, stood dumb, his jaw slack. I wished I could have taken a picture.

My first reaction was that that wasn't possible. Luckily, my mouth wasn't working yet, because obviously it was possible. I'd been there. I'd seen the way Percy's goons glowed and it made sense. They'd been wrapped in stolen magic.

Madison's hands knotted together. Her eyes were haunted. "Percy has the ragpickers collect spirits from the people he kills. The wraith spirits are in tatters by that time. Something about the effects of Sparkle Dust, I guess. At that point, their talents are easier for the quilters to work with. Whole spirits are hard. Anyhow, even neuters can use the talent cloaks. Percy sells them for a lot of money."

At the word *neuters*, Price's fingers tightened on my shoulders. It referred to people who had no magical talent—like Price. There were other words—*mundanes, ordinaries, defects, brokens*. Lately, the derogatory *neuter* had caught on. It had to be hard, living in a world of magic and not having any. Percy's talent cloaks would be in serious demand. Especially if you could have more than one. Hell, talented people would covet having access to new powers. It was half the reason people claimed to use SD.

Price was the one who pulled himself together first, jumping into cop mode. "Now we know why Percy keeps your father and sister. He'll have them well guarded. Do you know where they are kept?"

Madison shook her head. "I get blindfolded. All I know is that there's an entrance somewhere in Percy's living quarters."

"We've marked those on the map," Touray said, shifting a page and pointing. Price examined them.

"How accurate is the map?" he asked Madison.

"I've explored a lot in these areas, so I'm fairly confident in the layout," she said, pointing. "Over here, Percy makes the SD. I'm not allowed back there at all. This is the prison corridor and here are his offices, kitchens, and common areas. Employee residences for that level are back along this side. I'm not allowed into this upper section or the lower sections. I know a lot of the miners are housed in those areas, along with equipment. There's storage there, and that's where the deliveries come in."

"He's got a drop shaft," Touray said. "I pulled the blueprints from my contact at the mining department. It's proprietary. He doesn't share it with anyone. That's our best entry point."

"Wait—you're not going in through the tunnels?" I asked. "Knocking in the front door is a whole lot more dangerous, isn't it?"

Price shook his head. "Not really. Percy will be expecting a back-door assault. If you got away, then it's the only way in you know, so he'll be watching. The front door is probably always watched, but he's not likely to have added security at this point." He smiled grimly. "We're good at this, Riley. Trust us."

Good at this. Invasion of an armed stronghold? I believed it. That, and Price had long experience with the police flushing out criminal warrens.

The more they talked and planned, the less I felt a part of the action. They didn't really need me for anything. I wouldn't be able to find Madison's family with trace since I had no trace to track. She couldn't remember anywhere that I might be able to pick it up, either. Going in the front door meant little likelihood of booby traps or the blanket traps. Nulls—of which Touray had a massive stockpile—would take care of the talent cloaks and hopefully any exposure to SD. That left me with nothing to do.

I guess that was Price's plan all along.

I'd like to say I didn't resent it, but I did. Not that he said anything directly. He knew I was smart enough to figure it out and that I wouldn't endanger everybody else by insisting on coming along. Leo was more welcome than I was. In fact, he was a key player. His metal talent meant he could subdue enemies and dismantle guns without even seeing them. The entire team would wear a series of handcuffs on their clothing or cables wound around their arms that he'd be able to use if no other metals presented themselves. It was all very tidy and exclusive.

At some point, when Touray, Price, and Leo were deep in a discussion over the entry, I got up and left.

I stood outside the dining room, trying to sort out just where I wanted to go. I was pouting, and that was ugly. I maybe could have contributed something if I stayed, but this was not my area of expertise whatsoever. Maybe I could go do laundry or clean bathrooms. I made a face at myself. Criminy. Pity party, much? I swallowed down my unreasonable hurt. I'd pretty much used up my attention quota when I needed rescuing several times in the last couple of days. I sighed. The others were doing what needed to be done and didn't need me whining at them because I wasn't getting enough attention.

That still didn't give me anything to do. At least when Price followed me into the hallway, I didn't whine at him.

"Riley? What's wrong?"

"I'm not much help in there," I said and was pleased to note that I sounded matter-of-fact. "I might be able to boost some nulls. I'd like to send you in with the strongest nulls possible, given the Sparkle Dust threat."

His gaze narrowed suspiciously. "Send us in?"

"I'm not going to be much use, now, am I? Seems stupid to take me along when all I'll do is distract you."

He couldn't hide his relief, which both exasperated and gratified me.

"You don't have to look so happy about it."

"Any time I don't have to worry about you, I'm happy," he said, refusing to be in the least bit daunted.

"Price?" Touray looked out of the room, giving me an implacable look like he wasn't going to back down from shutting me out any more than Price was.

I did not roll my eyes at him, or stick out my tongue, even though I wanted to. Junior high still runs thick in my blood. Before he could say anything condescending and John Wayne little-lady-ish, I cut him off.

"Where are your nulls? I was just telling Price I'd like to boost some. May help if you get exposed to SD." The thought made me sick, but I kept my happy face plastered on.

Touray's brows rose, no doubt surprised that I wasn't throwing a hissy fit all over the ground. "I'll show you."

Price started to follow us, but I shooed him away. "I'll be fine, and you've things to do here."

He gave me a suspicious look, but for once I had no need to feel guilty. My conscience was clean. For now. I smiled brightly at him, which only made him scowl.

Touray led me down several stairways into an underground bunker, for lack of a better word. It had a steel door protected by magic. He stepped inside the massive vault, and golden light flared to life. We stood in a room the size of a basketball gym, with a broad aisle running down the center and lines of shelves, drawers, and cabinets branching perpendicular from it. A computer sat up front on a tall desk with a swiveling barstool for a chair.

"This way," he said, leading me down the center aisle and then left. He stopped short, indicating the entire set of shelves jammed full of everything from coffee cups to cathedral crystals. "These are all nulls. I'll leave it to you to decide what you think we ought to take with us."

"All right," I said, deciding that since he wasn't into small talk, I wasn't going to be either. Not that I had much to say at this point.

He started to walk away, then turned around, his black eyes boring through me. "You know that staying behind is the right thing to do, right?"

"I'm not arguing," I said, not looking at him.

"That's what worries me."

I smiled. Ordinarily, he'd be right to be worried. This time, though, I didn't have any mischief planned. "I hear that sort of thing sharpens the edges, keeps you alert."

"I'm plenty sharp and alert, thank you."

"Ah, well. Then it's good I'm on board with your plan."

"Are you?"

"Do you want me to swear on a stack of Bibles?"

"Would that in any way prevent you from lying?" He countered, both brows rising.

"As far as you know," I said, then waved my hand to dismiss him. "Go away now. I want to have these ready when you need them. How long before you figure to leave?"

He clearly wasn't convinced that I wouldn't go do something on my own, but he had no choice but to believe me. And maybe duct-tape me to a chair before he left. I wouldn't put it past him. Note to self—hide a knife in my bra.

"Two hours."

"What time is it?" I asked, realizing that I had no idea. "Hell, what day is it?"

"It's Wednesday." He glanced at his watch. "Ten after one. Afternoon," he added.

Wednesday? How was that possible? I'd gone into the tunnels on Thursday. I must have lost a few days between getting lost in the dreamspace, sleep, and today's episode with the mental blocks. I kept my happy mask on, refusing to let Touray see how shaken I was by my time loss.

"I hope Percy hasn't abandoned ship already. How long do you expect your strike on his compound to take?"

He shrugged. "We'll hopefully capture Percy and get Madison's family out within a couple of hours. After that, we'll send a larger force in to shut the rest down."

"What about the other prisoners?" I asked. "And the people he's turning into wraiths? And Luke? He helped me. I don't want him to get hurt."

"We don't know if he still has any prisoners. We've got Luke's description. We'll do our best not to harm him. As for the wraiths, I don't know what will happen to them. Our priority to is to shut down the operation, and keep anyone with knowledge of the SD production from escaping and starting up a new drug factory. Since the wraiths are caged up, I assume they'll be fine until the dust settles and we can free them."

I frowned. "Free them? They can't just go free. They're addicts. They'll kill to get SD, or they'll kill themselves trying. They need to be detoxed and cared for."

Touray smiled in that gentle, pat-on-the-head way that indulgent parents smile at children who still believe in Santa Claus or the Easter Bunny. The way the world talks to artists and dreamers.

"That's not the way it works. Detox requires money, and I doubt any of them have it. Percy scraped up the street dregs so that nobody would miss them or come looking for them. Even if they could raise the funds, detox is effective only three percent of the time. To hit that three percent, you'd need a world-class dreamer. You'd never find one to take them on, not even Cass. It would kill her to attempt that big a healing. I'm sorry to say it, Riley, but any way you slice it, these people are screwed. Once Percy got hold of them, they never had a chance. They'll be lucky to die sooner rather than later. Going cold-turkey off SD is more unpleasant than you can imagine, and few survive. The best I can do is to promise that they'll be cared for until the end."

He was right. Totally logical and reasonable. I, however, had never been accused of being logical or reasonable, and the thought of letting hundreds of people die without trying to help them made me want to scream. I rubbed my hands over my face. Maybe *I* could do something to help them. I'd nulled away the magic of the Sparkle Dust. Was it too late to do that for addicts?

I didn't know, but I sure as hell was going to try. I pulled back on my galloping thoughts. That problem would have to wait until later. First I needed to get nulls ready for the invasion of Percy's domain so that the SD victims could be rescued.

"You'd better let me work, now," I told Touray.

He didn't move. "You've got that look like you're up to something," he said. "What are you thinking?"

"I was thinking I could use a massage."

The corner of his mouth quirked. "Easy enough to arrange. I've got several masseurs on staff. You can have one now."

I probably shouldn't have been surprised. I mean, the man had more money than he had room for. He probably burned stacks of it in the fireplace to keep warm. "I'll take care of the nulls first," I said weakly.

"I'd still like to know what's running on that hamster wheel in your head," he said.

Since he wasn't going to go away without an answer, I decided to give in gracefully. "I was wondering if I could null out the addiction. It worked for me."

He looked thoughtful. "Worth a try, though for that many people, it could take the rest of your life. Riley—I know you want to help, but you do understand that these people may not be innocent victims? Most of them likely weren't forced to take SD. They wanted to. Even if you cured the addiction, they'd be likely to go back to it. You might be able to take away the magic that binds them, but you can't take away the memories of the euphoria, or the desire to feel that good again."

I felt myself deflate. I wanted to argue, but once again, he was totally logical and reasonable, and worse, he was right. I'd encountered enough junkies in my life so far to know that. "Yeah, okay," I said.

"I'm sorry."

He sounded like he meant it. I lifted a brow at him. "Not your clowns, not your circus, right?"

He grimaced. "My town. My circus. My clowns."

I couldn't help staring. "Seriously?"

167

"I told you before, Riley, I may do some terrible things, but I intend to clean up Diamond City and make it safer."

"You do realize that's like the devil saying he wants to clean up Las Vegas?"

He grinned, and once again I was struck by how human he could be. "The irony is not lost on me. But I told you before, ugly things are happening in Diamond City. War is not clean and I'm fighting a war against evil people. Percy is just one head of a massive hydra."

"Doesn't the mythology say that chopping off one head only makes it grow more?" I asked, remembering the stories my dad used to read to me.

"With luck, we'll seal up the compound and keep anybody from learning how to make Sparkle Dust."

"You don't sound all that hopeful," I said.

"I'm not. Percy isn't the only one making it. I'm hoping he's the only one who knows how to make it from people. I'll leave you to your work."

I watched him leave. He was complicated: ruthless, brutal, and yet he loved Price, and he was totally loyal to him. And now to me, and my family, too. He still scared the piss out of me, and yet he also made me feel weirdly safe, because he'd wrapped the shadow of his protection around me. I made a face at myself, surprised to find that I actually liked him. Of course, that was the devil's specialty: seducing you, luring you, making you feel good, all right before he dragged you off to hell.

"Next stop, Fire and Brimstone Station," I murmured, and then laughed quietly in the silence of the vault. It wouldn't have been funny if it weren't so true.

Chapter 17

The number and variety of nulls in the vault was ridiculous. I was impressed by the skill level and creativity in some of them. It was a learning experience I didn't have time to absorb. Instead, I searched until I found what I was looking for. One entire shelving unit held pegboards with a variety of necklace nulls. I pulled down three with heavy gold chains and rectangular gold ingot pendants. *Rapper-wear*, I thought, but gold was a dense metal and as good as lead for holding the maximum amount of magic. Each was loaded with a powerful trace null. I could work with that.

I carried the four necklaces to a table near the front of the vault. Then I went back and gathered a bunch more nulls, the most powerful I could find. Three armloads later, I figured I had enough to make a start.

I began by unwinding the trace nulls in each of the necklaces and restructuring them as magic-absorbing nulls. That would be their best chance of combating the effects of SD as well as the talent cloaks. I just didn't know if I could load them with enough power to do the trick, especially if they were hit by multiple magical attacks and the nulls drained, or if they were left exposed too long to Sparkle Dust.

No. I couldn't think that way. I had to believe they knew what they were doing and would strike quickly and cleanly and that my nulls would be enough. To even think otherwise would send me around the bend. I just wished I had the time to create a null that would absorb and then bind the magic to power the null. That took more time than I had, though, so I had to be content with packing the necklaces with as much power as I could.

I unwound the stock of nulls and fed the magic into the necklaces. The work was slower than I liked, but I'd drained my first load and gone back for more when Price, Leo, Touray, and Madison arrived. Time was up.

I sat back from the table, tying off the last null. Even though I hadn't had to produce the magic to reinforce the nulls, I still ached. I'd sat in one position too long, and my mouth was dry as dust. Nevertheless, the nulls were packed almost as full of magic as the gold would bear.

"I'd wait to activate them until you're down inside the tunnels," I said, trying not to sound as worried as I was. I kept the table between me and Price. I wasn't sure I wouldn't wrap myself around him and beg him not to go, or to take me with him. Not that I would be helpful. I hadn't created a null for myself, and the one on my belly needed to be recharged before it would do me much good. I was flat out a liability at this point.

They were all dressed in tactical gear, except for Madison, who wore a bulletproof vest, but didn't carry any weapons. She did have a metal cable double-looped around her waist and fastened with a padlock. Metal for Leo to use if he needed it, and more importantly, to find her with if she got lost or taken. Touray, Price, and Leo wore similar cables, with a pair of handcuffs hooked to each of their wrists like fashion jewelry for masochists.

"So, all ready to go?" I said brightly, still looking anywhere but at Price, or Leo for that matter.

"On our way now," Price said.

"Great!" I sounded like such a Stepford wife.

"If things go well, it shouldn't take long," Touray said. "Our people will move in if we aren't out in four hours. We've got them staged at several entrances. If things go according to plan, they'll move in and shut everything down behind us."

"Okay," I said and pasted a fake smile on my lips. "Don't let me hold you up."

Touray flicked his brows up at me, clearly amused by my attempt at cheerfulness in the face of disaster. "There's a phone outside on the desk. Dial zero and someone will come to show you the way back to your rooms." He didn't wait for an answer, turning away and striding out.

Leo pulled me into a hug. I kept myself stiff as I patted his back.

"Take care of yourself," I said, a knot building in my throat.

"Don't worry. We'll be fine." He leaned back to look at me. "So, Price? Really?"

I flushed. "You know he's standing right here," I pointed out. "He can hear you."

Leo shrugged. "I can't seem to get a chance to talk to you alone." He frowned. "You've been through a lot. Are you really feeling okay?"

I nodded. "Except for finding out Dad tied knots in my head, yeah."

"We'll talk when I get back. Promise?"

"Sure."

"See you soon." He kissed my cheek and hugged me again. I squeezed him tightly, letting him go with heavy reluctance. He disappeared after Touray.

I turned to Madison, still avoiding Price, even though his presence filled the room to smothering. "Take care of yourself," I told her, giving her a hug. "Don't do anything stupid."

"I won't," she said. She hugged me back, whispering, "Thanks."

I let go. "Don't thank me. Luke got you out and these guys are doing all the rest. I'm just sitting in the cheap seats on this one."

She tipped her head. "That's what you really think?"

"I got lured into a bad place, got caught, and got tortured. If you want to call that helpful, then you're welcome. Otherwise, I can't see that I've done much that's useful, except this—" I touched the gold pendant around her neck. "Hopefully that will keep you safe from magic."

She gripped my hand. "Because of you, my sister and father have a chance of escape. That's a lot."

That's when I realized she thought I was having a pity party for myself and was trying to bolster me up. "Thanks," I said. "But the heroes here are Luke, Touray, Price, and Leo. You, too. It takes guts to go back in and face Percy."

Touray leaned his head in the door. "Let's go. We're burning daylight."

Madison squeezed my fingers again and trotted out, leaving me with Price. I edged away from him. "Be careful, okay?"

"You know," he said, coming around the end of the table to corner me against the wall. "You really suck at good-bye."

"I don't want to say good-bye."

"Okay, see you later, then."

"See you later," I parroted, my lips wooden. If he stood there much longer, I was going to pick the locks on the handcuffs and fasten us together so he couldn't leave without me.

"Hey." He put his fingers under my chin and lifted until I met his brooding gaze. "We're going to be fine."

"Sure. I know," I lied, because who wants to hear that he's probably going to die a horrible death when he's about to beard a dragon in its lair?

He brushed his lips against mine. I fisted my hands on the sides of his flak jacket, inhaling his scent. When he straightened, I bit my lips.

"We'll be careful."

"I know." And they would be, but that wouldn't help if Percy got creative. Price knew that, too.

"I've got to go."

I nodded, and forced myself to release his flak jacket. If I hadn't been leaning up against the wall, I'd have slumped to the floor. He started to walk away, then twisted and kissed me again, this time hard, pulling me tight against him. It was over before it started. He pulled away, and I made a whimpering sound. He gave me a crooked grin and then strode out. I slid down the wall to the floor, trying to calm my breathing, and trying not to either panic or cry.

I'm not sure how long I sat there in my daze. Five minutes. Ten. Maybe fifteen. I waited until I figured they had to be on the road. At least I couldn't run after them and beg them to let me go with them.

I tried to picture their route in my head, but the closer I moved them to Percy's, the more tense I got. Eventually, I stood up. I couldn't sit there forever. I had no idea what to do with myself to pass the time, but I had to do something. Anything. I ended up lining all the spent nulls up on the table, smallest to largest, and sorting them by material and color. That took another ten minutes. I looked around at the vault. I doubted that Touray had meant to leave me inside. He might never do it again. I should explore.

Since I didn't have anything better to do and it was more interesting than just pacing back and forth and driving myself batshit crazy, I decided to take stock of the place and see what he might have stored away. That worked for about a minute or two, but then I kept thinking about where the team was now. And then now. And now again.

I snaked slowly up and down the aisles without noticing much of anything. Right until I came face-to-face with a locked glass cabinet. It contained an assortment of things, but my attention riveted on a jar on the top shelf. It contained shards of purple glass. I knew without a doubt that those were the shards from the glass heart that had belonged to my mother and hung over our kitchen sink when I was a kid.

I couldn't tear my gaze away. I was hypnotized. I wanted to touch them. It didn't make any sense, but even so, I pulled on the cabinet doors. They were locked. I examined the two locks. Not that hard to pick. Of course, I didn't have my pick set on me. I foraged for something that would work. I found several necklaces strung on wire and pulled those apart and made what I needed.

It took me a good half hour to make my tools and then get the locks open. I pulled open the doors and took down the thick-walled jar. The flip-top lid was made of glass fastened down by a bale. Now that I had it, I hesitated to open it. I decided I'd go back to my sitting room. Or maybe not, since Price and Touray's fight had destroyed it. Maybe the dining room, then. Suddenly, the vault felt claustrophobic.

I closed the cabinet, pocketing my makeshift pick set, and headed for the door. I wondered how long it had been since the others left. Had they reached the entry shaft yet? Were they down inside?

In the room outside, I found a phone on the desk, and a clock that said 3:55. They'd been gone nearly an hour. I considered a moment, then set the jar down and took a steadying breath. I couldn't stand not having some contact with them. I could fix that. All I had to do was pick up each of their traces. Which meant reaching into the trace dimension. Which meant risking getting grabbed again.

It was worth it. Besides, I was ready this time.

I dropped into trace vision. I had no trouble picking out Price's trace. It was burgundy with streaks of blue. Touray's was a brilliant yellow edged with black. Leo's emerald ribbon was as familiar as my own silver-green. Madison's trace was dark gold, the color of squash blossoms. I reached into the trace dimension and gathered Leo's and Touray's trace, pausing to wrap them around my wrist. Cold washed up my arm, making my elbow and shoulder ache. I grabbed Madison's trace next and reached for Price's.

Something brushed against my hand. I jerked away. My heart sped. I scrabbled for Price's trace, snatching it triumphantly and intending to yank it out of the trace dimension.

Nothing happened.

I jerked back again, and then again, but I was stuck fast, my hand locked in solid nothing. I sent null power down into my fingers. The invisible grip loosened. Before I could draw back, a blue-white hand circled my forearm. Cold washed through me. My heart clenched with the pain. I didn't have time to think. A tug pulled me off my feet and right into the trace dimension.

Ice invaded my body. My heart stuttered. I could no longer see Touray's house. I was surrounded by velvet purple-black. Wisps of opalescent energy swirled and drifted through a jungle of a billion vibrantly colored ribbons of trace. But none of that captured my attention. I followed the hand holding my arm up to its owner's face.

Shock quaked through me, and my heart stopped beating.

The face was opalescent and transparent, the eyes reflecting the ribbons all around. All the same, I couldn't doubt who it was.

Mom.

I mouthed the word as sudden sobs broke apart in my chest. Old grief poured out, and she pulled me into her embrace. It was cold, but I could feel the energy that was uniquely her wrapping around my soul. She ran her hands over my back and head and murmured to me.

"Hush, hush, sweetling. Oh, Riley, don't cry. You're breaking my heart."

That only made me cry more. I buried my head in her shoulder. I could almost smell her perfume. She pet my head and then pushed me away from her.

"Oh my baby! You have grown to be so beautiful! But there's no time.

I have things to tell you and you cannot stay in this dimension long."

I didn't get a chance to answer. Another spirit crowded between us, bulling my mother out of the way. I recognized her immediately. Lauren Morton. Percy had killed her after all. Despite my anger for what she'd done, I was sorry. She hadn't deserved to die. She'd been trying to save her nephew.

Her form wavered and melted inward, then firmed. Her mouth was moving. At first I couldn't understand the twisted syllables, then the sounds solidified into sense. "Percy escaping. Killing everybody. Trap. He knows. Plane." She flickered again and repeated the last word. "*Plane.*"

Then she lost cohesion, turning into one of the opal blobs of energy. Terror gripped me. I grabbed at her, but she was no more than icy smoke in my fingers.

"What did she mean? Can you talk to her?"

My mother pressed the flat of her hand against Lauren's pulsing spirit. Then shook her head. "I get images. I don't understand them, except she's wants you to know so you can do something. She's panicked about something."

"I have to go. I have to warn the others," I said. "How do I go back out of here?"

My mother hesitated. "I have things to tell you. About what happened to me. About your father. They can't wait long."

My father again. "I'll come back as soon as I fix this."

She shook her head. "No. Wait until you warm up. You might need healing. The trace realm is not meant for the living. It leaves its marks on you. But don't wait too long. Danger is coming." She brushed her fingers over my brow and along my cheek. "I love you. little girl."

With that, she grew businesslike. "To come back to me is easy enough. To enter this dimension, simply to open yourself to the trace realm and let yourself fall into it. I'll be waiting for you. Now you have to go before you become ill. Follow your own trace back to where you entered. Push magic down into your hand, reach through to the living world and grip your trace to pull yourself out."

I followed her instructions, my fingers almost too numb to feel my trace. I glanced at my mother. "I'll come back as soon as I can."

She smiled. She didn't look any older than when she died. Almost the same age I was now. We looked a lot alike, though her hair had been auburn and mine was coppery red. I held still a moment longer, not wanting to let go. What if she disappeared before I came back?

"Go," she ordered gently. "You're dying now. You need to warm up. Be careful."

She stepped back until she disappeared in the tangles of trace. I hauled myself back into the vault's outer room. I sprawled on the carpet. I ached. I couldn't feel much of anything. And yet there was no time to waste. I made myself stand up. My hands were blue gray and my fingernails and tips of my fingers were totally blue. If someone was filming a murder movie, I could have been cast as a body in a morgue.

I grabbed the phone on the desk and punched zero. It took two rings for someone to pick up.

"Hello. May I help you?" asked a pleasant and professional voice.

"This is Riley Hollis. I need Cass—" I stumbled. I couldn't remember her last name. Maybe I didn't even know it. "I need Cass down in the vault room five minutes ago." I didn't recognize my voice. I sounded like an eighty-year-old man who'd smoked a pack a day since puberty.

"Certainly, Miss Hollis."

"It's an emergency. Your boss could die. Hurry up," I added without any force at all, then dropped the phone and wilted into the chair.

It felt like hours before anyone came, but it was less than two minutes, according to the clock on the desk. I waited because I couldn't do anything else. I couldn't feel anything, like I'd been shot up all over with Novocain.

The first person into the room was a tall brunette, her hair pulled up in an elegant bun on the back of her head. She took one look at me and called back over her shoulder. "Get the healer!"

I recognized her voice from the phone. Two women followed her, both wearing black canvas pants and gray polo shirts. An embroidered logo of a black circle with a crescent inside was stitched on the left sleeve. Both women wore police-style gun belts, fully kitted out with extra magazines, handcuffs, extending batons, and no doubt a bunch of magical accoutrements.

"Explain," the first one demanded, not wasting any words.

She also wore a gun under her suit jacket, I realized. I wondered if Touray's maids went armed, too, just in case goblins or something crawled out of the toilets.

"Warn them," I said, concentrating on forming the words. My tongue didn't want to bend. "Trap."

"What kind of trap?" asked one of the gray-shirted women. Her dark blond hair was woven into a French braid down the back of her head.

"I don't know. They need to get out."

The brunette from the phone grabbed her cell and dialed. She swore when no one answered, then hung up and typed out a text and sent it. If the team was down in the shaft, they couldn't get a signal. The text would do no good.

"Need Cass," I said.

Just then, she arrived, led by a muscular gray-shirted man. "What's going on?" she asked.

"We have to warn the team to pull out. I've got their trace."

She hesitated. "I don't know if you can handle it. You look like shit, and me going in again so soon after your brain meltdown could really fuck with you."

"Don't care. Do it." She hesitated a second and then took a hold of my hand. I tried to relax as she invaded.

Easy, now.

Hurry, I urged.

What happened?

I'll tell you later. Just tell them to get out and fast.

She burrowed deeper into my head. I was almost glad to feel the pain, since I couldn't feel anything else. Finally, she broke through. I felt her magic chasing down my arm to the trace I still held on to.

Did you reach them? I asked after about ten seconds.

Hold on. Silence. Then, *okay, I got them. Touray wants to know what the problem is.*

Just tell him to stop wasting time and get out.

Hands settled on the crown of my head. Magical worms squirmed beneath my scalp, indicating Maya had arrived. I shuddered in disgust. On the other hand, feeling anything was better than not feeling anything at all, and she was healing me.

"What have you done to yourself, *querida?*" Maya murmured, her hands sliding down to cup the sides of my head, then lower to my shoulders.

Delicious warmth spread through me, bringing with it spiny prickles. I was grateful to feel something.

Cass was still in my head. *Touray says he needs to know how sure you are.*

Very sure. A dead cop told me when I went into the trace dimension, I said baldly.

Cass's astonishment rippled through me. *When you did what, now?*

Just tell them it's not safe and to come back. Tell Gregg that family is telling him to come the hell home. Percy's already on the run.

Realization crashed into me as I fully registered Lauren's last word to me. *Plane.* But no, I was being paranoid, wasn't I? Percy didn't know that my sister, Taylor, was a pilot. Even if he did, he'd use someone he knew and trusted to fly out of Diamond City. He probably had his own pilot and plane all ready.

Except he *was* the type to get revenge. He'd burned my arms because I'd sassed him. He used Madison's family as a weapon against her. Used her as a weapon against them. Going after family is what he did.

I think he's going to fly out—

He'd known enough to send Lauren to lure me down to his compound. He'd known just what she needed to say and do. Why wouldn't he know about Taylor? He probably knew everything there was to know about me. It wasn't crazy to think he'd do something vicious to get back at me. After all, because I'd escaped, the cat was out of the bag on how to make SD. Plus I'd taken Madison, his leverage against her father and sister. He had to be pissed. He was the type to want to make a statement. Lauren's spirit had been so determined to tell me about the plane. She'd said it twice, like it was the most important thing I needed to know.

Any doubts I had vanished. I had to get to Taylor.

I'm going to Taylor's hangar. Tell them to meet me there. Tell them to hurry. Pull out. I need to go.

Purpose drove away any remnants of cold or weakness left behind by my sojourn in the spirit realm. I braced myself for Cass's withdrawal. As she pulled back, a sunburst of pain exploded in my head and black spots spun across my eyes. I blinked, waiting for the pain to recede. When my vision cleared, I started to stand.

Maya's hands gripped me harder. "Not yet, *chica*," she said.

"I have to go. Percy's going after my sister." Saying it out loud made it feel even more right.

"Yes, but you have injured yourself again and you must be as ready as you can to fight. You cannot help her if you are prey. You must be strong. You must be the hunter."

She *tsked* as a surge of hot energy dumped into me. I started to sweat.

"Get her something to eat," Maya said in a distant voice.

The brunette from the phone picked up the receiver and hit a couple of numbers. She put in a food order to be delivered within the next five minutes. "High protein, high calorie," she said, then put the phone down.

"What can we do?" she asked without preamble.

I really liked her all of a sudden. "I don't know. Percy's paranoid. Even if he plans to get away without anybody catching up with him, he'll be ready for an ambush. He likes to use Sparkle Dust against his enemies, and his people have these spirit cloaks that give them concentrated talents. Paralyzing victims within the vicinity is one. I don't know what else."

"If I'm right, and I'm pretty sure I am, he's going to kidnap my sister to fly him out of Diamond City. She's a pilot and she's got her own small fleet of planes."

"Where?" She was rapidly typing into her phone.

"Hollis Air and Freight," I said. "It's up—"

"I've got it." Elegant dark brows arched. "Burdock Terrace? Nice."

My sister's hangar was up on the Midtown shelf, where a lot of money lived, and an air service was an abomination. She was suffered to exist there partly because it was convenient to have her there and partly because she used magic and illusions to reduce the noise and visual pollutions from her air traffic, and she only flew helicopters out of there. The main airport was up on the rim, a few miles northeast of the caldera. She kept another hangar there for her jets, and chauffeured clients between via helicopter.

"They'll be up on top of the rim at the main airport. If not now, that's where they'll have to go to board one of the jets."

"I'll put people on both," brunette woman said, tapping away. She glanced at her two companions. "Jo, you take the Burdock Terrace team. Tash, you get up on the rim. Go by air."

The two gray-shirted women were halfway out the door before she finished giving her orders. Now the brunette looked at me.

"Which team will you accompany? What will be useful for you to take with you?"

I was going to travel through the spirit realm. I knew how. I should be able to track my trace to the hangar. I'd been there enough. If I couldn't, I'd return here and go with the team. I wasn't sure what would travel through the spirit realm with me, but better prepared than sorry. Ignoring the first question, I answered the second. "A gun. Nulls. A heal-all or two, just in case."

She nodded. "What about binding spells? Maybe some hexes that could serve as distractions?"

I shook my head. "He'll be using nulls or his own binding spells. They'll kill anything I want to use." I didn't have time to make anything really useful. "I'll take a flak jacket if you've got it. Been shot once in my life, I'd rather not do it again."

She smiled in that way that said she'd been there, done that, totally agreed. Her fingers danced on her phone as she sent another text. "Anything else?"

She called this over her shoulder as she vanished inside the vault. She returned a minute or so later carrying two null necklaces and a double-pointed quartz crystal, which had to be the heal-all. She set those down before me. Just then, a breathless man wearing white kitchen clothing arrived with a tray. He set it on the desk and left.

On the tray were cold cuts and cheeses, crackers, several small cartons of whole milk, an assortment of dried fruits, and several small cups of nuts. I'd nearly finished gulping it down when the flak jacket arrived, along with a gun belt.

I took it from my brunette helper. "Thanks. What's your name?"

She looked taken aback, then flushed. "My apologies. I should have introduced myself."

"Instead of wasting time with introductions, you competently responded with speed, which I by far prefer. Thanks for that, too, by the way."

Her flush deepened. "Thank you. I'm Elinor Bartholomew. Call me Elle."

"Which team are you going with?" Cass asked. "Maybe I should go with you. If you could touch someone or pick up trace once you get there, I could take some people out of the game."

"No," I said. "This isn't your fight. Besides, I'm not going with a team."

"You're not what?"

"There's a faster way."

She narrowed her eyes at me. "You're going to try to travel through the spirit realm, aren't you?"

Cass was not stupid.

"I think I can do it. It's the fastest way."

"And significantly dangerous, given that you came out this time half frozen."

"I have to risk it." I said.

"I know. I get it. She's your sister."

I'd been prepared for a lot more argument. "Thanks."

"Don't die."

"I don't plan to."

"Who does?"

I drank the last of the milk. My hands were back to flesh tone, and I no longer felt like a corpse. "It's time," I said, urgency starting to claw at me. "Maya, I have to go now."

She said nothing, but I felt the wormy tendrils of her magic drawing back out of me. After a minute, she patted my shoulder. "I have done what I can, *chica*. Try not to stay too long with *los muertos*. They steal your life essence, even when they do not wish to."

"I'll go fast," I promised. I stood and gave her a hug. "Thanks."

"You are welcome, *querida*. Perhaps if you wanted to visit with me, you might invite me to dinner, rather than get hurt? I would not be offended if you didn't need my services."

The otherworldly white filming Maya's eyes cleared.

"I will," I said. "I promise."

"Good. And *buena suerte*. Good luck. I will be ready if help is needed."

"Thank you."

I looked at Cass. She held up a hand to keep me from saying anything. "No good-byes or anything mushy. I'll be here, too. But I'm thinking Maya has the right idea of it. Girls' night. Elle, you're invited, too."

"Of course. I'd love to," she said as she helped me into my flak jacket. She tightened it on, then put a bracelet around my wrist. "It might not help, but if anything can withstand the cold, it's this. It's a shield spell for extreme weather."

"Thanks." I glanced past her at the vault. "Maybe I should go look for helpful spells."

"I got it," Cass said, and went to look.

I buckled the gun belt around my hips, then took out the .45 and checked it, chambering a bullet before holstering it again. Elle dropped the null necklaces over my head and I slid them under my shirt so that they touched skin. She tucked the heal-all into one of my pockets. She frowned, vanished into the vault, and came back with two more.

"Better to be overprepared," she said.

"I hope I'm overprepared," I said darkly. I had a feeling nothing I carried would be enough. *I don't need to stop Percy*, I told myself. *I just need to keep him busy until the cavalry arrives. I can do that.* Even so, I had a feeling I was going to have to get win-the-lottery lucky.

I drew a breath. Since my luck didn't usually run toward the good side, I had another plan in mind. Percy was a narcissistic asshole, as far as I could tell. My best bet was to piss him off and hope he did something I could take advantage of. Being pissed screwed with a person's decision-making skills. I could work with that. At least it was playing to my strength. If there's one thing I knew how to do, it was piss people off.

Cass returned empty-handed. "I checked the electronic inventory. It's fairly well-categorized. The search didn't bring up anything on spirits or ghosts. Since you're a tracer heading into traceland, nulls will likely be your best bet."

"I've got those."

"Then you're set." She took my hand, then pulled me into a hug. "Whatever, happens, don't die. We can fix almost anything but death. Remember help is already on the way. All you've got to do is not get killed before they get there."

I hugged her back, grinning despite myself. "I'll do my best. So far, I've got a good track record."

She pushed away. "Good, because Price is going to want to murder you himself for going in on your own."

"That's not exactly motivation to stay alive."

"Nope, but I hear makeup sex is fabulous."

"Isn't that called necrophilia? I mean, if I die."

"Hmm. You could be right. Wouldn't be nearly as fun as a corpse. Best not die then."

Famous last words. "I won't."

Chapter 18

Before I went back into the trace realm, I mentally sorted through the belongings I had with me. Was there anything that might have Taylor's trace on it so that I could pull through right to her? I had nothing. I was going to have to count on using my own trace to get to the hangar.

I touched the bracelet Elle had given me and activated it. Magic swirled around me. My stomach churned uneasily as I dropped into trace mode. I reached inside, uncertain what I should do next. Usually, I grabbed for someone's trace. I decided to pick up Cass's, letting myself fall into the soul-chilling cold.

Once again, I found myself inside the ribbon jungle. The shield spell vanished. The cold seeped into me, faster than before. Maya had healed me all she could, but my body—no, my soul—hadn't fully warmed. I couldn't be here long if I hoped to help Taylor at all.

I hadn't been to my sister's hangar for about five months or so.

"Riley? What are you doing back so soon?"

I jumped and faced my mother. With such unrelenting silence to this dimension, I'd imagined I'd hear her coming somehow, or see her.

"Taylor's in trouble," I said. "I need to get to her hangar before she gets hurt."

"Taylor?" My mother frowned. "Who's that?"

I wanted to disappear. "My sister. Half sister. Dad remarried after you were killed." That was a sentence I'd never imagined I'd be saying. I carefully didn't mention he'd remarried within a year. "I need to help her. I'm the reason the sadistic fuck is going after her."

Though it was difficult to read her ghostly expression, I could tell it was pinched with pain. "Have you been to the place you want to go? This hangar?" she asked.

"I have, often. I null my trace a lot. I'm not sure when I wasn't nulled at the hangar."

She nodded. "It makes it a little harder if you nulled away your trace, but not as much as you think. If you're as strong as I think you are, no trace can ever truly disappear for you. You need to let go of all other distractions—"

The conversation was surreal. My mother had been a low-level tracer, as far as I knew. But then, what did I really know for sure? Everything before my dad disappeared could be fiction. The whole foundation of my life, of everything I thought was true and solid, was crumbling away from beneath my feet, leaving me adrift. Was anything I remembered about my parents, about my childhood, real?

She waited while I untwisted Touray's, Price's, Leo's and Madison's traces.

"Now take up your own. Gather your power and shove it out into your trace. Follow it back to wherever you need to go. Pay attention, because it will be very fast, and you must stay focused or you will lose your trail at those points where you've nulled out. If so, you have to start all over. Remember that your trace is there, but it will be faint. When you get where you want to go, do as you did before. Go quickly. You've been here too long. Be careful. And don't forget to come back." With that, she vanished like a light going out. Dramatic.

I followed her instructions, focusing on my trace. I gathered my power and pushed it out along the ribbon. It might as well have been confetti, for all the times I'd nulled out my own trace. Still, my mother was right. I could follow it, even when I could no longer see it. It was a thickening, a current of electricity that flowed through all my trace, no matter how suppressed.

I could feel everywhere I'd been as I raced along. I traveled so fast that I shot past the last time I was at the hangar. It took a minute to figure out how to reverse myself. I retreated until I could feel my trace bisecting the right spot. I gripped hard and pulled myself out.

I staggered into Taylor's office, tripping over a trash can and sprawling onto the floor. Thick carpet absorbed the noise. I clambered to my feet. I was alone. I still wore my flak jacket, but the shield spell was depleted. The window blinds were drawn. I couldn't see out into the rest of the hangar. Not that there was much to see. The place was covered in a steeply pitched roof that was heated in winter to keep the snow off. The far end of it opened to allow a copter to lift off. Taylor had a fleet of eight. They sat in their own garage stalls on magically modified cement pads that hovered inches off the floor. Those could be easily guided out under the roof opening and back using only a pallet jack, or three or four strong bodies.

She had a crew of ten pilots whom she rotated shifts between, plus another dozen ground crew, mechanics, and office staff. They all shared a bullpen next door that also contained a communal kitchen, a lounge, ping-pong and pool tables, dart boards, and card tables. Beyond that were a dozen crash rooms outfitted with bunk beds and showers, where employees could refresh themselves during long shifts. A door in the back corner of Taylor's office led first into a private bathroom, and then into her own comfortable apartment. She stayed there whenever business got hectic. Between wealthy travelers, business people, summer and winter vacation traffic, and the fall hunting season, Hollis Air was often hectic. Her rim-top hangar had a similar setup, though it was much larger to accommodate the jets. The trouble was, I wasn't going to be able to handle another trip through the spirit world if she wasn't here. Someone would have to fly me up.

It occurred to me then that Taylor might not be in Diamond City at all. Hope bloomed in my chest. She ran a lot of her own long-distance flights. She could be in Paris right now, or halfway to Singapore.

I circled around her desk and plopped into her chair. She had three monitors hooked up. I tapped the calendar icon.

"Dammit!" She wasn't on a flight. In fact—"I am so going to kill that bastard," I said, my teeth clenched so hard I was surprised I could make any coherent sounds.

On Taylor's appointment calendar, she had scheduled a helicopter flight for one P. Caldwell, along with five passengers. I glanced at the clock. That was over an hour ago. Had they already left?

I cleared the screen and brought up the security cameras, flipping through as I searched for Taylor.

What I found was so much worse than I expected.

Chapter 19

Bodies littered many of the security screens. Blood leaked across the floor like streaks of black ink. I recognized almost all of the people, most having worked for Taylor for years. I didn't realize I'd begun crying until my vision blurred. I swiped away the tears, but they kept coming. On the waiting-area camera, I found a family slumped in their chairs. The youngest kid was probably twelve. She sat in utter bewilderment, a dark hole in her forehead.

I flipped past. I couldn't think about that kid. But just because I didn't want to think about it, didn't mean it was so easy to wipe the image from my mind.

I found Taylor in the main hangar. It was set up almost like a stage. Taylor sprawled in a recliner chair someone had dragged from the lounge. She wore no bonds. A length of chain circled the chair on the floor. Her body twitched and shook and her expression was rapturous.

Oh shit! No, no, no!

I was too late. Percy had infected her with Sparkle Dust.

Percy perched on the arm of the chair, watching Taylor succumb to the drug. His long white-blond hair was caught behind his head in a neat ponytail, and despite the weather, he wore a dark suit. He glanced up at the camera and smiled gloatingly, then waved. I flinched away, my heart leaping into my throat. How could he know I was here?

Slowly the answer came. He couldn't know that I was here, that anyone else was on the way. He thought he had all the time in the world. He expected me to see this later. He knew at some point I'd see it, and then he'd have his revenge. He was enjoying imagining my helplessness and horror. If I could have killed him right then, I would have.

Luke hulked behind Percy, as stone-faced as ever. He had two pistols on his hips and an assault rifle cradled in his arms. My hands flexed into fists. I didn't want to believe it, but I knew he was at least partly responsible for all the deaths in the hangar. I thought of the family in the waiting area. How *could* he?

My fury at him startled me. It's not that I'd thought he was a good guy. I knew better. I just hadn't figured he was such a cold-blooded killer. I'd thought he'd tell Percy to fuck off before he ever slaughtered an innocent family. I owed him, but if I survived the day, I was going to make sure *he* paid for that, if nothing else.

Off to the side was a blond man and a younger girl, both bound with their hands in front of them. They looked terrified, and the girl looked like she was about to faint. I guessed they were Madison's father and sister.

Other than that, there were another two goons. Both looked like muscle-bound military types. They bristled with weapons, including assault rifles. They had their backs to the others as they watched for incoming trouble. Percy plus five companions is what it had said on Taylor's appointment calendar. They were all I was up against. All. Like I wasn't outnumbered and outgunned. I didn't have a snowball's chance in hell of defeating them.

How long before the strike team Elle had sent got here? How long before Price, Touray, Leo, Madison, and their little army moved in?

It didn't matter. Right then, time ran out.

Percy slapped Taylor's cheek. Her face jerked to the side with the force of it. He slapped her again, then gripped the front of her shirt and pulled her upright. I didn't realize I'd moved until I was at the door, my hand on the knob.

I stopped myself, taking a breath. I couldn't just barrel out there. I couldn't take Percy and his men alone. I had to keep him busy until help arrived.

All right, so I'd keep him busy. He liked to taunt and gloat and torture. What if I walked down there and let him do just that? I'd survived that once; I could survive it again.

I reached up and touched the hidden null on my scalp. Things had never been so bad that I really considered activating my scalp null. Now—Should I? Was this that rainy day of imminent death? Was I down to the nuclear option? Could I gamble everything on an experimental null?

I knew what I planned for it to do, but hadn't risked testing it. The null was just as likely to kill me as save me, so I figured I'd wait for more dire circumstances.

Dire had arrived.

The null was designed to work even after I passed out. It not only nulled out all magic within twenty yards of me, it sent out a pulse of crippling pain to anyone in the vicinity. I'd had it since I was eighteen. I'd created the null and then hired a tinker and a dreamer to weave in the pain part of the spell. After that, I only had to continually reinforce it. Unlike the null on my belly button, the hidden one on my skull was already and constantly tied directly to the flow of my magic. It only exhausted itself when I was dead. Which meant that if I passed out before I could deactivate it, the chances of it killing me were pretty perfect. Plus, if I ended up in a coma or needed medical help, I was screwed. And all of that was with it working properly. Then there were all the ways it could just go haywire and fry me like a bug in a zapper.

I'd always just liked knowing I had it. The null was a way to fight, and a way out, if it came down to being owned by someone like Percy. If I was forced to activate it, then it would be because I saw no other way out, and death was better than living. I figured that was my own silver lining to a shitstorm. I never imagined I'd need it to rescue my sister. I just hoped it would work.

I turned the knob on the door and peered out. The office door faced the main part of the hangar. At center stage, maybe twenty-five yards away, was Percy's demented little circus act. Between us was a tiny ultralight helicopter made by Dynali. It was mostly windshield and seats, and sat only two people. Taylor used it for sightseeing trips, or to take photographers up over the mountains. I dashed over to it, easing around under the tail to see what was happening.

Percy had managed to get Taylor's attention. She stood on her feet beside Luke, who had a hand hooked under her armpit to steady her. Handprints in red decorated her cheeks. She swayed.

"She isn't ready," Luke growled. "She can't fly like this."

"Thank you for stating the obvious, Luke. I thought she'd be more resistant, as her sister was."

"Half sister," Luke said.

That earned him a rebuke from his twisted boss. "Never correct me. I should hate to have to delay your next dose."

Luke's teeth bared in a silent snarl, but he said nothing. So he'd been given Sparkle Dust, too. Did that mean he'd told Percy his talent? Or revealed that he'd helped me and Madison escape? Logic said no. Percy wouldn't have let him live if he knew Luke had helped me.

That's when I noticed the yellowing bruises on his face. The black and white security cams hadn't revealed them. What other damage was he hiding beneath his clothes? A surge of empathy ran through me. Percy had hurt him, hard, and he still hadn't revealed his secrets. That said something about the man. That's when I remembered the dead family in the waiting room, the hole in the little girl's head. My lip curled. That said something, too. So Luke had been tortured and force-fed SD. That didn't let him off the hook for acting like a human being.

"Miss Hollis," Percy said.

I tensed at the sound of my name, then realized he was talking to

Taylor. When she didn't respond, Percy slapped her again, raising his voice as he spoke her name again.

"Fuck you. Why do you keep hitting me?" Taylor asked in a slurred voice. Her head rolled back on her shoulders so she could look Percy in the face. Her mouth was swollen from the blows, and one of her eyes was starting to turn black. A trickle of blood rolled down over her lips.

"It's time to come back to reality," Percy said crisply. "Your talents are required."

Taylor said something that sounded like "*mmphmmph.*"

Percy slapped her again, then turned to Luke. "Bring me a container of ice and some water. Big enough to dip her head into. There's a kitchen in the lounge."

Luke looked like he wanted to say no, along with some other choice words, but marched off to do as told. Should I go after him? Take him down while he was alone? The lounge had a wall of windows facing the hangar, and only some of the curtains were closed. I risked being seen by Percy and his other goons. Not a great idea.

That left my original plan: delay Percy until the cavalry arrived. How long would it be? A half hour? An hour? Probably closer to half, despite the snow. I could survive that. Hopefully. I took a breath to steady myself as Luke returned with a gray dish tub full of ice water, his assault rifle slung over his back.

He set the tub on the floor. Percy grappled Taylor by the back of her collar and forced her down to her knees. He started to shove her face into the tub.

I held myself still. It wouldn't hurt for Taylor to come out of her drug haze. He wasn't going to drown her. He needed her to fly for him.

Percy held her down for the count of ten. Taylor started to thrash around the count of seven. He yanked her up, and she took a great gulp of air. Before she could speak, he repeated the process. Then again. And again.

Each time, Taylor fought him harder, but her movements were still clumsy and uncoordinated. Percy was starting to hold her down longer. I couldn't risk that she could take much more. Time to get in his way.

"You seem to have a fetish for helpless women," I called out, stepping into sight. "Some might think you're compensating." I waggled my little finger suggestively at him.

Percy whirled, dropping Taylor. She sprawled on the floor in a puddle of ice water, coughing. Luke stared at me like I was a spider he'd like to squish. The other two goons swung around, aiming guns at me as they marched toward me.

"You should stop there," I said as I dropped into trace vision. They both wore bright spirit cloaks. Not for paralysis, or the others wouldn't have been able to move. So what was their borrowed talent? I wasn't about to find out.

Neither of the two men stopped. I activated the two null necklaces, and at the same time drew my gun and leveled it at them. They stopped. Mexican standoff. Except—

"Please remember your sister, Miss Hollis," Percy said, having overcome his surprise. "That is, Riley. Forgive my informality. I shouldn't want you to be confused about whom I'm addressing. If you should like to see the other Miss Hollis remain unharmed, lower your weapon."

I didn't move. "Unharmed? You've been beating the crap out of her."

"I have not. Beating her would be something more akin to this."

I heard a heavy thump. Taylor made a squalling sound.

"I suspect she might have a broken rib or two, though she should still be able to fly. Shall I continue? Or will you listen to reason?"

I hated to give in, even though I'd planned to all along. I made myself lower my gun.

"Very good. Now drop it and kick it away."

I did as I was told.

"Search her, Barnes."

I held myself still as the darker haired goon on the right slung his rifle around to his back and strode toward me. He pulled off the flak jacket, then frisked me, though it was more of a groping. Bastard. He hooked fingers under my necklace nulls and pulled them over my head, then stripped off the useless shield spell bracelet. As he did, his mouth curved up in an expression of pure malice.

"Clear," he said.

"Good. Bring her here."

Barnes gripped my arm and shoved me along in front of him until I stood in the center of the hangar with Percy, Taylor, and Luke, whose primary job seemed to be wrangling Taylor.

Percy examined me, walking around me once like I was a cow he was thinking of buying. "You've proven quite resourceful. I thought you'd be rotting away deep in the mountain. Who is with you? Surely you did not arrive alone?"

"Hell no," I said. "I've got a boatload of goblins and orcs in the back office. My pet T. rex is in the bathroom. He's had some intestinal trouble, but he should be out soon."

Percy was clearly not amused. He gave me a long look, his pale eyes as remote and unforgiving as a cobra's. A vivid memory of him burning my arms made sweat spring up all over my body. The man was a psychopathic control freak. Challenging him might not be the smartest idea at this particular juncture. On the other hand, he'd lost interest in Taylor for the time being, which was a win for me, and every second that went by was a second closer to help arriving. Taylor's breathing sounded liquid, with a high-pitched wheeze at the end of each inhalation. I hoped to hell she'd be okay until help arrived. It proved he could be pushed out of his cold control, though. He needed her to fly. Kicking her had only risked his escape.

He raised his hand slowly and slapped me hard, half spinning me around. I responded before I had a chance to think. I grabbed two handfuls of his long hair and smashed his head down on my knee. Hands tore me off him and threw me back onto the floor. I bounced on the concrete. Black splotches swirled around my vision. I started to jump back up, but a foot landed on my neck and a gun barrel pressed into my left eye.

"Move and die, bitch."

That was my good buddy, Barnes.

"Stand down, Barnes," Percy said.

"He'd like to torture and kill me himself," I said, rasped really, given that a boot was crushing my larynx. "Sad for you, I know. Maybe next time." I was trying real hard not to pee my pants. My captor lifted the barrel of the rifle off my eye about an inch and set his foot flat on the floor. I rubbed my throat.

"Barnes!" Percy barked, threat snapping in his voice.

The other man's lip curled, but he backed away a couple steps. I sat up. Percy was pressing a wet cloth to his nose. It was my sister's shirt. He'd stripped it off her and collected up some ice in it. She remained curled up in a ball, her hands clutched around herself. Her face was swollen and bloody, and a bruise had started to blossom across her ribs. Percy didn't look much better.

"Ooh, that has to hurt. You probably want to get a heal-all on that stat."

"Get me a heal-all," Percy said to no one in particular. He was busy oozing venom at me.

Barnes's goon partner responded, going to a stack of luggage piled up near Madison's father and sister. Those two huddled together, watching the spectacle unfolding. She hadn't stopped weeping since I'd first seen her on camera. Her father held her tightly, looping his manacled arms over her head and shoulders, hunching so that his back was between her and potential gunshots.

After rifling in one of the packs for a moment, the goon returned and handed Percy a cuff bracelet. He bent and touched the chain on the floor that had been kicked askew while wrestling with Taylor. As power flared and died, I realized it was a null. I hadn't paid any attention to it before, but now realized they'd used it to suppress any sudden magical talents Taylor might have developed when they gave her the SD.

Percy tossed aside the ice-filled shirt and clasped the silver cuff over his left wrist. I couldn't help grinning. I had smashed his nose, but good. It was pulpy and skewed to the right. The heal-all wouldn't be able to straighten it out. Percy would have to do that himself or have a tinker break and heal it again later.

He surprised me when he put his fingers on either side of his nose and pushed it back forward. He didn't bat an eyelash at the pain he must have felt. I watched in disgust as the damage I caused vanished. Within a minute, he was essentially back to normal. I'd been hoping to run more time than that off the clock.

"That was very rude of you, Riley," he said, sniffing and dabbing blood away with his handkerchief. "Unfortunately, I don't have time enough to teach you another lesson in manners at the moment. However, since you'll be joining us on our journey, I'll look forward to spending some quality time with you. Now, let's see about your sister, shall we? Can't have our pilot mewling about on the floor."

He slid the silver cuff off his wrist and put it on Taylor. I watched as the bruises and swelling faded. Soon her breathing calmed. When she appeared mostly back to normal, he took the cuff and pocketed it. Then he grabbed Taylor by the hair, wrapping it around his fist. He dragged her over to the ice-water tub. He pulled her up onto her knees and then shoved her head under water again. This time, she instantly started to struggle, thrashing and kicking. I could hear her muffled screams. She shoved her hands against the floor, trying to get purchase. Percy was impervious. Once again, I held myself still, reminding myself that a sharper Taylor could only help get us out of this mess.

After a good half minute, he wrenched her up. She swore and shoved at his legs. "Let go! What the fuck is going on?"

"Oh good. You're back among us. Are you ready to fly?"

"Who the hell are you? Get your goddamn hands off me!" That's when she noticed me lying on the floor. "Riley? What are you doing here?"

"Wanted to see if you'd started talking to me again," I said. *We're in serious fucking trouble* seemed a little obvious. "I guess you have."

She scowled, her expression tightening. "This is no time for jokes. What's going on?"

"Yes, Riley. Explain to your lovely sister just what's happened to her and why," Percy said. His smile at me was oily and made me want to wash in acid to be certain every bit of his filth was gone.

"This asshole wants you to fly him and his friends out of Diamond City," I said. "He was your last flight appointment of the day."

There was silence, until Percy figured out I wasn't saying any more. He shook his head. "Riley, how very terse of you. My dear Taylor, I've just given you a dose of Sparkle Dust. If you want more, and you will, you'll need to obey my orders to the letter. That starts with flying us out of here. Do not think to refuse me. I'm generous with my loyal employees, but you will not like what happens should you cross me. Try to recall how good it felt when the Dust flooded your system, and how your body went incandescent with heavenly bliss. I will make sure that you feel that way every day, if you cooperate. If not . . . the cravings for and withdrawal from Sparkle Dust are dreadful. I have seen addicts peel the skin from their own bodies." He gave an exaggerated shudder. "I should hate to see such a beautiful woman suffer like that."

"Yeah, right," I said. "You get off on other people's pain. Don't fall for it, Taylor. Don't fly him anywhere. He's just trying to scare you."

"Am I? Well then, let me demonstrate to you both how very sincere I am. Alan, go fetch me a pair of cutters from one of the mechanic bays. Something that will slice through a finger."

Barnes's partner strode away without a word. Taylor flashed me a scared look.

"Is this guy for real?"

I nodded, my mouth dry. "He's as evil as they come, and yes, I'm guessing he's going to cut off my fingers to get you on board. He's killed all your employees and a family you had waiting. You don't want to mess with him."

Taylor's mouth fell open, and a storm of grief and then fury spun across her countenance. She covered her eyes with both fists.

My sister and I had our problems. She hadn't talked to me in weeks, and we frequently butted heads over just about anything, from where to find the best pizza, to whether or not it's raining outside, or even if grass is green. But I love her more than I love my own life, and I'd do anything for her—for my whole family. I had every intention of getting her out of Percy's clutches alive. After that, I'd get Cass and Maya to work on the addiction. They'd helped Josh—Taylor's former fiancé, and he'd been force-fed a steady diet of Sparkle Dust. Taylor had only one exposure. That had to be easier to fix. As far as I knew, Josh had managed to stay off it. Then again, I hadn't seen him since Cass and Maya worked on him. For all I knew, he'd wraithed away in a gutter somewhere.

Wasn't going to happen to Taylor. I'd let him dice me into tiny bits before I let that happen. I had no way to tell her help was coming without clueing in Percy and giving up the advantage of surprise. On the other hand, I didn't want her to give in. I had to find another delay.

I wondered if Percy had a big enough ego that he'd fall for the evil villain mistake of every B movie and have to brag his plans out to his victims, wasting enough time for the hero to swoop in and save the day. It was worth encouraging him.

"Must smart like a bitch to have to run away with your tail between your legs."

Percy's mouth tightened, and he sat down on the chair, crossing his legs. "My departure from Diamond City is quite planned, and I am not running away."

"So that's a yes."

He shrugged. "My business is no concern of yours."

So far the triumphant bragging wasn't working out. "What happened to your Dr. Frankenstein?"

His brows rose. "Doctor Inawa? Now how did you know about her?"

"Did you kill her or did she escape?"

"You are certainly full of questions."

"I'm surprised you aren't. I thought you'd at least want to know how I could shake off the SD like a dog coming in from the rain."

"Actually, I am, though I've no doubt you will simply lie to me." He smiled. "Never fear. I have the means to get to the truth. Barnes? If you will?"

The surly pile of muscles stepped up behind me and planted his hand on the top of my head. Magic flared from his talent cloak, spiraling around me in sticky loops. My body turned heavy. I tried to lift my arm. I couldn't move.

"That's better," Percy declared. "Now, tell me how you managed to avoid the SD addiction?"

I opened my mouth to say something like diet, exercise, and clean living. Instead, the truth popped out. "I nulled it."

Once again his brows rose. He leaned forward, his pale blue eyes glittering. "However did you manage to do that?"

I wanted to tell him to fuck off and die. I wanted to keep my mouth shut. I wanted to do anything but sit there and spill my guts. "I have a null tattooed on my stomach. I activated it and it nulled out the drug."

"Ah. That *is* interesting. Why haven't you used it to counter the spell holding you and making you talk?"

"I couldn't recharge it."

"Ah. That is good news."

I heard boots on the cement floor behind me. Percy's other goon, Alan, was returning with whatever finger choppers he'd found among the mechanics' tools.

I was running out of time. I had no doubt in my mind that Percy was going to do as promised and demonstrate to Taylor that he would, in fact, cut off my fingers.

He reached down and picked up my limp left hand. I struggled to pull it away, but I might as well have been Gumby. He turned it over, palm-side up.

"Which finger to start with is always the fundamental question," he mused. "A person can easily lose the pinky without losing any hand function at all. Truthfully, even losing the forefinger could be fairly easily compensated for with the other fingers. Losing the thumb, however, means that you no longer have an opposable thumb, arguably the only significant difference between animals and humans.

"Generally, given the choice, offenders prefer to lose the pinky. I sympathize with that, but obviously, the impact is consequently much less, and therefore, the offender risks not learning his lesson. I find it much more practical and educational to begin right with the thumb. We'll start below the first joint. Then we'll move down to between the middle and upper joint, and finish with a close cut at the base of the hand. I find that taking an appendage in pieces also carries far more impact. Wouldn't you agree?"

He looked at Taylor, who'd gone pale. She twisted and vomited on the floor, her body jerking with the violence of her reaction. My throat burned with the bile that rose on my tongue. I swallowed and forced myself not to show fear. I wasn't going to give Percy the satisfaction.

Alan handed Percy a small bucket full of various pliers and snips. He pulled each out and considered them. "I think this is the best choice, don't you?" He held up a pair of metal shears with heavy jaws. "I should think they'd do quite nicely."

He stood, resting my hand on the arm of the chair and drawing the silver heal-all cuff out of his pocket. He put it on me. "You may not be aware, but there's an artery in your thumb. You're not likely to bleed to death, but certainly this will help. Alan, did you happen to see anything back there that might work to cauterize the final wound? Some rags might not go amiss. Move quickly, though. Taylor has recovered enough to fly and we should be on our way as soon as possible."

"I'll do it," Taylor rasped. "I'll fly you anywhere you want to go. Don't hurt Riley."

Percy patted Taylor on the head. "I wish I could, but it's important for both you and Riley to fully understand what it means to disobey me. I can't have you rebelling at the last minute. Unfortunately, your sister did not take her first lesson to heart. That was my failure. I underestimated her ability to learn. Some people are quite slow in that regard. I hope you are faster."

"Please," she begged.

I tried to tell her not to bother, but with Barnes's hand still on my shoulder, I couldn't speak, except, apparently, to answer questions. As I heard Alan's returning footsteps echoing through the hangar, my simmering panic exploded into a full boil. My hand remained perched on top of the recliner's arm like an offering.

"All right then," Percy said as Alan set a pile of red mechanics' rags on the seat, followed by what looked like an aerosol can topped with a blow-torch apparatus. "Looks like we can get started. Now Riley, this will hurt quite a bit, but I think this time the process will be more effective in teaching you that obeying me is the wisest choice."

"Please! Don't do it!" Taylor begged.

She lunged forward on her knees and shoved my hand off the chair. Alan grabbed her by the arms and dragged her backward. She kicked at him, twisting and elbowing as she fought his iron grip. He grunted and swore when she smashed her head into his mouth. He staggered back, and she pulled an arm loose . Swinging around, she kicked him in the side of the knee. It went out from under him.

Before she could do more damage, Luke was there. He put his arms around her, clamping her arms to her sides, and picked her up. He carried her back to where Madison's father and sister sat and set her down. Clamping her wrists in one hand and locking one of her legs between his, he efficiently fastened her wrists together with riot cuffs. He pushed her down to the ground and grabbed a roll of duct tape I hadn't noticed. He wrapped her ankles, then slapped a piece over her mouth. Her enraged yells cut off abruptly.

"Thank you, Luke. I see your lessons have been well learned. Alan, do stop whining. You ought to have been more than a match for Taylor. I'm very disappointed."

Alan paled and went silent as he pushed himself to his feet, his left foot barely touching the ground.

"Now, let us begin, shall we?" Percy said and gave me a smile of pure malice. "I'll try not to hurt you too much."

I translated that into he'd hurt me as much as possible and enjoy the fact that I could do nothing but sit there and take it.

Except—I didn't have to.

I had one weapon. All my enemies were within range. All I had to do was activate my skull null, and everyone would be incapacitated with pain. My null should free me from the spell holding me prisoner, and I'd be able to duct-tape all of them and deactivate the null.

Easy.

You'd think by now I'd have learned that *easy* is never a word that describes anything in my life.

I activated the null as Percy reached for my hand.

Then screamed as he chopped off the end of my thumb anyway.

Chapter 20

Blood spurted over the arm of the chair. Shock froze me in place, even as the spell imprisoning me vanished. Barnes moaned and staggered away. He crashed to the floor, seizing with pain. His body shook and shivered. His legs, arms, and body bucked and flopped as every inch of the forty-some-odd miles of nerves in his body came under attack. Alan and Luke did the same.

Nerve pain hurts more than just about anything.

Except maybe having your thumb cut off.

I rolled away as Percy lunged at me, the shears held high like he was going to clobber me in the head with them.

How was he still in control of himself?

He didn't have any nulls. I'd have felt them.

Blood continued to pour out of my thumb. I folded it inside my fingers and gripped tight to help stanch the flow. Unfortunately, my null was sucking the juice out of the heal-all. Percy stalked forward, his head lowered, his eyes narrowed to slits. Adrenaline and a thrill of danger rushed through me. I tensed to run. I'd never seen this side of him. He was always so three-piece-suit uptight. I backed away.

I flicked a quick glance about to see where I was. I was nowhere near where they'd stripped away my flak jacket and gun belt. I'd backed up too far to reach Barnes's or Alan's weapons, and worse, Percy stood between them within easy reach of either. He hadn't realized it yet. I edged to my right, hoping he'd keep following.

He didn't.

"I surprised you, didn't I?" he said, turning to face me as I backed toward my gear.

"How are you doing it?" Keeping him distracted seemed like a good idea, plus I really wanted to know.

He smiled, a pirate smile. "Turns out I'm immune to most magic. It is, quite ironically, my magical talent. Healing magic does work, thankfully. Sparkle Dust is another story, though I had high hopes for it. I still do."

"Are you insane? That stuff is toxic. I wouldn't wish it on my worst enemy." Actually, I'd wish it on Percy in a heartbeat. He was immune to magic? If I hadn't just seen it for myself, I wouldn't think it was possible.

"Eventually I'll learn the secret to stabilizing its effects. I will also learn how to use it. If healing magic works on me, then I can make SD work as well."

I actually stopped, too stunned to remember that I was trying to get away. "You are fucking crazy. How many people are you going to kill in your harvests? How many people are you going to turn into wraiths on the streets? It's poison."

His head tilted, and a dangerous glint appeared in his eyes. "I was not aware you knew the secret to making Dust," he said and started toward me again, moving fluidly on the balls of his feet.

He was stalking me like a lion after a wildebeest. I didn't want to know what would happen if he caught me this time. Probably the same thing that would happen to the wildebeest. Given the viciousness of Percy's expression, losing fingers seemed like the least of my worries.

I backed up. I didn't dare take my eyes off Percy. Given the slightest opportunity, he'd plow me down. I guided myself in the general direction of my gun belt and flak jacket, hoping I'd bump up against them. I had no idea how I'd get the gun before Percy grabbed me and jammed the point of the shears into my eye socket.

The only sounds in the hangar were moans and whimpers and my own harsh breathing. Sweat broke out on my forehead, and along my back and ribs. Percy continued to pace steadily toward me. My hand throbbed with fiery heat, and I was starting to feel woozy as if my null had started drawing on me for power. It was way too soon for it to have used itself up, I assured myself. The shock and blood loss from losing part of my thumb was making my brain spin inside my head. It had nothing to do with the null.

Percy's relentless silence had started to unnerve me. Abruptly, he shifted speeds and came at me faster. The twenty feet between us turned into ten. He held the shears low, like he was going to gut me. My brain screamed *run!*

Instead, my training kicked in. My dad had started me through a constant wringer of defensive training starting after my mom was killed. I was no martial arts master. That hadn't been the point. He wanted me to be able to save myself if someone jumped me. He taught me to fight dirty and fight smart. So instead of running, I waited until Percy closed the distance to five feet, then three. His arm cocked back, and he thrust at my stomach. I stepped to the side, dodging his strike. In the same moment, I grabbed his wrist in my right hand and his elbow in my left, clamping tight so I didn't lose my grip. My blood made his skin slick.

In dodging to the left, I'd left my right leg slightly extended. I pulled him across it, twisting his arm down and around as he fell, letting his weight do the damage. His arm made a crackling, popping sound as his shoulder dislocated and bone broke. The metal shears clattered to the ground.

He let out a high-pitched shriek. I didn't wait for him to recover. My gun belt was a dozen feet away. I snatched it up and drew the .45. Without hesitation, I smashed the butt into the side of his head twice. He sagged and went unconscious.

I stood over him, panting. I shoved my gun into my rear waistband. Blood dripped across the floor in a nearly solid line as I fetched the duct tape. I grabbed one of the red mechanics' rags and pressed it to the exposed stump of my thumb, trying not to look at it and trying not to throw up. I wrapped duct tape around the rag to hold it in place, doing my best to ignore the pain.

I returned to Percy and bound his feet and hands, using the shears to cut the tape. Next I did the same to the now incapacitated Barnes, Alan, and Luke, after disarming them and searching them for knives or other weapons. By now I was staggering. My shirt was soaked in sweat, and my heart was beating like hummingbird wings. I couldn't chalk it up to the thumb anymore. It had to be the null. Why? But then it clicked. Taylor's hangar and helicopters used an enormous load of magic to suppress noise and create a permanent glamour around it. The protections rose up for a half mile. On top of that, she had security, and the ordinary comfort magics that went with the business and life. My null had been sucking up all those. Stir in the fact that traveling through the trace realm had drained my reserves, it was no wonder I was woozy. I was running on fumes.

I needed to deactivate it before I passed out, otherwise I wouldn't be able to. I glanced around to make sure I hadn't forgotten anything. My gaze settled on Luke. He'd burn through his bindings in nothing flat. I found my discarded necklace nulls and dropped them over his head. That should do the trick. I realized then that Taylor remained bound. I cut through the bindings on her hands and peeled the tape off her mouth. She watched me, her body shuddering and twitching with vicious pain.

Damn. I should have deactivated my null and not waited until I cut her loose. It took me a couple of seconds to focus enough to turn it off. Almost instantly, I dropped to the ground, a marionette with cut strings. I landed on my butt. My left hand banged against the floor. I cradled it against my stomach, rocking back and forth as waves of agony crashed over me.

"Riley?" Taylor's voice was hoarse. "Are you okay?"

I couldn't unlock my teeth to answer. If I did, I'd have screamed. I couldn't even cry, I hurt so bad.

"Oh my God," Taylor whispered. "He did it. The bastard cut you."

I'd have laughed if I could. Cut me? That sounded so harmless. Percy had amputated my thumb. A piece of me was sitting over on the recliner. Remembering that galvanized me. If I wanted to salvage the thumb, I should put it on ice. Even magic couldn't reattach rotted flesh.

I startled to struggle up off the floor. I got to my knees, and Taylor put a hand under my arm to lift me.

"What do you need?"

"Thumb. Ice."

Her body went rigid, but she remained calm. "Right. I can take care of that. I'll go get some ice. Are you okay here?"

I nodded, and she slowly released her hold, her hands hovering in case I fell. When I didn't, she turned and ran to the lounge.

"Use the heal-all," Luke said from the floor on my right.

It took a second to process his words. In the fight with Percy, the cuff had come off my wrist. It was made for a man. I got up and looked for the cuff. I found it beside the chair and put it on. There wasn't much juice left in it. Still, I could feel it working on my thumb.

"Is Madison all right?" Luke asked.

I looked at him. He didn't look like he had any wraith symptoms. I wonder how long before they started to show. I was tempted to tell him she'd died or something, by way of revenge for killing that family out front and all of Taylor's employees, but I couldn't muster up the hate.

"She's safe," I said. "Why did you kill that family out front?"

"I didn't kill anyone. That was all Barnes and Alan," he said, his eyes closing as he slumped. He made a made a noise that was half laugh, half anger. "Percy didn't trust me to do it. He put me on guarding your sister."

"Right. And every murderer on death row was framed. Even if that was true, it didn't stop you from helping to make it possible. You're just as guilty as they are. You could have shot every one of them before they knew what hit them."

Luke lifted a shoulder. "Percy said he'd go ahead and torture Bill and Robin if I crossed the line."

I assumed Bill and Robin were Madison's father and sister.

I didn't know what to say to that, but I didn't have to answer. Taylor returned carrying a plastic container full of ice and a plastic baggy. She was crying, her face white. Her bottom lip was clenched between her teeth. She'd seen the bodies of her employees and friends littering the hangar and lounge.

"Why?" she asked raggedly.

Guilt tied my stomach in knots. "Because of me. I got away from him and he was going to make me pay. You and your people got caught in the crossfire."

I didn't wait for her answer. I twitched the plastic zip baggy from her fingers and went to find the missing stub of my thumb.

It had fallen to the seat of the chair. I almost couldn't bear to touch it. My stomach lurched, and it was all I could do to keep it down. There was something infinitely terrible about seeing part of you lying separate from your body. It was so unnatural, it felt like the world was operating under different rules, where down was up and hot was cold and everything I ever knew to be true was suddenly wrong.

I wasn't sure how best to pick it up. Then Taylor was beside me.

"Here," she said, taking the baggy back. She flipped it inside out around her fingers and picked up my thumb. It was less than an inch long. She pulled the bag off her hand, leaving the stump inside. She sealed the baggy and put it on top of the ice inside the plastic container and put its lid on. "That will take care of it. You need to get to a tinker soon."

"Help is supposed to be on the way." My gaze fixed on the dark bloodstains on the arm of the chair. My blood. But I was alive. My thumb could be reattached. That's all that mattered.

I made myself turn around and wiped my face with my good hand. The throbbing of my decapitated thumb had lessened, but not quit. The heal-all had run out of power. "I've got friends coming. They should get here soon."

"Who?"

"Price. Touray. Leo, too."

She gave me a sharp look.

"Price is moving in with me," I said randomly.

"Okaaay," she said. "You trust him now?"

It was a legitimate question, especially given the fact that up until a few days ago I'd been determined not to trust him. Which may not have been me at all.

"Yeah, about my trust issues . . . Dad messed with my head. Changed me. He made it impossible for me to trust anybody."

"No, he didn't," she said, brows furrowing. "Dad would never do that."

"I thought so, too. Until the shit he put in my head nearly killed me."

"Wait—what? Killed you? What do you mean?"

I shook my head. Now wasn't the time. I didn't need an audience for my dirty laundry. "It's a long story, and—"

I broke off as a helmeted squad flowed into the hangar in military formation, weapons raised to eye-level. They came in through the doors leading into the front lobby. I didn't know if they were friendly or not. I thrust an arm out to push Taylor behind me. She ducked and ran to get one of the assault rifles I'd piled out of the way. I was startled at how efficiently she managed it. Dad had taught both of us to shoot, but she hadn't been a willing student, and had weaseled out of range sessions more often than not. She'd learned more than I thought.

I had my .45 tucked in my waistband. I drew it, but I was a sitting duck. I couldn't get to cover before I was dead. On top of that, my hand shook. I wasn't sure I could hit anything I aimed at.

"Riley!"

Price's shout echoed, and he broke through the ranks in front of him. I wobbled with relief. The cavalry had finally come.

I found myself pulled into an iron hug. I'd never imagined I'd be so happy to see anyone in my life. Price made me feel safe. Because of him, I'd broken through the walls my dad had built inside my head. With Price, because of Price, I could show the true me, with all the flaws, fears, and insanity. It was a gift. I squeezed my eyes shut against a sudden wash of tears. I'd pushed Price out of my life. What if I hadn't decided he was worth getting back? What if I hadn't broken down my mental blocks enough to realize how much I wanted to be with him?

Percy and my father were no different. They'd both mutilated me. Only Percy had had the decency to make sure I knew it. Right then I hated my father. I could hardly breathe as it filled me. *Maybe he had a good reason*, a rebellious voice whispered in my head. He said it was for my own good. I couldn't see how.

Price pushed me away, his gaze running over me like a jeweler examining a diamond for flaws. He scowled at my hand as I cradled it up to my stomach. Using it made the pain return, and I felt blood beginning to seep.

"What happened?" he demanded. His fingers curled into my hips like hooks.

"My thumb got cut off."

His face went white. His cheeks splotched red. He looked angry. No, that wasn't enough for it. Enraged. Savage. Rabid. "Who did this to you?" He shook me once.

I sucked in swift breath, wincing.

"Sonofa—" He hunched down to look me straight in the eye. "Who did this?"

"I'll be okay," I said. Not to protect Percy, but to dull the bite of wild ferocity crackling around him. His control was frayed. Every muscle knotted tight. Virulent emotion flittered across the granite set of his face and churned in his eyes. Logic was gone; he was running on pure instinct and animal protectiveness. That, and hatred. I could see it eating him, chewing away the edges of his humanity.

"How did your thumb get cut off?" His tone was almost gentle.

"Percy." I rested the flat of my good hand against his face. "I'm okay."

"You're not. He burned you. He cut you. He can't get away with it." The last words were guttural, ripped from that dark place inside that none of us talk about, that we pretend doesn't exist. That place where all our worst fears live and thrive.

That's when I realized that this wasn't just about my thumb, or even the cigarette burns. Losing me, no—not being able to protect me—was Price's worst nightmare. The thing in the closet and under the bed that kept him awake at night and chased him through hell. Especially when I went dangerous places he couldn't follow, like my own head.

Price was spoiling for a fight because he needed something he *could* fight. This whole adventure with Percy had put him on the sidelines while I was battling on the front lines. He'd not been able to lift a finger to help, and it was killing him.

Except, all along he'd been my anchor. I knew I could count on him to be there for me, to heal me, to hold me, to accept me, and above all, to love me. He hadn't tried to change me, to turn me into something I wasn't. He'd let me be myself, even though it tore him to shreds.

My heart swelled and my chest hurt. God, I loved this man.

I wound my arm around his neck and pressed myself against him. "I will never let you lose me," I said against his ear.

His hands clenched on me, then he pulled me back into his arms. Shudders ran through him.

"You don't stop. You don't back down."

"Tell me what will help." In that moment, if he'd asked me to crawl into a bunker with him and never come out, I would have. Anything to stop the worry bleeding his soul dry.

His chest jerked as he gave a silent bark of laughter. "How does full body armor sound? Maybe a tank, snipers, and a couple dozen body guards?"

"You name it. If you ask me, I'll do it."

He went still. "You mean that." Cautious wonder filled his voice.

"I should warn you that I may argue. In fact, it's likely. Possibly with name-calling and flying debris."

He chuckled. "I can imagine."

"Tell me what will help," I repeated, relieved to hear the brittle tension leaving his voice. He was still drawn too tight. I wanted, no, I *needed* to take care of him, to pull him from the edge. The same edge I'd pushed him to, my fault or not.

"Just—"

Words seemed to fail him. He swallowed and pressed his lips to my hair, inhaling my scent. He stiffened again and pushed me away. He caught my wrist in his hand. Blood drenched the rag I'd taped around my thumb, and more trickled down over my hand. "I'm an ass," he said. "We need to get you to Maya."

"That seems to my theme song lately," I said lamely. Then, not willing to let the conversation go, "Price—"

He cut me off. "Shut up."

"But—"

He put his fingers over my mouth. "I didn't fall in love with the Riley you might become if I twisted you into the right shape, I fell in love with *you*, the cocky, irreverent, bullheaded Riley who scares the living shit out of me and gets into trouble like nobody's business. I'm not asking you to change. I don't want you to. I'm a big boy. I'll handle it."

I smiled so wide I thought my face would crack and my heart would stop.

I barely heard the noise as something clattered loudly on the concrete floor.

Then everything changed.

Chapter 21

I was no longer standing in the middle of the room with Price. I was hanging upside down over a man's shoulder while he carried me across a snowy parking lot. It was dark. My hands were bound at my sides and my feet were tied together. I was looking straight at some guy's ass, and he was kidnapping me.

I twisted my head. I wasn't the only one they were taking. Madison, her father and sister, and Percy had also been bound. I didn't see anyone else. I wriggled and jacked my legs up, but my captor only clamped his arm tighter around my knees. I twisted my hips, levering myself so I started to roll of his shoulder. He swore and hoisted me up with his arm, then with his other hand, he grabbed my bloody hand and squeezed hard. White fire spun through my head, and I screeched.

"What's the problem, Riggs?"

Dalton. Un-fucking-believable. He'd come back, only this time, he wasn't trying to protect me.

"Nothing I can't handle," my captor said.

"Don't damage the goods. The boss won't like it."

Fear chilled the swagger in my captor's voice. "Yessir."

"Get moving, then. Nice to see you again, Princess." Dalton patted my ass and walked away. The bastard carrying me followed him.

My mind flipped rapidly through my options. That sound I'd heard just before I found myself being carried must have been some sort of spell to incapacitate us. Dalton had had time enough to get us out of the hangar, and no doubt had left everybody else tied up.

Help wasn't coming.

Unless . . . Two people might help, if I could help them first. I was sure that ever-careful Dalton would have nulled Leo or knocked him out. I'd nulled Luke. Both of them had magic that could free themselves and everyone else, but first I had to get rid of the nulls. I'd start with Luke, since I knew exactly what kind of null I was up against.

I reached out with my senses, but I was too far away. I had a way to go farther, if I didn't kill myself trying. I dropped down into trace mode and focused on my belly null. There wasn't a lot of power left in it, but what there was, I used to reinforce the skull null. If I did this right, I could ride the wave of magic of the skull null out until I could reach those circling Luke's neck. I could drain their power and pray he'd realize he had the use of his magic back. After that, I'd do the same for Leo, if he was nulled and not—

I gasped, my blood freezing. He could be dead. They could all be dead. My reaction was electric and instinctive. I bucked and twisted, unleashing my null. Pain swept over the group. The man carrying me crumpled to his knees. I fell into the snow and rolled onto my back. I flung my senses out along the wave of null magic, searching for the two necklaces around Luke's neck. It took only a matter of seconds to home in on them. They had to be suppressing the pain of my scalp null. Good. When he started feeling pain, he'd know they'd stopped working.

I ripped the power of the nulls out, channeling the energy into the skull null. I was too weak from blood loss and using it previously to let it stay active for long. Once I passed out, it would eat me. Not even a stronger null could stop it.

Dalton's crew had left behind another dozen nulls. I couldn't tell which might suppress Leo's power. One by one, I destroyed them. Each took a toll on me, wearing me down. I fed their power into the skull null, but it didn't matter how strong I made it if I was too tired to turn it off properly, or if I lost consciousness. It would eat through all the new power and then start back on me.

I worked through the first six. Sweat dampened my body, and it turned to ice in the near-zero temperature. The seventh and eighth took considerably longer. I shivered, and my focus slipped. I caught myself, and the ninth and tenth went swiftly, as fear hardened my resolve. My focus fractured on the eleventh, and I felt minutes ticking away as I made my sluggish mind pull apart the spell and draw the energy into my own null. Finally, I was at the last one. I closed my eyes, unable to keep them open. I no longer shivered. I lay on the snow, unable to feel anything, even the molten pain of my missing thumb. I must have smashed it when I fell.

I don't know how long the last null took. I only knew when it released. I made myself deactivate my skull null. It took me four tries. I rested after the first two. The third time I dozed. I woke with a start. I had no idea what pricked me back to consciousness. Maybe the agonized sounds of Dalton's people. Maybe the whimpering cries of Madison and her sister, or the strained breathing of their father.

I was so tired. So *very* tired. I felt warm and so comfortable. But I had one last task, one last thing to do. What was it? The null. Yes. I fumbled at it with my mind. Thick mists crowded thoughts. *Sleep*, they told me. *Rest.*

I almost gave in. Then I remember that I promised Price he wouldn't lose me. I couldn't let him down. I made myself focus. One last push, and the thing was done. I opened my eyes, the black sky brilliant with stars. Diamond dust. Sparkle dust. If I'd had the strength, I'd have laughed at the irony.

Movement stirred around me as the debilitating pain I'd broadcast ended. Dalton shouted orders, called names. Confusion. That was funny, too.

"What did you do?" he leaned over me, his silver eyes flat. He didn't wait for an answer. He grabbed my arm and dragged me upright, then hoisted me over his shoulder.

He started slogging forward, calling his people to follow. "Make sure you have Percy and the others. We want them all!"

We might have gone twenty steps when the night turned orange. Fire roared in a ring all around us. Flames reached high into the air. From upside down, they seemed to lick the stars. Dalton turned.

I heard shouts. I told myself to wriggle and buck, to get free of Dalton's grip, but I had nothing left in the tanks. I might as well have been a wet blanket for all I could move at that point.

More shouts, and a few shots popped off. Snow melted, and the air turned humid. I waited for Dalton to do something, but he didn't move. Then feet splashed toward us through the rotting snow, and once again, Price was there. He pulled me off Dalton's frozen shoulder and stood me on my feet. I sagged. He held me, slashing at my bindings with a knife. He cut my wrists apart and then my legs.

"Talk to me, baby. Tell me what's wrong. Did they hurt you?"

"Tired," I whispered, barely able to make my lips bend around the words.

I don't know if Price heard me. He swung me up into his arms. My head fell against his shoulder. Now I could see that Leo had done what I'd hoped. He'd caught Dalton and his team in shackles made from the metal of their own guns. He now cut Madison free while Touray freed her father and sister.

"Riley needs to go, now," Price told his brother.

"A minute. Who are these people?" Touray asked.

"This one's Dalton, the one who was leading her bodyguard squad," Leo reported, coming to stand in front of the man in question. "The one she thought was working for you."

Touray looked demonic in the flickering shadows of the fire. "Who *are* you working for?" he demanded.

Dalton's mouth pulled into a flat smile. He didn't look scared. Didn't even look a little bit nervous. That made me worry.

"I'm not at liberty to say," he replied.

Touray shrugged. "Very well. There are ways to take what you refuse to give."

"You can try."

His total lack of concern didn't seem faked. My worry tightened.

"Damned right, I will." Touray turned his back on Dalton. His own people had arrived on the scene and were gathering up the prisoners. "Take them to the bunker. We'll get answers there."

Another day I'd have flinched from the cold brutality in his voice. At the moment, I couldn't manage to scrape up even a little bit of fear or judgment. I was surprised I was still conscious. I didn't think I was dying. Not this time. Vaguely, I wondered where my thumb might be.

Taylor appeared out of nowhere with blankets. She shook two out and wrapped them around me, then helped wrap Madison; her sister, Robin; and their father. He was looking haggard, and his breathing was harsh.

"We should get in out of the cold," Taylor said. "Turn the flames off, would you? We don't need the fire department here," she told Luke. Her voice was thin and strained, but she remained ice cold. Whatever else you might say about her, when the shit hit the fan, my sister had nerves of steel and brass balls. She'd fly a helicopter into a hurricane without breaking a sweat.

The flames doused at once, but sirens blared. Too late for discretion. Touray turned to Price. "Get Riley out of here before the cops arrive. Leo and Taylor, you go with them. Take Madison and her family with you."

"The hell I will," Taylor said. "This is my place and these are my people. I'm not going anywhere."

"I'll stay, too," Leo said.

"Fine, but I want Percy out of here. Throw him into one of the vans and take him to the bunker, along with Dalton."

"What about him?" Leo asked, pointing at Luke. I got a good look at him then. He looked hollow and worn. He was shaking. He was going to want a fix soon. He watched Madison comforting her sister and father. He reminded me of a man out in the cold, looking through a window into a room full of treasure he could never touch.

"Null him out and take him, too."

Luke woke up at that. He gave a little shake of his head. He glanced at me and gave me a little salute, then stepped back. A wall of fire roared up between him and us. It spread outward. I didn't doubt that when it died, he'd be long gone.

"We're leaving," Price said. He carried me to an SUV parked out on the street a hundred yards away.

"Are you okay, Riley?" he asked. "I need you to stay awake, baby. I know you're tired and cold. You're soaked through. You did it, though. I don't know how, but you made it so Leo and Luke could get free. You're amazing. Terrifying, but amazing. Come on, now. Talk to me."

I muttered something that wasn't all that polite.

His chest rumbled as he laughed. "That's my girl. Almost there. We'll get the heater going and have you back in Maya's care in no time."

"She's going to want overtime pay."

"I'll pay her anything she wants," he said, pressing his lips to my forehead. "I'll give her the moon, if necessary."

"How will you get the moon?"

Another rumble. "I don't know."

"Maybe you shouldn't promise her that, then."

He paused, looking down at me. I couldn't see his eyes. The night turned them to velvet shadow. "If she wanted the moon to make you safe and well, I'd sell my soul to get it for her."

My heart clutched in my chest. "I meant what I said, earlier. Tell me what you need and I'll do it."

He took a long breath and let it out. "I just need you, baby. Just you."

He pressed a fast kiss to my lips and started walking again. I stared up at him, so full of emotion I could hardly breathe. I couldn't believe he'd asked nothing. He gave everything, and took just me. I was enough.

I was never going to let him regret it.

Chapter 22

"I hate this," I announced as we drove up through Midtown, heading to my stepmother's house. Our Saturday date with the family had arrived. Only we weren't alone. Bodyguards traveled ahead of us and behind, with more waiting at Mel's and along the route. Our SUV was fully protected with both ordinary armor and magic.

Price took my hand, rubbing the back of it with his thumb. "I'm not risking you."

"I didn't say I was arguing, I just said I hated it." I stared out the window.

Dalton had escaped Touray's bunker. Nobody knew how, just that suddenly he wasn't there. Worse, he'd taken Percy with him. The idea that someone had either rescued the sick bastard or was now squeezing him for information on producing SD made me sick with fury. His tunnel headquarters had been quarantined. He'd rigged it to blow up, while at the same time releasing SD everywhere. No one could get in. The risk of getting infected with SD made it too dangerous to go look. At least Taylor was on track to recover. Cass had done her thing to pull the addiction from her mind, and Taylor was determined to fight the physical cravings. I'd tried nulling her, but it was too late to get at the drug's magical roots. At least for now. With Percy and Dr. Inawa still out there, I was determined to develop a way to cure the addiction. I thought of Luke. I still owed him. That would be a good way to pay him back.

"That's my girl," Price said.

"Let's hope you still think so after dinner tonight," I said.

He laughed. "I already know Leo and Taylor. Surely your stepmother and other brother aren't terrifying."

"That all depends on your point of view."

I adored Mel. She'd loved me like a daughter, and she'd always respected me and done everything she could to protect and care for me. She was also an FBI reader with a spine of steel. She wouldn't bat an eyelash at facing down a Tyet army all alone. Price had no idea what he was up against if she decided she didn't like him.

I sighed. Didn't matter. One way or another, I'd bring her around. I sure as hell wasn't giving up Price.

"Two weeks," he murmured, lifting my hand to his mouth and kissing the back of it.

A shiver of hot anticipation ran through me. Since the incident at the hangar, I'd not seen a lot of him. Mostly I'd been with Maya—who'd reattached my thumb—or sleeping or telling what had happened to me. The part about traveling through the spirit world had turned Touray white. He hadn't told me why. Not yet. But I had a feeling that conversation was coming soon. I was sure it had something to do with the Kensington artifacts and finding the superweapon that he wanted to use to bring the other factions of the Tyet to heel. It was the reason he'd wanted me in the first place. The artifacts could be put together to make a weapon that would let him squash his Tyet enemies and take over Diamond City. He needed me to find the rest of them, and the instructions on how to use the weapon once it was built.

Right at the moment, I was willing. Another Percy couldn't be allowed to exist. Hell, the first Percy couldn't be allowed to exist, and yet he was back out there. Then there were all the kidnappings and murders, the shakedowns of store owners, the many illegal manipulations and games, and the fear. Too many people living in fear. I didn't know if I was going to like the future that Touray had in mind for Diamond City, but I'd fight that battle when I got to it. For now, he was the best hope I could see, especially since he listened to Price, and I'd sure as hell make sure he listened to me. Between the three of us, maybe we could help.

"Where did you go?" Price asked me.

I turned to look at him. "What do you mean?"

"I mention our two weeks alone together and all of a sudden you go quiet and brooding. Where did you go?"

"Thinking about Percy and your brother. Touray isn't going to let you just vanish for two weeks, and he's sure as hell not going to let you go off the grid to my house with me."

"Us," Price said, kissing my hand again. "You're important to him, too."

I snorted. "Of course I am. He wants me to follow Kensington's trace to the last artifacts."

"That, too. But he likes you. And even if he didn't, I love you and that makes you family. He'd die for you."

"We should have invited him tonight. Let him really get a taste of family," I said. "I'd pay to see him and my stepmom going at it. Wonder if Diamond City would even survive?"

"If she's anything like your sister, it could be fun to watch. From what

I hear, he nearly snapped Taylor's neck during the hangar's cleanup."

"Everybody thinks she's a pushover because she's gorgeous and looks like she walked off the fashion pages. They think she'd be so afraid she break a nail or get a hair out of place that she must be a doormat. She flew in Iraq for military contractors and ended up fighting off insurgents in order to pull troops out of harm's way. She's got nerves of ice. After losing Josh, after your brother's part in it, she's not going to forgive him any time soon."

Price shrugged. "Gregg isn't used to having people challenging him. It's good for him. Anyway, he didn't kill her, the cops have been handled, and he's made sure the place was cleaned up and better security established. She didn't like that last one, either."

"But . . . she's family now," I said, the corner of my mouth quirking up. Poor Taylor, she'd gone from having two obnoxious, overprotective brothers to four. Thanksgiving dinners were going to be entertaining, at the very least.

"Gregg's bulked up the security on my place, too. We can go there if you like," Price said.

I stared out the window a long minute. "You wanted to come to my house."

"It's not secure enough given what's going on." I could feel him looking at me. "What's the matter?"

I lifted one shoulder. "It doesn't really matter where we are as long as we're together."

"I know, but something's still bothering you."

"You wanted to know I trusted you. Coming home with me, living with me, that's how you were going to know."

We'd come a long way since that moment, but it felt wrong to back out of that deal. I didn't want him to think I was weaseling out of it. I didn't want him to doubt me.

He sighed. "I shouldn't have pushed you that day. I was so out of my mind that I couldn't see straight. Let me be very clear: I don't care where we stay, so long as we're together and I can keep you safe. I can't do that at your home without letting a whole lot of people in on the secret of its location. I know you don't want that. My place is the better option. Plus if you ever need somewhere to run to ground, you still have one, and I know where it is. Not that you'll need it," he added tightly.

"I like your place," I said. "Especially your shower."

"I like you in my place," he said. "And in my shower." He let go of my hand and slid his arm around me, snugging me against his side. Good thing I wasn't in the habit of wearing seat belts. He pressed a kiss to my head. "I really like you in my bed."

The gruff note of desire in his voice lit my body on fire. My stomach did a delicious flip as I imagined just what we'd be doing later, after dinner. I could hardly wait. Price and I hadn't had any time to make love since he'd brawled with his brother in my sitting room. I squeezed my thighs together, remembering the feel of him, his touch on me, the glorious shattering he lifted me to.

"Maybe we should just go to your place now," I said, twisting to nibble his ear, my hand drifting down to stroke him through his pants.

He groaned. "Don't tempt me. Jesus, Riley. If you keep that up, I'm going to crash."

I drew my hand away slowly, trailing my fingers along his hardening length. "I wouldn't want you to crash."

He sucked a breath in between his teeth. "I will get you back for teasing me," he promised.

"You'd better."

Mel lived in Uptown. It was one of the smaller places, but she had twenty acres of parkland that surrounded the main house. There were tennis courts and two guest houses. A brick-and-iron wall prevented intrusion. The guard at the gate let us in. We drove up the long drive beneath arching trees, their snow and ice-covered limbs gleaming in the moonlight. We arrived at the house. Several other cars already lined the circular driveway. Leo, Jamie, and Taylor were already here. We were the last to arrive.

Price parked, and I started to get out. He came around quickly, taking my door and offering me his hand. I took it and stood. He looked me over admiringly. I'll admit, I'd dressed for the occasion. Maybe not all glitz and shine like Taylor, but I'd put on a sapphire wool dress, its soft fabric clinging to all my curves. It had a deep V-neck. It came down to just below my knees, and I wore a pair of black ankle boots with spike heels. My hair tumbled down my back and around my shoulders. I'd even put on some lip gloss and mascara.

Price put his hands on my hips and drew me against him. His cock was still hard. He rubbed himself against me, and it was my turn to moan as I gripped his shoulders. He chuckled triumphantly. "Turnabout is fair play, right?" He bent and nibbled my neck where it joined my shoulder, then sucked lightly. My knees sagged.

"Oh hell," I whispered, tilting my head to give him better access.

His mouth nibbled lower. I trembled at the sandpaper scratch of his jaw against my skin. He licked the cleft between my breasts, and I shuddered, my nipples hardening as strands of lightning desire whirled through me.

"You are not playing fair," I whispered.

"No? Then I suppose I should stop."

He straightened. Instantly, I wanted him back. I squeezed my eyes shut, trying to get a handle on my raging hormones. Stepmom. Family. Dinner. I opened my eyes. Price was grinning wickedly at me.

"You are not a nice man," I said.

"Never said I was."

"You'd better eat a good dinner, because when we get home, I'm giving you a workout."

"Home," he repeated, taking my hand. "I like the sound of that."

"You won't when you find out that I leave my dishes in the sink," I said as we walked toward the front door. Nerves fluttered in my stomach. I wanted Mel to like Price. I was pretty sure Leo did, and Taylor—well, she was still pissed over Josh in general and she'd lumped Price into her fury. She'd come around.

I rang the doorbell. My stepmom answered. She was dressed in a green silk sheath with a gold necklace made of skirling wires and delicate tracery, and set with diamonds and emeralds. Jamie had made it for her a few years back. Her red hair had cranberry highlights and curved around her pale face in an elegant bob. Her fingernails were glossy burgundy. A matching bracelet circled her left wrist, and she wore several rings.

I started to smile and move in for a hug. But she only nodded and lifted her fingers to warn me back.

The fluttering nervousness in my stomach hardened into worry. Did she already hate Price? Without giving him a chance? It wasn't like her. She always gave everybody a fair shake.

"Riley. I'm glad you've come." She gave me a penetrating look, meant to tell me something, then held out a hand to Price. "You're Clay Price? I've heard about you."

As they touched, I felt a pulse of magic from her. Whatever she communicated made Price's head snap back. Instantly, he went into predator mode. His gaze swept the foyer behind Mel, his body coiling.

"What's wrong?" I whispered.

Mel gave a brittle smile. Then, "we have unexpected company for dinner tonight. It's quite a surprise."

"Who?"

"Come see." She cast another look at Price. I'm not sure what she wanted him to know or do, but he held my hand tightly, staying slightly ahead of me.

We followed Mel into the sitting room. "Look who's here, everyone. Riley and her beau." Mel stepped aside.

Jamie and Leo stood rigidly on opposite sides of the room. Taylor was at the bar. She looked shell-shocked. All of them stared at the person sitting in the chair by the fireplace. He stood slowly, and I felt the air leave the room. My mouth fell open, and I was filled with a tangle of hope, hate, fear, and love.

"Dad. You're back."

The End.

Acknowledgments

As always, writing a book, while a solitary experience in many ways, is also a group production. First, I want to say thank you to the best readers in the world. You have both inspired me and made it possible for me to write books. I can't thank you enough. Nor could this book be possible without my amazing editor, Debra Dixon, and my agent, Lucienne Diver. Both are creative and hard-working, and I couldn't do this without them. Thank you also to the fantastic staff at Bell Bridge Books. You have been so amazing to work with. I also want to say thank you to the Word Warriors. Every day they provide encouragement, snark, commiseration, and celebration. The writing process can be difficult, but they smooth the way. Thank you also to Devon Monk for her support and friendship, for teaching double points, and for long coffee breaks. Finally, I want to say thank you to my family. I couldn't do this without them. And wait! One more finally! I want to say how much I appreciate all the support of my friends online and off. It's been a tough year on several fronts, and you've made every day better.

Author the Author

Diana Pharaoh Francis is the acclaimed author of a dozen novels of fantasy and urban fantasy. Her books have been nominated for the Mary Roberts Rinehart Award and *RT*'s Best Urban Fantasy. *Edge of Dreams* is the second in her exciting new urban fantasy series—The Diamond City Magic novels.

Visit her at dianapfrancis.com and find her on Facebook.

CPSIA information can be obtained at www.ICGtesting.com
Printed in the USA
LVOW10s1448190415

435209LV00005B/793/P